WITCH HUNT

Also by Ruth Warburton

Witch Finder

THE WINTER TRILOGY
A Witch in Winter
A Witch in Love
A Witch Alone

WITCH HUNT

RUTH WARBURTON

Hodder
Children's
Books

A division of Hachette Children's Books

To Ian, with all my love

1

Phoebe Fairbrother groaned as the light filtered through the tattered red brocade curtains. She had a head on fit to burst, and beside her George Wainwright was snoring like a pig, though that wasn't what had woken her up. Something else had – a noise from the street. But it was George stopping her from falling back to sleep.

'Get out!' She hit him with one of the stained satin pillows from her bed.

'Wha . . . ?' He sat up, his hair comically rumpled on one side.

'I said get out! Nobody paid me for no board and lodging.'

'But, Phoebe darlin'—'

'You deaf? Get out!'

She pulled the pillow over her head as he clumped around the room, pulling on his britches and boots, and then stomped crossly down the stairs to the street door. At last it was quiet and she rolled on to her back, trying to recapture the warm languorous dream she'd been having before she'd been woken – but just as she was slipping into unconsciousness it came again. A crack against the windowpane. This time there was a cry, a voice low and hoarse.

'Phoebe! You awake?'

'Oh shurr*up*!' she groaned. But the rattle of stones came again and this time she got up, pulling the eiderdown around her shoulders, and marched angrily across to the window to fling it open. The sky above the rooftops was paling to grey, but in the narrow alley next to the pub she could see nothing but shadows and the small puddle of light beneath the gas lamp.

'You can eff off, whoever you are,' she called. 'We ain't open.'

'Phoebe.' A tall figure stepped into the light from the lamp post. His face was covered in soot but when he pulled off his cap the lamplight glinted off his straw-coloured hair.

Phoebe's mouth fell open.

'Luke Lexton? What the hell are you doing here?'

'I'm sorry it's so early, Phoebes. Please let us in.'

'What's happened?'

'Never mind that.' He shivered into his greatcoat, his breath a cloud of white in the grey dawn light. 'Let us in before we freeze.'

2

She was halfway down the stairs before it occurred to her to wonder who 'us' was.

Luke let the stones fall from his hand on to the pavement and stood, his arms wrapped around himself, trying to keep in the warmth. Something gusted in the light from the lamp and when he looked up he saw dark flecks against the brightness, like specks of ash in the draught from a fire. But it was not ash. It was snow.

Then there was a sound and he turned back to the door.

'Bleedin' thing,' he heard, muffled from behind the wood. 'Always did stick, the bastard. Give it a shove, Luke.'

Luke put his boot to the foot of the door and pushed, until it gave suddenly, opening with a rush that tipped him into the narrow vestibule and almost into Phoebe's arms.

'Oi, mind yourself,' she said crossly, pushing him back and straightening her clothes. She was in a stained flowered tea gown, her face streaked with last night's paint and her breath smelling of gin. Luke could have kissed her.

'Thank you, Phoebes, *thank* you. I—'

'Yes, all right, all right. Shut the door or you'll let all the warmth out. You can tell me yer bleedin'-'eart story when you're in front of the fire.'

She made as if to close the door, but Luke put his hand out, stopping her.

'Wait. I'm . . .' He took a breath. 'I'm not alone. Rosa, come here.'

She stepped forward out of the shadows, her face blue with cold and covered in soot and smuts, her grey silk gown still stinking of smoke and the match-factory chemicals. Her long red hair had come loose from its pins and tumbled down her back, full of ashes.

'What the—' Phoebe looked amused at first, but then her mouth fell open. 'What in Gawd's name are you doing 'ere?'

'You know each other?' Luke looked from one to the other. They looked so different – Rosa small and pinched with cold, Phoebe warm and golden and bold. But as they stared at each other they both did a strange thing; each let a hand creep to her throat. Luke recognized the gesture in Rosa; it was what she did when she was nervous, putting her hand to the locket her father had given her as a child, as if it could give her strength. But Phoebe?

'Yes, we know each other,' Phoebe said shortly. She let her hand drop and pulled the tea gown tightly around herself, up to her throat. 'She's a lady. She can't come in 'ere.'

'I have no choice.' Rosa spoke for the first time, her voice hoarse with smoke and tiredness. 'P-please. Look at m-me.'

'Darlin',' Phoebe's face was hard, 'let me spell it out for you: there's only one kind of woman comes in 'ere, and it ain't your kind. Understand? If you're seen leavin' here your reputation won't be worth a bent farthing.'

'I know what you're saying.' Rosa stepped forward and

4

her face was as hard as Phoebe's. Luke saw her fist was clenched. 'But we're all f-f-fallen in one way or another. I don't c-c-care about my reputation. Please, let me in before I f-freeze.'

For a moment Phoebe hesitated. There was something behind her careless expression, something wary. Then she shrugged.

'Your funeral, love.'

'Thank you.' Rosa pushed past her, into the dusty little parlour of the pub. The embers of a banked-up fire smouldered in the small grate, and Phoebe knelt in front of it for a moment, raking it apart and piling on more coal. Then she brushed her hands on the hearthrug and sat back on her heels.

'All right then. What's going on? You two runnin' away together?' She didn't laugh; the idea was too preposterous to need spelling out as a joke.

Luke looked at Rosa and, for a moment, her gold-brown eyes held his. Then she looked away. He bit his lip.

'We're in trouble.'

'I can see that,' Phoebe said tartly. Her sharp eyes caught something, a flash in the dimness. 'What's that on your finger, love?' She was across the room in a moment, her eyes wide. 'Strewth, don't tell me that's real?'

'It's real,' Rosa said dully. She let Phoebe pick up her hand, turning it this way and that in the light of the fire, her face a mixture of grudging respect and plain envy.

'Good job you 'ad gloves on when I met you last, love. If you'da walked through Spitalfields with that in plain view, you'd of lost more than your locket.'

'It won't come off.' Rosa pulled at the ring and for the first time Luke saw that the skin around it was red and swollen and beaded with blood. 'See? They'd have had to cut off my finger to steal it.'

'There's plenty wouldn't let that stop 'em,' Phoebe said shortly. 'I'll get the kettle from the bar and we can all have a brew.'

As soon as she had gone through to the next room, Luke turned to Rosa.

'What did she mean about losing the locket?'

'Oh.' Rosa's hand went up to her throat again, and when she let it fall he saw that there was nothing there. The locket was gone.

'What happened?' His voice came out harder than he'd meant it to, but she shook her head.

'Nothing, Luke. Please leave it.'

'What happened?'

'Nothing!'

'Phoebe?' He moved to block the girl's path as she came back into the room, the full kettle in one hand, tea caddy in the other.

'What?' she asked, but Luke knew she must have heard his conversation with Rosa, and the expression on her face told him what he already knew. Reaching out, he pulled open the neck of Phoebe's tea gown.

There it was, hanging just below the hollow of her throat: Rosa's locket.

'Gerroff!' Phoebe shoved past him, banged the kettle down on the grate and pulled the tea gown closed. 'I didn't invite you in to paw at me, Luke Lexton.'

'Did you take her locket?'

'No, she give it me!'

'You liar!'

'It's true!'

'I sold it to her.' Rosa's voice cut through their argument. 'That's quite true. It was fair exchange, Luke.'

'Exchange for what?'

She bit her lip, looking at the floor, and he turned back to Phoebe.

'Exchange for *what*?'

'If you must know,' Phoebe said huffily, 'I told her where to find you. Took her there, in fact. And so what if I asked payment for my time? I'm a working girl, ain't I? And she's no friend of mine. If you wanted to see her so bad, you should've given her your address. You got a funny way of showing a girl you care, Luke Lexton.'

'Give it back to her,' Luke said, through gritted teeth.

'No!'

'Give it back.'

'No.' It was Rosa who spoke this time, quietly, but firmly. She put her burnt hand on Luke's arm. He winced at the sight of it, swollen red from the fire. 'No, it was fair exchange just as I said, Luke. I didn't have to pay the price she asked.'

'There you go.' Phoebe gave the fire a vicious poke and then walked to the door. 'You heard her. I'm going up to change. You can sort your own tea out.'

There was a silence after she'd gone. Rosa moved to huddle in the corner of the settle with her knees up, wrapping her skirts around her legs like a child. Luke stood, facing the fire, leaning against the mantelpiece and looking bitterly down into the flames. He was angry at them both – Phoebe for cheating Rosa out of her locket, Rosa for letting her. Most of all he was angry at himself for being the unwitting cause.

'Luke.' Rosa's voice cut through his thoughts. 'What are we going to do?'

'I don't know,' he managed. He turned back to face her. She looked very small and pale sitting in the corner of the settle, her magic just a thin wisp of red-gold in the darkness. The firelight caught her hair and the ruby on her hand, sending back echoes of the flames. 'We've got to get away. So we need horses. Or *a* horse at the least. And money.'

Where could they find either? William had money – Luke thought of the iron box beneath the floorboard of his uncle's room – but his heart failed at the thought of creeping in there while William was asleep and stealing his savings. And William had no horse. Could Rosa magick them up some money?

No: he pushed the thought away. He refused to ask. It felt like stealing, and he would not ask a woman to do his dirty work for him.

'We could sell this.' Rosa held out her hand, the ring glinting up at them. 'If only I could get it off.'

'That's not a bad idea . . .' Luke said slowly. 'It's too conspicuous as it is. I could get it off at the forge. William has all the tools I'd need. But we'd have to be quick. He was out drinking last night so with luck he'll be sleeping in today, but not for long.'

The kettle gave an ear-splitting shriek and they both jumped. Luke moved to the grate, pulled off the kettle, spooned leaves into two cups and poured on the water. He passed a cup to Rosa and then drained his own.

'I'm sorry about the locket,' he said gruffly, as he set his cup on the edge of the mantelpiece. The lees had made a strange flickery swirl in the bottom of the cup. They reminded him of flames.

'It's all right,' Rosa said. She put her hand to her pocket of her dress, feeling for something. 'I've still got the portrait, that's the main thing. The locket didn't really matter. It was the memories.'

'Portrait?'

She pulled it out, a little dirty scrap of paper, slightly sooty, cut oval to fit the shape of the locket. He took it in the palm of his hand, cradling it carefully as he turned it to the light of the fire, trying to see what it was. It was a child's drawing of a man with large dark eyes and a full beard, the perspective a little skewed and the proportions wrong. But she had caught something in the expression, something kindly and perhaps a little sad.

'Who is it?' he asked, but he knew, or thought he did, even before she answered.

'My papa. It doesn't look much like him really. In fact, Alexis—' She stopped.

'What?'

'Alexis said . . .' She gave a short laugh, a little bitter. 'He said that it reminded him of Charles Dickens crossed with a potato. But Papa liked it.'

Luke said nothing as he looked down at the scrap. He had no portrait of his own father and mother, not even any memories, save that one earliest blur: of himself, a small boy crouched beneath the settle as their blood ran red down the walls and a hand crept towards him, feeling for the snake's-head cane that had rolled across the floor through their pooling blood. The cane that he had last seen in Sebastian Knyvet's hand as he leapt from the factory window to freedom . . .

He could have followed. He could have followed and found out the truth about his parents and why they'd had to die. But instead he had turned back, for Rosa. He had chosen friendship over vengeance. And now it was too late.

He handed the scrap back to Rosa and she took it and tucked it into her pocket.

'Ready?' he asked.

'Ready,' she said, and stood, looking as if she were

steeling herself for something.

'Ready for what?' Phoebe stood in the doorway. She had put fresh paint on her face and the locket hung defiantly between her breasts, above her knotted woollen shawl.

'Thank you for the tea,' Rosa said. 'We have to leave.'

'Ain't you gonna tell me what all this is about?'

'I'm sorry.' Luke took her hand. 'I can't explain. But thank you, Phoebes. You don't know what you did for us. You might've saved our lives.'

'What *is* all this about, Luke?' For the first time she looked alarmed. 'You're not joking, are you? Are you in some kind of trouble?'

'Yes. Bad trouble. Phoebe, if anyone comes asking for us – doesn't matter if it's Leadingham, even my uncle – you never saw us, right?'

'All right.' She looked at him for a moment, her eyes worried, and then she leant forward and kissed him on the cheek, softly. 'I dunno what you've got yourself mixed up in, but you take care of yourself, Luke.'

'Goodbye, Phoebes.'

At the door she watched them go, biting her lip. They were halfway down the street when she called out, 'Wait!'

Luke turned as she came running down the alleyway towards them.

'What is it?'

'Here.' She pulled at the shawl, yanking it off over her head, and pushed it towards Rosa. 'Take this. Part-exchange for the locket, yeah?'

11

For a minute Luke thought Rosa was going to refuse. Then she nodded and wrapped the shawl around her shoulders.

'All right. Thank you, Phoebe.'

'G'bye.'

She watched them go, until the shadows closed around them all.

2

Luke probably didn't mean to walk so fast, but his legs were longer than Rosa's and he wasn't hampered by skirts and petticoats. She found herself half running to keep up, a painful stitch in her side where her corsets pinched. She told herself she could keep up, that she wouldn't beg, but at last, as he turned yet another corner in the dark and narrow maze of streets, she burst out, 'For God's sake, slow down!'

He turned to look at her, his mouth open in surprise.

'I'm sorry, I didn't mean . . .' He stopped, looking around. The quarter wasn't yet busy, but there were people about. 'I just . . .'

He swallowed and then said almost under his breath. 'The Malleus. The Brothers work these markets. We can't afford to meet 'em. Any of them.'

'Will they recognize me?'

'Maybe. I don't know.' He looked at her appraisingly, as if trying to see her with a stranger's eyes. Rosa hung her head. She could guess what she looked like, walking through the streets at dawn, with her head bare and her hair loose and her gown ripped and filthy.

'I must look like a tramp,' she said bitterly. To her surprise, Luke's worried face broke into a reluctant smile.

'You ain't seen many then. Or not many East End ones. No, you don't look like a tramp. But you don't look quite like a lady either. No, no, that's good,' he added hastily at the sight of her expression. 'They'll be looking for a lady, for Sebastian Knyvet's fiancée. Hang on a minute.' He pulled her into a quiet doorway, away from passers-by, and then took hold of the shawl, pulling it up around her face, covering her bright hair. 'Your gown's ripped and sooty from the fire, but the cut's too good, and these flounces are too fancy. We can't do much about the cut but . . .' Rosa felt a tug, there was a ripping sound and Luke let some torn silk and lace flutter to the ground. 'If only we could do something about that bloody ring. Phoebe's right. If anyone sees it and thinks it's real . . .'

'I'll hold the shawl like this.' Rosa twined her left hand in the wool, hiding her fingers. 'Is that better?'

'It'll have to do. Just don't let the shawl slip.' He turned up the collar of his coat and huddled into his muffler. 'Listen, is it all right . . . ?' He stopped.

'What?'

He stepped towards her. It was hard to see his expression

14

above the scarf, but she could have sworn there was a flush on his cheek.

'It'd look better if . . . if we looked like . . . sweethearts. Like a married couple off somewhere.' He was definitely blushing now; even in the thin winter dawn she could see his cheeks were scarlet. 'I don't want to be familiar, but . . . can I take your arm?'

She wanted to laugh, it was so preposterous that he was worrying about such things at a time like this.

'Luke! Stop being ridiculous.'

He flinched as if she'd slapped him and began to walk away, his head down. He was muttering something under his breath.

'. . . presumptuous . . . my place . . . servant . . .'

'Luke!' She ran to catch up. 'Luke! I meant of course you must take my arm. For heaven's sake, staying alive is the only thing that matters. I don't give a damn about presumption or anything else.'

'Really?' He turned to face her, his expression doubtful above his tight-wound muffler.

'Really.' She held out her arm and he took it, tucking her hand beneath his arm. He didn't mean to, but she couldn't suppress a gasp of pain as he crushed her burnt skin.

He let go instantly.

'My God, your arm, Rosa. I forgot.'

'It doesn't matter,' she said, through gritted teeth. Then her racing heart slowed and she was able to smile through the stab of pain. 'It's all right. I'll be able to heal it soon – when I've had some rest. Put your arm around my shoulders instead. It'll look more natural.'

For a moment he hesitated, and she was not certain if it was because he was unsure of himself, or of her. Then he did it, letting his arm rest stiffly across the nape of her neck, as if he was afraid to touch her.

They began to walk, and slowly she felt his muscles relax, the weight of his arm began to rest on her shoulder, and he drew her into his side, as if they were a real couple.

How easy to pretend, Rosa thought. *To just go on, pretending that this is the truth, just two people walking home, and all the rest, Sebastian, and the Malleus, and the factory – if only all of that were the crazy impossible fantasy.*

'What are we going to do?' she asked again, as she had at the pub, but this time it was without curiosity, with a bleak hopelessness that didn't expect an answer. 'Sebastian will never let me go, I know that, Luke. He told me before he left, he would rather kill me than lose me.'

'He thinks you're dead.' Luke's voice was low and steady, close to her ear. She felt his breath on her hair, through the shawl. 'Remember that. He has no reason to think we survived the fire at the factory. There'll be bodies enough to keep him puzzled for a while; I didn't get everyone out. It'll be a long time before anyone comes looking for us.'

She didn't believe him. An outwith might have been fooled – but not Sebastian. But she didn't argue. Instead she felt Luke squeeze her shoulders, a rough, comforting gesture that made tears spring to her eyes.

'It'll be all right, Rosa. We'll get the ring off at the forge, and then we'll sell it, and use the money to get a horse from somewhere. It'll be all right, I promise.'

His promise comforted her, not because she believed him, but because she knew he lied for her sake.

The forge was still in darkness. There were no sparks coming from the chimney as they walked quietly up the lane. Luke lifted his arm from Rosa's shoulders and put his finger to his lips as he lifted the latch of the gate and pulled it ajar, holding its weight so that the hinges wouldn't squeal out and wake William.

Rosa slipped through the gap into the cobbled yard, and Luke pulled the gate shut behind her, latching it so that no one would see the open gate and think the forge open. The snow was still falling and the cobbles were slick with ice as they crossed them carefully. Luke glanced up at his uncle's window as they passed, but it was still dark. He had no watch, but it must be gone seven, and even when he was sleeping off a hangover William rarely slept past eight.

Inside the forge he pulled the door shut against the cold and began to search through William's tools. He laid the likeliest out on the bench – a narrow rasp, nippers, the smallest hacksaw . . . He and Rosa stood looking at them, and he could see the fear in Rosa's face. He felt it himself, looking from the huge heavy tools down at her small hand, bloodied and dusted with soot.

'It's not going to work,' he said at last. 'William's got nothing small enough. We need a goldsmith's tools, not these.'

'Try,' she said. 'At least try.'

With a sick heart he picked up the nippers and tried to angle them to pinch just the gold band of the ring, keeping clear of the skin of her finger, but it was nearly impossible. They were too large and too heavy, and the ring dug so tightly into Rosa's finger that he couldn't get a purchase on the metal without pinching her flesh. At last he thought he had it, and began to tighten, gently, and then harder.

'Stop!' she screamed, and he let the nippers clatter to the floor. There was sweat on her forehead, sticking the red-gold hair to her face. She closed her eyes. Blood was running down her finger. 'No, take no notice of me,' she said, her voice shaking. 'Try again.'

'No.' Sickness rose in Luke's throat, the sight of her blood turning his stomach. 'No, I won't.'

'Coward,' she said bitterly, and Luke's stomach clenched as if he'd been punched.

'*What* did you say?' His voice came out louder and more dangerous than he'd meant. 'If you were a man, I'd—'

He broke off, suddenly hot with shame. Had it come to this, that he was so afraid of his own cowardice that he was reduced to shouting threats at an injured girl? Not just a coward, but a bully too. At least Knyvet, loathsome though he was, was brave in his own way.

18

'I'm sorry.' He couldn't bear to look at her as he walked back to the tool rack to put them away, avoiding her gaze. 'I didn't mean—'

'It's tightened,' she said in a small voice, breaking into his stumbling apology. 'That was why I screamed. It wasn't the cut – I could have stood that. But the ring – when you tried to clip it off, it tightened.'

'What?' He moved across the forge and snatched up her hand. She was right. The ring, previously just too narrow to get past her knuckle, but loose enough to turn, was now so tight he couldn't move it, though her skin was slick with blood. 'Are you sure? Couldn't it just be your finger's swollen?'

She shook her head.

'My finger's been swollen ever since I tried to take it off yesterday. That's not it – this is different. I *felt* it tighten when you tried to clip it. It was like it . . . knew.'

They looked at each other, and Luke saw his own fear and doubt reflected back in her eyes. He opened his mouth, trying to think of something to say that would reassure her, something that would get them out of this unholy mess – when he heard a noise in the yard. He stiffened and then, as the forge door latch began to rattle, he pushed her roughly down behind the big stone hearth and stood in front of her, his heart banging in his throat, waiting to see who would come through the door.

It was William's voice he heard as the door began to swing open.

'Whoever you are, messin' about in my forge, I'll have your – eh?'

William stood in the doorway, his hair rumpled from his bed, his boots on beneath his nightgown.

'Luke! What are you doing here at sparrow fart, lad? I thought you were abed.'

'I couldn't sleep.' It was almost true, after all. He hadn't slept, though in truth he hadn't had the chance.

'But . . .' William took a step forward into the forge, towards where Rosa was hiding. Luke held his breath and prayed. 'Your coat, it's all charred and burnt. What happened? Were you in a fire? You stink of smoke . . . and summat else. Where've you bin?'

'I've been to the Cock Tavern.' That was true too, but it was not the truth. 'There was a fight.' Another truth, another twist. 'I got pushed into a street brazier, boy selling chestnuts.' *Lies*. He felt sick with deception.

'But your skull, lad! You shouldn't be drinking and brawling. You're not two days out of bed!'

'I know.' Luke clenched his fingers inside his coat pockets, begging William in his head to leave, *begging* him to go and stop asking questions. He could hear Rosa's stifled breathing behind him, and from the corner of his eye he could see the shift and swirl of her magic. *Please leave* . . .

William shook his head. He turned on his heel and Luke held his breath. Then just as William reached the door he turned back.

'Lad, listen.' He came back across the cobbled floor towards Luke. Luke held his breath. Any second now he was going to come round the corner of the forge hearth and he would see Rosa and it would all be over. Behind him he heard Rosa's panicked gasp and knew she knew this too – he felt her magic flare up like a fire in a draught, knew that she was gathering herself together, readying herself to cast—

'No!' He swung round, took a step backwards to put himself between her and William. 'No! Rosa, don't – not William.'

There was a sudden, perfect silence. A silence so complete he could hear the wind in the chimney, and then Rosa's skirts rustled and she stood, in full view of William.

William's mouth dropped open.

For a minute none of them said anything, then William gave a great guffaw.

'You were with a *girl* last night? That's what all this secrecy was about?'

Luke bit his lip, wondering if he could stand here barefaced and carry off the lie, pretend that Rosa was a tavern girl. But it would be all over as soon as she opened her mouth. She might not look much of a lady at the moment, but she still sounded like one.

'What's your name, love?' William was asking Rosa. 'Rosie, did he say?'

Before Luke could stop her, before he could jump in with a false name that would protect them both, she

21

answered, her voice as clear and grave as if she were giving evidence against him.

'Rosa. Rosa Greenwood.'

For a moment William didn't connect the dots. He stood, his brow furrowed. Luke could almost hear the ticking of his thoughts: *Heard that name somewhere . . . not a local . . .*

Then the penny dropped. Luke could see it, to the very second. His uncle's face went ashen and he looked from Luke, to Rosa, and then back again with a kind of horror.

'My God, it's *her*. It's the witch!'

'Yes.' It was all Luke could say. There was no point in lying any longer – it was much too late.

'Are you mad?' William spoke in a kind of screaming whisper. 'Why in hell's name did you bring her here? You can't do the job here, Luke. We'll all be for the chop.'

For a minute Luke was too surprised to speak – then he almost laughed. After all this, after everything that had happened, William still thought he was going to do it. He felt as if his treachery were written on his face – and yet even *William* hadn't guessed the truth of it. He had no idea of the depth of Luke's betrayal.

'I'm not going to kill her,' he said. He felt light with the relief of speaking the truth, and dizzy with the stupidity of saying it aloud. 'I can't.'

'She's bewitched you.' William spoke hoarsely. He was backing away towards the door, trying to put distance between himself and Rosa, his eyes flicking between her and Luke as if she were a tiger in the corner of the forge, not a frightened, injured girl. 'That concussion, I knew it weren't natural. She's addled your head, Luke. Think, man! Think what this'll mean – to you, to the Brotherhood. Her life or yours, Luke. Her life or yours!'

'She hasn't bewitched me,' Luke said impatiently. He took a step forward, towards William, holding his hand out pleadingly. 'Come on, Uncle. You can see it's me, for God's sake! Do I look bewitched? I tried to do it, not once but twice, God forgive me, and it nearly killed *me*. I tried to tell you what it was like when I came back to the forge that time – I'm not a murderer.'

'But why in God's name did you bring her here?' William groaned.

'I didn't bring her – she came for me, and d'you know why? To tell me her fiancé, Sebastian Knyvet, was enslaving men and women and girls at his match factory off Brick Lane, and to ask for my help. And I turned her away with a curse and a threat to kill her. She could have gone home and left them there to rot, but she didn't. She went back to free them herself, and got half killed in the process. Look at her!'

He didn't say the rest: that he'd not only spared Rosa but had let Knyvet go – and with him the truth about Luke's parents' death. He'd turned away and gone back for Rosa. He had chosen her.

'She's been chosen!' William hissed, echoing his thoughts

23

so strangely that Luke flinched. 'God's chosen her to die, Luke! And I'll not lose you for—'

'God didn't choose her,' Luke broke in roughly. 'I did. I stabbed that bloody pin. I picked her name. If God had anything to do with it, maybe it was to show me the madness of what we're doing. Killing people because of their birthright? Men should be punished for their deeds, not for something they can't help!'

'Her life or yours!' William shouted.

'I don't care!' Luke bellowed back, the veins in his throat standing out. He slammed his fist down on the anvil, his face dark with anger. 'I don't care,' he said more quietly. 'I don't believe it anyway – I know it's what they say, but I don't believe they'd do it. What, men who've known me since I was a nipper? Send me to the dogs because I wouldn't kill a girl half my size?'

But William was shaking his head.

'Don't mistake the Brothers, Luke. They'd do it all right. Remember Ethan Wilder? Tall lad, skinny, apprentice at the printworks in the city?'

Luke nodded, remembering a lanky figure from his childhood, a shy lad with peach-down cheeks that burnt rose-red when he blushed.

'Yes, I remember him. What of it?'

'He boasted of it, of the Malleus. Told a man at the works he'd been taken into the Brotherhood. Not a witch – no one who mattered, but that wasn't the point. He'd broken the oath of silence.'

'And?' An uneasy coldness pooled in the pit of his stomach.

'They took his tongue. Cut it out at the root.'

'Who?' Luke's voice caught hoarsely, as if there was smoke in his throat, but the air was clear.

'Never you mind who. But I was there. I helped hold him down, God forgive me, though I didn't wield the knife. He was a boy like you, no older. And he didn't do the half of what you're proposing. You've not just failed in your task, you've turned – you've turned . . .' His voice cracked and he turned away, scrubbing at his face in an agony.

'Traitor,' Luke finished dully. 'A traitor to the Brotherhood.'

'Kill her, Luke,' William begged, as though Rosa couldn't hear, as though she wasn't huddled against the wall just feet away, her eyes wide and dark with fear. 'Do it now and this can all be over. Think of your parents, man! They'd be turning in their graves if they knew.'

'I won't do it!' Luke cried. William's words were almost more than he could bear. 'Don't ask me again, William. Now, get out of my way – or would you rather I knocked you down? At least then you can tell the Brotherhood you were overpowered.'

'No!' William's voice cracked and he held out one large hand to Luke, pleadingly. But Luke looked away, held his arm out towards Rosa.

'Come on, R-Rosa.' He stumbled over her name. It still felt so strange saying it, stranger still in front of William.

She nodded, her expression still full of shock, and they moved together towards the forge doorway. For a heart-racing moment, Luke thought that William was going to bar their way – he stood in the doorway, his big frame blocking it, his hands hanging helpless by his side. But as they drew close he seemed to flinch from the sight of Rosa, and he fell back as they walked out into the snow-dusted courtyard.

'Keep walking,' Luke said in a low voice. 'Don't be afraid.'

'I'm not afraid,' she said fiercely, but he could tell it was a lie. Luke flung a quick glance over his shoulder as they reached the gate to the lane.

'It's all right. He's gone back into the forge.' *He doesn't want to watch me go . . .*

He pulled at the gate latch with fingers that were suddenly numb and cold. The metal tongue had frozen to the catch and he had to drop Rosa's hand to wrestle with it. It sprang free with a bang, and he was about to yank open the gate and walk through when some other sound made them both turn.

William was standing in the doorway of the forge, a pistol in his hand.

Rosa's eyes widened and she crouched instinctively, like an animal going to ground, making itself the smallest target it could.

'No!' Luke bellowed. He flung himself at Rosa and at the same time there was a deafening crack, and he felt a thump in his shoulder as if he'd been punched. He gasped, and William cried out, a terrible cry.

'Luke!'

'Oh my God!' Rosa leapt to her feet, her hands feeling for his shoulder, but he pulled away, dizzy and staggering, shaking his head.

'I'm all right, I'm all right,' he gasped. But he was not. He could feel he was not. The pain was spreading like a pool of fire across his shoulder and down his arm.

'Luke!' William cried again. He let the pistol fall from his hand, his face white and bloodless. 'I never meant—'

'No, you meant to kill her, not me,' Luke managed. He steadied himself on the gatepost. He felt sick and dizzy, and he thought he might fall. Pain raced up and down his arm with every heartbeat.

'I only thought—'

'Goodbye, Uncle.' He took Rosa's arm and together they walked through the gate, letting it slam behind them with a crash to wake the dead.

3

In spite of Rosa's pleas, Luke wouldn't stop but carried on doggedly up the lane and into the street. At last, a hundred yards away from the forge, he turned into a narrow alley between two warehouses and slumped against a wall, feeling the sweat prickling his skin in spite of the cold air. Rosa began to pull back the thick, blood-wet fabric of the greatcoat, searching for the wound.

'It's all right,' he said dully, as she peeled back his muffler and then his coat. The blood steamed in the cold air, mingling with her short quick breaths. 'I can feel it's all right. I can move my arm. Must have missed.'

'It didn't miss,' she snapped furiously. Her cheeks were scarlet with some strong emotion – anger, or perhaps fear. Her magic crackled. 'You're covered in blood.'

'Missed anything important.' He thought of John Leadingham's lessons on killing a witch. Aim for an artery or a vital organ. Spleen, kidney, carotid, femoral – not the lung or the heart: too many ribs to get through. Failing that, a tendon that could incapacitate long enough for you to get away.

At last she had his shirt unbuttoned and pulled back to the skin, and he craned round, looking at the damage. As he'd thought, it was nothing like as bad as William must have feared. The bullet had torn a shallow furrow along his bicep, but it'd heal.

Rosa was looking at it, her brows furrowed in concentration, and for a minute he didn't understand what she was doing. Then he saw her lips move, and felt the hot tingle of her magic rush through his muscles like a drug.

'Stop it!' He began to struggle in her grasp, but she hung on, digging her nails into his bare skin and the material of his coat. 'I don't want your magic!'

'Stop cutting off your nose to spite your face!' Rosa cried. With a great effort he twisted himself out of her grasp with a wrench that sent her stumbling to her hands and knees in the alley. But when she looked up she was smiling, and as he pulled his shirt roughly back over his shoulder he could feel the skin was whole again.

'Damn you! Don't ever do that to me again!'

'Why not? What's *wrong* with it, Luke?'

'It's not—' He stopped, struggling for words, his breath coming fast and white in the still air of the alleyway. Then a small fox-faced boy came down the street, kicking a stone in front of him, and stopped to look at them.

'Bit early for a lovers' tiff, ain't it?'

'Shut up and mind your own business,' Luke growled.

'Gissa penny and I'll leave you alone,' the boy said with a grin.

'I said, get lost!'

'Farthing?' the boy called, dodging the stone Luke threw at him, and then he ran off up the alleyway. 'A'right, I'll settle for a kiss!' he shouted out as he rounded the corner. Luke couldn't stop a smile from twitching at the corner of his mouth, and somehow, as he buttoned his coat, the blood sticky beneath his fingers, he couldn't find his anger of a moment before, only a ghost of it.

'I'm sorry,' Rosa said quietly as they began to walk back towards the main street. 'But you let me save you in the factory, Luke. Why is this any different?'

'Because . . .' But he trailed off. Why was it different? Because he had been about to die when he fell through the factory floor? Because, in that instant, he didn't care whether he was saved by Rosa's magic, or divine intervention, or a fairy godmother – he just wanted to live? He couldn't answer. He just knew that it felt different, and that to sit there, helpless, consenting, as her magic burrowed into his skin was too much, too intimate. 'Because I didn't need saving this time,' he managed at last. 'I would've healed.'

'Maybe,' was all she said. They walked in silence until at last Rosa asked, 'Where are we going, Luke?'

'I don't know. Far away from here. We need a horse.

Unless we can get enough money for a train ticket.'

'No,' she said with certainty. 'Not a train. When they find out I've gone they'll ask at the train stations, and if the ticket office remember us, they'll know exactly where we went, and when we get there we'll be sitting ducks without any transport. No, a horse is better. With a horse, we could be anywhere.'

'Well then, we need a horse. And the only horse I can think of . . .'

'Brimstone.' Her face was pale. 'Or the carriage horses. That's what you're thinking, isn't it? Oh God, Luke, I don't know if I can do it. I don't know if I can go back there. What if they see me? What if Sebastian—'

'I'll go. You can wait in the park.'

'No – if the servants see you . . . they know you've been turned off. Oh God.' She put her hands to her face and he saw the ruby give a flash of fire.

'Cover that up!' Luke said urgently, and Rosa gave an exclamation of frustration and thrust her hand inside her shawl. 'Look,' he said more quietly, 'we'll wait until dark, then go round by the mews. No one will hear us.'

'But they've engaged another groom already, and he's sleeping above the stable. Mama was spending money like water on the promise of my marriage to Sebastian. No, I must go. I can make myself invisible if the worst comes to it.'

'But will that work against a witch?'

She flinched, and he said, 'What's the matter? Did I

say something wrong?'

'It's that word,' she said quietly. 'W-witch. It's not . . . not polite.'

'What do you call yourselves then?'

'Nothing. What do you call yourselves? Normal. We call your kind "outwith", do you know that?'

'No.' He felt again as if he'd fallen down a rabbit hole. 'At least – I think I heard Sebastian call me that, once. I thought it was an insult.'

'It's not insulting,' she said slowly. 'Although he might have meant it that way. It's just . . . the word we use to describe someone without magic. But to answer your question, it's complicated. Another, well, someone like me – we can see through a spell an outwith might not be able to penetrate. But we would have to try. We would have to notice that the spell was there in order to break through it. I suppose it's a bit like being a confidence trickster. Maybe you're more likely to see through a deception because you know how it's worked, but that doesn't make you infallible, it doesn't mean you'll never be duped yourself.'

'So – you're less likely to get caught, but it's not impossible?'

'Yes.'

'But if they catch you . . .'

'I don't know.' Her voice was bleak. 'I don't think Sebastian will let me go. I know what he did at the factory. I could give evidence against him. And my mother and brother will be bankrupt without this marriage. I think

32

they would force me into it, or try to.'

'No one can force you to marry!' Luke burst out angrily. 'This isn't the Middle Ages, Rosa!'

'It's not that simple,' Rosa said. Her face was tight, her lips pressed together. When she spoke again her words were clipped. 'I've had no choices, no freedom, Luke. Not ever. It's not like I can earn a living – I have nothing but what Alexis and my mother give me – whether that's food, or clothes, or freedom.'

'But no one can *make* you say, "I do"!'

'Oh really?' She looked at him, her small pale face full of a weary kind of anger. Luke shook his head, ready to argue his point, but found his head was no longer shaking but nodding. He opened his mouth to tell her to stop, to shout at her for playing with his mind like this, and he found his unwilling lips forming words that were not his own.

'I . . . *do* . . .' It came out like a strangled gasp, through lips that were stiff and teeth clenched together, but they were unmistakably words. Then, abruptly, she loosed the spell.

'I'm sorry,' she said. 'That was cheap and cruel. But you see what I mean.'

He shuddered, but still his mind refused to accept it.

'But you're a witch! You could fight them – fight the spell.'

'I have magic, yes.' Rosa pulled the shawl tighter around her shoulders. 'But I'm not particularly strong.'

'You're stronger than Alexis.' He said it with certainty, remembering Rosa's dazzling blaze of fire, compared to Alexis's weak green haze.

'Yes.' There was no boasting in Rosa's voice, just a statement of fact. 'But there's Mama too – I cannot fight them if they work together against me. This marriage is vital to them both. For her it's her fortune, but for him it's something more – it's his future, it's power and influence. And in any case, none of that would matter if Sebastian took their side. I was never able to best him, even as a girl, and he's only got stronger.' She shuddered again, suddenly, convulsively. 'Since his father died – I don't understand it, Luke. No one should have power like he does. It's like a hurricane.'

Luke thought back to the black swirling cloud of hate that he had seen in the warehouse, before Sebastian jumped. Yes. He could see how no one could fight that. The thought of drowning in that darkness . . .

'We must be quick,' he said stubbornly. 'And careful. That's all. And once we have a horse we can be out of London in a few hours.'

'But what about money? Even if we could get this ring off, would we be able to sell it? Wouldn't they think we'd stolen it? I don't exactly look like the kind of woman who wears a ruby ring any more.'

Luke bit his lip. It was true. And worse – it would draw attention to them. Even if they found someone shady enough to give them money for the ring, it wouldn't be a

34

fair price, and it would more than likely set Sebastian on their trail.

'Can't you magic some up?' he asked crossly, hating to ask. But she shook her head. 'Why not? Not now, I mean, I know you're tired, but later . . .'

'It's not that simple,' she said again. Her face looked pinched and tired. 'Look, there's two ways of creating something like money. Either you do it for real – change the real, base nature of the elements – and that's very difficult magic: alchemy, it's called. You need to be very strong and very practised and it can go horribly wrong.'

'Wrong?' Luke echoed. 'How?'

'Think of Midas,' Rosa said shortly. 'Once you start changing things, it's not always easy to know when to stop, *how* to stop.'

'And the other way?'

'Illusory magic. You don't really change boot buttons to sovereigns, you just make the shopkeeper *think* it's a sovereign in his hand. But that's dangerous in its own way too.'

'How?'

'Because the illusion can only hold as long as the spell holds – as long as I concentrate on keeping it up. So I can make you *think* I have a bacon roll in my hand . . .'

He blinked, and suddenly there was a bacon roll on her outstretched palm. He reached out for it, but it felt wrong in his grip – thin, insubstantial – and when he sniffed it, it didn't smell of bacon, but like the memory of

35

bacon – an ersatz nondescript savouriness. It was like food in a dream. As he watched, Rosa exhaled and the roll dissolved into nothing, leaving him grasping at air.

'It's dangerous because it's very obvious,' she said regretfully. 'If we walk away and the innkeeper finds he's holding dried leaves instead of banknotes, how long do you think before he comes after us? And how long until the story spreads – back to Sebastian, or back to your kind?'

Luke nodded, a bitter resignation spreading through his bones. It seemed as though witchcraft should be good for *something* at least. And yet Rosa, in her own way, was as powerless as him.

'Clemency . . .' Rosa's voice broke into his thoughts.

'What?'

'Clemency. My friend, Clemency. She has money. And she might—'

'No.' Luke cut across her furiously. 'We can't trust her!'

'Because she's a witch? Is that it?'

'No, because . . .' *Because she's a toff – one of them*, was what he'd been about to say. But wasn't Rosa one of *them* too?

'Look.' She grabbed his arm. 'I let you take me to that place, that pub. You vouched for Phoebe and I trusted you. Won't you trust my word on Clemency? Luke, she *won't* betray us, I promise.'

He took a deep breath – held it – counted to ten while he thought. Then he let it out with a gusting sigh.

'All right. It's your funeral.'

36

'I hope it won't come to that for either of us,' Rosa said, with slight acidity. Then she pulled her shawl around her shoulders and stood up straighter. 'Let's get walking.'

God, it was a long way. What made it worse was that Luke seemed immune to it. He never complained, never stumbled over piles of rubbish on the pavement, never slipped into a puddle of filth. He just strode beside her, not panting, not grumbling, but walking tirelessly. At Covent Garden he took her arm to forge a path through the throngs – it had seemed as if they would be stuck for ever in the shifting mass of traders and carts. Rosa let herself be pulled in his wake as he shoved and pushed with one shoulder, ramming through the tight-packed crowd. After that he kept hold of her arm, tugging her along, helping her to keep pace.

Even so, Rosa's feet in their tight-buttoned boots were crying out, and her free arm throbbed painfully. It was too bad that she had spent all her magic healing Luke's shoulder. Not that he was grateful for it, she reflected bitterly as they crossed Piccadilly. She should have saved her energy and healed her own skin first. Now she would be lucky if it didn't scar.

She thought again of the smooth pale skin of his shoulder, the veins blue beneath the glaze of blood, the muscles shifting and tense as he strove to pull away, and the soft brush of hair beneath his arm. She could not remember ever having touched a man's naked body before.

She had seen boys, of course: Alexis and his friends bathing in the lake, and once, as she spied through her bedroom curtains, Luke himself stripped to the waist and bathing beneath the pump in the yard. But touching a full-grown man so confidently, so intimately? That, never. The thought of what she had done – stripping back Luke's clothes even as he struggled away from her – both amazed and appalled her. Where had she found the courage?

Luke didn't speak as they tramped across London, and for that she was grateful. Other men would have made solicitous small talk, remarked on the weather, the crowds, the likelihood of rain. Not Luke. He walked in silence, his arm firm beneath hers, just glancing at her from time to time to make sure she was keeping up. And she herself had no breath to spare for chat.

At last they passed Fortnum and Mason's and she was able to let out a sigh of relief. Not far to Clemency's now. Pray God that Philip would be at the Ealdwitan for business. The thought gave her sudden pause and she stopped.

'Luke.'

'Yes?'

'Clemency is married.'

She waited for him to respond, but he did not, and she was forced to continue. 'I trust her, but not her husband. He is a member of the Ealdwitan, our ruling council, and he reports to Sebastian. What shall we do?'

Luke thought, still in silence. Then, just as she was about to prod him in despair, he said, 'Well, we'll have to find out if he's home. The servants would recognize you, right?'

'Yes.'

'So I'll have to ask.'

'Yes, but, Luke, they'll tell you he's not home anyway. He's not going to come to the door for a—' She stopped, not wanting to wound him, but she could see he understood. It was a part of his life as much as hers, after all. He had had eighteen years to get used to her class looking down on his.

'No . . . he won't come to the door for a stable-hand, but I don't need to see him.' He began to walk again, and they continued in silence up Piccadilly until they reached the turn-off for Clemency's house.

'Left here,' Rosa said, and then, as they rounded the corner, 'the third house on the right is Clemency's – the one with the rhododendrons in the front.'

'Stay here,' Luke said. He dropped her arm.

'What are you doing?'

'Going to find out if her husband's there – what's his name, by the way?'

'Philip. Philip Catesby. But, Luke—'

But he had already gone up the road, knocking on the big polished front door.

Rosa flattened herself against the railings, her heart in her mouth, and listened as a maid opened the door. She heard Luke's murmuring voice and the maid's tart response.

'No, he ain't at home to the likes of you. And next time,

come to the tradesmen's entrance.'

Rosa watched through the rhododendron leaves as Luke pulled off his cap, his straw-coloured hair tumbling over his forehead, and smiled at the girl.

'Sorry, miss,' she heard. 'I'll know for next time. It was only I had a message for him, from Mr Greenwood.'

'Well, he's down at his office,' the girl said, mollified. She brushed an imaginary speck of dust off her white apron. 'If you fancy coming back later, he'll be here around four. Or you can leave a note.'

'Not to worry,' Luke said. He flashed another smile and a dimple appeared in his cheek. 'But I might take the excuse to come back if I thought I'd get a smile from you. Think you could manage one before I go?'

'Oi, cheeky!' the girl said indignantly. But she *was* smiling, looking at him under her lashes as she shut the door.

So Luke could flirt! Who would have thought it – silent, taciturn Luke. Rosa watched through the leaves as he came back down the path, the smile gone from his face, his expression serious again.

'He's out, did you hear?'

'Yes.' The question only remained, was Clemency? There was only one way to find out. 'You'd better wait here while I go and speak to Clemency.'

'All right.' He bit his lip, looking down at her, the dimple buried as if it had never been. 'Be careful.'

'I will be.'

Her heart was pounding as she went up the path to the front door, where Luke had knocked only a moment before. She plied the knocker again and heard the girl's footsteps.

'I told you,' she heard as the girl opened the door, 'smile or no smile, it's the tradesmen's— Oh! Who're you?'

'I'd like to see your mistress,' Rosa said. The girl frowned, taking in her shabby, burnt clothes and cheap shawl, but puzzled by her accent. 'Mrs Catesby. Is she at home?'

'Not to you.' The girl came down with a thump on the side of suspicion and folded her arms. 'What of it?'

'I don't want any of this "not at home",' Rosa said impatiently. 'If she's here, she'll be at home to me. I'm an old friend.'

'Oh really!' The girl raised one over-plucked eyebrow. 'Queen of Sheba, are we?'

'If you don't go and get your mistress immediately,' Rosa hissed, 'I'll see to it that you're sacked. Tell her Miss Greenwood is at the door and you've kept her waiting by refusing to pass on a message. Look.' She fumbled in the pocket in her skirt and pulled out a card – smudged and sooty round the edges – bearing the name 'Miss Rosa Greenwood'. The girl looked down at it, chewing her lip, and seemed to make up her mind.

'Wait here,' she said haughtily, and shut the door in Rosa's face. When she opened it again it was with a slightly sour expression. 'You'd better come this way.'

Rosa followed her down the hallway into the drawing

41

room, where Clemency was sitting on an overstuffed sofa. She had a needle and thread in her hand, but she flung down the embroidery hoop at the sight of Rosa and hurried across the silk Turkey rug with her hands outstretched.

'Rosa! My God, what's happened to you? That's all right, Millie,' she added to the maid. 'You can go.' As the girl withdrew reluctantly, she turned back to Rosa. 'When Millie said there was a shabby woman at the door with your card I didn't know what to think. Rosa, are you all right?'

'No.' Her chin began to wobble at the sight of Clemency, so normal and so concerned. 'No, I'm not all right. Oh, Clemency, we're in such trouble – I didn't know where to turn.'

'We?' Clemency took Rosa's hand and tried to lead her across to an armchair. 'Who's "we"? Sit down, for pity's sake, Rosa. I'll call for tea.'

'No, I can't stay, and I can't sit, I'll ruin your chair.'

'Damn the chair!' Clemency said. Her plump, comfortable face was anxious. 'Rosa, please tell me what's happened? Your dress – it's all burnt! Where's your hat? And where in heaven's name did you get that horrible shawl? It looks like a dishrag!'

'It was Sebastian—' Rosa began, but she couldn't finish. Suddenly the strain, not just of the night, but of the past days and weeks, seemed to well up inside her and she found she was sobbing. Clemency pushed her to a chair and forced her to sit, and somehow Rosa found the

42

whole tale spilling out – how she had agreed to marry Sebastian against her better judgement, in spite of her growing fear of him, and how Luke had caught her crying in the stable after she had become engaged, and they had ended up kissing.

'Sebastian walked in on us,' she said, wiping her nose with her sleeve. Nothing could make the dress more soiled than it already was. 'And, oh, Clemency, he was so angry. He . . . he beat me. And he must have beat Luke, although I didn't see that.'

Clemency said nothing, but Rosa could see the thoughts flitting across her face, her sympathy for Rosa mixed with revulsion at the idea of kissing an outwith and a servant, and with the thought that any man of pride might have lashed out if he caught his new fiancée in the arms of a stable-hand.

'I thought he would break it off,' Rosa continued, her voice low and hoarse. 'The engagement. But he *didn't*. And I realized that somehow the whole episode had only made him want me more. I never thought a man would want a woman who didn't love him, but, oh, Clemmie – it was as if the more I hated him, the more he was excited by it, and the more he *had* to have me. Does this make any kind of sense to you?'

'I'm not sure,' Clemency said. Her blue eyes were fixed on Rosa, her rosebud lips were tight, reserving judgement. 'Perhaps. Some men are creatures of strange tastes, that much I know, and I can see that perhaps your . . .

indiscretion, let's call it – might have hurt his pride and made him more determined to hold on to you. But that doesn't explain all this . . . What happened with your dress?'

'Luke was turned off, when we got back to London, of course,' Rosa gulped, and Clemency nodded.

'Of course.'

'I was trapped. If I broke it off with Sebastian he would expose me, and worse, he would very probably take his revenge on Luke. And I felt so guilty – it seemed to me that if Sebastian were prepared to forgive me, shouldn't I be able to forgive *him*? So I tried to carry on, I tried to be a good fiancée and take an interest in his family's work and their charitable concerns. So I went to the East End, to his factory, and – oh, Clemency, what I found . . .' She broke off, reliving again the horror of those dimly lit rooms, glowing with the ghostly luminescence of the phosphorus, and the men and women and children with their faces eaten away by the chemicals. She remembered the smell of it – flesh and bone liquefying into a stinking, oozing putrefaction. 'They were dying, Clemmie. The outwith workers. There was no way they could have stayed in that poisonous place willingly. They were drugged with magic – chained there – like slaves.'

Clemency bit her lip. Her face was very still, very serious.

'So what did you do?'

'I tried to persuade them to leave, but they wouldn't

44

listen to me. The charms were too strong – I don't know how, but they were like iron, far stronger than I could break. I pleaded but they just ignored me and carried on. And then I recognized one of the workers – a girl. She was a friend of Luke's. And I thought if I went and got him, he might be able to help, she might listen to *him*, if not me. But . . . ' She stopped.

This was the one part she must not tell Clemency. She could betray her own secrets, but not Luke's. Luke's identity as one of the Malleus Maleficorum must remain secret at all costs, even from Clemency, or they were *both* dead. Clemency would never agree to help them if she knew. And there was also the cold immutability of a fact that she had not yet quite faced: Luke had been tasked to kill her and, though his nerve had failed him at the last moment, he had tried to carry that task out. She did not know if she would ever be able to forget the sight of him raising the hammer above his head, the hate in his eyes . . .

'Yes?' Clemency prodded. Rosa took a breath, picking her way carefully between the truth and the omissions.

'He didn't remember me. I took his memories when he went away, and he no longer knew who I was. So I returned alone and confronted Sebastian – to try to make him lift the spells.'

'It didn't work,' Clemency said, in confirmation rather than question.

'No. And he shut me in the warehouse and set fire to it

'– I suppose to hide what he'd done, and perhaps because in that instant he realized that he had lost me, and he could not bear for that to happen.'

'He locked you in?' Clemency's normally rosy face was pale, and her wide blue eyes were even wider than usual. 'He left you to *die*?'

Rosa nodded.

'Yes, but Luke must have remembered something, because he came after me in the end, and helped me escape. But now, Clemmie, you must help us. We have to leave London, before Sebastian finds us.'

'Oh God, Rosa.' Clemency stood and began pacing the Turkey rug back and forth, back and forth. 'What can I do? I really think – surely your mother—'

'Mama?' Rosa knew the bitterness in her voice was unpleasant, but she couldn't hide it. 'Ha. She's so afraid of losing Sebastian's money – she'd sell me to him in an instant. She'd sell *herself* even, I think.'

'But, darling, think!' Clemency's plump comfortable face was contorted with distress. 'Think what you're saying . . . You're proposing – what? To run away with – with this *stable-hand*? You'll be ruined! And how will you live? Go home, please, darling.'

'Clemmie, listen to me. Sebastian Knyvet tried to *kill* me. Do you understand what I'm saying? I think he is mad. I saw it before, but never so clearly until that night in the factory. I cannot go home – even if Mama and Alexis believed me, Sebastian would know I was there. I must get away before he finds me – before he kills us both.' *Or worse*, she added silently in her head. To be married to Sebastian, that could be a living death in itself.

'But . . .' Clemency wound her fingers in her handkerchief until they were bloodless, and then released them. 'But Philip has the carriage. What can I do?'

'I can manage horses. We just need money, Clemmie Only a little!' she added pleadingly, as she saw Clemency about to protest that she had none, that it was all Philip's. 'Please! Whatever you have in the house – enough for a meal and a bed – I have nothing, Clemmie. I haven't eaten since . . .' She suddenly realized that she could not remember when. Yesterday, certainly, and she'd had no dinner. Had she had tea? Lunch, even? 'Please, Clemmie,' she said again, swallowing against the lump of helpless rage in her throat. '*Please*.'

Clemency bit her lip again, and then seemed to decide.

'You can have whatever I have in the house. Let me go to my room and see what I have in my change purse – Philip may have left some notes in his dressing room. But oh God – Rosa – why did you give the maid your real name? What if Sebastian comes here?'

Rosa shut her eyes, suddenly realizing the truth of what Clemency said. Even if Clemency denied her visit, the maid would not. Did she dare risk a spell to wipe the girl's memory? But Clemency's servants were not outwith; the maid would know what she was attempting, would fight.

'You must tell me that you cannot help, in front of the

47

servants,' she said slowly. 'We must have a fight.'

'Yes . . . yes, that might work. Let me get the money and then . . . then we'll decide what to do.'

She left the room and Rosa sank back in the armchair, her hands over her face, trying to push away the sense that her world was collapsing around her. Yesterday had held the promise of all this – a house off Piccadilly, servants, tea-trays, comfort, wealth. Today? She had nothing, except a spoilt dress and her magic.

And Luke, something whispered at the back of her mind. *You have Luke*. But it was not true. He was not hers. He was not her servant, nor her lover. They were just – what? Friends? But that one simple word did not describe what lay between them – the complicated web of hurt and gratitude and betrayal, and beneath all that, a great gulf of class and magic. Luke had tried to kill her, and he had saved her life. He was an outwith, and yet he could see her kind as no other outwith could, as no witch could, even. All these impossibly contradictory truths bound up in one being.

Friend was too small and too simple a word for what Luke was.

He was something else. Something bigger, more complicated and, perhaps, more dangerous . . .

'Rosa.'

Her head shot up. Clemency was standing in the doorway. She came inside and closed the door with her elbow. Her hands were full of something.

'Darling, I found this . . .' She poured a shower of silvers, coppers and a single gold piece into Rosa's cupped hands. 'It's not a great deal, I'm afraid – not quite a pound. But Philip had these in his dressing room.' From her sleeve she unfolded two pound notes, thick white sheets the size of Rosa's pocket handkerchief. Rosa bit her lip. Those notes would keep them for a week, perhaps a month if they were careful. She realized she had no idea what board and lodging cost – but surely not more than a few shillings a night? Her hand stole up to her throat, to where the locket had always hung, comforting – but it closed only on air.

'Won't he notice?'

'He might,' Clemency said. 'I truly don't know. He's not very careful with his belongings, but two pound notes . . . There was a five-pound note too but I didn't dare to take it. He would certainly remember that.'

'I think I should only take one.' Rosa made up her mind. 'Fold it back as if there were two – he'll think that he misremembered.'

'Very well.' Clemency handed Rosa one note and slipped the other back into her sleeve and then, as Rosa stood, she cried, 'But wait – you're not going? Won't you have something to eat at least?'

'I can't.' Rosa picked up the shawl from where it lay on Clemency's canary silk armchair and wrapped it around her head and throat. She gave one longing look at the warmth of the fire, but Luke was outside, without any fire in the December cold. 'I must go, before Philip gets back. Now, remember – you must throw me out.'

'But where will you go?'

'I'm not sure – but even if I was, I couldn't tell you. I'm sorry, Clemmie.'

'Don't you trust me?'

'Of course I do.' Rosa put one hand against Clemency's cheek, feeling its smooth warmth, and as Clemency closed her eyes a single tear traced down over Rosa's fingers. 'I wouldn't be here otherwise. But I don't want to make this more difficult for you than it is already. Now, come – throw me out.' She took a breath. 'Please, Clemmie!' she shouted. 'How could you be so heartless?'

Clemency gave her a last despairing look and squeezed her hand until the ruby bit into Rosa's flesh. Then she took a breath herself.

'I said, get out! How dare you come here with these absurd tales.'

'I thought you were my friend.' Rosa found her voice was shaking, and there were real tears in her eyes. Clemency's grip on her hand was painfully hard, the stone of the ring biting into her skin until it felt like it would bleed.

'Go home!' Clemency cried. Her voice cracked despairingly. 'Go home and let us forget this whole painful episode, Rosa!'

There was a knock at the door and Clemency dropped Rosa's hand.

'Come in,' she said, with a voice that was convincingly shaken and upset. Millie's frightened face appeared around the gap.

'Mr Wilkins asks if everything's quite all right, ma'am?'

'Quite all right, thank you, Millie. Miss Greenwood was just leaving.' She turned a stony, expressionless face towards Rosa. 'Please show her out.'

'Clemency,' Rosa said. It was all she could say. She had not thanked Clemency for this terrible, daring thing she had done – this act of friendship in defiance of her husband and their kind. And now she could never thank her – not in front of the maid. She could only repeat, hopelessly, 'Clemency' and hope that her voice and her eyes said everything she could not.

'This way, miss,' said the maid firmly. There was a hint of triumph in her voice, and Rosa realized that she was pleased, in some odd way, that her initial suspicions had been justified. 'Or should I ask the footmen to show you out?'

'No,' Rosa said. She made her voice bitter, and she stood and walked to the door, her back very straight, her right hand folded tight around the coins and the note Clemency had pressed into her fist. 'No, I'm going. You don't need to get the hired thugs to throw me out. Goodbye, Clemency. My *friend*.'

Goodbye . . .

4

Luke said nothing as they walked quickly across the park to Knightsbridge, and the last stretch towards Osborne Crescent. Rosa had been crying, he could see it in her red eyes and the clean tracks on her dusty, sooty face. But he didn't know what he could say that would comfort her, so he took refuge in silence.

Still, the best part of two pounds – forty shillings, as near as made no odds. That was a king's ransom in Spitalfields. The coins jingled in his pocket, the pound note was tucked inside Rosa's dress. How much for a room in an inn – a shilling perhaps? They would have to share, but he closed his mind to that difficulty. Time enough to worry about that when they'd found a horse.

It was growing dark as they rounded the corner into the mews behind Osborne Crescent, and the fog was starting to draw in, as it always did on cold evenings around this time, but that was all to the better. Less chance of anyone noticing. The clock above the stable struck six as Luke put his hand to the latch of the stableyard gate. It was good timing. Mrs Ramsbottom would be in the thick of cooking, Mr James would be counting the wines for dinner, the servants would be preparing to sit down to their own meal. And the family – would they be out still?

Rosa was close behind him as he pulled the gate cautiously open, and he turned as he was about to step into the yard.

'You don't have to do this.'

'I must. If they catch you, you will need my protection.'

'They won't catch me,' he said gently, but she shook her head, and together they slipped through the narrow crack of gate and into the cobbled yard. The windows above the stable were dark – evidently the new stable-hand was not at home.

Luke unlatched the door to the stable and they moved quietly inside and shut the door behind themselves, waiting for their eyes to get used to the darkness. They could not light a candle or risk a witchlight. Anyone glancing out who saw a light in the window would be instantly suspicious.

As Luke's eyes adjusted his heart fell. One empty stall . . . two . . . three . . . Where were all the horses? Cherry was gone, of course, but Castor and Pollux – had they come all this way for nothing? He swore quietly beneath his breath. There was an answering whicker from the furthest stall, and his heart leapt.

'Brimstone?'

In the darkness he was almost impossible to see, but Luke caught sight of the white blaze on his nose as he shook his mane.

'Brimstone! You beauty.'

He moved forward, moving more surely in the darkness now, and felt for the saddle on the peg between the stalls. There it was.

'How can we manage with only one horse?' Rosa whispered. 'Mama must have taken the carriage out.'

'It's better,' Luke whispered back. 'Horses cost money to stable and feed – this way we can travel cheaper.'

'Can he carry us both?'

'He can if we nurse him. And I can walk. Anyway, we have no choice. We can't wait for the carriage to come back, can we?'

'No.' Rosa's shape was a dim ember in the darkness, but he thought he saw her shiver. 'Luke, it's gone six. They'll be back soon for dinner. We must hurry.'

'I know.'

He opened the stall door and saddled Brimstone up, petting his nose and whispering to him, praying that the horse wouldn't whinny and give them away.

'It's a man's saddle,' he whispered to Rosa as he did up the girths. 'Cherry's isn't here, and anyway, we wouldn't both of us fit side-saddle. Can you manage?'

He felt, rather than saw, the look of scorn she gave him.

'I can manage,' she whispered back fiercely.

'All right, all right. Keep your hair on. I was just asking,' Luke said. 'Now, are you ready? We'll have to be quick. There's nothing we can do about Brimstone's hooves on the cobbles and if they hear those . . .'

'I'm ready,' Rosa said.

Luke nodded and was just about to lead Brimstone outside when he stopped, his hand on the latch.

'What?' Rosa whispered. 'Can you hear something?'

'My knife. And the bottle.'

'*What?*'

'I left them upstairs in the stable block. I should get them.'

It was the witch-hunting kit John Leadingham had given him when he first set out. The thought of the implements made him feel sick now, the long knife with the wicked point, the iron gag. The garotte. The syringe. The bottle, wrapped in rags, that could slay a witch – or a man. They had been meant for Rosa, and that thought made him curl with self-hatred. But they would be useful, undeniably, if Sebastian or Alexis came after them . . .

'No,' Rosa said. 'No, we get out of here now. You can buy another knife.'

Luke made up his mind.

'Wait here. Hold Brimstone.'

'*No!*' Rosa hissed after him, her voice a furious whisper. But she was too late. He was already out of the door and padding quietly up the stone steps to the room above the

55

stables. The *empty* room – or so he hoped.

His heart was thudding in his throat as he pushed gently at the door and slipped inside. The room was empty – but not unoccupied. There was a case by the windowsill and a pile of dirty linen on the floor. They'd lost no time in engaging a new groom.

The loose board was still loose, and he prised it up, his fingers shaking as they dug into the splintered board and pulled it back. Inside the hollow he pulled away the bottle of whisky and erotic cards left by the previous occupant, and behind them was the bundle with the familiar sharp-sour smell leaking from the bottle. The smell made his head swim and his eyes water, even through the tightly stoppered cork and wrapping of rags.

He yanked them out and looked around for something to put them in. The new stable-hand had a suitcase but that was far too unwieldy to carry on horseback. Instead he yanked a thin moth-eaten blanket off the bed and made a hurried pack roll. There were plenty of spare girths in the stable; he could rig something up.

He was just about to leave when the sound of hooves turning into the mews caught his ear, and he leant against the window, trying to see sideways down the long dark mews, through the gathering dusk and the fog. A carriage had just turned into the right-hand side of the mews, with two horses hitched at the front. It was difficult to tell in the dimness, but he was almost certain the horses were Castor and Pollux.

For a minute he stood frozen, the pack roll in one hand. Then, all thought of caution gone, he flung open the door and ran down the steps, his boots thumping on the stone.

Rosa looked round, horrified, as he burst into the stable.

'Hush! Have you lost your mind?'

'They're back,' he gasped. 'Come on, we've got to get out *now*. Two horses, coming up the mews from the right. If we get out now we can turn left and maybe miss them.'

He saw her eyes, huge and black in the darkness, dilated with fear. Then she gave a single sharp nod and opened the stable door. Luke strapped his bundle to the back of the saddle with shaking, hasty fingers, then grabbed Brimstone's reins and led him out into the courtyard, trying not to communicate his fear to the horse.

'Up,' he said to Rosa. 'I'll open the gate.'

For a minute he thought she would argue, but then he held out his cupped hands and she vaulted up on to Brimstone's high back with a single movement and picked up the reins, and he ran across the cobbles to pull open the gate to the yard. He could hear the hooves, terrifyingly close now, coming along the mews. Thank God the horses were tired and pulling slowly – but it would not be enough, he realized with a sudden lurch of horror. They were only a couple of doors away. At this rate they would meet in the mews, directly outside the house.

He stopped with his hand on the gate.

Rosa's face was white in the darkness and he could see she'd realized how close they were too, and was filled with the same indecision. She closed her eyes, her hands tight on the reins, and for a moment he thought she was about to be sick. Her lips were moving in some kind of silent prayer. But it was not a prayer: both she and Brimstone suddenly disappeared from view. It was a spell.

'Go!' her voice hissed from an invisible mouth. 'I can't hold this for long, not for all three of us.'

Three? He looked down at himself and saw – with the strangest sense of sickening disorientation – that he was no longer there. He could see the impression on the mossy stones where his boots stood – but no boots. No legs. No hand when he held it in front of his face.

'*Go!*' she whispered again, with quiet desperation.

Luke gasped and then yanked open the gate, just wide enough to let them out. They slipped through – the sound of Brimstone's hooves on the stones horrifyingly loud – but the carriage just a few houses away did not falter; perhaps they could not hear the sound above the rattle of the wheels and the horses huffing. Luke turned to look. It was definitely them. They were too close to be mistaken, and he would have known Castor anywhere.

He yanked the gate shut behind them – no time to latch it – and scrabbled for the invisible Brimstone. For a moment he couldn't find him – and then, just as he was about to panic, he felt Rosa's hand grab his.

'I'm here,' she whispered. 'Reach down, feel for the stirrup.'

It was there, and somehow he managed to get his

foot into it, grab for the reins and swing himself up. For a moment there was a confused scramble as he almost toppled across the saddle, and he felt Rosa's hair in his face and a great flurry of skirts as he scrabbled for a hold. Then, somehow in the middle of the confusion, his hand met skin: smooth, soft, hot skin. Her knee? Her thigh? He heard Rosa's gasp, jerked back and felt his face flood with blood – only the knowledge that they were invisible, and that she could not hold the spell much longer, kept him from letting go and stumbling to the floor.

Then he was up behind Rosa, his arms around her waist, his thighs gripping Brimstone for dear life. He felt her arms move as she tugged on the reins, and they were off, clearing the gate just in time for the horses and carriage to take their place.

'Whoa!' a man's voice called. Castor and Pollux clopped gratefully to a halt, and Luke heard the strange groom slither from his perch.

They were almost at the end of the mews, almost away, when a shrill barking split the night air and a small brown shadow lolloped through the open gate and began to run, wheezing, up the mews behind them.

'Bloody dog!' Luke heard from the groom. 'Who let you out, you little sod?'

He felt Rosa stiffen at the sound of the barking, and she dragged on the reins to bring Brimstone to a halt.

'What're you doing?' he hissed furiously.

'It's Belle!' she gasped. Brimstone faltered and Luke felt

him turn back under the pressure of Rosa's hands. The dog had almost reached them; the groom was perhaps twenty yards away.

'Keep going!' Luke snapped.

'It's Belle!' she snarled back, just as furious. 'I can't leave her, Luke! I'm all she's got – Mama never liked her, Alexis hated her—'

'For God's sake, the groom'll run into us!'

He reached around her waist and grabbed for the invisible reins, feeling the leather in his hands, and yanking right to pull Brimstone back around.

'Come on, boy! Come on, gee up!'

Brimstone took a few faltering steps and Rosa began to struggle in the saddle. Luke couldn't see what she was doing, but he guessed she was trying to swing one leg up and over Brimstone's neck.

'Rosa, stop it!' He clenched his fingers on the reins, trying to hold Brimstone, who was beginning to panic. 'You'll kill us both for a dog. We *have* to go!'

'Luke, let go of me!' Neither of them were bothering to whisper now, their voices ringing in the narrow mews, and the groom looked around in astonishment, trying to work out where this unseen struggle was taking place. Brimstone snorted with fear and Luke felt him try to rear. He threw his weight forward, crushing them both against the pommel as he tried to stop Brimstone from rearing up.

'Take your hands off me!' Rosa shouted, and she pulled at his arm, trying to wrest herself free, digging her nails into his hand as she tried to pull his fingers off the reins. Brimstone swerved to the left as she tugged and began to back, panicked by the struggle. With a huge wrench Luke brought the horse's head back around and he gave him a kick, harder than he'd meant, that made Brimstone neigh with indignation and start forward. Then he was off, cantering down the mews in spite of the double weight on his back.

'Belle!' Rosa cried. Looking back, Luke saw the groom catch up with the little pug and pick her up, holding her to his shoulder. The man stood open-mouthed, staring after the sounds, and then they rounded the corner and disappeared into the enveloping fog.

'He's got her, Rosa,' Luke panted above the noise of Brimstone's hooves. 'She's all right. The groom's got her.'

Rosa began to weep, and as they turned into Osborne Crescent the spell wore off with a shocking suddenness. One moment Luke could see nothing but the fog and the muddy road, flying past as if of its own volition, the next he was blinded by Rosa's tangled red curls, and he became aware that at some point he had let go of the reins with one hand and was holding her, his arm wrapped around her waist, hugging her against him. He let go abruptly and she slumped over Brimstone's neck, sobbing as if her heart would break.

'Rosa . . .' He'd not felt so helpless since she'd lain dying in his arms at Southing from the wound he'd inflicted. Even then she hadn't cried. 'Rosa, we'd have been caught

– and even if we weren't, what could we do with a lapdog on the road? She's meant for sitting on cushions and eating minced chicken, not life on the road. Did you want to see her hungry and footsore?'

'I have nothing left.' Rosa's voice was cracked with sobs. 'Papa. Cherry. Now Belle. She was the last. Oh, Belle . . .' And she began to cry again, but now with a kind of resigned hopelessness.

Luke slowed Brimstone to a walk and they made their slow way through the darkened streets, taking turnings at random but always bearing roughly north, for reasons he hardly knew, except that Sebastian was to the south, and William to the east and Osborne Crescent to the west.

The roads were unexpectedly quiet but it had begun to drizzle, a fine light mist of rain that mingled with the fog and hung in Rosa's hair, dewing her skin, mixing with her tears.

He thought they would be stopped, perhaps. A bloodstained man and a crying woman on a thoroughbred horse. But they were not. Perhaps he should not have worried. After all, a woman weeping was not a strange sight on the streets of London.

5

'Rosa,' she heard as if through a fog. 'Rosa, wake up.'

She lifted her stiff neck. They were in the courtyard of an inn; she had no idea where, but they must have left the city, for the night air was clear and clean, and the moon was full. The air smelt of wood smoke and horse manure. Brimstone stood, tired and panting, his breath a cloud of white in the darkness. She was cold, her fingers frozen where they had clutched the pommel. Only her back was warm, where Luke's body had pressed against it as they rode.

Now he slid from the saddle, leaving her shivering.

'Where are we?' she whispered, and then coughed. Her throat was dry. She had never felt so thirsty or so hungry in all her life.

'I'm not sure,' Luke said. 'Somewhere north of Chipping Barnet, I think. But Brimstone's spent. Two riders ain't good for him. We need to put up for the night.'

Rosa nodded, feeling a headache begin to pound against her skull. She sat shivering, holding Brimstone's reins while Luke went around the corner of the inn, looking for the night door, but there was no danger of the horse making off. He was even more tired than she was.

They stood, drooping together in the quiet yard, waiting for the sound of Luke's boots. When it came Brimstone heard it first; she saw his ears twitch before she heard the sound herself. Then Luke came into the yard with another man.

'I'll tek the 'orse,' he said briskly. 'You tek your sister inside. She looks perished.'

Luke held out his hand, but Rosa shook her head and managed to slide stiffly from Brimstone's back without his help. Nevertheless, she stumbled as her foot touched the ground, and would have fallen if Luke hadn't caught her arm.

'Don't speak,' he whispered in her ear, his breath warm against her neck. 'I've told them you're my sister, but your accent'll give us away in a second.'

She nodded, and followed him round the building to a low porch, and into a smoky parlour. Two men were still drinking beer in the corner and they looked up as she entered. Rosa ducked her head and pulled her shawl closer around her face, digging the ruby into its folds. She waited in the shadows of the doorway while Luke made his way across to the bar and spoke to the landlady.

'Luggage?' Rosa heard her say, and saw Luke shake his head.

'. . . weren't expecting to have to stay,' she heard. 'We got caught up in London.'

'You'll 'ave to share a bed wi' yer sister,' the woman said irritably. 'We've only got the one free. But you can have the room to yourselves.'

Share a bed? Rosa felt her face flush scarlet, and then silently chastised herself for being such a child. Of course they'd have to share a bed. They couldn't afford to pay for two rooms.

The woman came across, holding a key, and looked her up and down sharply.

'Quiet little thing, ain't you? Cat got yer tongue?'

'She's tired,' Luke put in shortly. 'So am I.'

'All right, all right. Only making perlite conversation. Here's the key to your room. Payment's now.'

Luke nodded and fished a couple of coins out of his pocket.

'My sister's hungry; we haven't eaten all day. Is there anything she can have?'

'Cook's gone home,' the woman said sourly. Luke pulled out another coin and she looked at it for a moment and then tossed her head. 'But you can 'ave bread and cheese. Not down 'ere, we're closing up. I'll bring it up.'

'Bread and cheese? That's the best you can manage for a shilling?'

'Take it or leave it.'

65

'At least give us a glass of beer.'

'All right. Bread, cheese and beer. And you're lucky with that. The room's the second floor, right-hand door as you come up the stairs. Don't open the window, the catch is broke. And here, take this.'

She shoved a lighted oil lamp into Luke's hand and Rosa followed him up the rickety stairs to the attic.

At the top of the second flight they paused for a moment, catching their breath, and then Luke pulled the key out of his pocket and set it in the door. But it was not locked – as he went to turn it, the door swung open of its own accord and they went inside, Luke ducking his head as he passed under the low door frame.

He set the oil lamp on the mantelpiece, turned up the wick and they surveyed the room.

'I know it's not what you're used to . . .' Luke said uneasily. There was no space for anything except the bed, pushed hard against the wall, a single stool that doubled as a bedside table, and a narrow washstand wedged into the alcove by the fire.

'It's fine,' Rosa said in a low voice. But the only thing she could think as she gazed around the cramped chamber was how *small* the bed was. Smaller than her bed at home. The thought of her and Luke sharing the narrow mattress . . . She felt blood flood her face again and turned away, hoping he couldn't see her furious blush and misunderstand it for shame or anger. She walked to the window to press her face against the cold glass, trying to cool her burning cheeks and quell the ache in her head. *He's Luke*, she told herself as she stared out into the night. *He is your brother*. For now.

'Rosa . . .' Luke came up behind her, and in the dark reflection of the window she saw his hand hover over her shoulder, not quite touching. 'I—'

'Bread and cheese.' The voice came from the doorway. 'And beer.' Rosa turned to see the landlady bang the plate down on the stool by the bed, and the tankard after it, the beer slopping as she did.

'Thank you,' Rosa said automatically and without thinking. Almost at the door, the landlady stopped and looked back, as if puzzled. Then she shook her head and left, banging the door shut behind her.

Rosa felt herself go hot and then cold with horror as she realized what she'd done.

'Oh, Luke. I'm so sorry – I forgot! Do you think . . .'

'It doesn't matter. It was just "thank you",' Luke said, but his face was uneasy. 'She won't remember tomorrow. But we should get away as early as we can. Before dawn, if possible.'

He sat on the edge of the bed, the springs squeaking, and rubbed his face, his hands rasping against his unshaven cheeks.

'Well, at least she didn't stint on the bread.'

It was true. The cheese was nothing but a cracked noggin, 'fit for the mice', Mrs Ramsbottom would have said. But the bread was piled high and was fresh, or

67

reasonably so. Rosa took the piece that Luke held out to her, but suddenly she was not sure if she could eat it.

Perhaps it was the landlady's gaze, but she suddenly felt sick with the realization of what she was doing. *You are alone with him, alone in a bedroom with a strange man . . .* The thought made her almost dizzy with disbelief. It was against everything her mother had drilled into her – and Luke was not just a man, but a servant, a witch finder, an *outwith*: everything alien and forbidden.

But when she bit into the bread, feeling the taste flood her mouth, she realized how hungry she was, and she took another bite, and another, all thoughts driven out of her head except for her hunger and the taste of the bread. The crust crunched between her teeth and she thought that nothing, not the finest smoked salmon or the creamiest foie gras, had ever tasted so good.

There was silence as they both crunched, and then, as she swallowed the last salty crumb of cheese, she realized something else.

'I'm thirsty.'

'D'you drink beer?' Luke said shortly, around a mouthful of bread. 'Sorry there's only one glass.'

'I'm not sure. I've never tried it.'

'Here.' He held it out, tankard handle towards her.

Rosa took it from his hand and sniffed at the golden liquid. The smell was not particularly pleasant, but she was horribly thirsty and, wrinkling her nose, she took a great swig.

Her first impulse was to spit it out, but she screwed up her face, pressed her lips together and swallowed heroically.

'Urgh!' she spluttered when her mouth was clear. 'That's *revolting*!'

'Your face!' Luke was laughing properly now, but not too hard to grab the tankard before she spilt it in revulsion. 'You've really never tried it?'

'How can you drink that stuff? It's so – so *sour*!'

'It's not sour! It's – well, it's beer. It's the hops that make it bitter. I suppose I can remember not liking it much when I was a kid. But I was six, I didn't like cabbage or Brussels sprouts, neither!'

Rosa shuddered, and went over to the washstand to see if the ewer had water in it to wash her mouth out. The jug was half full, but there was a layer of dust on the surface and a dead fly floating in it.

'Come on,' Luke said, his face still twisted in a grin. She saw that the dimple was back, skewered deep into his right cheek. He patted the bed beside him. 'It's not that bad. Try another go.'

'I'd rather die of thirst!' Rosa retorted as she sat beside him, the mattress squeaking. But she took the glass and managed a tiny sip. It was not so bad, now she was expecting the bitterness and she took another, slightly larger mouthful. 'It's still revolting. But it's better than drinking dead flies, I suppose.'

'Glad you approve.' He took a gulp himself and then passed her back the tankard.

'Do you think Brimstone's all right?' Rosa asked. Luke nodded.

'He'll be fine. They had a good stables round the back. Nice and clean. Four other horses besides him.'

'I wonder what Alexis is doing right now.' The thought made her draw her knees up to her chest, hugging them uneasily. 'Scrying maybe.'

'Scrying?' Luke stood and put the tankard down on the washstand. 'What's that?'

'You can use water or oil, or runes. It's like a form of divination. Some people use it to tell the future, but you can see the present too. Find things.'

'Find things?' Luke's face was suddenly alarmed, the grin gone as if it had never been. 'Like, people?'

'Yes. But it's not very accurate. Not unless you're very good. And Alexis isn't.'

'God damn it.' Luke sat again on the bed, the springs squeaking, protesting under his weight. 'Isn't there anything we can do?'

'Keep moving. And get as far away as possible. It's most accurate with still objects, and the closer you are, the better chance you have.' She felt muzzy-headed and wondered if this was the drunkenness Mama had warned about, or if she was just tired. 'There are charms too – countermeasures, ways to confuse the searchers. I don't know much about it. If only I had Mama's Grimoire . . .'

Luke was chewing his lip.

'Magic might be the least of our worries. We should try

70

to dye Brimstone tomorrow – maybe cover his blaze. They'll put out a description soon, and we're pretty recognizable put together. There's not much to say about me, except for my height maybe. That's the only thing anyone'd notice. I don't know what we do about you though.'

'About me?' Rosa frowned. 'What do you mean?'

'There's not many red-haired sixteen-year-olds on the run, specially not ones brought up in Knightsbridge with the accent to match.'

'You – you don't think I'll pass for your sister then?' Rosa said. Luke shook his head.

'I don't know if the landlady believed us, but even if she did, there's others won't. We don't look like brother and sister. I wonder . . .' He took a handful of her hair, pulling it away from her face, looking at her appraisingly. 'D'you think you could pass for a boy if we cropped your hair?'

'Maybe,' Rosa said doubtfully. Luke sighed and let his hand drop, and they sat in silence, Rosa watching the backs of his hands as he played with the empty plate in his lap, turning it this way and that. They were covered with burns, old ones from the forge, fresh ones from the factory.

'Thank you, Luke,' she said quietly. He looked up, his face puzzled.

'For what?'

'For coming back for me. You didn't have to. I had no choice in this but you did. You could have—'

'No, listen.' He cut her off, his voice rough, his words

tumbling in their urgency. 'This was my fault, all of it. When I chose your name, when I did – what I did, God forgive me . . .' He still could not bear to say it, what he'd tried to do. 'What I'm trying to say is, we neither of us had much of a choice. Thank me? God! What for? You went back when I wouldn't – you saved Minna. I'll never be done being sorry for what I tried to do to you.'

'But what about what I tried to do to *you*?' Rosa said, her voice very low. 'I took your memories, I ripped them out of your mind. And my people enslaved yours.' She dropped the words like cold pebbles of truth into the pool of silence between them. 'I'm one of *them*, Luke, the people you're sworn to kill.'

'Not any more,' he said. 'I'm not a Brother any more.'

His face in the lamplight was all shadows, impossible to tell if he spoke the words with sorrow, or relief. Perhaps both.

She was trying to think of something to say when, with a little sigh, the lamp went out, leaving them in darkness. Rosa heard Luke swear, soft and vehement.

'That bitch. I might have known she'd cheat us on the oil on top of everything else.'

'It doesn't matter.' She put out a hand, feeling for the bed to stand up, but touched his knee instead. She snatched it away. 'I'm t-tired,' she stammered. 'It's time for bed anyway.'

Bed. There was a sudden silence, full of feeling, as the word hung between them, and then dropped, like a stone

72

into a well, sending its ripples into the darkness.

'I'll sleep on the floor,' Luke said gruffly.

'Don't be silly.' Her voice caught in her throat. 'There's only one blanket. You'll freeze. There's plenty of room for us both. It's a big bed.'

He did not call her on the lie.

She heard a thump, as Luke pulled off one boot, very slowly, and then the other. And she let a tiny witchlight flare in her palm as she did her own boot buttons, wishing for a button hook. If only she could loosen her corset . . . but she could not possibly start undressing in front of Luke. She would just have to endure the discomfort.

She let her boots fall to the floor, pulled out the last of her hairpins and then turned to face Luke. His face was grave, uncomfortable.

'Are you sure?'

'Sure,' she said with a braveness she did not feel. She crawled across the bed to lie pressed against the wall, with the chill of the plaster against her right side. The last thing she saw before she let the witchlight die out was Luke sitting on the edge of the thin mattress, his hands clasped as if he was praying. Then she heard the bed springs squeak and felt his warmth as he lay beside her, barely touching, their bodies just the fraction of an inch apart that the space permitted.

She pulled the thin blanket up, over them both.

'Goodnight, Luke,' she whispered into the darkness, and she felt his weight shift minutely beside her as he tried

73

and failed to find a comfortable position, his body perched precariously on the metal edge, as far away as he could get without falling out.

'Goodnight, Rose,' he whispered back. His voice melded into the darkness, its Cockney twang comforting: *G'nigh' Rose . . .*

And then silence . . . just the sound of his breathing, first shallow, then slowing and deepening by degrees.

She should have been tired. She should have been exhausted. But she could not sleep. She lay in the darkness, feeling Luke's presence beside her and pondering the impossibility of it all.

You're ruined, she thought, remembering Clemency's words. *If anyone knew you'd spent the night with a man . . .* And not just a man. A stable-hand. An outwith. Luke.

Beside her Luke's muscles had begun to relax in sleep and his arm had fallen by his side, touching hers. She thought again of the smooth bare skin beneath his coat and shirt, the blue veins, the muscles that flexed and shaped as he moved, and the mark of the brand on his shoulder – how different it was from her own sharp curves and narrow bones. He was the first man whose body she had touched, and now she was lying in bed with him, so close she could have reached out and slipped her hand beneath his shirt as he slept.

At the thought she felt blood flush through her like a fire, her cheeks blazing. The ring on her finger seemed to pinch agonizingly tight, and she could not breathe.

It's Luke, she thought furiously. *Stop it, stop thinking like this.*

Thank God he was asleep and knew nothing of what was passing through her mind. She closed her eyes in the darkness, listening to the slow, regular rhythm of Luke's breathing, and slowly, slowly, she let it lull her into sleep.

6

'Well!'

The voice cut through Luke's dream like a knife, and he jerked out of sleep, his heart pounding wildly, trying to work out where he was and what was happening.

There was something heavy on his chest and shoulder, a warm and yielding weight, and as his blinking eyes adjusted to the light he realized, with a tingle of shock, that it was Rosa, curled inside his encircling arm. Her cheek was pressed against his shoulder, her mouth warm in the crook of his neck, and her arm was flung across his ribs, pinning him down as he struggled to sit up and face the landlady standing at the foot of the bed.

'Funny way for a brother and sister to carry on,' she said with a sour triumph.

'Get out!' Luke found he was shaking with rage. He managed to extricate himself from beneath Rosa's arm and stood, pulling his shirt straight with hands that trembled. 'How dare you come into a room we've paid for?'

'It's past ten. You've paid for one night and unless you want to pay for another, it's you that'll be getting out, my lad, and your "sister" with you. *Little slut,*' she added under her breath as she turned away.

Luke's fist clenched. He shut his eyes, forcing himself to count to ten as William had taught him as a boy. *Nothing to be gained by hitting out, Luke lad. That only puts you in the wrong as well.*

'We'll be out,' he said stonily. 'We need to be on our way in any case.'

'Ten minutes,' the woman snapped. 'A moment longer and I'll send Henry up here to throw you both out.'

'Get out,' Luke snarled.

'With pleasure,' the woman snapped, and she banged the door behind her so hard the windowpane rattled in its frame.

In the bed, Rosa opened her eyes and sat up, blinking and astonished, raking her long red hair out of her eyes.

'What was that noise?'

'Landlady,' Luke said shortly. 'We overslept.'

'Wh-what?' She gave a great yawn. 'What time is it?'

'Gone ten, she said.'

'Ten?' Rosa was up and out of bed in one movement. 'You said we had to be on the road by dawn!'

'Like I said, I overslept.'

'Oh God, we need to leave, now.' She began pulling on her boots, her face pale.

'You need to heal yourself,' Luke said, watching her as she struggled with the small buttons, her burnt, blistered fingers clumsy.

'I know.' She spoke shortly. 'I will. But I haven't got much magic to spare. I want to conserve it – you know, in case.'

In case Sebastian turned up. Luke shivered. He wanted to argue, but he could see her point. Better a scarred arm than a dead body. And he could see she was right to be worried about having enough to spare: her magic was still a thin, pale thing compared to the roaring flame of a few weeks ago. The realization made him frown.

'Look, your magic . . .'

'Mmm?' Her head was down, tugging at the buttons.

'How long does it usually take, to – you know, to come back?'

'Depends. On how tired I am. On how much rest I get.'

'But still . . .' He trailed off. But still, he wanted to say. Shouldn't it be coming back by now? It was true that she'd given all she had at the factory, wrung out every drop of magic in an effort to keep them both alive. But that was one, two nights ago. And she had barely more strength now than when they'd woken up on the banks of the Thames, wet and cold and covered in ashes.

'I need gloves,' Rosa said, looking ruefully at her burnt

hands, and the ruby, like a great red eye on her knuckle. With a wincing effort she turned the ring, the tight band grating over her sore red skin, so that the stone was inwards, towards her palm.

'I don't know,' Luke said. 'You're supposed to be my sister. My kind doesn't wear gloves.'

Rosa bit her lip and stood, twisting the shawl about her shoulders and head.

'Well, if it comes to it, that didn't go so well, did it? The brother–sister thing. I don't think the landlady was fooled, even last night.'

'They don't need to be fooled,' Luke said impatiently. 'They just need to give us a bed and not drum us out of the place for adulterers. What else can we tell them – that we're married?'

'Maybe,' Rosa said defiantly. There was a flush high on her cheek. 'It's more believable than pretending we're related. We look nothing alike.'

Luke turned away, pulling his greatcoat on, and snatched up the bundle from beneath the bed.

'Come on. Let's get Brimstone before they try to charge us another night's lodging. We've already been robbed once. I'm not giving that woman any more money.'

Down in the yard Rosa waited, huddled into Phoebe's shawl, while Luke fetched Brimstone from the stables. It was a cold, crisp morning, the sky as blue as speedwell, and there was ice in the puddles. She rested her boot on

79

the thin skin, waiting for the satisfying *crack* as she put her weight on her heel.

'Hey, you!' A man's voice rang across the yard, above the sound of a horse's hooves, and she looked up. 'Yes, you,' he said impatiently. He was a runner of some kind, in a uniform. 'D'you work here?'

She was about to say *no*, but he pulled a piece of printed paper out of his saddlebag and shoved it into her hand, without waiting for an answer.

'Here, get that put up in your mother's bar, will you?' he said, and then turned his horse around and cantered out of the yard.

Rosa was about to call after him that she was a guest, not his errand girl, when her eye fell on the page. It was a poster.

She crumpled the paper in her fist, her heart beating. Then slowly she edged the shawl further up around her face, trying to hide her bright, incriminating hair. It seemed almost impossible that the man should have failed to notice, failed to make the connection. Thank God she had not spoken.

The sound of hooves came again, from the other corner of the yard, and her heart quickened horribly until she thought she might throw up, there on the straw of the yard.

But as the rider turned the corner she saw, with a great lurch of relief, that it was Luke.

'Rosa?' Luke stared down at her from Brimstone's high back. 'What's happened? You look like you've seen a ghost.'

MISSING

Miss Rosamund Evangeline Greenwood
OF OSBORNE CRESCENT, KNIGHTSBRIDGE

DESCRIPTION

Age, 16 years	Hair, Red
Eyes, Brown	Build, Slight

Last seen wearing a silk grey morning dress, dark blue wrapper and bonnet, and sable muff

May be in the company of a bay stallion with a white blaze

£100 REWARD

OFFERED FOR SAFE RETURN

(Information to Southing House, Southing)

For a moment she could not speak, she only scrabbled desperately for a hold on Brimstone's saddle, until Luke grabbed her arm and hauled her up in front of him.

'What's the matter?' he asked again. 'You're shaking.'

'I'll tell you in a moment,' she managed, and she gave Brimstone a kick that set the poor horse into motion with an indignant lurch. 'Let's just get out of here.'

'Hair dye!' laughed the young lady behind the counter. She put her hand to her own beautifully sculpted coiffure. 'What's that for then?'

'That's my business,' Luke said uncomfortably. He felt in his pocket for the shillings that rattled there. Already the cache felt uncomfortably lighter than last night.

'Surely you're too young to be going grey?' the girl said. She looked up at him through lowered lashes, her eyes sparkling.

'As the gentleman said, that's his business, Millicent!' barked a man from further up the counter. He came down and put a small box in front of Luke. 'I do apologize, sir. Young ladies like their joke. Will this shade do, sir?'

Luke looked at the box. It was called 'Autumn Gold' and a coloured spot on the lid showed an odd clay-like beige.

'I'd like it a bit darker if you have it, please.'

'In that case . . .' He rummaged in a cupboard behind his head and then turned back with a second little box. 'Try Beech Grove, sir. Gives a lovely mahogany tone.'

'And how do I – you know . . .' Luke wished the stupid

girl behind the counter would stop making eyes and laughing at him from behind her hand. He wanted to sink through the floor. 'How do you put it on?'

'Make a paste with a little water, rub it on and then wash off after half an hour. It will stain clothing while it's wet, so we recommend drying the hair thoroughly before dressing.'

'Thanks.' Luke took the box. The spot on the top looked mud-coloured, which was probably as good as they were going to get. 'How much?'

'One and thruppence.'

Christ. Luke nearly groaned aloud. Another chip off their precious stash. He pushed the coins across the counter and pocketed the small box, and then strode bad-temperedly across the town square and down to the river where Rosa was waiting.

Brimstone was still grazing in the field where Luke had left him, but there was no sign of Rosa as he crossed the stone bridge to the far side of the shore. He was just getting worried when her small worried face peered out from beneath its shadow.

'Who's that trip-trapping over my bridge? Ain't that what you're supposed to say?' he called down. It was a thin enough attempt at a joke, but she was smiling as he slid down the bank to join her by the shallows.

'Are you saying I look like a troll?'

'About as much as I look like a billy-goat gruff. Bad news. We're another shilling down.'

'A shilling!' Rosa was scandalized. 'Is that how much hair dye costs?'

'I've no idea. I'm not in the habit of dying my hair. A shilling and thruppence, to be exact.'

'I had no idea it would be so expensive. We'd better get our money's worth. Should we do me first or him?' She nodded up the bank at Brimstone. Luke bit his lip.

'Dunno.' He looked down at the packet. 'It looks pretty small. Let's do him first. I'm worried there won't be enough to cover your hair.'

'I might end up being cropped for a boy yet,' Rosa said. Luke felt a smile twitch at the corner of his mouth.

'You'll need to ditch the corsets first.'

They squatted by the river's edge, mixing the powder to a paste on a flat dipped stone. It smelt foul, and Rosa made a face as Luke stirred it with a stick.

'If I were Brimstone I'd run a mile before I let you put that on my nose.'

'First of all, you'll be Brimstone in a second,' he said. 'And second, who says I'm the one daubing it on? I'll be holding his head.'

Rosa pulled a face and, dipping her fingers into the gunk, made as if to swipe at Luke's nose with it. Laughing, he scrambled up the bank.

'You'll have to be quicker than that. And be careful, that's about half a shilling's worth you've got there.'

She followed him up slowly, hampered by her skirts and only one free hand. Luke gave her his to pull her up the last few feet, and they walked together across the field to where Brimstone was grazing contentedly.

'All right, me old mate.' Luke caught him by the bridle and stood for a moment, petting his nose. Then he took a firm hold of his bridle and reins. 'Go on then.'

Rosa took a breath, and stood on tiptoe to stroke the stinking gunk down Brimstone's nose. To Luke's surprise he stood quietly as she stroked it gently down, and when the white was completely covered he let go of the halter and the horse trotted off to graze in another corner of the field.

'Blimey. He must have lost his sense of smell!'

'I know.' Rosa sniffed her fingers in distaste. 'Me next, I suppose.'

'Come on then. Let's get it over with.'

They knelt together at the water's edge and Rosa pulled the pins slowly out of her hair, letting it tumble down her back, rich and glorious, all the colours of fire and flame. Something in his chest swelled at the thought of staining it a muddy brown, and for a moment he hesitated, his hand hovering over the flat stone.

'Wait,' Rosa said.

'What is it? Have you changed your mind?' He was not sure if he was relieved, or angered. It was only hair, he told himself. It'd grow back.

'I don't want to stain this dress – well, stain it any worse, anyway. It already looks like I've been digging ditches in it, but it's still silk and it might just be saleable.' She was dabbling her hands in the river, washing off the last of the dye paste. Then she stood and began unhooking the front of her bodice.

Luke sat frozen, not certain whether to turn away or close his eyes. Instead he did neither, but just watched as she undid hook after hook, after hook.

A kind of coldness washed over him as he thought of how strangely similar this was to the last time they'd been by a river shore together, Rosa in his arms, a horse quietly grazing the bank above. Only then it had been him pulling apart her clothing in an attempt to undo what he'd done.

He remembered the bone sticking out of her corset, deep in her lung. He remembered the blood and the bubbling wound . . .

'Luke?' Rosa's voice broke into his thoughts. 'Luke? Are you all right? You're very pale.'

'I'm fine,' he managed hoarsely.

She shrugged off the grey silk bodice and laid it carefully on a dry stone. Beneath, she was dressed in some kind of petticoat, and beneath that her corset and chemise, thin as gauze. Try as he might, Luke could not stop looking – at the softness of her pink-white shoulders, at the curve of her breast above the tightness of the stays, at the pristine unstained whiteness of her chemise, where before there had been nothing but spreading blood . . .

'Ready?'

She knelt at the water's edge, her head bowed, and

pulled her hair apart at the nape, for all the world like a prisoner baring her neck for the executioner's sword.

'R-ready,' Luke said, and to his fury he found that his voice shook as he said the single word. *It's only hair.*

He picked up a handful of the dye, black and stinking, and for a minute he didn't think he could bring himself to touch her.

'Come on!' Rosa's voice came impatiently from beneath the shimmering curtain of hair. 'I'm g-getting cold. It's f-freezing with no clothes on.'

'Sorry.'

He knelt behind her and touched his hand to her nape, where the fine hairs were red as fire, and the tendons of her neck rose and dipped. She shivered at his touch.

'I'm sorry,' he said again. 'The stuff's cold, I know.'

'Not half as cold as it'll be rinsing it off. Be quick.'

He felt her shudder as he smeared it in.

'Keep going,' she said, her teeth gritted.

He put his fingers back into the black gloop and smoothed on another handful. And another. And then another, running his hands down the long, silky length of her hair, feeling it grow thick and clagged beneath his fingers.

'R-rub it into the roots.' Her teeth were chattering. 'I d-don't want a r-red p-parting.'

He pushed his fingers deep into the roots of her hair, rubbing her scalp, and she shuddered again, a long slow almost luxurious shudder, and he saw her fingers dig hard into the silk of her skirt as if she needed something to hold on to.

'Lean back,' he said hoarsely. 'I've got you, don't worry.'

He piled her hair up in a heavy, gunk-filled mass and she tilted her head slowly upright so that he could smear the last of the dye on to her hairline, above her forehead.

'Is it d-d-done?' Her teeth were chattering so hard she could barely speak. Luke nodded.

'Here, take my coat. You'll perish.' He held out the stiff woollen greatcoat and she pulled it on, but the shivering didn't stop. Her cheeks had lost the angry red flush of cold and had gone bloodless white, and her lips were starting to look blue.

'Rosa . . .' He knelt beside her, shivering himself, now he was clad only in his shirtsleeves. 'Rosa, you need to get warm. Use some magic.'

She didn't speak, just nodded. Then she closed her eyes and he saw her lips begin to form a strange silent prayer, and felt the familiar mix of awe and horror shiver across his skin as he waited, watching for the flare of magic, the halo of fire crackling around her that would tell him the spell had worked.

It didn't come. Rosa opened her eyes.

'Luke, it's not working. What's happening?'

'Try again,' he said. But there was a cold feeling in the pit of his stomach and he knew, even before she tried, that it was not going to work. He could see there was nothing there. It was as if some vital fire in her had burnt out.

"Luke w-what's happening?' Her cold shaking hand closed on his wrist. 'What's wrong with m-m-me?'

'I don't know.' Suddenly he didn't care about her hair any more. 'Let's get that muck off your hair and get you warmed up.'

She knelt again, shaking so hard now, even with his greatcoat on, that he had to hold her still with one hand while he poured water over her head from a tin can he'd found by the water's edge. It was rusty and the water trickled from the holes in the side, making it hard to pour carefully. She gasped and flinched beneath his grip as the water ran down inside the collar of his coat. The river at the water's edge turned muddy brown, and he poured and poured, and still the stream ran dark from her hair. At last he gave up and helped her stand.

'Come on, you've had enough.'

She was blue and shaking, her hair like a drowned rat's close to her head, dripping dark down his greatcoat.

'W-w-what's wrong with me, L-Luke?'

'Shh, you're cold, that's all.'

'It's n-n-n . . .' she tried, but she couldn't finish. He pulled her up the bank into the thin winter sunshine, and helped her to sit, huddled with her back against a tree, her teeth chattering helplessly.

'Rosa . . .'

He didn't know how to say it. If he didn't warm her, she would likely die, or catch her death of cold. But she was small and wet and unclothed, and he didn't know how to ask her.

Instead he moved closer and put his arm around her, inside the coat. Her skin was cold and wet and she was shaking. He'd thought it would feel strange and wrong to touch her, but it did not. He pulled her close, as if she were Minna or some other small thing, and with shaking hands she tried to push the coat over his shoulders, so that it covered them both.

He felt one small, cold hand steal tentatively around his ribcage, making him shudder in sympathy and suck in his breath as her icy skin struck cold though the thin cotton of his shirt. Then slowly the heat of his body woke an echoing warmth in hers, and the shivering subsided, and they grew still together, huddled inside the rough shelter of his coat.

'God, you're nesh,' he said.

'I am not!' Rosa's indignant voice came from somewhere near his chest. 'What does that mean anyway?'

He laughed at that, feeling it shake through them both.

'You're so ready to deny it before you even knew what I'd said? What if it was a compliment?'

'It wasn't. I could tell from your voice. Go on then, what does it mean?'

'It means you're a bit feeble – you can't take the cold.'

'What! I'm not feeble! You'd have been cold if someone poured icy river water down your neck for two hours!'

'Two hours? Ten minutes. You should've grown up washing under the yard pump like I did.'

'More fool you, if you couldn't work out how to boil a kettle,' she said, but there was a smile in her voice.

They lapsed back into silence after that, for a long time. Luke wasn't sure quite how long, but he knew that the tree trunk at his back had grown hard and uncomfortable, and that his arm around Rosa's shoulders had gone to sleep. And yet he didn't want to move – in fact, he thought he might never move again, that he would be quite content to sit here for all time, feeling the warmth of her bare skin against his chest and the weight of her head on his shoulder.

'Come on,' he said at last, and she lifted her head so that his shoulder felt cold, suddenly, and empty.

'What?'

'We should get going. The sun's gone in. We need to keep moving, find a place to spend the night. And we need to wash that stuff off Brimstone. Is your hair dry?'

She felt it, pinching it with the tips of her fingers.

'Dry enough. How do I look?'

She looked . . . different. And yet the same. Her fire was muted, and the dark hair made her face look smaller and paler, the nutmeg freckles standing out against her nose and cheekbones. But she was still beautiful – the most beautiful girl he had ever touched. He felt an almost overwhelming urge to kiss her, as he had in that moment of madness in the stable before Sebastian found them both. Instead he turned away, his heart thudding painfully.

'You look fine,' he said brusquely, speaking to the river. 'Good thing your eyebrows are dark.'

'Yes.' She gave a short laugh as she stood. 'Alexis wouldn't fool anyone with dark hair. Orange eyebrows are a bit obvious. Ow . . . My foot's gone to sleep.'

'My shoulder an' all.' He rotated his arm, feeling the joint click and crunch and the blood rush back into the starved muscle. 'Come on, I'll fill up that can from the river while you get dressed. Then we'll try to catch Brimstone.'

'I've ruined your shirt,' she said as she handed him back the coat. 'I'm sorry.'

He looked down. There was a brown stain, like tea, where her wet head had rested on his shoulder.

'Doesn't matter.'

It took a long time to wash the stuff off Brimstone's nose. It had dried on, and where he'd been so good about letting Rosa put the dye on, he was skittish and cross as Luke tried patiently to scrub it off.

'Come on, you bastard!' Luke said at last, as Brimstone pulled his head free and skittered sideways across the field for the fifth, or maybe sixth time. 'Will you just stand bloody still?'

'Don't swear at him!' Rosa said crossly. She'd dressed again, the shawl clutched around her shoulders, her dark hair pinned as well as she could without a mirror.

'I wasn't swearing.' He grabbed Brimstone's bridle and pulled his head round. 'If you think that's swearing – Christ, I could really give you something to complain about if you want.'

'Don't be such a bully,' she snapped back. 'God, are all men bullies? I thought I'd been unlucky with Alexis and Sebastian but—'

'Sebastian?' Luke swung round, his face white with anger. There was dye spattered across his face where Brimstone had shaken his head, trying to get the water off his nose. 'Is that what you—'

'Oh, don't be such a . . . Look, I wasn't comparing you, I was just—'

'It bloody sounded like you were,' Luke growled. He went back to scrubbing Brimstone's nose.

'I'm sorry,' she said more quietly. 'I'm just . . . Look, I'm worried, all right?'

He stopped, his hand on Brimstone's nose.

'I'm sorry as well. You're right, I was being a bully – or a shit anyway. Which maybe comes to the same thing in the end. Anyway . . .' He took one more swipe at Brimstone and then dropped the handful of dock leaves he'd been using to scrub at the dye. 'It's not perfect, but it'll do.'

Rosa looked doubtfully at the horse. His blaze was no longer white – but it didn't match the rest of his beautiful mahogany coat either. Instead it was a strange muddy patch on his long nose. No close observer would be fooled, but it might make them harder to spot to the casual passer-by.

'Come on,' Luke said. 'We need to get going.' He held out his palms, and she put her boot into his locked hands and swung her leg up, trying to forget the impropriety of what she was doing, trying not to think of what Mama would say. But as she pulled herself into the saddle, she caught the flesh of her palm between the stone of the ring and the pommel, and it dug viciously into her palm, so painfully that she couldn't stop herself crying out.

'What happened?' Luke put out a hand to Brimstone's bridle, steadying him as he shifted uneasily at Rosa's cry. 'Are you all right?'

'My finger,' she managed. She held up her left hand and heard his sucked-in breath as he saw the blood oozing from her palm.

'We've got to get it off.'

'But how?'

'I don't know.'

'Eleven shillings,' Luke said.

'What?' Rosa looked up from where she was sitting on the far side of the bed. The inn they had found in Baldock was nicer than the one in Barnet; the room was larger with a good fire, the landlady kinder. They had eaten roast pork and crackling and then made their tired way upstairs, but not to sleep.

'Eleven shillings. That's what I've got left. Plus the pound note.'

'Eleven shillings!' Rosa went pale. 'Is that all? That means we've spent, what – nine shillings in two days? How did we manage that?'

'Two shillings at the first inn, plus a shilling for bread

and beer. A shilling on the dye. Another shilling on food at that village we stopped in. Three at this place for bed and dinner for us both . . .'

'And the last?'

'I don't know – pennies here and there, I suppose.' He put his head in his hands. 'Two pounds felt like a fortune when you got it. In Spitalfields that could've lasted us weeks. What're we going to do when it runs out?'

'I don't know.' Rosa looked down at her hands where she was holding a boot button. Her heart felt like lead. She had spent the last half-hour trying and failing to turn the button to gold. Not for real – just a simple little illusion charm that should have taken a few moments, and yet there it sat, still black as coal, glinting in the palm of her hand in the firelight, as if winking malevolently. What was *wrong* with her?

Once when she was twelve and had the influenza, she had nearly died. She remembered Papa crying outside her chamber. And when she recovered, her magic had lagged behind. Long after she was sitting up in bed, sipping soup and asking for her storybooks to read, her magic had sulked and refused to come back.

But that had been different. She had felt it, stiff and halt, like a cramped muscle that refused to flex and twinged sulkily when pushed.

Now – there was simply nothing. She could feel nothing wrong. And yet the magic was not there. It was as if it was being siphoned off at the source, before she could use it.

But that was impossible. It didn't help that she could not concentrate – when she shut her eyes and searched inside for that well of power that *should* have been there, that had never failed her yet, all she could think of was Sebastian, like a hound on her tail, and the ring that bit into her finger.

As if to remind her, her finger gave a painful throb and she looked down. There was blood in the groove around the ring and her finger was swollen and pink. The ring was tighter than ever.

'Are you all right?' Luke asked from the other side of the bed. He stood and put the change in his pocket and came around to her side. 'You've been very quiet.'

'Just thinking . . . Luke, we need to make a plan.'

'I know.' He rubbed his face. 'We can't keep spending at this rate, or we'll be broke.'

'But not just that – what are we doing?' She felt a desperation rise up inside her. 'Where are we going? We're heading north, but *where*?'

'I don't know!' He stood and walked to the window, his face unhappy. 'How far do we have to go before Sebastian can't find us?'

To the ends of the earth, she thought, but she didn't say it. Instead she took a breath. It was not just Luke's job to decide what they did; she should not be pushing the burden of decision-making on to his shoulders.

'We should try to make some money,' she said, more firmly than she felt. 'You should look for work – they take on jobbing smiths, don't they?'

'Yes . . .' he said slowly. 'Though it depends. I could ask at the forge tomorrow. But can we afford to stop here longer?'

'Yes, if it gets us more money. Money will give us more options, more possibilities. We push on north – it's as good a direction as any, after all, and you'll keep looking for work.'

'And when do we stop?'

'When the posters stop.' She felt her courage returning with her words. Forming the plan was helping. 'When people stop looking. They'll have to give up eventually. And *somehow* my magic will return, I know it.'

She did not know it. But she had to believe it – for her own sanity. The other possibility was too awful – that her magic was gone for good. But it *couldn't* be.

'Now,' she said with a briskness that didn't quite conceal the awkwardness in her voice, 'do we have enough for you to have a pint in the bar?'

'I suppose so – why?'

'Because you need to put the word out about work, and I . . .' She stopped, swallowed, feeling a stupid flush rising up her throat. 'I need to wash.'

'Oh!' He flushed as well, his cheeks red beneath the stubble. His embarrassment should have added to hers, but somehow it did not. Instead his sudden awkwardness was strangely endearing. 'I – I see. All right. I'll go down; I'll get the landlady to send up a jug of hot water.'

97

Rosa watched him go, and then she began to unhook her dress.

Later, much later, Luke climbed the stairs of the inn, holding fast to the banister as he came up the second, narrow flight. The beer had gone down well, a little too well perhaps, and he'd had more than one pint. At the door he steadied himself and then knocked.

'Come in.' Rosa's voice came small and faint through the thick black oak, and he pushed at the door clumsily and then shut it too hard, with a bang that made him jump. It was almost dark inside, a single candle burning on the bedside table. For a long, long moment he fumbled with the bolt, and then finally it shot home, and he half walked, half felt his way to the bed, where Rosa lay with the covers pulled up to her chin. As his eyes adjusted to the candlelight he saw her, looking up at him out of the unfamiliar mass of black-brown hair that tangled on the pillow, her eyes huge and dark.

'Sorry I took so long.' He pulled off his boots, one by one, trying not to let them thump too loud on the floor and wake the sleepers below. 'There was a man in the bar, was telling me about some work might be had at a smithy out of town.'

He pulled back the covers, with some difficulty, for Rosa hung grimly on to her side, keeping them fast to her chin, and swung his legs into bed. And then he noticed, with a kind of lurch, that Rosa's dress and corset were hanging on the chair by the washstand. He went very still, feeling the beer-clumsiness in his hands and limbs, and suddenly understanding her death-like grip on the sheets.

'Luke,' she said in a small voice, 'I . . . I took my dress off. I'm only wearing my chemise. Do you mind?'

Mind? He swallowed, his throat suddenly dry, unable to think of a single thing to say.

'Only,' her words were suddenly tumbling over themselves, unsure, 'it was so uncomfortable sleeping in my stays. I know it's what fashionable ladies do, but I can't think how they bear it; you can't imagine the relief of taking them off at night. And I can't fit into the dress without the stays so . . .'

She trailed off, and he lay, listening to his heart beating in his ears, wondering what he would have said a few months ago if someone had told him it would come to this, that he would be lying in bed next to a half-dressed girl – a lady – a *witch* – listening to her talk about her corsets. What part would he have laughed at the most?

He didn't feel like laughing now. Anything but.

'Luke?' she said again. He shut his eyes, not trusting himself to speak, but knowing that he had to.

'No,' he said at last. 'No, I don't mind.'

'Good,' she whispered. Then she blew out the candle and turned on her side.

They lay in the darkness, Luke staring wide-eyed into the blackness above, and listening to Rosa's breathing and the scratch of the starched sheets as she huddled them closer around herself.

He was drunk, but not very drunk. Not drunk enough to reach across the narrow gap between them and touch her hand.

But drunk enough to think about it. Drunk enough to lie there stiff and shaking with the thought of it.

He clenched his hands into fists and turned his back on her, screwing his eyes shut in the darkness, trying to shut out the picture of her warm soft body beneath the sheets, just inches away.

She's not yours. Not yours to touch, not yours to kiss. Remember that, you fool.

'Are you asleep?' Rosa's whisper cut through the silence.

'No,' he whispered back, though there was no need to keep their voices down.

'I can't sleep.' He heard the rustle of the sheets as she turned.

He rolled on to his back again, and turned his head to face her in the darkness. The curve of her hip was silhouetted against the embers in the grate, but he could see nothing of her face in the shadows that lay between them.

'What're you thinking about?' he asked.

'About . . .' She stopped and swallowed; he heard the movement of her throat in the silent night. 'About my magic. Luke, I'm frightened.'

He sighed and rubbed his face, feeling the rough three-day beard that had started to shadow his cheeks and chin. He wished there was something he could say to make it all right, something to chase away her fears. But he had no answers – how could he? He knew nothing of what she was.

'Have I done something?' she asked desperately. 'Do you think by betraying my family and Sebastian, I somehow broke something inside me?'

'More likely he did something to you. If every witch who betrayed their lover lost their magic, I doubt there'd be many left. Is there a spell he could have put on you, d'you think?'

'I don't know. I've never heard of such a thing, but he knew a lot of dark magic. So did his father.'

'When did you first notice?'

'I don't know. The last couple of days, mainly. I just never seemed to recover from the factory. It should have come back, but instead it seemed like every spell was just draining an emptying well.' There was silence, only the wind moaning softly in the chimney and the dying coals guttering in its draught. 'Maybe before that, if I'm honest,' she said slowly. 'I haven't felt right since – well, since . . .'

'What?'

She swallowed again.

'Since I kissed you,' she said very low.

'No.' Luke turned his body to face hers. 'Is that what you've been afraid of, that you did this? That *we* did this?'

'Maybe.' Her voice was a whisper in the black.

'No! God, no! You can't tell me you're the first witch

101

ever to kiss a man, surely?'

'N-no . . .' Rosa said slowly. There was something a little more hopeful in her voice. 'No, that's true. God knows, Alexis has kissed enough outwith servants.'

'Well then.'

'I just . . . I feel naked without it. I never knew how much I relied on it, even when I wasn't using it, just the knowledge that it was there, and now – now it's not.' There was a sob in her voice as she said the last word.

'It's still there,' Luke said fiercely. He gripped her hand in his, feeling her fingers, small and pliant, in his grasp. 'It will come back. It's Sebastian, it *must* be, and if we put enough distance between you and him . . .'

Maybe it was the beer that gave him courage at last, or perhaps the touch of her hand in his, but he put his free arm out, beneath her neck, and she curled into his arms where she had slept the night before, her head on his shoulder, her face pressed into the soft crook of his neck. He felt her breath, warm against his collarbone, and the beating of her heart against his ribs. And at last he slept.

A long way away, perhaps a hundred miles to the south, a man was awake, crouched over a silver bowl of water that glimmered in the light of a single candle. He stirred the surface with the tip of his finger, watching as the ripples shivered out from his touch and bounced back from the polished sides of the bowl, making a thousand reflections and refractions in the dim light.

102

As the ripples died away a face looked back at him from the surface of the water, pale and distorted by the shimmering light. But it was not his own. It was the face of a girl, her eyes closed in sleep, her dark hair straggling over her cheek. Dark hair? The man frowned and leant closer, trying to see better, and his eager breath disturbed the water so that momentarily the picture dissolved. When it coalesced again, he saw that the image had changed; she had turned to lie on her side and her cheek was pillowed against . . . against . . .

The blow sent the silver bowl scudding across the mahogany table, the water splashing and hissing as it drenched the candle. It rang like a bell as it struck something in the darkness and came to rest – and as the sound died away the man stood in the inky blackness, his breath tearing in his throat, the smell of smoke and spilt wax from the fallen candle filling his nostrils as he panted.

Without the candle, the room was utterly dark. But the image still burnt in his mind's eye as he fell to his knees. A girl, her cheek pillowed against a man's shoulder, her lips against his skin.

The man stood, shaking, and ground his heel on the shadowy white shape of the fallen candle, hearing the wax crack and snap beneath his sole as he ground the slim white column into the carpet.

'Rosa,' he whispered through clenched teeth, the sharp edge of his boot grinding the wax into splintered shards. 'Oh, Rosa. What have you done?'

7

'It's all right, boy.' Rosa stroked Brimstone's neck and pulled the shawl more closely around her shoulders. 'He'll be back in a bit.'

She wished she had a watch. It felt like hours since Luke had left for the forge. Overnight someone had put posters up in the marketplace with her description, so they had agreed that Rosa would wait near the woods to the north of the town where neither she nor Brimstone would attract too much notice. Then, depending on what Luke found, they would either carry on north, or try to find a cheaper lodging in Baldock while he earned enough to build up their dwindling stock of money.

The wait had to be a good sign. Maybe he had found work, or was showing them his skills.

Her stomach rumbled, but she had eaten her half of the bread long since. And she was thirsty too. She looked around her, but there was no river to be seen, just fields and woods. Did she dare risk the drinking trough in the town centre?

Then she remembered the bottle she had seen Luke tuck inside the blanket roll at the base of Brimstone's saddle.

She felt a prickle of something as she undid the strap that held the blanket roll. Not guilt exactly, for Luke hadn't told her not to touch the bundle. But he had not shown it to her either. In fact, quite the reverse. She'd almost forgotten it was there, after the flurry of getting away from the house, and since then Luke had taken care not to leave its contents lying about. But this morning, as he saddled up Brimstone, she'd seen the shape of a bottle inside the blanket and heard the slosh of liquid. Was it alcohol? Spirits, maybe?

At last the girth came free. The bottle slipped out of the pack first and she caught it before it could fall to the ground, but the rest tumbled on to the frozen mud at Brimstone's hindquarters. They lay there, glinting up at her in the winter sun. A sliver of wire with a metal bar at each end. A rope. A shiny syringe. A piece of metal with a leather strap either side, ending in a buckle – she had no idea what that could be. But the long knife, with the hammer design embossed into its hilt, and its blade sharpened to a wicked point, she could be in no doubt about what that was for. It was designed to kill.

He is a witch finder. The words pounded in her head – a

105

truth she had tried to forget. *These are the tools of his trade*.

And the bottle? She knew even before she uncorked it that it was no drink. The fumes made her reel back, dizzy and sick. If her magic had been any better than a spark, it would have quailed at the stink of that stuff, she knew it.

She shoved the cork back in and stood, panting and dizzy and trying to work out what this meant.

This was Luke. *Luke*. Whatever he had tried to do, he was not a killer. She knew it in her bones, in her marrow. He had not been able to kill her, even when she lay in front of him bleeding and helpless, even though it would have saved his life.

But this bundle was horrible proof of his past – and perhaps of his present too, for why else would he have gone back for them, when they were running for their lives?

She was still standing stock-still, her heart beating hard, when a low wolf whistle came from behind her in the woods.

It was a strange man in a cap and overcoat, a shotgun broken over his arm. She turned away, back to the blanket and its spilt, horrible contents. She did not want to touch them, but she could hardly leave them here, in the field, for anyone to see.

After a moment she pushed them into a pile and flung the blanket over the top. Let Luke deal with them later, if he liked.

The whistle came again, but this time she didn't turn

back. *Young ladies do not speak to strange men*: her mother's voice rang in her head. *A gentleman awaits an introduction.*

Something told her that this man was no gentleman. She certainly didn't want an introduction.

'Oi, miss,' his cry filtered through the trees. 'Yes, you. Too hoity-toity to talk to a fella, are ya?'

Rosa bit her lip. Damn Luke and his bundle. She half wanted to jump on Brimstone's back and ride away, but she couldn't leave that knife in the field, still less that stinking, poisonous bottle. She began to pack them up, carefully at first, and then faster as she heard the man's footsteps striding through the undergrowth, twigs cracking under his feet. There was another man too, she saw as she glanced over her shoulder. They were calling to each other now.

I have no magic. The thought was like a drumbeat in her heart. *No magic. No means to defend myself. I have no magic.*

The man came closer and closer . . .

'Listen, miss,' his voice was very near now, 'don't run away, I just want to talk.'

At last she had the pack done up, and she began to buckle it beneath Brimstone's saddle. Then she swung her foot into the stirrup, ready to heave herself up.

Too late. She heard pounding steps as the man ran the last few feet and then a hand grabbed for Brimstone's bridle and another for her skirts, hauling her firmly back down to the ground even as she tried to scramble for the saddle.

'Din't your mother teach you it's not polite to walk away

107

when someone's speaking to you?' his voice hissed, close to her ear. Rosa winced.

'Let go of me. I'll – I'll . . .'

She stopped. There was no threat she could make that had teeth. Call out? They were alone. Fetch the police? How, when he had hold of her dress?

I have no magic.

She turned to face him. He was a labourer perhaps, or a small farmer. Someone who worked on the land. His face was deeply tanned and there was a scar on his jaw that showed white when he smiled. He was smiling now. She was more afraid of the smile than his anger.

'Don't be afraid. Like I said, I just wanted to talk. What's your name?'

She kept silent, and the other man came up close behind them both and grinned.

He said, "What's your name? Cat got your tongue?"

'Minna,' Rosa said wildly. It was the first name that came into her head.

'Minna what?'

'Minna S-sykes.'

'See, I hate to call a lady a liar,' said the first man. He took a step closer and put his hand on her shoulder. 'But I seen a poster in the town square. Sixteen years old. Slight build. Brown eyes. And a horse, a nice bay with a white blaze.'

'He's got no white blaze,' Rosa said fiercely. 'And take your hands off me.'

108

'And I wasn't born yesterday, girl.' The man twisted at her shoulder so that she gasped with pain and her knees gave way suddenly. She knelt in the mud in front of him. 'I bin stealing horses since before you were born and I know a cheap dye job when I see it. Women, as well as horses.' He flicked contemptuously at her hair. 'Red-head, are you, Miss *Rosamund Greenwood*? I know a way to tell.'

Rosa went utterly cold.

'A hundred pounds,' she managed. 'For safe return. *Safe.*'

'There's safe and then there's safe. I don't reckon they'll quibble.'

Her heart beat in her breast like a panicked bird, and from somewhere very, very deep, a thin thread of magic flickered in time with her panic.

She shut her eyes, nursing its tiny flame, concentrating every atom of her being on the single fragile spark . . .

Her hands clenched at her side.

She drew a breath.

'*Fýrgnást!*'

'Argh! You bitch!' The man let go as if he had been burnt and wrung his hands helplessly, holding them between his legs in an agony of pain. 'She shocked me! The little—'

Rosa didn't wait to hear any more. She scrambled up and leapt for Brimstone's back. But she wasn't even halfway into the saddle when the second man had her, hauling her roughly back to the ground, stamping on her hand so that she screamed and cried out.

'You little bitch!' The first man was half swearing, half

sobbing. 'You burnt me!' Then something in his face changed.

'Christ, Chalky.' He looked from Rosa, to his friend, and then back. There was something calculating in his expression, a cold clarity beneath the pain. 'She *burnt* me. D'you know what that means?'

'Oh my God,' the second man said. He looked down at Rosa, as if frightened that she would engulf him in flames at any moment, and crossed himself fearfully. 'What do we do? There's the hundred quid, but the Inquisitor—'

'A witch! A bloody witch.' The first man stood, wringing his burnt hand and staring at Rosa lying on the ground, a mixture of hate and avarice on his face.

'We can't take her back to London if she's a witch,' the second man said. 'She'll send us mad before we get to Hatfield.'

'Let me go.' Rosa tried to keep the sob out of her voice, tried to sound like the witch she was, the witch she had been, but it was hard to sound fearsome when you were lying on the ground, your hand bleeding into the mud. 'Let me go, or I'll burn more than your hands. I'll burn your heart inside your living body while you stand there.'

The second man shivered but the first man only stood, watching her, sucking his burnt palm. Then he shook his head, very slow.

'Nah. If you could've burnt me alive you'd have done it then. I know women. I know what they're like when they

110

strike out. They don't hold back. That was all you had for the moment, I reckon.' He turned back to his companion. 'Get a rope. And a gag – that's important. See if Fletcher's got any chloroform.'

'Let her go.'

Rosa jerked her head up. It was Luke. He was standing behind the two men, and his face was pale with fury. She had never felt more glad to see anyone.

'And who the hell are you?' the first man said over his shoulder. 'Piss off back where you came from. That's a hundred quid lying on the ground right there, and I've better men than you want a piece of her.'

'Let her go.' Rosa saw him reach slowly for the pack roll under Brimstone's saddle, and she held her breath. If only she had repacked it right. If only he could find the knife . . .

His fingers closed over something and he repeated, very low, very quiet.

'Let. Her. Go.'

'Go screw yourself,' the first man said with casual contempt. And then in one sudden move, Luke was at his back, the knife in his ribs. The man went very still.

'Let her go,' Luke whispered, 'or I will gut you like a pig.' Rosa didn't doubt for a second that he would. This was a Luke she had never seen before. A cold, frightening Luke.

'Hey, hey – calm down,' the man tried for a laugh, but there was fear in his voice. 'Chalky, take your foot off the girl, all right?'

Rosa felt the crushing weight on her hand lift, and she scrambled up.

'Rosa, get on to Brimstone's back,' Luke said. His voice was very calm, but his face was quite white. She obeyed, her hands shaking as she climbed into the saddle, trying not to get blood on the tack. 'Now, you,' he spoke to the first man, 'you're going to walk away – right?'

'Damn you, you son of a bitch,' the man whispered under his breath, but he nodded. 'All right.'

Luke let the knife point drop and the man took two steps forward and stood, staring at Luke with hate. Luke put his hand to the bridle and was about to swing himself up alongside Rosa when the man's mouth fell open, and he pointed to the knife, still in Luke's other hand.

'Your knife – it's got the hammer.'

Luke stopped, very still. He and the man stared at each other.

'Are you a Brother?' the man demanded.

Rosa held on to the reins, her knuckles white, willing Luke to get on the horse and get away. But he only stood frozen, his hand on Brimstone's bridle. She could see from the way his eyes flicked from one man to the other, and then up at her, that he was thinking, calculating, trying to work out what answer to give, what answer would get them out alive.

'Yes,' he said at last. Rosa let out a breath she did not know she had been holding. The feeling in the air had changed, but she could not say how.

'Show me your mark,' the man demanded in a growl. 'Show me, or by God I'll drag you in front of the Inquisitor for an imposter!'

Luke unbuttoned his shirt and pulled it down at the neck, baring his shoulder. There it was on his shoulder, the livid red-white mark of a half-healed burn, in the shape of a hammer. The man sucked in his breath and looked from Luke, to Rosa, and back again.

'What's going on here?'

'She's mine.' Luke spat the words. The tension between them had not gone; if anything it was stronger than before. He put his mouth close to the first man's ear and whispered something, too low for Rosa to hear.

The man pulled back, his face twisted with anger.

'Screw you then, you tight-fisted bastard.'

Rosa held tight to the reins and behind her Luke heaved himself into the saddle in one quick move. She felt him give Brimstone a great kick that sent the horse curvetting and stamping. Then they were off, across the frozen mud, and away.

They rose in silence for a mile or more, Luke too filled with fury and fear to speak. Rosa sat straight-backed in front of him, her hands gripping the reins much too tightly, so that Brimstone pulled anxiously at her grip and tossed his head.

At last, deep into the countryside, he pulled Brimstone to a halt and slid from his back. They were away from the men and the horse couldn't keep carrying two of them.

113

'I can walk,' Rosa said, but he shook his head silently and tugged at Brimstone's bridle.

'Luke, I can walk!' Rosa said again, but he didn't answer. The tenseness of the muscles in his neck and shoulders told her that he'd rather walk alone, so she let it drop.

At last, as they passed into a deep wood-shadowed lane, he spoke.

'So now you know.'

'Know what?'

'What kind of a man I am.'

He looked up and saw her eyes flicker towards the bundle at the back of the saddle, and he knew that the memory of the knife, quicksilver in the sun, must be shivering through her, as it was him; but she shook her head angrily, as if pushing the thought away.

'You're not like them.'

'I *am*. I was. Only I'm not. Christ.' He put his free hand over his face. 'I should have killed them; the story'll be halfway back to London by now.'

'So why didn't you?' she snapped. 'Why didn't you kill them?'

It was the question Luke had been asking himself for the last mile. For a moment he couldn't answer. But it was easier speaking to the silent trees than to Rosa's face.

'Because I'm a coward.'

She pulled Brimstone to a halt and leant down, trying to look at his face in the dim pine-scented shadows.

114

'Don't be ridiculous.'

'Fine. I'm ridiculous.' He tugged at Brimstone's bridle again and the horse took a step, but Rosa pulled him up.

'No, wait, you don't get to stop this conversation now you've started it. What are you talking about?'

'I'm a coward.' He spat the words as if they were bitter on his tongue. 'Can we carry on, please?'

'No!' She was looking at him with a mixture of astonishment and anger. 'No, we most certainly cannot. You're not a coward! You're . . .' She was almost spluttering, lost for words. 'Luke, you came for Minna, you faced witches to free those men and women, you walked into a *furnace* for me.'

'I've spent my life walking away from fights. I walked away from those men, I walked away from Knyvet, I hid – I hid . . .' He couldn't finish. It was like something physical in his throat, something he had swallowed, stopping him, choking him. The spectre of the dream rose up in front of him, a hand groping, a child cowering under the settle, and for a horrible moment he thought he might cry.

'Can we just bloody carry on?' he managed.

'Walking away from a fight doesn't make you a coward, you fool!' She was as angry as him. 'It's not bravery makes a man take on a fight he can't win, or kill a man he could afford to spare. It's stupidity!'

'You don't know nothing about it.'

'Fine.' She sat up straight, stiff with anger, and he knew that if she'd had any magic left it would have been spitting and crackling like damp coal on a hot fire. But she had none. Instead she slapped Brimstone's reins down on his neck and the horse trotted on.

8

There were no inns. That was what he had failed to realize. They had turned off the Great North Road some five or six hours back, and at first the going had been better, and quieter. He'd felt reassured by the dwindling towns and villages. Fewer people meant fewer posters, fewer spies, less chance of being caught.

But now dusk was falling and they had been going for hours. Brimstone was tired, and Luke and Rosa were both faint with hunger. They'd drunk from a stream by the roadside, Luke trying not to think of dead sheep and leaking dung heaps upstream. But there had been no food, not since breakfast.

It was cold too and, as the sun slipped beneath the horizon, it began to snow, very gently, then harder, in soft white smothering flakes that got into their hair and eyelashes, and made everything wet.

They needed to stop. They needed to sleep. But there were no inns.

Another corner was coming up and Luke told himself that this would be it, round this corner there would be a village, or even a farm, a cottage. But there was nothing. Brimstone was going slower and slower in spite of Rosa's encouraging clicks, and now he stumbled in the slush as they came round the corner. Rosa pulled him up with shivering hands and they stopped.

'What are you doing?'

'I'm g-going to walk. He's t-too tired to keep on like this. And b-besides, it's n-not fair that I k-keep riding while you walk. I'm n-not a wilting f-f-flower.'

'I rode.'

'Only a m-mile or two.' She slid from Brimstone's back. Close by, he could see how cold she was, her dress wet with the falling snow.

'We make better time like this,' he said brusquely. 'If you had proper boots instead of those stupid button-up things . . .'

But, more than the boots, they had to find her a proper coat. That silly shawl of Phoebe's was meant for scurrying from one pub to another, not walking miles in the frozen countryside where there was nothing to break the wind but the trees and the odd barn. For a minute he thought about offering her his greatcoat, but he knew she'd turn it down. Instead he moved around so that she was squashed between his body and Brimstone.

'W-what are you doing?'

'Nothing. It's more comfortable like this.' It wasn't, but she would freeze, stuck on the outside. At least like this she could get some shelter from Brimstone's body. After a few yards he put his arm around her, trying to share the warmth of his thick coat. He half expected her to protest, but she didn't.

They needed to stop. Neither he, nor Rosa, nor Brimstone were fit to go on much longer without rest, and something hot inside them. God, if only they were in London; there you were never far from *something*, a pub – or a doss house even – but something with a roof and a fire. And even if you couldn't get a roof, there were pie-sellers and hot chestnut vendors, or a tramp with a brazier to let you warm your hands. But out here, in this great frozen waste of fields . . . He thought again how pitiless the countryside was compared to London. There were none of the piles of refuse and filthy beggars. But death lay just as close beneath the surface. Even a pile of rubbish might hold a meal or the wood for a fire. What could you eat in these desolate, frost-frozen fields and woods? Grass? Twigs?

'Look.' Rosa's voice broke into his thoughts and he glanced up, following the line of her finger into the swirling snow. She was pointing further up the bend, but all he could see was trees, the woods clustering thick against the road.

'What?'

'Don't you see it? Smoke!' She quickened her pace, until

she was half running in the muddy slush and Luke had to jog to keep up, pulling the tired Brimstone in his wake.

'Rosa,' he panted angrily. 'Rosa, wait!'

But the protests died on his lips as they rounded the bend and there it was – a tiny cottage tucked almost into the woods, and a thin coil of smoke coming from the chimney. The windows were dark – but there was no denying that wisp of smoke disappearing into the forest.

Rosa was through the garden gate and banging on the door before Luke had a chance to catch his breath. He stood by the gatepost holding Brimstone's bridle, his heart thumping with the effort of the run and his breath coming white in the night air, but the blood cooled in his cheeks as they waited for an answer. None came.

'Open up!' Rosa banged again on the door. 'We're freezing out here. We'll d-die on the road. Open *up*!'

They stood silent, Luke holding his breath and listening for a step, watching the windows for a candle's flicker.

Nothing. There were people there – a fire could not light itself. But they were not opening the door after dark, that much was plain.

'What shall we do?' Rosa turned to face him. Her voice cracked on the last word. 'Damn them! They must be home.'

'Knock again?'

'I'm going to try the door.'

'No!' he cried, but she was already rattling the handle. 'Are you crazy? We'll be shot for trespassers!'

'We won't be shot. But it's locked anyway.' Her shoulders slumped, defeated. She put her hand up to where the locket had hung, forgetting, and then let it drop with a choking sound. For a moment Luke thought she was going to cry, but she pressed her lips together, choking down whatever noise she would have made. Then she tossed her head, that funny proud gesture he had come to know as so completely Rosa.

'It is they who should be shot, for letting travellers die on the road rather than open their doors. Do you hear me?' she shouted up at the silent windows. But there was no answer.

'Hell and damnation.' Luke clenched his fists inside his jacket pockets as she turned and walked up the path, back towards the road.

'If only I had my magic! I could get us through that door in a second. But I can't even make a witchlight!'

She was nearly crying with frustration, and Luke was torn between wanting to put his arm around Rosa and wanting to punch something. The desire to turn tail back to London and the warmth of the forge was almost overpowering. But he could not. He could never go back.

'What shall we do?' he said, very low.

'We can't keep walking.' She was shivering again, the borrowed warmth from the run fading as fast as it had come. 'We'll have to sleep in the woods.'

'We'll freeze!'

'The tramps used to do it. We'll make a shelter. Build a fire.'

'How?' He would not show himself for a coward and a weakling. But he was very close to despair. 'We've got no matches, no tinderbox. How?' He shut his eyes, pushing back the bleak thought of the match factory and the row after row after row of drying matches, the thousands upon thousands of boxes. Damn Knyvet. Damn him to hell and beyond, for what he'd driven them to.

'C-come on.' He felt Rosa's hand in his, cold as ice, and they began to walk into the woods.

'Here will do.' Rosa looked around them. They had not found the barn or field-workers' shelter she had been hoping for, but at least in this small copse the trees were dense-packed and the ground thick with leaves. The snow still fell, but not so thick, between the close-set branches. She set about unbuckling Brimstone's saddle.

'Make yourself useful,' she said over her shoulder to Luke, standing helplessly, his hands by his side.

'How?'

'Get some sticks, some kindling.'

'But we've got no—'

She gave him a look, and he turned and began searching on the forest floor for dry twigs and leaves. Rosa turned back Brimstone. Her fingers were too cold to work the buckles easily, but at last she had them loose and pulled first the blanket roll, and then the heavy, shiny saddle free.

Brimstone gave a little snort as it came loose and made all the skin on his back twitch and shiver in the moonlight.

'There you go.' She spread his saddle blanket over him and stroked his warm mud-coloured nose. 'Don't freeze, darling Brimstone. You're all we've got.'

She shivered as she said the words and Luke looked down at the pile of twigs.

'What now?' he asked. 'I've heard tell that tramps can light a fire by just rubbing a stick, but I don't think this wood's dry enough for that. Why didn't I pack my damn tinderbox?'

Rosa swallowed.

'Let's see what I've got left.'

'What you've . . .?' For a minute he didn't understand, then he said, 'Oh,' and fell silent.

He said nothing as she crouched over the little pile, a piece of birch bark between her fingers, remembering, thinking of all the fires they had set as children in the woods and fields around Matchenham, roasting fish from the lake and eggs stolen from the hen coop, potatoes pulled from the kitchen garden when the gardener was at his own lunch, wild garlic from the stream bed. Alex had always sworn by dry grass, she by birch bark. But she had never had to do it without magic.

She knelt, feeling the cold strike though her clothes.

Come on, just a spark, just the smallest, smallest spark . . .

Nothing.

She pushed harder, her lips forming the different spells,

the words to call heat, the words to call fire, the words to bring forth light from the darkness.

Nothing at all.

'God!' It burst out of her like a sob. 'I never knew how much I relied on it!'

She turned, looking at Luke's face, white in the darkness.

'What can I do without magic? Nothing! *Nothing!*'

'Don't say that.'

'It's true! I was never taught any other way to take care of myself, any other way to live – I know nothing at all.'

She rubbed her hands over her face, feeling the emptiness inside, and the ruby ring scratched at her skin, drawing a bead of blood on her cheek. She put her finger to the cut, and looked at it in the moonlight. 'And I hate this ring. I hate it. I hate *him*!' She began to pull at it, dragging it up her finger, her teeth clenched against the pain, until at last she stopped in despair.

'We'll get it off,' Luke said. There was something almost angry in his voice. 'I promise. We'll get the damn thing off.'

'How?'

'I don't know.' He took a step forward and then crouched beside her, putting his arm around her. 'You're shivering. Let's sit for a bit, rest. Maybe with a bit of rest . . .'

'I'm scared, Luke.' She heard the crack in her own voice and hated the weakness. *I will not cry. I will not.* 'If I don't have magic – what am I?'

'You're still you.' He got up, and for a minute Rosa thought he was going to leave, but he only moved across the clearing to where she'd left the saddle and began unwrapping the rolled-up blanket. The long, wicked knife flashed in the darkness and she heard the iron gag chink against the bottle as they slid to the forest floor. She felt her heart beat faster in spite of herself. *This is Luke*, she told herself. *Luke. He is not one of them.*

But he came back with only the thin blanket and wrapped it around her shoulders. Behind them Brimstone gave a great sigh and heaved himself awkwardly to the forest floor, his head on the ground, and Luke and Rosa sat, leaning against his warm back, side by side, the ache spreading through their tired limbs.

After a few minutes she reached out and put her arm around him.

He went quite stiff and still for a moment, just long enough for her to think better of it, to consider pulling back, and to wonder how she could do it without looking like a fool. But then he put his own arm around her shoulders, pulling her close into his side, so close that she could feel the movement of his chest as he breathed. She sat in silence, thinking how strange it was, how wrong by all society's codes and rules. They were not related. They were not married. They were not even of the same class. And yet his arm around her shoulders and the furrows of his ribs beneath her palm both felt completely right.

'Luke . . .' She took a breath, feeling his arm rise and fall with the rise and fall of her shoulders. 'What made you join them – the Brotherhood, I mean? Who are they?'

There was silence again, backed by the sigh of the woods and the patter of snowfall, until she began to wonder if he would answer her at all. Then he sighed.

'D'you remember, I told you I was a coward, earlier today?'

She nodded in the darkness, knowing he would feel the movement.

'Well, this is how I know: when I was a child my parents were killed – by a witch.'

Rosa let out a small sound. She had not meant to speak, but she could not help it. It was not quite a cry, but something smaller, more ashamed. She put her free hand over her mouth and waited for him to continue.

'He came to our house in the night. My mother woke me up and I hid beneath the settle while he butchered them. Their blood ran down the walls and pooled where I was lying.'

Rosa pressed her hand harder across her mouth, stifling the sob that was trying to rise up and choke her.

'And I did nothing. I just lay and listened as they died.'

For a moment she didn't trust herself to speak. She pressed her knuckles against her mouth, breathing through her nose and swallowing hard. Then she spoke, trying to keep her voice steady.

'Luke, you were a *child*. What could you have done against a full-grown witch?'

'I could have looked,' he said, very quietly. 'I know I could never have stopped it. But I could've looked and seen the man who did it. But I did nothing. I just watched his cane rolling across the floor towards me. I see it still when I shut my eyes at night; black with a silver snake, eating its own tail, rolling, rolling closer, and the hand, groping for it, ready to touch my leg. And I did nothing. I just closed my eyes and prayed.'

'Oh my God.' She shut her eyes, trying to shut out the picture that rose in front of her in the darkness: a terrified child, a killer, a couple dying in each other's arms.

'I've waited fifteen years to avenge my parents' death.' His voice was all the more terrifying for being so flat and soft. 'And I thought the Malleus was the answer. I passed the test of fire and the test of the knife. And the last test was to kill a witch. Kill *you*. Do what I'd been waiting to do all these years. And I failed. I was too much of a coward.'

'You were *not*.' Her voice shook. It meant so much that he believed her. '*Listen* to me, you showed me mercy. That was not the act of a coward. A coward would have killed me as I lay there dying, and gone back with the news to the Brothers.'

He said nothing. She wasn't sure if he was even listening.

'Luke.' She twisted against him, pulling her arm out from behind his back, and took his face in her cold fingers, turning it to look at her in the dark, trying to read his expression. 'Luke, do you hear me? You are not a coward. My God, you – you . . .'

She stopped, the words deserting her.

Luke looked away, over her shoulder. His lips were

127

pressed shut and she knew he would say no more.

Damn him. Damn his silence. How could you argue with a man who said nothing, with someone who hid everything inside?

For a moment she almost longed for Alexis, who blurted out the first thing that came into his head, whether that got him laughed at or punched. But Luke – she had never known what he thought beneath that quiet, unsmiling face.

She thought of that soft deep dimple that came and went so quick she had to remind herself that it had really been there.

'I wish you'd smile,' she said, knowing it came out of the blue, that she sounded crazy. Luke said nothing. Then he sighed.

'I don't have much to smile about at the moment.'

9

Luke was very cold. He was lying on the hard stone floor of his parents' cottage, beneath the settle, the cold stone striking through his thin shirt. It was the old bad dream – his parents were dead again for the hundredth time, perhaps the thousandth time. And just like all the other times before, he could do nothing. Nothing but wait.

The pool of blood came nearer and nearer. And he waited, for the clatter of the ebony cane, and the creep, creep of the black-gloved hand searching for it.

But it didn't come. Instead the blood carried on lapping, and rising, and suddenly he realized he was wet, floating, up to his chest in a stream of gore, struggling to keep his footing. He tried to reach out for something to steady himself, but his hands were full of Rosa's limp dying body. He stumbled for the bank, through the river of blood, and her breath rattled in her throat, a stream of gore running from her mouth. And he realized that the river had been coming from her all along, that it was her life blood running away, threatening to drown them both.

In the red swirl he saw the snake's-head cane – Sebastian's cane – bobbing away on the tide of blood, far out of reach, and he loosed one hand from Rosa, reaching, reaching after it . . . but it was gone, and he needed both his hands to clutch at the riverbank, dragging Rosa's heavy blood-soaked body up the muddy shore.

'Rosa,' he tried to say. 'Rosa, you can stop this!'

But his voice was swallowed up in the roar of the river and the dying rattle of Rosa's breath.

He grabbed her, shaking her, shaking her furiously.

'You're not to die! Hear me? You're not to die!'

And then suddenly, cutting through the dream like a silver sharp knife, he heard a voice.

'Well, well, well. What do we have here?'

Luke woke abruptly, so fast that it took a moment for him to disentangle reality from the dream. There was no river; the roar in his ears was only his own blood and the frantic beating of his heart. But the cold – that was real. A thin veil of snow had fallen in the night and his cheek was burning with the chill of it. When he tried to open his eyes there were snowflakes on his lashes and his hand was frozen. The weight of Rosa's body in his arms was real too. Her sleeping form was curled against him, her spine firm against his chest, his arms holding her hard, trying to keep them both warm. His coat was open, wrapped around them both, and the thin threadbare blanket was spread across them and as much of Brimstone's rump as it could reach.

But the voice . . . Was the voice real?

For a moment he could not tell. Then it came again.

'Take your hands off her, you filthy outwith.'

There was a flare of magic, bright in the darkness of the wood, and Luke found himself suddenly snatched upwards and away from Rosa, so fast that he barely knew what was happening. The wind whipped past his cheek and then he was hanging in mid-air, pinned there by some unseen magic that gripped him almost too tight to breathe. There was a six-foot drop beneath him, to the forest floor.

Below him Brimstone scrambled up, snorting with alarm.

'Put me down!' Luke gasped. 'Who are you?'

'Put you down?' The figure stepped into the pool of moonlight, his orange hair dimmed to a washed-out yellow in the pale light. It was Alexis. 'And have you punch me like the great ham-fisted oaf you are? Not on your life. Do you think I'm stupid?'

Get up, Rosa! Luke willed her. *Wake up!*

'Well, you can't be as stupid as you look,' he croaked, in a half-gasp. 'No one could manage that and keep breathing.'

For a second the unseen hand tightened on his throat and he gave a strangled choke – and then Alexis gave a careless, brittle laugh.

'Funny, aren't you? Well, you'll find it hard to crack

a joke when Seb's finished with you. I promised him I'd take you alive, but I imagine that state of affairs ain't going to last long.'

'Stop it!' The voice rang out from somewhere below him, and there was a scrambling sound as Rosa staggered to her feet. Luke tried and failed to look down at her, but his heart flooded with relief. 'Alexis, you bastard. Let him go!'

'Sister dear,' Alexis drawled, but there was a pant in his voice, and Luke could see that he was tiring. His face hadn't changed – his self-satisfied smile was stuck just as firmly to his lips as ever. But his magic was flickering like a flame in a strong breeze. He was not a strong witch – not nearly as strong as Rosa. Or at least – not nearly as strong as Rosa had been . . .

'Put him down.' Rosa spoke dangerously, her voice calm and low, but Luke could hear the almost imperceptible edge of fear beneath.

'Or what?' Alexis said carelessly. 'Seb told me he'd clipped your wings. Said I wouldn't have any trouble from *you*.'

'Put. Him. *Down*.'

Alexis shrugged nonchalantly, but his magic was a strangled flicker. Surely he couldn't keep this up much longer?

'Very well then.'

Suddenly, as if he had meant to all along, he let the spell go with an abrupt rush and Luke fell to the forest floor with a bone-rattling thud that left him gasping and winded, his head ringing with the blow. He tried to get up, but there seemed to be no muscles in his gut – he could only lie on the pile of leaves that had broken his fall, trying not to groan aloud.

'What did you mean?' Rosa was edging round, trying to get between Luke and Alex. Luke wanted to groan, tell her to stop, point out that she couldn't protect him without magic – but he couldn't get the breath to say the words. 'Clipped my wings – what's that supposed to mean?'

'Sorry, can't help you there,' Alexis drawled. He was enjoying this little moment of power. 'According to the sot, I'm too stupid to know what I'm saying. Now, get over here. You too, Brimstone.' He clicked to the horse, who gave a nervous snort and backed away.

'I'm not coming.' Rosa's voice shook. 'You can't force me back.'

'Oh really? I think you'll find I can. I'm your legal guardian, until you marry Seb.'

'I will never marry him!' Rosa choked out. 'Don't you understand that? Why would I give myself up to a life of – of *abuse* and misery? He doesn't love me! He hates me – he hates all women, I think. Why would I condemn myself to a marriage like that?'

'Because,' Alexis came very close, and put his hand on her arm, his fingers digging into her flesh, 'because Mama and I say you will. Because you made a promise and I intend to see that you keep it. And lastly, dear little sister, because you have no other choice. Who else will want you, after you've spent three days whoring and slumming around the countryside with *him*?'

'How dare you!' Rosa snarled. She drew back her hand and smacked Alexis round the face, a ringing slap that cracked through the silent wood like a gunshot. For a moment there was complete silence, broken only by the screech and caw of birds startled out of sleep by the noise and the shocked scream of an owl. Then Alexis began to laugh and he flung out a blast of magic that sent Rosa tumbling to the forest floor, sprawling at his feet.

'How dare *I*? My God, that's rich! You little slut. You should be thanking God on your knees that Seb still wants you, not teaching me my manners.'

'Why does he still want me,' Rosa said thickly, 'if I'm such a worthless slut?'

'God knows.' Alexis looked down at her with contempt. 'But he seems to. Perhaps it's precisely *because* you've run. There's no fun in hunting, after all, if the fox doesn't run. All those pretty English girls in India on the prowl for a husband, who sighed and gave up the prize for the asking – where's the fun in that? What a man likes is the chase. The hunt. The fox at bay. And when a chap can have anything, perhaps it's natural to want the one thing you *can't* have. Perhaps Seb's had enough of kissing girls who swoon. Perhaps he wants one that shudders instead. To be frank, I don't really care.'

'You bastard,' Rosa's voice shook.

'Don't swear, you horrible child,' Alexis said in a bored voice. 'Now.' He pulled a twist of rope from his belt. 'I'm going to tie your hands. Don't make me gag you as well. It won't look nice when we stop at inns.'

'You're going to drag me home to London with my hands tied!' Rosa said scornfully. She climbed to her feet, brushing the leaves from her scorched and stain-marked skirt. 'And you expect people to stand by while you do this?'

'I've got the carriage, you little fool. You didn't think I walked all the way here, did you? No one will know what's happening behind the doors, much less care. Now, keep still.'

He said the words of a spell, there was a brief flare of magic and Rosa turned suddenly rigid against the moon, still as a post while Alexis bound her wrists together with laborious thoroughness. Luke seemed to have been forgotten about – almost. Just a few feet away across the clearing he could see something silver-pale glinting in the moonlight. The knife. If only he could reach it before Alexis noticed . . .

He edged himself across the carpet of leaves, keeping low, trying to time the rustle of the leaves with Alexis's bouts of swearing. Four feet away. Three. Two.

Then he heard Alexis give an exclamation of satisfaction.

'There, get out of that, if you can! Now, where's the sot?'

Abandoning caution, Luke leapt for the knife and scrambled to his feet, holding its blade out in front of him.

'Keep still,' he snapped at Alexis. 'I know you're a witch, but I can gut you before you finish a spell and, trust me, I will.'

'What?' Alexis said delightedly. He gave a long, sneering laugh, as if this was the best joke he'd heard all day, and took a step towards Luke. 'Gut me? You couldn't pick your nose, unless I let you.'

He spat out a word in that foreign spell-casting tongue they all used, and Luke found himself suddenly as heavy as molasses, his limbs stuck to his side. He swore, but he was not motionless, not by a long stretch. With a huge, trembling effort he took a step towards Alexis and then another. Alexis's eyes widened and, for the first time, Luke saw fear there.

'What? God damn you! *Belúcan!*'

This time it was easier – Luke shook off the words like shaking off a heavy tiredness. He took another step. Another. And then he gripped Alexis around the throat.

'Who are you?' Alexis gritted out – it was half a snarl, half a whimper. His skin felt clammy beneath Luke's fingers and his pale-green eyes were wide and wild with fear. 'Who *are* you? You're no God-damned outwith! No outwith should be able to do that.'

'Who am I? I'm a man.' Luke was panting heavily with the effort of holding off the spell. There was sweat running into his eyes, in spite of the coldness of the night. 'Which is more than I can say for you. How do you want to die?'

'I don't want to die.' Alexis looked suddenly ill with

fear, as though he'd realized his predicament. In the moonlight his face was fishbelly-white, his freckles standing out dark against the bleached skin. 'P-please. Don't kill me.'

The knife was against Alexis's throat, the tip pressing into the pale skin above his cravat.

'Please!' Alexis moaned. His voice cracked, high and shrill with fear. 'Please don't do it!'

Luke pressed harder and harder, thinking of John Leadingham's words. *Carotid artery. Stick 'em quick and get out, before they can bewitch you. Don't look back.*

A bead of blood appeared at the tip of the knife and Alexis gave a high, keening cry . . .

And Luke stopped.

It was not the spell. He could still feel it, weighing down on him, sucking at his limbs like thick mud, trying to stop his every movement. But it was not what was stopping him from killing Alexis. All that would have taken was one small shift – but he could not do it. It was the same story. The old story.

Coward.

He hesitated just one second too long – and then there was a sudden blinding crack of light and Alexis was no longer in his grip. Luke whipped around, the knife outheld – but he couldn't see; he was blinded by the flash and Alexis seemed to be nowhere in the clearing. Where was he? Where was he?

And then he felt something thick and strangling

137

drop over his head and tighten around his throat, and he heard Alexis laugh, a long, half-hysterical cackle that went on and on.

'You fool!' Alexis's voice was high and shaking with relief. 'You dumb sot! Why didn't you do it?' He laughed again and tightened the blanket around Luke's face and throat until Luke began to see stars. He dropped the knife, clawing with his fingers to try to pull it away from his throat, buy himself a little air, a little time . . .

And then there was a ringing crack and a cry of pain – but *whose*?

Luke stumbled forwards, still blinded by the blanket, but it was loose around his face and he was pulling free, able to breathe – only the air was full of terrible, choking fumes . . .

At last he dragged the blanket away and drew a breath of the choking air, looking wildly around.

And then he saw.

Rosa was standing over Alexis's prone body, her bound hands still clutching the neck of the broken bottle she had smashed over her brother's skull. Her eyes, as she stared down at Alexis's unconscious body, were wide and dark, dilating into black.

'The bottle!' Luke managed, hearing his voice hoarse and croaky in his own ears. 'You broke the bottle! For God's sake – cover your face!'

The smell was making him feel faint and woozy, even as he wound the blanket back around his nose and mouth, trying not to breathe as he snatched up the rest of their belongings.

Holding the knife awkwardly, he slashed the rope around Rosa's wrists. She was still standing, gasping, her mouth and nose uncovered to whatever poison was in that bloody bottle.

'Come on!' he yelled. 'Move!'

She stumbled against him and he grabbed her shoulders, half dragging her along, away from the dizzying, choking fumes.

'Is he . . . ?' she slurred. 'Will he . . . ?' But she couldn't finish. Instead she stopped to heave into the bushes at the side of the path.

'Come on!' Luke pressed the blanket against his face; the fumes were still making his head swim even ten, twenty, thirty feet away from the clearing. Rosa shuddered, wiped her mouth and let Luke pull her the rest of the way to the road where she vomited again, trying to hold her skirts away from the mess, tears watering down her cheeks.

'Don't look!' she managed to choke out as Luke held her hair back from her face. 'Go away!'

At last the vomiting stopped and she was able to sit by the side of the road, her face white and her hands shaking.

'Will he live?' she managed. 'I didn't want to kill him. I didn't know . . . What was it?'

'I don't know.' Luke shuddered at the memory of the stench, at the memory of John Leadingham's words as he handed it over: *Whatever you do, don't break the bottle or the witch'll be the least of your worries.* 'Something like chloroform, I think. John Leadingham gave it to me. You're supposed to put it on a rag – just a drop – press it over their mouth. It stops them from casting spells, sends 'em unconscious. I don't think it's supposed to kill them.'

Not used as he'd said, no. But having a full bottle broken over your head and lying unconscious in a pool of the mixture?

'He'll be all right,' he said at last. 'He has to be.' He had to be, because if he was not, Rosa would never forgive herself, would never be able to move on from this thing she had done, to save him, to save Luke. 'He'll be all right. Come on.'

But Rosa didn't move. She sat with her arms wrapped around her knees, shivering in the falling snow, her eyes wide and dizzyingly black. Her huge black pupils reminded him of the opium addicts down at the docks. What *was* in that bottle?

'What did he mean?' she said.

'I don't know – look, come on. We need to get out of here.' Sebastian might not have come himself, but he would certainly be keeping close watch on Alexis's movements. It would not take them long to find Alexis – dead or alive.

'Sebastian clipped my wings, he said. What did he mean?'

'I don't *know!*'

'I do.' Her voice was slurred, but there was a queer

140

determination in her face as she held out her hand. 'Give me the knife.'

'What?' He had not even realized he was still carrying it, stuck into his belt. Rosa stood, drunkenly, and pulled it from his waist.

She spread her left hand out on a fallen tree stump, the fingers spread wide, the ruby ring flashing in the moonlight. Her other hand she clenched around the knife. Then she shut her eyes.

The tip of the knife rested against the thin gold band.

'Rosa . . .' He was suddenly alarmed, more than alarmed – frightened. 'Rosa, what are you doing?'

She drew a whimpering breath.

'Rosa!' he shouted and leapt forward – too late.

There was a sickening crunch and Rosa screamed. Her hand was clutched to her breast and there was blood pouring down her dress – pouring, pouring as if it would never stop. Her magic blazed suddenly like a fire in the black night, blindingly bright and beautiful.

And Luke could only stand, gasping in horror, as the ring fell to the ground. Rosa slumped after it, her eyes closed, her face pale and still.

His blood was screaming in his ears, and his breath tore in his throat, and he found he was sobbing, 'Rosa, Rosa, oh my God, what have you done, oh, Rose, oh my God . . .'

He fell to his knees in the mud beside her and picked up her limp hand, where it lay cradled against her breast.

The third finger of her left hand was gone, cut away at the joint.

Luke vomited into the ditch. Again and again he heaved, where Rosa had been sick just a moment before, though there was little in his stomach to throw up, just spit and acid.

Then he crawled back to Rosa, not wanting to look at her butchered hand, but unable not to.

'Oh my God,' he sobbed again. 'Oh Jesus. What should I do?'

Her finger was bleeding heavily and, at last, remembering what William had done one time when he'd ripped off a nail in the forge, he tore a strip off the bottom of his shirt. It was not clean, but none of their clothes were clean. He wrapped it around the stump of Rosa's finger, trying to knot it as tight as he could to stem the bleeding. If only she would wake up.

Her magic blazed around them both with a terrible dark beauty, and he realized how much a part of her it was, how she had seemed to be fading in front of him without it. He had never thought he could be glad to see the flare and burn of magic, but he *was* glad – more glad than he could put words to. It was part of her, as much part of her as her lost finger, and seeing her without it was just as wrong.

At last her finger was bound and the blood seemed to be slowing. He had done as much as he could, and now the sky was paling in the east. Dawn was coming.

He left Rosa while he tracked Brimstone to a nearby

142

field, where he must have blundered in the night. He was peaceable and easy to catch, and stood patiently while Luke saddled him up and repacked their meagre belongings.

He returned to Rosa, hoping she would have woken, but she lay still, very pale, her dress dark with blood down the front.

'Come on,' he muttered, touching her cheek. 'Wake up, Rosa. Wake up. You can heal yourself, I know you can. Just, oh God, please wake up.'

But she didn't, and at last he managed, somehow, to heave them both on to Brimstone's back, in a desperate slithering rush that left him frightened and sweating, and Brimstone sidling and snorting.

'Come on, boy.' He clicked his tongue to Brimstone and gave the horse a gentle kick with his heels. 'You've done well tonight; just give me a few more miles and we can all rest when we're away from here. Oh, God damn you, Rosa!' He wanted suddenly to weep. 'Wake up, please!'

He had never felt more frightened or more alone. What would he do if she did not wake up? Was it the effects of the fumes, or the shock of cutting off her own finger? What if infection set in and he was powerless to prevent it?

Only one thought kept him going as Brimstone clopped through the quiet night: Rosa had her magic back. She had been right – and whatever the price, perhaps it was worth it.

It lapped around them as they rode, a dark flameless fire, a red-gold blaze of power, so beautiful and so terrible he could hardly bear it. And it seemed, or so he thought, to warm him as he and Brimstone rode in silence through the snowy darkness, filling him with a strange kind of comfort.

As long as her magic burnt, she was alive. And as long as she was alive, that was enough.

It was only as they passed the milestone marking 100 miles from London that he suddenly thought of the ruby ring, lying in the mud and blood where they had left it.

For a moment he pulled up, Brimstone's ears twitching curiously. Then he shrugged and pressed his heels to Brimstone's flanks again.

It was gone. Good riddance to it.

She was free.

She was free.

A hundred and fifty miles further south, a man jerked upright in the darkness of his bedchamber, his heart pounding as if someone had touched him while he slept.

He felt it, her magic wrenched away, slipping through his fingers like water as he struggled to hold on to it.

And then it was gone.

How? How had she done it?

He snarled and swung his legs out of bed, cursing in the darkness. Alexis. He should never have sent that fool to do his work for him – like an idiot he had thought that Rosa might trust her brother, might even surrender to him. He was not naive enough to think that she would give herself up to *him*, but to her own brother? Perhaps. And if not,

144

what was one un-magicked witch and one helpless outwith against a full-grown witch like Alexis?

The answer, incredibly, seemed to be that they were not just a match for him, but more than a match. They had bested Alexis, they *must* have.

Alexis, he did not care about. But the ring – what had she done with the ring?

10

Rosa woke, but didn't move. She lay blinking in the soft rose-coloured light that was breaking across the hills.

For a long time she just lay, feeling the glorious ripple and flex of her magic bubbling like an irrepressible spring from within her. *I'm back!* she thought exultantly. *Do you hear me, Sebastian?*

The thought crackled over her skin and suddenly, unable to help herself, she sent sparks shooting into the air in the sheer exuberance of being alive and with power. She knew she should be keeping her magic for what mattered – healing her hand and protecting Luke and herself from Sebastian – but just at that moment she did not care. She watched them as they flew into the air like fireworks and drifted back down, fading as they came.

She was lying in a hollow beside a hedge, Luke's

greatcoat thrown over her like a counterpane. Turning her head she could see Brimstone stood placidly grazing at the edge of the field, his ears twitching occasionally in the breeze.

She was cold. At least, her face and feet and right hand were cold. Her left hand was not. Instead it throbbed agonizingly, with a worrying heat.

Cautiously she sat up and began to pick at the blood-crusted bandage.

'You're awake.'

The voice came from behind her and she turned. Luke was sitting on the bank and he was smiling, the dimple deep and soft in his right cheek.

'Hello.' She was suddenly shy. It was stupid. She had lain in his arms three nights now, and ridden astride in front of him in the saddle for three days.

'I was worried. You passed out – I don't know if it was the stuff in the bottle or your . . .' He stopped and she saw his face shut at the memory. She knew him well enough to know that it was when he was at his softest and most vulnerable that the shutter came down, closing his face into blankness. Though he couldn't quite hide the shudder that passed through him in the silence between his words and hers.

'I'm all right now,' she said simply. She knew she did not have to explain, that he could see her magic as well as she could feel it – see it flex and shimmer and burn beneath her skin. What was a finger, compared to that?

147

'What do you think happened?' he asked.

She shook her head. 'I don't know. It was the ring – Sebastian's ring. I don't know what he did to it, but it was doing something to my magic, draining it, taking it away . . . I've never heard of that before, but it must be.'

'You gave yourself to him . . .' Luke said slowly. 'And he took everything.'

Everything. She shivered.

'Your finger. Can you heal it?'

'I don't know.' She looked down at the bloodied bandage and again felt the hot throb of infection, its heat shooting up her arm. 'I can't grow another finger, if that's what you mean. Magic can do what your body can – no more, no less.'

'But that's not true! Sebastian's mother – when you were dying . . .'

'I'm no healer, Luke. Her gift – I've never seen one like it. But even then, I wasn't dying. I was just gravely wounded. Punctured lungs can mend. Ribs can heal. But if a wound is unhealable, it's unhealable by magic. And this . . .' She touched the bandage gently, then winced. 'I think it's infected. I can probably keep the infection away, but . . .'

'You need to get it looked at by a doctor.' Luke's face was closed, but she could tell he was worried.

'Doctors cost money.'

'You need to get it stitched.'

Rosa bit her lip. It was true. She could keep the infection at bay and stop it hurting, but only by constant, draining use of magic she should be saving for other things. She had no idea how a severed finger would heal. *If* it would heal.

'All right.' She sat up straighter, pushed her hair out of her face. 'So we have to find a doctor. And then . . .'

Then what? She might have got her magic back, but this cat-and-mouse chase couldn't go on for ever. She and Luke running, Sebastian sending his hounds after them, and then coming in for the kill.

'We have to fight back,' she said slowly. 'We can't keep running blindly. It's what the unsuccessful fox does, the ones who end up getting caught. They run scared. The clever ones, the ones who live – they think ahead. They lead the hounds down to the river where they can break the scent. They plan. They go to ground.'

'We're not foxes, Rosa.' Luke sounded weary and irritable, as if he was trying not to snap back. 'And there's nowhere we can go to ground, is there? There's nowhere Sebastian can't find us eventually.'

'No, but . . .' Rosa bit her lip. An idea was forming at the far corner of her mind, something almost unthinkable, so crazy it would be the very last thing Sebastian would ever expect. But would Luke ever agree?

'Rosa?' He leant forward, as if he was reading her mind, though that was impossible. His forehead was furrowed. 'What are you thinking?'

'Nothing.' She shook herself and began pinning her hair with the last remaining hairpins, not nearly enough to hold her heavy mass of curls safely, but enough to look respectable at least. 'Come on. We'll need to brush ourselves up if we're to gain entry to a doctor's office.'

Luke said nothing. But he stood and began tucking in his shirt.

'Come on then. Let's get going. Which way?'

Rosa stood too and scanned the horizon. Then she pointed.

'Look. There are carts going along that road across the field. There's another. Laden with chickens. It must be market day at some town. If we follow the carts we can't go far wrong.'

'Doctor's?' The woman selling apples looked them up and down as she handed over the fruit. 'The only doctor in this town is Doctor Faulkes. He lives at the white house by the clock. But he charges a pretty penny.'

'We can pay,' Luke said flatly. 'Come on, Rosa.'

They wound their way through the throng of people picking over the fruit and vegetables and haggling over the shrieking chickens, eating an apple each as they went. After the quiet of the countryside the din was almost dizzying. The crowds should have made Rosa fear – after all, the more people, the more chance of being identified. But paradoxically she felt safer in their midst – a needle in a haystack of townspeople.

At the horse trough by the clock, Luke looped Brimstone's reins over a railing and put their last apple on the side of the water trough. Someone had already punched a hole in the thin ice and the horse stood, gratefully sucking the cold water and twitching his ears in the breeze.

It was clear which house the woman had meant: there was a brass plaque beside the tall black door.

Dr. N. M. Faulkes.

Consulting hours 10 to 11a.m. and 4 to 5p.m.,

except Wednesday.

They both looked up at the clock. It read five past ten. Luke shrugged and rapped at the door.

A maid answered, her white streamers fluttering in the breeze.

'Yes?'

'We're here to see the doctor,' Luke said without preamble. 'We . . . my . . .' He looked at Rosa and she saw something in his eyes, a kind of doubt. What story would the doctor be most likely to believe? 'My . . . um . . . my wife has hurt her finger.'

The word gave Rosa a strange little shiver and her fingers tightened on Luke's arm.

'Hmm.' The maid looked them up and down, clearly doubting their ability to pay, but she stood back and opened the door wider. 'Come in, then, Mr . . . ?'

'Williams,' Luke said, after a moment's pause.

'Come in then, Mr and Mrs Williams. The doctor has a patient just now, but he will see you shortly.'

They sat on a hard bench in the dining room and waited.

Rose felt her finger throb in time with her heartbeat and listened to Luke fingering the coins in his pocket. She wished she knew how much this might cost. For all Luke had said they could pay, the truth was they could pay only up to a certain amount. She doubted they had more than a guinea left, and this doctor looked prosperous and well-to-do. Well, if the worst came to it, she would just have to magick the pennies into sovereigns, and pray the enchantment lasted long enough for them to get out of the village. She did not like the thought though. It was not just the risk of being caught, or attracting attention. It was more the fact that however you looked at it, using magic that way was a kind of stealing, no better than taking sovereigns from a purse. *I shall let the outwith be, and no harm will come to me . . .*

Luke was silent too. She sneaked a look at his face, but it was shuttered and blank. His head was bowed and she could see the tendons at the nape of his neck standing out, tense as ropes.

'Mr and Mrs Williams?' the girl said suddenly. Luke jumped and Rosa saw the muscles in his cheek move as he clenched his jaw. She wondered if he was regretting that choice of name.

'The doctor will see you now.'

'Dear, dear me.' The doctor came around the polished mahogany desk and turned Rosa's finger to the light. 'How did you say this happened, my dear?'

'I . . .' She looked at Luke, feeling panic rise in her breast. It was one thing they had not discussed. 'I – I was chopping wood.' She tried to speak shortly, to blur her consonants and bend her vowels as Luke did. The result sounded nothing like his accent, more like a Welsh parlourmaid they had had once. She felt herself wince and Luke gave her a strange look.

'Hm.' The doctor did not seem to notice her odd accent, but only looked at her finger more closely through his pince-nez. 'It's simply that it's unusual to damage this finger in isolation. You must have been holding the wood in a very awkward manner.'

'I – I was.' Damn him. Damn him.

'Well, it's been cleanly severed. It must be stitched, of course. And then you must pray that gangrene does not set in.'

Luke stood outside while the wound was stitched. It was not his choice, but the doctor called in his nurse and sent Luke away. He stood in the waiting room, his hands gripping the back of the chair, and listened to Rosa's muffled scream and then her shaking voice telling the doctor to go on.

After that there was silence, apart from the soothing professional murmurs of the doctor. Then the door opened and she came out.

'Rosa?' He stepped forward, barely able to hold his anxiety. She smiled, though her face was white and her hair was damp with sweat in spite of the cold day. Her left hand was swathed in a white bandage, wound with military precision.

The doctor came out behind her. He took Luke's hand and shook it heartily.

'Your wife is a brave lady, sir. Barely a peep. I wish half my patients were as tough.'

'Thank you, Doctor.' He swallowed. 'And . . . your charges?'

The doctor looked them both up and down, appraising them. Then he seemed to make up his mind.

'Half a guinea will be adequate.'

'I do not believe that is your usual charge, sir. We do not need charity.' Luke knew his face was hard and ungrateful, but he could not help it. Pride made him stiff and awkward. Behind the doctor's shoulder he saw Rosa's incredulous glare and knew what she was thinking as clearly as if she had hissed it in his ear: *Take the offer and don't be a damn fool!*

'I said, half a guinea will be adequate,' the doctor repeated with a smile. 'It was a simple procedure, no chloroform or ether. I believe it will heal well.'

'Very well.' Luke tried to force a smile as he felt in his pocket and counted the coins out on to the table. Both he and the doctor left them there, ignoring the little pile as if unworthy of notice.

'Good day to you both,' the doctor said with genial benevolence. 'If there are any unfortunate sequelae, please don't hesitate to return.'

'Thank you.' Rosa smiled. She pressed her right hand into his. 'I could not have been in better hands, I feel sure of that.'

'You are most welcome, my dear. Godspeed.'

Outside, Luke held on to Rosa's uninjured arm as if she might fall, his grip almost painful.

'Luke.'

He didn't answer.

'Luke! I can walk, for goodness' sake.'

'Why didn't you do something? To stop the pain?'

'A spell, you mean?' She almost laughed. 'Good God, it's come to something when you of all people are begging me to use magic to save myself discomfort.'

He flinched as if he had been slapped and she felt instantly unworthy.

'Luke – I'm sorry, I didn't mean—'

'Don't be. I deserved that.'

They had made their way back to the trough where Brimstone was still tethered, and now they sat, the stone bench striking cold through their clothes. Rosa took Luke's hand in her good one, feeling the unaccustomed weight of the bandage on her other.

'Luke, listen—'

'You don't need to explain yourself to me.' His face was hard and closed and she felt fury rise up in herself.

'Stop it!' she burst out.

155

'Stop what?'

'Stop being like this – so, so shuttered and *silent*. Say something! How can we argue, how can we say what's in our hearts, if you close up every time you feel anything?'

'Is that what you think?' His face was blank with surprise and shock. She nodded. 'Rosa, I – I don't mean . . . God.'

He bowed his neck and put his hands to his head, and for a horrible moment she thought that perhaps he was crying, but he was only rubbing his face in a weary gesture, as if he were trying to rub away all the lies and suspicion and blood that stained both their hands.

'Just because I don't speak,' he said at last, his voice very low, so low she could hardly hear it, 'doesn't mean I don't feel. I *do*.'

'What?' she challenged. 'What do you feel? Anger? Fear?'

'All of those. But mostly – mostly . . .' He stopped, swallowed, turned his face away so that she could not see his expression.

'Luke,' she took his face in her hands, turning it back towards her, 'don't turn away. What?'

'Mostly I feel a horror at what I did to you, to your life,' he said simply. His face was full of a sadness she could hardly bear, and this time it was she who turned away, in case he saw the tears in her eyes.

'Luke . . .' She held on to his overcoat with her good hand, her fingers digging into the thick black wool. 'Luke, I . . .'

156

He shut his eyes at that. And suddenly she could not bear it any longer. She leant forwards and kissed his lips, there in the square, like the slut Alexis had called her. Except that she did not feel like a slut, she felt – she felt . . . She did not know what she felt. A confused tumbled desire that had been building and building, every day that they had ridden together and every night that they had lain chaste in each other's arms. She wanted to take Luke in her arms and kiss him until he stopped hurting, until he knew what he was, what kind of man she saw when she looked at him. Not a coward. Not even close to being a coward. A man who had made mistakes, yes, terrible mistakes. But one who had tried so hard to put them right . . .

For a long, long moment Luke kissed her back with a hunger that echoed her own, his mouth hot and open against hers, his breath coming hard and ragged. Then he broke away, but kept his hands on either side of her head, holding her both close and apart, as if he did not trust himself to kiss her any longer, but could not bear to pull away.

A milkmaid walked past, shooing her cow ahead of her, and then a girl with a flock of geese, but they did not move, only sat in their own little world, their foreheads pressed together, their noses still touching.

'I didn't take away the pain,' Rosa said very quietly, 'because sometimes it is better to feel. Sometimes we need people to see what we feel, and to know what is being done

157

to us. Yes, he hurt me. But he helped me too. Nothing comes without a price.'

He let his hands drop and she sat back, feeling the stitched finger throb in anticipation of what she was about to do.

'Luke, I have something I need to ask.'

'Anything,' he said, low and intense, but she shook her head.

'Don't say that, not until you've heard me out. You will think I'm crazy but – please think about it, all right?'

'All right.' He sat quiet and watchful as she drew a deep breath and held it, trying to work out how to begin. But there was no way of leading up to this. She must have the courage of her convictions. She looked him straight in the eye, his clear, hazel gaze meeting hers with absolute trust.

'Luke, will you – will you marry me?'

'*What?*'

It was not what he had been expecting, that much was plain. He rose from the seat and stood staring down at her with – what? Horror? Shock? She could not tell.

'Please.' She stood too, facing him, her good hand clenched. 'I know – I know you think it's foolish—'

'Foolish? It's insane!'

'No, please, listen—'

'You've cut yourself free of him, at what cost?' He gestured angrily at her bandaged hand. 'And now you'd shackle yourself to me for a lifetime? D'you understand what marriage means for a woman?'

'Of course I understand. Don't patronize me!' she said hotly.

'Well then, act like it! You'd have *my* station, *my* income, *my* name! You'd be nobody, *nothing*!'

'I'm nothing *now*!' she cried. 'Remember? God knows, I've been told that often enough! I'm just a pawn in my mother's game of chess, to be sacrificed for the highest scalp she can achieve! And I will not be pawned, I will *not*! I will never escape Sebastian as long as he wants me – and once I'm married the law says I'm his, body, mind and soul. Well, the only way to make sure I'm safe from him is to put myself *beyond* the law. No man can marry another man's wife.'

He stared at her and she saw the truth of what she said sink in, bone deep. Then he turned away.

'No, I will not.'

'What?' His answer stung like a slap. 'Why not?'

'Because. I won't admit defeat.'

'Would it really be that bad to be married to me?'

'That's not what I meant – and you know it.'

'Really?' Her throat was tight and sore with lacerated pride. 'Then what did you mean?'

But he had turned away and was busy checking Brimstone's girths.

'Luke!' She grabbed his shoulder with her unwounded hand. 'Don't turn away from me.'

'Come on,' he said shortly. 'We've been here long enough. We need to get on the road.'

'You can't avoid me.' Tears stung at the corners of her eyes, but she held her head high. 'Unless you propose to abandon me on the road.'

'Don't be ridiculous. I'm not abandoning you. I'm not avoiding you. I'm right here.'

'Yes. And so am I. So you'll have to listen to me sooner or later.'

He said nothing, just swung himself on to Brimstone's back and held out his hand.

'Are you coming or not?'

She let herself be pulled on to the saddle, feeling the soreness in her thighs as she and Luke settled into their now-accustomed positions.

'I'm not done,' she said mutinously as Luke clicked to the horse and they began to trot out of the town, heading north. 'Not by a long shot.'

'God save us,' Luke said. 'I'm starting to realize why William never married.'

They found a cottage that night – not an inn, it was not grand enough for that name, but it had clean sheets and a fire and that was more than they had hoped. The old lady, Mrs Cleave, charged them a shilling for a bed and a hot meal between them, and this time when Luke introduced Rosa as his wife, his voice did not falter.

After supper, Rosa took the hot brick in flannel that the old lady pressed into her hands and went upstairs to heat the bed, and Luke went out to check on Brimstone and give him a blanket, for the night was cold.

She heard his tread on the stair before he knocked at the door, and she opened it without saying 'come in'.

If he was surprised to see her still dressed and not huddled in the bed, he did not show it.

'So,' she said, as he walked across the room to sit on the side of the bed, and pull off his boots, 'you'll claim me as your wife when it suits.'

'Rosa . . .' he started, but then broke off.

'What?'

'What do you mean, *what*? You know very well we couldn't share a room as an unmarried couple. What's the alternative – pay for two rooms? Or would you have me sleep in the stable with Brimstone?'

'No.' She came across the room and put her hand on his arm, feeling the set of his muscles, tense and weary beneath his shirt sleeve. 'No. I would have you here, beside me.'

'Then what . . . ?'

She felt her heart begin to pound with the knowledge of what she must do. She would not use her magic against Luke. But she had one weapon still available to her.

She straightened. Then she put her hands to the buttons of her bodice, and began to undo the small silk-covered buttons at the neck of her dress.

As the first buttons slipped free and she felt the chill night air on the soft skin at the base of her throat, she heard Luke make a small involuntary sound – a kind of soft sharp breath, as if he were in pain. All his muscles were tense, as

161

if he was readying himself for flight – but she knew from the way that his eyes followed her every move that he would not look away, *could* not look away, even if he wanted to.

Button after slow button, her fingers shaking, her left hand stiff and useless. It seemed to be taking for ever. But his eyes never left her as the layers slowly dropped to the floor like wilting petals. First her bodice. Then her skirt. Then her petticoats.

The laces on her corset were tight and she bit her lip as she struggled one-handed with the knots, her fingers trembling and clumsy with nerves. If she'd had Luke's knife she would have been tempted to cut them – but at last they came free with a tug and she drew the laces out of their holes, one by one, until she was at the last layer of all: her chemise.

'Stop!' Luke spoke in a strangled voice. He was sitting on the very edge of the bed, his fingers clenched on the wood, and she could see a vein beating in his throat.

She stopped, her fingers on the lace ties.

'Please, Rosa, don't do this.'

'Don't do what?'

'Don't – this, I can't. I can't bear it.' His voice was hoarse, but he did not look away. His eyes followed her, hungrily, as she came towards him across the room and knelt at his feet.

'I'm sorry.' She felt her breath catch in her throat and

she meant it. But at the same time she was not sorry. 'But, Luke . . . '

'You know – you must know what it would mean for you, if we . . .'

'I know you're an honest man,' she said quietly, without looking up. She saw that her fingers were trembling and she gripped the sheet to hide the shake. 'I know you will not take what you cannot pay for.'

'Pay for?' he cried, his voice anguished. 'Is that what you think of this?'

'Why not?' She looked up, her fears drowned in a sudden wash of anger. 'What else is marriage, after all, but the bartering of a body for a ring?'

'No! God, no! If I'd wanted that I could have got it ten times over from Phoebe or Miriam or any of the other girls who were desperate enough to sell themselves to keep body and soul together. I won't do this, Rosa!'

'The price is too high.' She felt her mouth twist in self-hatred and bitterness. 'Is that what you're saying?'

'The price is too high for *you*.' He took her hands in his, burnt and roughened, and drew her next to him on the bed. '*Think*, think about what marriage to me would mean. I'm a blacksmith, Rose. I won't ever have a butler or a serving maid. I'll be lucky if I get an apprentice one day, but my wife will be pegging out her own washing all her days. She'll have to scrub her own floors, work all day from dawn to dusk – it's no life for—'

'For a lady? What is my life then?' she burst in

163

passionately. 'Marriage to Sebastian? *You* think, Luke. Think about what refusal will mean to me. Think about a life married to him, serving his every whim, with no hope of escape but death. God! I'd rather scrub a thousand floors than lie one night in his bed, I swear! Is it money, is that all? I'll conjure sovereigns from the air . . . I'll fix the Thousand Guineas so your horse wins . . . Anything!'

'Then you would make a whore out of me, Rose,' he said softly, so that she flinched and looked at the floor.

'How long, d'you think,' he said quietly, still holding her hands gently in his, running his thumbs across the soft blue-veined skin at the inside of her wrist. 'How long before *my* kind find us? You want me to think about what marriage to Sebastian would mean to you? Well, you think about what marriage to you would mean to me. It'd mean my death – and yours too.'

She recoiled at that. It was true. She had been so wrapped in her own selfishness that she had not seen what it would mean for him.

'I'm sorry.' She pulled her hands away and stood, wrapping her arms around herself, suddenly cold in her thin shift. There was an icy draught fluttering the gingham curtains. She shivered, but her cheeks were hot. 'I – I didn't think . . . I'm sorry.'

'Come here.' He put out a hand and drew her on to his knee, and they sat very still and quiet for a long time, his arms around her, her head on his shoulder. She felt a longing that she could not explain or assuage, and she knew that somewhere there was an answering longing in Luke, but that he would not give way to it, not here, not now.

'You don't need a husband.' His lips moved against her hair, his breath soft against her forehead. 'You'll be safe from him. I'll keep you safe.'

But you cannot, she thought. She thought of Sebastian coming for them both – and suddenly it was not herself she saw in Sebastian's arms, but Luke. Luke pinned to the ground, bleeding and motionless. Luke twisted and tormented and destroyed by Sebastian's whims.

She thought of Alexis's remark to Luke in the clearing: *I promised Seb I'd take you alive, but I imagine that state of affairs ain't going to last long.*

She felt her fists clench against Luke's back. The injured finger gave a great throb of hot pain and her magic blazed out, a blaze of fury and fear for Luke.

He looked up, his face full of questioning wonder, and she knew he was seeing her magic flare and blaze.

'What is it?' he asked softly. 'What's wrong?'

'Nothing.' She tightened her arms around him and felt as if she would choke with it, with the fierce burning determination to keep him safe from harm and far from Sebastian's clutches. 'Nothing is wrong.'

He hugged her back, his skin warm against hers.

'Don't let go,' she whispered. The candle guttered and the dying light of the fire cast shadows around them.

'I won't.' His voice was low; it made something shiver

inside her. 'Why, are you afraid?'

'No.' She shook her head fiercely. 'Never.'

But it was not true.

The poster beneath Blackfriars Bridge was frayed and water-stained but still legible, just, and the man reading it tipped his cap back and frowned as he spelt out the letters in the hissing light of a gas street lamp.

It took him a while to work out the message between the gaps, but when he had finished it was clear enough.

Someone else was looking for the girl. And not one of the Brothers. Someone with money, and no small amount of money either – a hundred pounds was an incredible sum, more than any of the Brothers saw in a year.

The man beneath the bridge scratched his head and picked a fleck of tobacco from his teeth, spitting it thoughtfully into the gutter as he considered what to do. Was this good news, or bad?

John Leadingham would know.

He considered trying to pull down the remains of the poster, but the wet peeling paper came to bits in his hands as he tried, and in the end he left it. It didn't matter. What mattered was that someone else shared the same aim as them – someone with money and resources. And that was going to interest John Leadingham very, very much indeed.

MISSING

Miss Rosamund Jane ___ ___wood

OF OSBO___ ___CENT, KNIGHTSBRIDGE

DESCRIPTION

Age, 16 ye___ Hair, Red

E___ Brown Build, ___ight

Last seen wearing a silk gre___ ___,
da___k blue ___ ___er and bonnet, and sable ___

May ___ in t___ ___ ___ a bay stal___ ___th
a white blaze

£100 REWARD

___ERED FOR SA___ ___T___

(Inforr___ ___on to ___thing House, Southing)

11

Luke sat in the window seat of the narrow dormer window, his feet pulled up beneath himself against the cold. It was tricky squashing his six-foot frame into the narrow ledge, but he could not have stayed in bed with Rosa, warm and languorous beside him, her face soft and flushed with sleep.

He thought again of last night and felt the blood rise in a tide from his chest to his throat and his cheeks. Did she know? Had she guessed how close he'd come to forgetting himself and his position, burying his face in her hair, pressing his lips to the soft shadowy curves that showed so painfully clear through the thin white chemise?

He thought perhaps she did, and he didn't know whether that made him want to laugh or cry.

The worst of it was that, in some ways, what she said made sense. But it was impossible to disentangle the logical, sensible reasons for marriage from the painful longing he felt in his breast every time she laughed, or tossed her head in that funny, proud gesture. How could he think, when his heart leapt every time she touched his skin, her magic prickling through him like a current, sending him mad.

He could not tell what he should do any more. He could only tell what he wanted. And what he wanted was Rosa. But that did not make it right.

He longed for the cold steel-bright certainty of before – for the black-and-white clarity of the Book, for the clear single-minded rules laid down by the Brothers. Witches were damned in the sight of God, so they must die. It was simple.

But where he was now, there was no Book to guide him. He was completely alone – save for Rosa, breathing softly in sleep just across the room, her bandaged hand on the pillow beside her cheek.

He looked out of the window, pulling the gingham curtain aside. It was still dark, but there was a thin pre-dawn sheen in the sky and the mist on the ploughed fields was luminous with its glow. Somewhere, not too far off, a horse neighed, and he wondered if it was Brimstone. Across the fields he heard the clang of cow bells. They were being led for milking, perhaps. Full udders wouldn't wait for dawn.

For no particular reason he thought of Minna, walking to the dairy in the pre-dawn light, her apron painstakingly laundered and dried in their cramped rooms, spotlessly white.

He wished he knew where she was now. He wished he'd had time to say goodbye. He thought of her as he'd last seen her, her face swollen with the phossy jaw. Would it heal, away from the factory? He didn't know.

He missed her like an ache in the heart. Her small impudent face, her thin dirty hands 'like a monkey's paws', William used to say, as she came scampering in at the back door to swipe an apple off the kitchen table, or a slice of bread from William's plate, back when Luke himself was just a skinny urchin and she a skinnier one.

Would he ever see her again? Would he see any of them again? William, John, Minna – and beautiful, dirty, heaving London. *His* London, not Rosa's – not the stuck-up white buildings and grand boulevards, but the real heart of London, the twisted foetid stinking streets that had raised him from a baby to a man.

Those streets had nearly killed Minna.

If only he knew if she were safe . . .

'What are you thinking?'

Rosa's voice made him jump. He turned, his heart beating angrily. She was standing next to him, the sheets clutched to her chest.

'Jesus! You nearly gave me an apoplexy.'

'I'm sorry.' She hitched the sheets higher and shivered. 'I thought you'd heard me.'

'Well, I didn't.' He swung his legs to the floor and was

170

about to stand when she said again:

'So, what were you thinking?'

His instinct was to shrug it off, but he thought of the other day, of her furious cry: *How can we argue, how can we say what's in our hearts, if you close up every time you feel anything?*

'I was thinking of Minna, if you must know,' he said reluctantly. 'I was wondering if she's all right.'

'Oh.' Rosa bit her lip. She looked at the ground, her dark lashes sweeping her pale nutmeg-freckled cheeks. Then she looked up again. 'Do you . . . were you sweethearts, Luke?'

'With Minna?' He almost laughed at the notion. Perhaps he would have, if his heart had not been so heavy. 'No! God no. It was never like that. She was always . . . I don't know. A mate. I never had a sister, perhaps like that.'

'But you do love her?'

'Yes.' He said it simply. His feelings for Minna *were* simple. He loved her, in spite of her faults – and God, she had enough of those.

'I . . .' Rosa took a breath and turned towards the bed. She picked up her skirt and stepped into it. Luke knew her well enough now to recognize the set of her shoulders and spine, to know that she was pretending carelessness, but that what she was about to say mattered very much. 'I could . . . you know. Scry. If you wanted.'

'Scry?'

'Look for her.' She began to lace her corset, wrapping

171

the laces around her middle before she tied them. She had her back to him, but Luke still turned away.

'H-how?'

Something rustled and he guessed she was putting on her petticoats, or her bodice. Her voice was muffled when she spoke.

'Water will do. Is there any in the ewer?'

'Yes,' he said automatically. Then. 'No. I don't want you to.'

'But why not? You're worried!'

'I can't – I can't explain it. Later, maybe.'

'Are you worried about it leading them to us? Or are you frightened of what I might see?'

'I don't know.' He bit his lip. Both, perhaps.

There was a silence, and then he heard Rosa make a small sound of frustration and pain, and he turned to see her struggling with the last of her buttons.

'Damn my finger!' she burst out at last.

'Here, let me.' He came across to where she stood by the bed and lit the candle, the better to see. He bent down to look. His fingers were too big for the tiny pearl-sized buttons, and for a moment he felt like laughing. A blacksmith – playing the lady's maid. But Rosa only stood quietly, trying not to breathe, looking down at the top of his bowed head, and at last the final button slipped into place.

'Thank you,' she said quietly.

'You're welcome. How's your finger?'

'All right, I think.' She held it out, but it was impossible to see much beneath the bandage. There was no sign of any seepage. But it looked horribly, horribly wrong – that shortened stump where her finger should have been but wasn't. Like a street magician's trick, gone grotesquely awry.

'Rose—' Luke began, but before he could finish there was a knock at the door. They both looked at each other, and then Luke tucked in his shirt and moved to answer it. The old lady, Mrs Cleave, stood outside, smiling.

'Porridge is ready, my dears. Come on down. You'll be hungry, I don't doubt.'

Luke scraped the last of the porridge from the bowl and licked his spoon. It was, if possible, even better than the meal of the night before. Then he had been too hungry even to taste the food; he had just gulped it down, inhaling the meat and potatoes more than eating them.

Now he looked up hopefully and Mrs Cleave smiled at him, her wrinkled face crinkling even more.

'I like to see a boy with an appetite. My late husband was just the same, three bowls he could eat, and not a pick of flesh on him.' She ladled another helping into Luke's bowl and topped it with a slosh of creamy milk, and he set to again, the hot porridge scalding his mouth.

Beside him Rosa was spooning busily, putting away her own portion with an efficiency that made the old lady smile and lean forward to top up her bowl as well.

'That's right. Flesh and bone won't heal itself on thin air, you know. What happened to your finger, duckie?'

'An accident,' Rosa said. Her eyes flickered to Luke and they exchanged a look. 'I was chopping wood.'

'Oh dearie me. How sad. And if there's one thing magic won't heal, it's a severed limb, heaven knows.'

There was a clatter as Rosa's spoon fell to her plate. They both sat, electrified but silent, for a long moment.

'I b-beg your pardon?' Rosa said at last. She picked up her spoon, but Luke could hear the tremble in her voice. He did not trust himself to speak. 'What did you say?'

'Oh, there's no need to pretend in front of me, my duck. I have no power myself, but I do have the sight.'

'*What?*' It was Luke's turn to drop his spoon, leaning forward across the scrubbed wooden table to where the old lady sat. He had to fight the urge to jump to his feet. '*What* did you say?'

'The sight. I see magic. As do you, perhaps?'

'I . . .' He felt the colour drain from his face and his fingers tighten on the tabletop. Beside him, Rosa's magic flared out in a panicked, directionless blaze.

'Or perhaps you don't?' Mrs Cleave stood calmly and walked across to the porridge pot hanging above the fire. She gave it a stir with the long stick that rested on the side of the hearth. 'You had a look to you of one who might, but perhaps I'm wrong.'

'I . . .' He found he could not breathe. Was it a trap?

Had they come all this way and escaped so much, only to walk into a trap?

'You have – what did you call it?' Rosa's porridge lay forgotten and cooling on her plate. Her eyes were fixed on the old lady, on her bent crooked back as she nursed the fire. 'The sight?'

'It's not a common thing,' Mrs Cleave said. She did not seem to have noticed their astonishment and alarm. She came to sit back at the table, wiping her hands on her apron. 'They say it's caused by magic turned inwards. My grandmother was one, of course.'

'A – a what?' Rosa said. Her voice was strangled.

'A witch,' Mrs Cleave said, as matter-of-factly as if she were saying *a dairymaid* or *a Londoner*. 'My grandfather was an outwith. And my father, their son, an outwith too, for all anyone could tell. But it came out in me as the sight.'

So there were others. Luke's head swam with the knowledge of it. He was not alone. He was not a freak. And perhaps his uncle was right. His father might have been gifted like him; it could have passed down through the generations from— He stopped suddenly, confronted with the one immutable, impossible fact: from a witch. Somewhere in his family tree there must have been a witch.

He turned to look at Rosa and he knew she was thinking the same thing; her eyes were wide with the strangeness of it.

A witch. The irony of it made his head hurt: he was a

175

witch's child – and he had turned his power to harm them. He had given it over to the Malleus, for the Brothers to bend and shape and use to their own ends. He thought of all the names inscribed in the Book of Witches because of him. Men, women, even *children* he had seen in the street, pointed out, identified, trapped within its pages.

And all the time, you were one of them.

'Luke—' She put out a hand towards him, but he pushed his plate away and stood abruptly, so that his stool fell to the floor with a crash.

'I'm sorry,' he said roughly. 'I – I can't . . . I'm sorry.'

And then he almost ran from the cottage, out into the wild wet fields and away.

Rosa found him at last. He was hunched in a small copse, his arms wrapped around himself against the cold, for he was only in his shirtsleeves. He was shivering.

In his drab clothes, with his head bowed and his gold-brown hair the same colour as the few autumn leaves still clinging to the branches, she would never have found him, but for a whispered charm and the wind showing her the way as she searched the fields.

'Come.' She knelt beside him and tried to drape his coat around his shoulders. 'Come home, Luke darling. You'll freeze out here.'

'Please leave me be,' he said miserably.

'No.' She took his lapels in both hands and forced a smile, in spite of the cold and the misery on his face. 'I'll stay here with you, and we'll both freeze together, if that's what you want. But I won't leave you out here in a field to wallow in your guilt.'

'Who was it?' He stared at her, unmoving, unable to shake the thought of what he'd done. 'Was it my grandmother? Wouldn't William have known though? Was it one of my great-grandparents? Was it even my *mother*?' His face looked grey with the horror of it.

'I don't know,' she said softly. She helped him to stand, his limbs stiff with hunching in the cold for so long. 'But, Luke, does it change anything? What you did – you were a child. You didn't know any better.'

'I know.' He put his hands to his face. 'It was a sin no matter what, but somehow . . .'

He did not say what he was thinking. The fear that somewhere on those lists that *he'd* helped to write was a relative of his own: one of the family he had never had, save William. A cousin. A great-uncle or aunt. Put there by his own hand and condemned to death.

It should not make it any worse. It was true what he had told Rosa – the sin was the same, the blood on his hands was as real and red as before. It did not matter if it was his own blood – did it?

But he could not help looking down at his hands, thinking of the men and women he had helped to murder – his own kin, perhaps.

They were almost back at the cottage when he put his hand on Rosa's arm and stopped.

'Wait. Before we go inside, there's something . . .'

'Yes?' She looked up at him, the wind blowing her curls into her face. She brushed them away, tucking them behind her ear. In the soft wintry light he could see the strands of red that had escaped the dye, like the scrap of fire that lurks in the centre of a burnt-out log, wanting only a breath to kindle into flame. 'What is it?'

'What you said – last night.'

'About . . . ?' she started, and then stopped. He saw emotions flicker across her face hope, doubt, a kind of fear, almost. He took her hands in his, feeling the bulk of the bandage and the slimness of her small fingers on the uninjured hand. 'D'you still want it?'

'Yes.' One word, spoken very short, as if she were afraid to say any more.

'Then . . . I agree. Rosa, will you marry me?'

He could not say why he had changed his mind. It was not what the old lady in the cottage had said – or not completely. It was everything. Rosa's small, worried face. Her bravery. The fact that she'd come for him, refusing to condemn, refusing to be pushed away.

To his surprise she did not answer – or not immediately. She was searching his face for something; he was not sure what.

'Is it what *you* want?'

'Yes,' he said, and suddenly he was sure. 'Yes. It's what I want. If it will help protect you, if it will keep Sebastian at bay for a little longer . . .'

She nodded, her small face very serious and pinched with the cold. Then she smiled, and in spite of himself, his heart gave an answering lift.

'Isn't life strange, Luke?'

He curled his fingers around hers, feeling their fragility, and their strength. Yes, life was strange – and painful, and perhaps wonderful too. He felt his heart fill with all the words he had not said. *Is this what you want?* she had asked. And he had answered with the truth, but not the whole truth.

The truth was that he wanted this more than he had ever wanted anything in his life. More than peace and his forge. More than revenge for his parents. More than anything – he wanted *her*, in his bed, in his arms, in his life. And the truth was that he had *always* wanted her, from the first moment he had seen her in the stable, with her magic blazing around her like a crimson fire.

But he said nothing. He just stood, holding her hand.

The wind gusted again, plucking at her skirts, at the worn and battered greatcoat.

'Rosa . . .' he tried. But he could not find the words.

'Come,' she said softly. 'Back into the cottage. There's a fire there and we can work out what to do next.'

So he nodded and followed her back into the warm, woodsmoke-smelling room.

12

They were both too young to marry without the permission of a guardian – in England, at least. Luke might have got away with it and passed for twenty-one, but not even the kindliest priest could believe Rosa was of age.

But in Scotland there was no such law. There, anyone older than fourteen could marry with a simple declaration. There was just one problem. They had to get to Scotland and live there for twenty-one days without being traced.

'We'll never do it.' Rosa paced up and down the little bedroom. They were supposed to be packing – that was what they had told Mrs Cleave. But they had already packed the only possessions they had: Luke's knife, rolled up in the blanket. 'We'll never make it for that long.'

Rosa reached the door and turned to pace the other way, back towards the window. As Luke watched, her uninjured hand crept to her throat, feeling for the missing locket, and then dropped again.

'We must,' he said. 'We must do it, that's all. Twenty-one days – how hard can that be?'

'God!' Rosa burst out. 'If only I had the Grimoire! We were so close to it in London – I should have taken it. I was such a fool.'

'It was best you didn't. Lugging a heavy book along with us – it would have just slowed us down. But listen, it can't be the only one in the world, surely?'

'No.' She bit her lip. 'There are others, of course. Most families have one, or something resembling one. Notes handed down from mother to daughter. Charms that never fail to take out a stain, or heal a fever. But I can't go knocking on doors asking if there's a witch in the house. Nothing would get us noticed quicker.'

'What about the old lady?' Luke said. Rosa looked at him, chewing her lip doubtfully. 'It's worth asking, isn't it? Her grandmother was a witch, she said it herself. And who else would she pass her book on to?'

'I could ask . . . But what should we tell her?'

'Tell her the truth – or some of it. Tell her we're not married, but eloping, and that you're on the run from a forced marriage. Tell her your family are on our trail and we need her help.'

'But what if she doesn't agree? What if she thinks I should be a good daughter, obey my family?'

'Then we're no worse off than we are now,' Luke

181

said grimly. Rosa thought about it for a moment and then nodded.

'All right.' She stood and brushed off her skirt. 'Wish me luck.'

'I see,' Mrs Cleave said, as Rosa finished her tale. She was knitting and there was a long pause as she finished her row. Rosa waited, her heart in her throat, twisting her fingers together so that the injured stump throbbed painfully. She almost welcomed the pain. It was a distraction from the fear that had haunted her since Luke had suggested the plan: the fear that the old lady would voice all the doubts in her own heart, tell her she was an ungrateful daughter, that she was flouting the fourth commandment, that she should keep to her own kind and return home and beg for forgiveness from her family and Sebastian.

'I have two conditions.' Her voice was old and cracked, but firm.

'Anything,' Rosa said.

'Don't be rash now, duckie. You don't want to go making promises you regret after. You've done enough of that already, if I'm not mistaken. No, my conditions are these: I'll let you have the Grimoire – to borrow, mind, not to take – if you do two things for me. The first is this: I have a deal of firewood out the back and it's a sore trial to me to split the logs. My eyes aren't what they used to be and neither is my back. Your young man, your Luke, he's to split the pile.'

Rosa almost laughed with relief, but she only smiled and said, almost giddily, 'Of course! He'd split a whole forest for you, if you asked. And the second?'

'The second is that you do my weekly wash for me. And put your dress and smallclothes in it. I'll give you another night's lodging and a hot meal into the bargain, but I'll not have any girl leave my cottage in the state you're in.'

'V-very well,' Rosa faltered. She looked down at herself. Was her dress really that bad? She peered at the soot stains and the blood, at the earth and grass stains and mud and all the rest. She had charmed herself into respectability for the doctor but it had worn off long since. Perhaps it was that bad. 'But what will I wear while I wash them?'

'As to that, you can have one of my old dresses.'

Rosa looked up from the copper, swiping sweat-soaked hair from her eyes. The promise of the Grimoire for just one week's washing had seemed like a good exchange at the time – now she was beginning to think she had been cheated. The fire beneath the copper smoked and smuts fell into the tub, and she was afraid the skirts of the borrowed dress would catch fire. And this was only the whites – she would have to do it all again for the darks and the silks. Had the maids at Osborne House really done this every week?

Out of the window she could hear the energetic *thwack*, *thwack* of Luke splitting firewood with the little axe the old lady had pressed into his hand and she felt, not for the first time, that the lot of women in this world was deeply unfair.

'I wish I was chopping,' she muttered under her breath. Mrs Cleave looked up from her knitting, the clickety-clack of her needles momentarily stilled.

'What did you say, dearie?'

'Nothing, Mrs Cleave.'

Think of the Grimoire. She gave the greasy white slurry a final twist with the dolly and then hauled the slippery wet mass out of the copper and into the rinse tub as Mrs Cleave had instructed, her back almost breaking with the strain.

'There's more rain water in the water butt if you need it, dearie,' Mrs Cleave said. She bit off her wool. 'And you can let the fire die down now. It doesn't need to be as hot for the darks.'

Rosa said nothing, but swilled the whites around in the rinse tub and then heaved them out to drain into the stone sink by the window. She would mangle them later in the yard. Or maybe make Luke do it. The temptation to use magic was almost irresistible, but she had a horrible feeling that whatever spell she found to keep Sebastian at bay, it would take all her magic and more.

'Pass me the pot, would you?' Luke collapsed on the settle just as Rosa passed through the tiny sitting room for the last time, the final armful of wet washing for mangling in her arms.

'What?' She stopped in the middle of the room, heedless

of the soapy rinse water dripping down her apron and on to the rug.

'I said pass me the teapot. My back's killing me. On your way back, I meant.'

'*Your* back's killing you!'

'Yes, that's what I said.' He looked up at her, his face puzzled. 'I just chopped and stacked a couple of trees' worth of wood, or didn't you notice?'

'Well, *I* just washed several thousand tons of wet linen, you lazy slob!' She felt a strong urge to fling the armful of wet dresses at his head.

'I only—'

'Get it yourself!' She gave the door a furious kick and stalked out into the yard. It was full dark now, but thank God the night was clear. The thought of pegging all that stinking, dripping washing inside the tiny cottage made her feel sick. She ran it through the mangle, listening to the buttons pop and squeak against the rubber rollers, and imagined she was mangling Luke's head. The bastard. '*Pass me the teapot*,' she hissed under her breath, twisting the mangle handle so forcefully that her injured finger gave a throb of protest at the effort. 'I may look like a bloody servant but—'

She felt a hand on her shoulder and turned to see Luke standing behind her. He said nothing, just pushed her gently aside and began finishing the mangling himself. She wanted to push him out of the way and snarl that if he thought he was coming in here now, right at the end, to claim credit for her work . . .

But she was too tired. Her arms felt like wet wool. Instead she sank on to the chopping block he'd been using, her soaked skirts around her legs, and felt her aching arms throb with thankfulness.

'I'm sorry,' he said, as he began to pin up the last couple of dresses with a surprising deftness. 'I know what it's like. I just forgot.'

'You do?' She couldn't keep the surprise out of her voice.

'Course. William sent out to a washerwoman most weeks, but I helped Minna often enough. She didn't even have a yard to mangle in, or hang the washing.'

'How did she dry it?'

'Around the house – if you can call it drying. Mostly in the winter it just hung there getting warmer and damper. You'd walk in and get a lungful of this sour smell of drying nappies – but they always had a clean tucker somehow. I don't know how she managed . . . There.' He put the last peg in place and then rubbed his face. 'Come on, let's get in and get tea for both of us.'

Mrs Cleave was at the table when they made their way back inside the tiny cottage, putting the lid on a fresh steaming pot of tea. She was smiling.

'Thank you, my duckies. You've earned this and no mistake.'

For a moment Rosa thought she was talking about the tea, and she reached out for the cup Mrs Cleave had poured. But her sleeve snagged on something on the near side of the table, and she looked down. There it was. Mrs Cleave's Grimoire.

It was nothing like her mama's one, with its fake binding and heavy brass lock to deter prying eyes. This was just a collection of papers sewn together by hand with painstaking care. The covers were plain board, no printer's mark or binding. But, leafing through the fragile pages, Rosa could tell it was the real thing. There were scraps from other books, older ones, in heavy gothic lettering, and pencilled notes copied out from other sources. Some were obviously folk remedies: *Let They who trauell Far cary a Sticke of Rowan to their side, to kepe their Path True. And To Cure a Babe of the Running Pox:– let him drinke only from his Mother's pap or, if she canne nat, the Well at Wycks Farm.*

Others were true spells. Spells to bind. Spells to heal. Spells to blight a crop, with the warning scrawled at the bottom: *Do nat emploie lightly. As Mistresse Alyce knoweth welle, this will rebound threefold upon the spell-caster.*

Rosa carried on turning the pages, her tea cooling by her elbow, her tiredness forgotten. Then she stopped at one.

A Spelle to Cache, Conceale or Throwe a Pursuer. Take an arm full of green wood – Birch if it can be had.

Lyght it to a Fier & lette the Room or Shelter or Clearing be filled w/ Smoke. Stand within & hold the Objet to be Hid.

Lete the witch cut her skinne & Pour her Blod upon the Fier & on the Objet, & while ðe Flammes feast uponn the blod,

187

Speake thrice these Words:

Hyde sé ðe Wylle, Hyde sé ðe Canne, Hydende be fram both God ond Man.

If the Pursuer be Known than let the Witch hold his face in her Mind's Eye an she Speake.

Thus it shalle be like as if the Objet hath been Consuméd by Fire, & wreath'd in Smoke.

She closed the book and looked up at Luke, nursing his cup silently on the other side of the table. His eyes met hers, his question unspoken, and she nodded.

'I've found something. We'll need to gather firewood. And bring your knife.'

They were deep in the woods. It was dark, but Rosa picked her way through the trees unerringly, collecting sticks as she went: a branch here, a handful of bark there. Luke trudged in her wake, marvelling at her ability to keep going in spite of the darkness and the cold, in spite of her tiredness of a few hours before. He did not know what time it was, but it was late, and they'd had no supper. *Time enough for that when we're safe*, she'd said when Mrs Cleave had suggested a meat pie, and he'd had to bite his tongue to stop himself from pointing out that Sebastian had waited four days and nights, and would likely wait for them both to eat a pie.

But now her anxiety to get this done and finished had infected him, and he willed her to stop walking, get the

188

damn spell over and done with.

He shivered. How had it come to this?

'Here,' she said at last. They were standing above a hollow where the soft leaf-strewn ground gave way to a short rocky drop a few feet deep. He followed Rosa down the boulders into the hollow itself and felt the trees above rise above him, their tall, pale trunks made taller still by the lowered ground. There was no denying it was the perfect place – quiet, sheltered, no wind to whip the smoke of the fire away. Instead it would pool in the hollow, wreathing them. But it gave him a feeling of foreboding.

'I hate the dreadful hollow behind the little wood . . .' he said in a low voice. Rosa dropped her armful of sticks and looked up.

'What did you say?'

'Nothing.' It was a poem they'd had to learn at school. He'd recited it and been given a penny as a prize, but even then it had made him shiver.

'Its lips in the field above are dabbled with blood-red heath,' Rosa said softly. 'The red-ribb'd ledges drip with a silent horror of blood, and Echo there, whatever is ask'd her, answers "Death".'

'You know it?'

'Yes. My father used to read us Tennyson. But I always hated that verse.' She gave a shiver and said, 'Don't spook me. I need to concentrate. Come – help me build the fire.'

Luke added his own armful to her pile.

'Keep back the green wood,' she said as they began to

189

build. 'We'll light the dry wood first, then add the green.'

Luke nodded.

At last they had a stack built in the centre of the hollow and Rosa bit her lip.

'Do you have your knife?'

Luke felt in his pocket and drew it out. The rag around the blade was still stained with Rosa's blood, and he saw her look at it – at the sharp, wicked edge – and felt her revulsion. How many witches had it taken in its long life?

'What about matches?' he asked. Rosa shook her head.

'We don't need them.'

She knelt in front of the wood, her head bowed, her hair twisted up so that it showed the white glimmer of skin above her shawl, and he saw her magic build and swell and flare out, bright as a fire, bright enough to burn and blind.

There was a spitting hiss from the twigs in the centre of the clearing and the sticks burst into flame, like no fire he had ever seen kindled before. One moment there was nothing but twigs and logs, and the next there was a roaring mass of heat, mingling with Rosa's magic into a shimmering column that reached into the sky, like a beacon.

He took a step back, but Rosa didn't flinch, only stood looking into the flames, her eyes reflecting their glow.

'What shall we use . . .' He found his voice was hoarse, and coughed, trying to clear his throat. 'For the object, I mean.'

'*We* are the object.' She looked at him. 'You and I. Now, come here. Give me the knife.'

Suddenly he didn't want her to do it. He thought of all the blood that had been spilt – their own, others' – by Sebastian's beatings, by the Malleus executions. The thought of adding another drop to the pool seemed unutterably wrong in every way. The hairs on his arms were prickling with some strong emotion – not quite fear, but close to it. He swallowed.

'Rose . . .'

'Come here.' She took his hand and pulled him close to the blaze and took the knife from his hand. The blade burnt bright in the firelight, so bright his eyes hurt to look at it. 'Ready?'

He wasn't. He never would be. But he nodded, and she picked up the mass of green wood and threw it on to the flames.

There was a sudden spitting and a choking mass of steam and smoke began to wreath around them, pooling in the hollow. Luke coughed, his eyes watering. Beside him, Rosa's hand felt for his, and he saw her standing in the wreathing white smoke, her magic mingling with the firelight and illuminating the cloud from within so that the whole clearing seemed to glow, setting them both aflame.

'Rosa,' he choked, 'I can't—'

'Give me the knife,' she said, her voice hoarse with the fumes.

'Wait—'

But she took it from his hand, her fingers groping for the hilt, and he saw her lift her arm in the white coiling miasma, the pointed blade silhouetted sharp against the flickering blaze.

'Rosa,' he said again, but his voice was lost in coughing, and she had her eyes shut. The point of the blade was against her arm. 'Rosa, *stop!*'

Lete the witch cut her skinne . . . The words rang in his head as if it were Rosa speaking them.

She gave a cry as it bit, and then suddenly blood was running down her arm, dark against the white skin.

'Luke!' she cried, above the roar of the flames, and he felt her grab his hand and press them both together against the wound, the blood hot and slick against his skin, so that his hand slipped stickily in hers. *Pour her Blod upon the Fier & on the Objet* . . .

Still holding his hand against her arm, she dragged their joined hands above the fire.

'We'll burn!' Luke shouted as the flames hissed beneath them. The heat was unbearable, scaldingly fierce. He tried to pull away but her fingers tightened on his, the blood running through her fingers and over his knuckles, drip by drip . . .

As it met the fire there was a crackle and the flames shot scarlet and green into the sky.

'*Hyde sé ðe Wylle!*' she cried, and he hardly recognized her voice. It was not the Rosa who had slept beside him, walked beside him, wept in his arms. It was someone else, someone full of an elemental power so fierce he was almost afraid of her. Her voice was harsh and hoarse with smoke, and the words rolled from her as if she had not learnt them, but had always known them, as if it was her mother tongue. '*Hyde sé ðe Canne, Hydende be fram both God ond Man!*'

Her grip tightened on his hand, her nails digging into his fingers with painful intensity.

'*Hyde sé ðe Wylle!*' she called again, her voice growing louder. '*Hyde sé ðe Canne, Hydende be fram both God ond Man!*'

Sebastian's face rose up in front of his eyes. The snake's-head cane. The Black Witch. Everything he had fought for and given up for Rosa. *Leave us alone!*

'*Hyde sé ðe Wylle!*' she cried again for a third time, her voice almost to a scream now, and he found his lips moving along with hers, his voice sobbing, the heat of the fire on his skin and in his veins. '*Hyde sé ðe Canne! Hydende be fram both God ond Man!*'

Her magic was like a beacon now, flaming out so bright he could not believe that everyone from a thousand miles around would not come running. As it flared to its height there was a sudden crack from the fire like a gunshot, and a piece of wood exploded outwards, hitting him in the chest. He dropped his grip and stumbled backwards, beating the sparks from his coat.

Rosa staggered backwards too, her face white, her magic cowed and small as if it had never been that huge blazing column. She tripped against a boulder and half stood, half slumped against the rocky side of the hollow,

193

her breath coming white in the cold air, her chest rising and falling as if she'd run a race. There was a steady drip, drip of blood from her hand and the knife dangled at her side.

'Rosa . . .' Luke ran across the clearing to her and caught the knife just as it dropped from her hand, point down, towards her boots. 'Rosa, are you . . .?'

She staggered and half fell into his arms.

'I'm all right,' she was saying hoarsely. 'I'm all right. It's just a spell. I'm all right.'

He held her, feeling her heart-rate begin to steady and her hoarse, gasping breaths slow. Her fingers clutched his coat as if she would never let go, like some small, terrified animal with its claws dug in. As the fire shifted and collapsed in a pile of sparks and began to die down, it came to him that he had seen true magic this night. Real magic. Not charms and deceptions, but heart-magic. Blood-magic.

His arms were around Rosa's shoulders and he felt her shivering begin to subside.

'Let me look at your arm,' he said at last, and she held it out like an obedient child and let him wipe it with the rag. The cut was not much – a slice with a sharp blade. She'd missed the artery, thank God.

'It's clotting already,' she said huskily. 'I'm all right.'

'It'll do. But we should wash it. When we get back to the cottage. And you need food.'

'I need sleep.'

'Come on,' he said roughly. He helped her to her feet, pulled her arm across his shoulders. 'Come on, let's get you home.'

He thought he would dream that night. He thought that, with what he had seen and done that night, that he would dream of the hand and the cold blaze of magic tearing apart the night, and the snake-headed cane. But he did not. Instead he slept, curled in Rosa's arms, and his sleep was dreamless, and soft and deep as fallen snow.

When he woke it was dawn and very cold, and he had to break the ice in the pitcher beside the bed to drink, but the sky was clear. It was a beautiful day.

Mrs Cleave fed them porridge and then kissed them goodbye. She gave Rosa the spare dress and Luke a muffler that she had knitted for him all the day before, while Rosa washed and Luke chopped.

Rosa climbed on to Brimstone's back and Luke looked up at her slim, dark shadow silhouetted against the sun. Her profile was sharp against the frost-blue sky, and he could see the little kink in her nose where Sebastian had broken it, that night in the stables.

Her magic made a bright, shining blaze against the blue and he thought, with a pain in his heart, that he'd never known a girl so gallant and beautiful, and so uncowed by all she'd been through.

'Goodbye, my ducks.' Mrs Cleave handed her up the bundle and a parcel of food, and then kissed Luke. 'You be careful now, it's a long way to Scotland, and a hard road ahead.'

'Thank you,' he said. 'Thank you for everything.'

He wished that he was a man of words, and could say what he felt and thought and meant. But he could only press her hand and hope that she understood what she had done for them both – with the spell book, but more than that: with the knowledge that he was not alone, that this gift of his was not a curse burnt into him by the Black Witch, but something else, something that was, perhaps, good.

She nodded, and he thought perhaps she did understand.

Then he swung himself up behind Rosa, his arms around her waist as she clicked to the horse.

'Goodbye, Mrs Cleave,' Rosa called as Brimstone began to trot. 'And thank you.'

13

She did not know where they crossed the border, but they must have, for it seemed at last they were in Scotland – and the purple-heathered hills were crested with snow.

'Langholm five miles,' Luke said as they passed the signpost. 'We must have done it. God knows we've been going long enough. And we've done it!'

'We've twenty-one days yet,' she reminded him, and she felt him smile. She did not need to turn around. Day after day of walking and riding beside him and she knew his silence, his quiet shifts of mood, from the tenseness of his arms and the muscles of his chest against her spine.

'Come on, let's stop,' he said. 'Celebrate with a bite.'

She pulled up Brimstone and he slid from the saddle and helped her dismount. Two hairpins fell to the road and she felt the weight of her hair against her neck. She was down to only half a dozen pins, not nearly enough to restrain the great coiled weight.

'I said we should have cropped me for a boy,' she grumbled as she pinned up the loose coils, the escaped strands blowing across her face in the soft, cold wind.

Luke smiled again, the dimple just showing beneath his deep beard, as he reached out to tuck a stray curl behind her ear.

'You're no boy. Look, it's coming back red. So much for that dye. If the shop weren't three hundred miles away I'd be asking for my shilling back.'

'I could dye it again. They must sell dye in Scotland.'

'No. Don't. I like it. And we're safe now, right?'

'Yes, we're safe.' She smiled back, finding her lips curving to follow his irresistibly. Why did he smile so little, when a smile like that could break your heart? If she had lips that curved like that and a dimple as deep as your little finger, she would have smiled all day and all night just to have her own way.

She hugged her knees as they sat on the verge beside the signpost and took the chunk of bread and cheese that Luke held out. The grass was frosty and crackled beneath Luke's boots as he sat beside her, but the sun was shining, the scudding clouds making shifting shadows on the far-off hill.

They chewed in companionable silence and then both spoke into the same pause.

'You know—'

'I was thinking—'

Luke stopped and laughed.

'You go first,' Rosa said.

'No, it's all right.' Luke bit off another mouthful. 'You first.'

'I was only going to say, do you know what day it is today?'

'No, what?'

'The shortest day. The winter solstice.'

'And the longest night. John Leadingham always used to say . . .'

He stopped.

'What?' Rosa asked.

'Nothing.' Luke's face shuttered again, the smile gone as if it had never been.

'No, what?' She leant forward. 'Come on, Luke, you know I don't blame you for what's past.'

Luke swallowed his mouthful, the muscles in his jaw and throat working beneath the beard. Then he sighed.

'All right. He said as witches love darkness, it was when their magic waxed highest, like a candle flame that flares brightest in the dark. Is that true?'

'I don't know.' Rosa hugged her knees again. She meant what she'd said. She didn't blame Luke for what was past, but that didn't mean that it wasn't strange and uncomfortable hearing about his past in the Brotherhood. 'Perhaps. It's true that magic does wax and wane. They say women . . .' She blushed suddenly, and stopped. It was said that women were weakest when they had their monthly bleed, and strongest halfway between. But she couldn't say that in front of Luke. 'That women are weaker at certain times than others,' she finished lamely, hoping that he wouldn't look up and catch her scarlet cheeks. But he was looking at his boots, playing with the frosted grass stems between his feet.

'What were you going to say?' she said to change the subject. 'You were thinking something.'

'Oh.' There was a long silence and she had the feeling that he was struggling with something, that he'd been relieved not to have to speak before, and was at war with himself over whether to speak now. 'I was thinking . . .' He took a deep breath and then when he spoke there was a sort of defiance, as if he were arguing his point before she'd even countered it. 'It was you saying twenty-one days and then we're safe. And I was thinking that if the spell really did work, if you really *are* safe from Sebastian . . . well, there's no need for us to get married, is there?'

'What?' Rosa put down her bread and turned to face him. She searched his face for emotion and found no clues. His brows were drawn into a frown against the sun, but that could have been just the light. 'What do you mean? You don't want to?'

'It's not about want.' He spoke testily. 'This was never a love-match, was it? It was about keeping you safe from him. And if you're safe already . . .'

This was never a love-match. It was true. Of course it

was true. So why did she feel like she'd been punched in the gut?

'So why are we here?' Her voice came out like a cry, like an accusation, though she hadn't meant it to sound so. 'What are we doing in Scotland?'

'I just meant—'

'I know what you meant.' She stood, her arms wrapped around herself, feeling suddenly cold. 'And you're right.'

'I'm right?'

He'd got to his feet and stood facing her.

'It was never a love-match,' she echoed back at him. 'Do you think I don't know that?'

'Why are you angry at—'

'I'm not angry!' But that was not true. 'All right, yes I am. I'm angry at *him*, for stealing my future and, and—'

She couldn't finish. She turned away from Luke, but heard him speak, stiff and stilted behind her shoulder.

'Then you should be angry at me. I changed your future as surely as he did.'

'Perhaps I am,' she snapped. Then she bit her lip and turned, seeing his stricken face. 'No, no – I'm not. Luke . . .'

She put her hands on his arms, feeling his muscles, as hard as if he were about to hit or flee.

'Luke, I'm sorry, I didn't mean . . .'

He shut his eyes. She was not sure if he were shutting her out or struggling with some emotion he could not afford to let out. She waited desperately for him to crack and say whatever it was he was refusing to say, feeling the tenseness running through him like magic crackling across his skin. But then he pulled himself free and turned his head away, towards Brimstone.

'Come on. It's late and cold. We should find a place to spend the night. And tomorrow I'll find work.'

Luke cursed himself as Brimstone clopped along the last stretch of road towards the town. Again and again he swore inside his head, berating himself for being a clumsy oaf – a sot, Alexis used to call him – and for the first time he felt that the word was just. Why couldn't he say what he meant?

He knew she was hurt – he wasn't a fool. He'd seen the look in her eyes as he said *It was never a love-match*. He knew what she thought – that he was pulling out of it at the first excuse because he didn't want to be shackled to a girl he didn't love.

How could he tell her the truth? His love wasn't the point. Whatever he felt for her, the point was that she'd been forced into this situation, as surely as Sebastian would have forced her into marriage with him. She hadn't chosen Luke any more than she'd chosen Sebastian; fate had pushed them together and fear had kept them that way. But there was no way on God's earth that Rosa would have chosen him of her own free will. Without his own knife and bottle, and without Sebastian's cruelty, she would never have been in this situation. She'd have married some kind, monied country squire with a fat belly and a big house, and had little fat-bellied children to fill it.

However he felt about her, whatever he felt, he was damned if he'd marry a girl because she was in fear of her life.

When it had been a matter of saving her life, it had been different. He wasn't so principled that he'd condemn a girl to death rather than put a ring on her finger, nor such a fool as to think that marriage to a poor blacksmith was worse than an early grave. But now . . .

They'd ridden for weeks without hearing so much as a whisper of Sebastian's pursuit. Through the Peaks, through the Lakes, through the Kielder Forest, through towns and countryside alike. The posters had vanished. The pursuers had gone. They were safe.

And if he married her in that knowledge, taking advantage of her fear – well, he was no better than Sebastian himself.

'Luke,' she said at last, as they rounded a bend. 'Luke, what are you thinking?'

'I was thinking . . .' Then he stopped. He pulled Brimstone up, shading his eyes against the winter sun. Far along the next stretch of road was a little building, squat in the landscape, with a thread of smoke coming from the chimney and the clear ringing sounds of a hammer on hot metal as familiar as his own heartbeat. 'There's a forge up ahead.'

'I've got work.'

Luke's face was shining as he came back to the horse. In

spite of her aching heart Rosa smiled back.

'Well done!'

'A day's trial at half-wages and then as long as I want at apprentice rates. His own apprentice is sick and he can't manage the work alone.'

'And you can do it? You're not worried about the trial?'

'Do it?' He smiled down at her, his worries forgotten in the elation of the moment. 'God, yes. I've no worries about that. I've been shoeing horses since I was up to your hip; I can do his job twice over. The wages aren't London rates but it's money, which is what we need. And the best thing?'

'Yes?'

'He's got a room above the workshop he's not using. The apprentice lives there, but he's gone back to his mother's to be nursed.'

'Where does the smith live?'

'In town, with his wife. He wants someone to live there and keep an eye on the place at night, build up the fire in the morning and so on. So he'll give it to us for free, as part of the wage.'

Money *and* a place to stay. It was almost too much. Her tiredness lifted like a fog rolling back.

'Well done.' She stood on tiptoe and kissed his cheek, feeling his short beard soft and rough beneath her lips.

'What was that for?'

'Nothing.'

They stood in the winter sun, smiling at each other,

with Brimstone nibbling the frosted grass at their feet, and Rosa felt herself smile and her heart lift.

'Nothing. Just you.'

The sky was darkening to lemon, the smith had gone home to his wife, but Luke was still down in the forge, tinkering, tidying up. She could hear him whistling, the tune filtering up through the little window beneath the eaves. She smiled, hearing his happiness, feeling the warmth from the smithy chimney, knowing Brimstone was fed and warm in the stable at the back.

The only thing marring her happiness was Luke's words of that morning: *It was never a love-match . . .*

She knew. She *knew* it wasn't. So why did his words niggle at her like toothache, lurking there ready to make her flinch with pain when she least expected it? He was only stating a fact.

She should have been happy that Sebastian was off their trail. She should have been singing with gratitude that she was free: free of him, free to be her own woman at last. She didn't want to marry Luke. She didn't want to marry anyone – she wanted to be her own woman, to own property, to choose where to live and where to love, not owned by some man, however kindly.

So why did her heart hurt whenever she thought of Luke's words by the roadside? *We're safe . . . it was never a love-match.*

The room above the forge was tiny – barely even an

attic. It was warmed only by the borrowed heat from the smithy chimney and had nowhere to cook or wash. She supposed the apprentice must have eaten his meal with the smith at lunchtime, and had bread and cheese for his dinner, and washed in the cold-water butt in the yard. There was a pump and an outhouse round the back of the stables.

But at least it was clean – or it was now. She had spent all afternoon sweeping and brushing and then, when the smith had left, she'd relented to her tiredness and whispered a spell to chase away the final cobwebs and brighten the small, grimy window. Now she was lying on her back in the narrow single bed, her hands locked behind her head, staring into the oak rafters and waiting for Luke to finish in the forge and come upstairs. And she was thinking. Thinking of Luke, of his strange contradictory nature. Of his silence, and his guarded face, and the softness of his lips when they'd kissed . . .

She let her eyes close.

'Rosa!' Luke took the stairs two at a time. He'd washed his face and sooty hands under the pump in the yard, and now he had his wages in his pocket and a light heart. 'Rosa! The smith was so pleased he gave me a full day's pay. Let's—'

She was lying on the bed in the candlelight, her cheek pillowed on her hand, fast asleep. The room was immaculate – so far from the dusty, cobweb-filled attic the smith had showed him that he could scarce believe it was the same place. How hard she must have worked . . .

'Rosa?' he said more softly, and she stirred, but didn't wake. Luke made up his mind. There was a scrap of wrapping from the loaf they'd eaten for lunch neatly folded on the table, and he took a pencil stub from a pot of odds and ends on the windowsill and wrote a note: *GONE TO TOWN TO GET BREAD. BACK SOON, LUKE.*

He spread it on the table and then bent over her, tempted to lean and kiss her cheek, golden in the candlelight. But he didn't. Instead he drew the blanket over her and then pulled on his greatcoat and left for the town.

In Langholm he bought bread and a bottle of beer. The shops were closing, the grocers selling off their wares cheap, and he got a good piece of ham for just tuppence.

He was turning back for home when he saw a sign that made him stop. *Post Office.*

He stood in the road biting his lip and, as he did, a woman came out from behind the counter and put her hand to the sign, turning it to *Closed.*

'Wait!' He ran forward, pushing at the door. She shook her head crossly.

'Sorry, we're closin'.'

'Please.' He smiled, doing his best to hide his impatience. 'Please, I'm so sorry. I only just got off work.'

'What d'ye want?'

'Just to send a letter, miss. I'll be quick.' He smiled again, trying to win her round. 'I got a job today; I wanted

207

to send half my first wages to my sister.'

She bit her lip and then rolled her eyes, a smile cracking through her irritated mask of politeness – and he knew he'd won.

'Come away in then, but be quick about it. I'll no have half the street followin' yer in to do their business after. It's this one thing and then I'm closin', like it or no.'

He followed her in. She was pretty – maybe twenty or twenty-five, her hair in a pompadour on top of her head.

'Ye'll be wanting paper and envelopes, I suppose.'

'If you can spare it. And . . .' Dare he risk his luck? 'And sealing wax, if I can ask for one more favour.'

'Get away wi' ye! You'll be wanting tea and scones next,' she grumbled. But she found him notepaper and an envelope and a stick of sealing wax with some matches. Luke took up the borrowed pen – and then stopped. What to say?

The girl stood, tapping her foot as he bit his lip, and he knew it didn't matter, he just had to write something.

Dear Minna, he wrote.

I was very sorry to go without saying goodbye. I hope you now that I would not have done so by choice.

I am putting a half-sovriegn

No, wait, that didn't look right. He crossed 'sovriegn' out and tried again . . .

soveriegn under the seal. It is all the monie I have. PLEASE do not let your dad get sight of it. Spend it on food for yourself & the kids.

If you need me

He stopped. He could not think of a way to put his address in that could not be traced. In the end he just sighed, crossed it out and wrote:

I will try to send more when I can.

Yours ever

Luke

PS Tell no one that you heard from me. Not even William.

He folded the letter, addressed it, and put the half-sovereign under the flap. Then he lit the end of the sealing wax, watching it drop down to cover the coin, turning it into an indistinguishable lump instead of a thievable piece of gold. He had no seal or ring, so he let the girl at the counter stamp it with the post-office seal and affix the stamp.

'Thank you.' He pushed his money across the counter and she smiled at him.

'You're welcome. I like to see a man who takes care o' his sister. London, eh? You're a long way fra home. Got a sweetheart up here, have ye?'

'I . . .' He stopped. The words gave him a sudden, unaccountable pain in his heart. *Yes. No.* 'There's a girl,' he said at last, picking his words.

'Oh aye.' She gave a sigh as she dropped the letter into the post-bag and tied the top. 'There aywis is.'

'Rosa.'

The voice came through her dream and she moaned

softly, pushing her face into the pillow, not wanting to wake from the warm drowsiness and contentment. 'Rosa. Wake up. I've got supper.'

'Luke?' She raised her head from the pillow, blinking and confused. He was sitting on the end of the bed, his face soft and golden in the candlelight. 'What time is it?'

'I don't know, but not much gone six. It's been dark since four though.'

'Urgh.' She sat up, raking her hair off her face. 'I've been asleep. I feel . . . I hate sleeping in the daytime. Have you been into the village?'

'Yes, it's more of a town really. I got bread and ham and beer.' He put them on the table. 'That's all our money gone but the smith's promised me at least two weeks' work. He says even if his lad's up and about before that, he'll have too much to do catching up.'

'*All* our money? I thought we had half a sovereign left?'

'We did.' He bit his lip. 'I'm sorry. I – I sent it to Minna.'

'You *what*?'

'Don't worry – I didn't give our address or tell her anything. But . . .'

But she knew. He'd been so worried. Minna had suffered as much as any of them from Sebastian's cruelty. She could be dying of phossy jaw right now, for all they knew.

'I could scry,' Rosa said softly. 'You know I'd do it in a heartbeat.'

'I know.' He was setting out bread and ham. They had no plates – just squares of waxed paper, but they'd do.

210

'I know. But I don't want you to.'

'Why *not*?'

'You know why not.'

But she didn't, not really.

'I wouldn't change anything . . .' She tried again, but he was shaking his head before she'd even finished.

'Don't you understand? *Looking* would change things. I don't want you to.'

'You still think it's devil's work?'

'No. I – I don't know.' His face was troubled and he took her hand in his. 'No, I know it's not. I know it's part of you – and I don't think any part of you was made by the devil. But I just . . . Look, I'm a man, Rosa. I wouldn't want a woman doing my dirty work for me.'

'You were happy enough for my magic to get you out of that burning factory,' she said, trying not to sound bitter; but to her surprise he smiled – a reluctant, wry smile that twisted half his mouth, but it was a smile.

'I was. I'm a hypocrite maybe, but not a fool.'

She had to laugh at that, and they both took a bite of their bread and ham, and she realized how hungry she was without even knowing it. They shared the beer, and then Rosa said, 'What now? To bed? It seems odd when I've only just woken, but there's only a stub of candle left.'

'Not yet,' Luke said. He ran his hand over the deep, soft beard shadowing his jaw. 'I'm going to shave.'

'No!' she began to laugh. 'What, now?'

'Why not? I don't know how old the apprentice was, but

he left his razor in the basin. And there's soap out by the pump.'

'You'll freeze! You'll cut yourself to ribbons with shivering.'

'I'm not that mad. I'll heat a kettle on what's left of the forge fire and bring a basin up here.'

She waited while he went out to the yard, and heard the clank, clank of the pump handle, and then the roar of the bellows as he kindled the remains of the forge fire into life. Then at last she heard his footsteps on the stairs outside and his boot kicked open the door. He was carrying a china basin full of steaming water, walking slow and steady with the concentration of trying not to spill it.

'I used to watch my papa shave,' Rosa said as he set it down gently on the little table and took up the soap and the cut-throat razor.

'Well, I've just realized there's one thing missing,' Luke said.

'What's that – a towel?'

'No, I'm not that fancy. A mirror.'

'I'll help,' she said, before she could think better of it.

'You know how to use a cut-throat razor?' Luke looked at her doubtfully.

'I think so. I watched Papa do it often enough. You can start off; I'll just do the bits you can't see.'

'All right. And I tell you what, if you cut my throat, I *will* let you use a healing spell. Deal?'

'Deal,' she said with a smile. He pulled his shirt over his

head and began to rub his face with soap. Rosa swallowed. It was not the first time she had seen him half dressed. Over the last few weeks she'd caught glimpses of him dressing and undressing, washing in the river, sometimes pissing, when there wasn't a tree around. But it was the first time he had sat in front of her completely shirtless, his muscles and bones all dips and shadows in the small intimate circle of the candlelight. His arms and throat were tanned dark gold, but the skin on his shoulders and chest was white – as white as her own – apart from the dark-red scar of the hammer branded on his shoulder blade.

She half felt she should look away, but he seemed unconcerned, and so she did not, but watched as he rubbed the soap across his jaw and then began to scrape carefully with the sharp edge of the razor, scraping away the rough growth of beard that shadowed his cheeks. Every now and then he stopped to wipe the razor on a rag and then he carried on, methodically working his way across his jaw.

At last he'd done almost all and he turned to her.

'I can't do the last bits without a mirror to see where I've missed. Are you sure you can do it?'

'I'll try,' she said. 'Come here. Put your head in my lap so I can see your face in the candlelight.'

He came to sit on the floor by the edge of the bed, in the dip between her legs where her skirts and petticoats made a soft dint against the mattress edge. He laid his head back against her and looked up with an expression so calm and

213

trusting – and the sight of him lying there, his throat bare to the knife, almost choked her.

'I'll do—' Her throat was dry, and she swallowed again. 'I'll do your lips first. Don't speak.'

She held his head with her left hand, feeling the rough silk of his hair between her fingers and the slow, soft beat of a vein in his temple where her fingertips rested. In her right hand she held the razor. She found her heart was beating fast.

'Hush now,' she said huskily. She began to shave him, very gently and cautiously at first, and then with more confidence as she got the feel of the razor against his skin and the knack of holding it at the right angle, so it shaved close as a whisper and did not nick.

'Now your throat.'

He lifted his chin.

'Mind my Adam's apple.'

'I'll be careful.'

She put her left hand on the other side of his throat to steady herself and she could feel his pulse beneath her palm, stronger than before, faster too. Was it possible he was not as unaffected as he seemed?

'You know,' he spoke carefully, softly, between scrapes of the blade, 'you could probably take that bandage off now.'

She looked down at her left hand. She'd almost forgotten it was there. It was so dirty she felt ashamed she had not changed it, but it had been impossible on their flight

214

through England, never staying more than a day in any place.

'You're right, I should.'

There was silence again while she finished his throat and then neatened the two short sideburns by his ears. He lifted his head gingerly and then turned to face her.

'Will I do?'

She smiled. He was soapy and gritty with shaved stubble, but his face was smooth again.

'You'll do.'

'I'll go down to the pump and wash it off. And while I do, you can take that off.'

'Take it . . . off?' For a minute she found her voice faltering and then she realized what he meant. The bandage. 'All right. You can fill up the ewer while you're down there, and I'll wash it in clean water when you come back.'

After he'd gone out she began to pick at the tightly tied bandage. It was hard at first to get a purchase and at last, in frustration, she slipped the razor under the topmost fold and snicked it loose. It unravelled and she shut her eyes, almost afraid of what would be under there.

When she looked, it was very strange. It was her finger – small and white and a little wrinkled and sweaty from so many days under bandages. But it was not her finger. Just a short stump that ended just before the knuckle. The skin had healed, though the stitches remained. They would have to be removed. Before she could think better of it, she picked up the razor, pulled at the knotted end and nicked the thread. It hurt coming out – but not unbearably. Just a stinging pull.

And then there it was. Her new finger. The mark of Sebastian's pursuit, of her desperation to get away. He had put his mark on her, as surely as the Malleus had branded Luke.

As if she had summoned him with her thoughts, he spoke from the doorway.

'Is it all right?'

'It . . .' She found her voice shook a little. 'It looks strange. I don't think people will . . . I think they'll be afraid, perhaps. Disgusted.'

'Let me see.'

He came close, crouched at her feet and took her hand in his, cradling it gently between his larger ones. She turned her face away, not wanting to see his expression, but when he spoke his voice was warm and steady.

'I'm not afraid. And I'm not disgusted. Rosa . . .'

He stopped and she found her heart was beating fast. They were quite still in the circle of candlelight, her hand caught in his. She could have reached out and touched the bare skin of his shoulder with her other. But she did not. She only sat, waiting, her heart beating hard and painful in her chest.

'Yes?'

'What I said earlier—'

'It doesn't matter,' she broke in.

'It does – it does matter!' He let her hand drop and got

to his feet as if he could not bear to be still, as if his feelings were too much for him to contain. He paced the small room. 'Rose, I can't talk like other fellows. I can't say what I mean, I don't know how, but you mustn't think . . .'

He stopped and put his hands over his face, so that she couldn't see his expression in the shadows beyond the candle, but she knew from his voice that whatever it was, he was close to tears. At last he let them drop and she saw his face, shadowed and full of a kind of desperation.

'I gave up everything for you,' he said. 'The Malleus, William, revenge for my parents – I gave it all up. I said it wasn't love between us, but that was only because, love – it's . . . Oh God, Rose, how can I make you understand? Love's too small a word. It's not enough for what you are to me.'

'Luke . . .' She tried to speak, but the words wouldn't come. She could only stare at his face, stricken, full of everything he wanted to say and could not. 'Luke . . .' she tried again.

And then, with a sigh, the candle flared up and went out, the wick collapsing into a puddle of melted wax where it glowed red for a moment and then died.

In the silence that followed Rosa could hear nothing but the beating of her heart and Luke's ragged breathing. Then she stood and groped her way across the room, her hands outstretched. Somewhere in the darkness her blind fingers met warm skin and muscle, and she gasped, and felt his arms come around her, and his lips seeking hers, clumsily, kissing at her cheek and her jaw, and then finally finding her mouth and kissing, kissing as if he would never stop.

Together they found the bed, tumbling backwards into it, with their limbs locked and their lips finding and seeking and missing and finding again in the darkness. His fingers were at her bodice, and she was pulling at the laces of her corset, wriggling off her stockings, and he was yanking at his belt and his britches and kicking free of his boots.

And then at last there was nothing between them but the darkness and their own skin, and his hands on her waist and her breasts, and her hands on him, feeling the smoothness of muscle and the hardness of bone and the soft, rough prickle of his hair beneath her palms and lips.

'We should not do this,' he whispered with a kind of agony in his voice. 'It's a mortal sin. We could . . . You might . . . Oh, God, Rose – I've wanted you so . . .'

She could find no words to argue with him, tell him that this was no sin; that what Sebastian had wanted, love without consent – that was sin. But this . . . But his hands on her skin seemed to have robbed her of all her words, save one: *'Yes . . .'*

And then nothing – even that last word was taken, and there was silence in the small room, silence except for their catching breaths and the wind that moaned in the chimney.

14

Rosa came down the stairs outside the forge and stood for a moment in the little windswept yard. She hugged her arms around herself, feeling the strangeness and the difference in her body. Everything was the same – and yet utterly changed in some indefinable way.

There were small icicles hanging from the eaves above the forge, and she thought that perhaps she was like the water in those icicles, melting from snow into something quite different and new.

Through the window of the forge she could see Luke bent over the hearth, hammering something in the heat of the fire. His movements were quick and sure, their purpose a mystery to her, but she could see the skill in the way he heated and twisted the metal, checking it each time, and the sureness of the blows of his hammer. The sound rang through the yard and the snowflakes scudded and gusted across the cobbles. From the stable she heard Brimstone, contentedly blowing down his nose as he chewed his hay.

'He's a good lad, your man.'

Rosa jumped and turned to find the smith standing behind her, his arms crossed.

'I'm James McCready, blacksmith. Ye must be Luke's wife, Rosa.'

'Yes.' She felt a great stupid blush rise from her breast up her throat, setting her cheeks ablaze. They had given the lie often enough – why was it only now that the intimacy of the word made her flush scarlet?

'Been married long?'

'N-not long.' Her hand went to her throat, searching for the locket, and then dropped. It was a long time since she'd done that, she realized with a pang. She was learning to remember that it was not there. Instead she put her hand to her pocket, feeling the soft, frayed shape of the portrait beneath her fingers.

'Come fra' Gretna, aye?' He smiled, misunderstanding her blush 'Don' worry yersel, pet. You're no the first lassie to ha a Border handfastin and ye'll no be the last.' But then, seeing her confusion, he kindly changed the topic. 'Aye, an like I said, he's a good lad, your man. A sight too good fr'an apprentice, if truth be told, but I'll tek his help and thank him for it.'

He patted her shoulder and then strode forward to throw open the door of the forge.

'How're ye doin', lad? Tek a break, make yer wife a cup o' tea now.'

Luke looked up from his hammering. He was frowning, wiping the sweat out of his eyes, and then he saw Rosa and a huge smile spread across his face, so that the deep dimple came and went and came again in his cheek.

'Hello.' He put down his hammer. It was impossible to tell if he was blushing; his face was hot and sweating already. But Rosa felt her own face flush with blood again at the sight of his hands and his lips, and the memories of last night came crowding in. She wanted to touch him, reassure herself that he was really there, that it had really happened.

'Hello,' she whispered. They stood, smiling foolishly at each other, saying nothing, not knowing what to do, and the smith rolled his eyes.

'Young love! Get away wi' ye both. You're due a break, lad. Tek the kettle upstairs wi' ye. There's tea in the caddy and ye can bring me a brew when you're done.'

Luke carried the heavy kettle carefully up the ice-dusted steps to the attic and set it on the little bare table, and they both stood, awkward and strange, in the quiet of the little room.

'You were asleep when I woke,' Luke said at last. 'I thought I'd just go down and start, not disturb you.'

'That's all right.' She found herself smiling again and, to busy her hands, she got out the cups and the tea. There was even a little battered strainer inside the caddy.

'Last night—' Luke said at the same time as she said:

'There's no—'

They both laughed, shakily, and Luke came around the table and took her in his arms and kissed her cheek, and her lips, and the soft skin at the curve of her jaw. She did not speak, but she made a sound like a whimper or a sigh, and she felt his arms tighten around her, as if he were afraid to let her go.

'Last night . . .' he said again, his voice soft against her ear, and she hugged him harder and pressed her lips against the warm skin of his throat, above his collar, and said:

'I know.'

'I never knew . . . I never thought . . .' His voice shook.

His closeness made her shiver with a strange faintness; she could feel his long hard body pressing against her through her dress, and she remembered the feel of him against her skin last night, and the feel of his hands on, around, inside . . .

She shut her eyes.

Then she pulled away, smoothing down her skirt.

'Come on. Tea. Mr McCready won't wait for ever.'

'Damn, McCready.' He caught at her waist as she poured, running his hands up her bodice to the thin sliver of skin that showed above the high neckline, and she felt a shiver of wanting run through her and laughed, a strange tremulous laugh that didn't sound like her own.

'There's no sugar.' Her voice was a gasp and her hand

222

shook when she picked up the cup. 'That's what I was going to say, before.'

He let go of her waist and took the cup, but his hazel eyes remained on hers as they drank. She watched the dimple come and go above the cup as he smiled, and the movement of his throat as he swallowed.

At last it was drained and he set down the cup on the table and came across to put his lips to her throat one more time.

'Go!' she said, laughing, pushing him away even while her lips sought his. 'No, wait, here's Mr McCready's tea. And the kettle. Go on, back downstairs. We *need* this job.'

'What will you do?'

'I don't know. I might walk into Langholm, buy something for supper.'

'We've only pennies left.' He fished in his pocket and put the last of their money on the table. 'Want me to ask McCready if he'll let me have my wages early?'

'No . . .' She counted the pennies and farthings. 'No, it'll be enough if I'm careful.'

'Good. Do that. Be careful.'

She followed him down the icy steps and into the yard, her shawl huddled around her, and at the door of the forge she kissed him, once, quick and chaste, the kiss of a sister or a good wife setting off to market.

He smiled and she walked off into the speckling snow.

* * *

223

All through supper they looked, but did not touch. It was as if they were afraid, now that the smith had gone home and the place was their own again, afraid of what was to come.

Or not quite afraid, Luke thought. That wasn't the right word. It was more like Christmas morning when he was a child and had felt the weight of the stocking at the end of his bed; instead of leaping up, he had lain there with his eyes tight shut, almost frightened to open his eyes for fear of it being too lovely to bear.

He watched Rosa as she ate, picking at her kippers and the potatoes they'd roasted at the edge of the forge-hearth. She had coiled her hair low on her neck and in the candlelight it looked almost back to its old flame-like glory. In the dim light, her skin seemed to glow, as if the candle was inside her, not stuck in a saucer between them, and when she looked up, her eyes were dark and shining as they met his.

She licked her fingers, one by one, and he watched, hungrily, watching the soft pink wetness of her lips and tongue as she sucked the last savouriness from her fingers. He swallowed and, looking down at his plate, he realized suddenly that he'd barely even touched his own food and was hungry.

'I didn't buy beer,' she said, her voice low. 'There wasn't much money; I thought food was more important.'

'That's all right.' He put a piece of potato in his mouth. He wasn't sure if he was glad or sorry that there was no beer to drink. He could have done with the borrowed courage – but he didn't need anything to make his head reel more.

The potato crunched in his mouth, half cooked, and he suddenly felt that perhaps he was not hungry after all. His stomach clenched with fluttering nerves.

He pushed the plate away.

'Rosa . . .'

She put out a hand towards him, her magic a shimmering fire in the candlelight.

And then there was a sudden pounding at the door. They both looked at each other, frowning, surprise giving way to puzzled apprehension.

'Sebastian?' Rosa mouthed. Luke frowned.

'Would he knock?'

She shut her eyes and her magic flared up, hurting his eyes, and he realized she was looking outwards, through the door, using her magic to see who was there. When she opened her eyes she shook her head.

'Strangers. I've never seen them before. Two. There's a carriage downstairs with two more.'

'All right.' He stood and took a breath. 'With luck it's just someone wanting directions or a loose shoe fixing. I'll find out. You stay here.'

Rosa watched as he strode across the room to the doorway and opened it. His silhouette filled the frame, and she couldn't see the faces of the men outside, but she'd already seen them in her mind's eye. Two fair-haired strangers at the door, muffled against the swirling snow, and another two men standing by the carriage: one a fat man wearing glasses, the other a little monkey-faced man with a grim expression.

'What is it?' Luke said.

'Shoe gone,' said one of the men shortly. He had a London accent. 'Can you 'ave a look?'

She heard Luke's sigh, and he glanced back over his shoulder at her. She shrugged and then nodded. The smith wouldn't be pleased if he heard Luke had turned away business.

'All right. I'll be a few minutes, Rose.'

He closed the door behind him and she heard his feet on the steps outside, voices murmuring. Then silence. She waited for the sound of the forge door, the roar of the bellows – but it didn't come. The wind moaned in the chimney and she heard the whisper of snow at the window.

She stood and walked to the door, trying to listen, then opened it a crack. Nothing. There was nothing there. Just the carriage, standing still and dark in the centre of the courtyard. Had they gone into the forge? But the horses were both still between the traces.

It was as if they'd all disappeared.

Something was very wrong.

Pulling Luke's greatcoat from the peg, she slung it around her shoulders and tiptoed out into the dark, swirling night. The snow was disorienting as she made her way silently down the stone steps and stood uncertainly in the courtyard. The windows of the forge were dark. Where had they gone?

She closed her eyes and let her magic unfurl, searching for Luke's familiar form, feeling for his presence. He was not in the forge, nor out in the lane. She turned her attention to the carriage.

Rosa let out a gasp. He was there. Inside the carriage. But not seated between the men, talking. Instead he was slumped on the carriage floor, face down, and a man was bending over him, efficiently binding his wrists.

Her eyes snapped open. She felt her magic roar and build like a scream inside her, ready to annihilate whoever had hurt Luke.

She opened her mouth to shriek a curse that would rip them all to shreds – but before she could speak, a hand came around her throat from behind, grabbing her jaw. A wet rag was stuffed into her mouth and she felt a blow on the side of the head that sent her staggering to her knees in the snow.

'No!'

It was supposed to be a shout, but the word came out hopelessly twisted and muffled by the stinking rag. She knew the smell, it was the same stuff in the bottle she'd broken over Alexis's head – the choking fumes were already making her head spin, and the smack to her head had left her gasping and reeling, unable to think . . . unable to . . . *Luke* . . .

She was on her hands and knees in the snow, trying to

claw the chemical-soaked gag from her mouth.

Luke . . .

She gathered all her magic, forcing it through her muscles to give herself the strength to stand . . . fight . . .

'Give up, you stupid bitch,' snarled a voice from behind her, and she saw a shadow fall over her shoulder and half turned in time to see a hand raised, holding some kind of cosh.

It came crashing down. And that was the last she knew.

Luke woke with a pounding headache and a feeling that he'd been carried a long way in a wooden box that was too small for him. As he came round he realized that was not far off reality. There was some kind of blindfold over his eyes, but he could tell he was lying face down on the floor of a carriage, bare boards beneath his face. He was penned in by legs on either side of his body and his hands were tied behind his back, so that he couldn't push himself upright but could only lie there groaning, feeling the pain at the back of his skull. Someone had hit him hard. But who?

'Who are you?' he croaked.

'D'you need to ask that?'

The voice was grim but somehow familiar – horribly familiar. And the smell in his nostrils was familiar too – sawdust and blood, and a kind of faint chemical underlay. For a minute Luke's jarred aching head could not put it all together – then suddenly it came.

'John! John Leadingham, for Christ's sake, what are you doing?'

'I could ask the same of you.' There was no laugh in the voice, none of the kindliness Luke knew so well. It was as hard and cold as stone.

'John, please.' He strained against the bindings, knowing it was useless, knowing he was caught – trussed like a pig for slaughter. 'John, mate . . .' His voice cracked and broke. 'You've known me since I were a boy. *Please*. Please don't do this.'

'No one made you join us,' John Leadingham said. 'No one asked you. You came of your own free will. You knew the rules.'

'Please,' Luke said. 'If you won't spare me for my sake, think of William. Think what this'll mean to him. John!'

But there was no answer, and eventually Luke gave up pleading to lie silent on the jolting floor of the carriage.

Yes, he knew the rules, God damn it. He'd had three tasks. The trial of the knife – to show he was obedient, and would not flinch in his duty. The trial of fire, to show he was unafraid and would never betray the Brotherhood. And the trial of the hammer, to kill a witch. And although he had passed the first two tests, in reality he had failed all three. He had betrayed the Brotherhood in every way imaginable. He had disobeyed their commands. He had betrayed the secrets of the order – and not just to anyone, but to a witch. And he had failed in the last and most important task of all: he had not killed Rosa. Instead, he had fallen in love with her.

He had known the rules. He had known the price he might pay for sparing Rosa's life. Well, now he was being asked to pay it, that was all.

There was only one bright spark in all of this: at least they did not have Rosa.

The hours passed, painfully, slowly, and Luke drowsed, lying on the floor of the carriage, jostled by the men's boots.

Then at last he came out of his half-sleep to find the carriage was slowing down. At first he thought it was just a crossroads, but it swung off the main track on to a stony courtyard and there was a sighing and a stretching of legs and the sound of men getting out.

He heard doors opening and closing, panting horses being changed. He heard a man gulping down a draught of something, and his throat ached with a powerful thirst.

Then the door of the carriage opened and Leadingham's voice spoke.

'Go on, lad. Get yerself a pint.' For a crazy moment Luke thought he was talking to him, and he raised his head blindly, but then he felt the boots against his spine shift and someone lumbered heavily out of the carriage, so that it groaned and squeaked on its springs.

'You too, Merriman. I'll keep an eye on the boy.'

'I won't deny, I'll be right glad to get a dram of beer and summat to eat. Seems like a long time since we had a bite.'

'We've been eight hours on the road,' Leadingham said, 'and we've got a deal longer to go. So get something wet down yer.'

The man shuffled off, his footsteps disappearing into the distance, and Leadingham climbed up into the carriage and stood in silence. Luke could see nothing, but he could feel the man staring down at him.

At last he spoke.

'I've got water here, d'you want it?'

'Yes,' Luke said croakily.

'I'll help you sit up.' As he did, Luke found that the reason he hadn't been able to twist round further was because his wrists were tied to a ring on the floor. Leadingham held the flask to his lips and Luke gulped blindly at the water, choking as it ran down his chin and soaked into his shirt.

'If you untie my hands,' he managed, 'I'll give you my word not to run for it.'

'You've shown us what your word's worth,' Leadingham said shortly. Luke flinched, but he couldn't deny the truth of it. He'd sworn himself to the Brotherhood and, not two weeks later, he'd betrayed them.

'How did you find me?' he said at last, leaning back against the bench. His wrists twisted painfully where they were tethered to the ring.

'Because you're a soft-hearted fool,' Leadingham said shortly.

'What does that mean?' Luke said, and then before

231

Leadingham answered, he realized, with a sickness to his gut that made him almost groan aloud.

Minna.

'Minna Sykes,' Leadingham said, echoing his own realization. Luke could almost see the twist in Leadingham's lip, his acknowledgement of the injustice of it; that it was not Luke's betrayal, but his loyalty to his own kind that had ultimately cost him his liberty.

'But – but I said nothing of where we were . . . I—'

'Ain't you heard of postmarks, you young fool?' There was bitterness in Leadingham's voice. Luke knew that he was not relishing this, that in some secret part of himself he might have been almost relieved that Luke had made a clean break. But, unlike Luke, he was a man of his word. A man of honour and courage, who would not flinch from a task, no matter how painful. 'And more than that, you let the postmistress put her seal on it. *Langholm P.O.*, it said, clear as day. Minna got it yesterday morning. By ten o'clock she'd sold it on to me.'

'How much did you give her?' Luke asked. His voice cracked. He was not sure what he wanted to hear; that at least Minna had sold their friendship dear, perhaps.

'Two shilling,' John said.

Two shillings. He had sent her five times that, under the seal. And for just another few pence, she'd betrayed him.

'And then?'

'Then we caught the train up to Carlisle, hired a carriage and a pair of hacks, and were at Langholm by dusk. It

232

didn't take us long to get word of a Cockney lad and a well-spoken red-head girl. We knew you'd be with her.'

Her. Rosa. What would she be thinking? She'd be frantic by now. Would she be scrying? *Stay where you are,* he thought desperately, hoping that if she was searching for him she could perhaps hear his thoughts. *Stay safe. You can't help me by getting killed yourself. At least . . .* He felt tears rise in his throat and swallowed them back down. He would not cry in front of Leadingham, he'd be damned to hell and back first. *At least if you're safe . . .* He pushed Rosa resolutely from his thoughts. Breaking down in front of Leadingham would solve nothing. And if he was to die, he wanted to do it with dignity.

'Did you bed her?' Leadingham broke into his silence.

'What?' Luke jerked upright, the ring in the floor creaking as he strove to free his arms. Hot fury flooded his body and the ropes bit into his skin as he pulled against them. 'What did you say?'

'I just wondered.' There was a shrug in Leadingham's voice. 'I wondered what hold she had over you, to make you betray the Brotherhood so fast. And what you got out of it, for your pains. Whatever tricks she turned, I hope she was worth it.'

'Shut your mouth, you filthy bastard,' Luke snarled. He was panting behind the hot blackness of the blindfold, the blood in his arms and hands pounding with the desire to hit someone very hard indeed, and keep hitting, until they begged for mercy.

233

Beside him, Leadingham began to laugh, a bitter, mocking laugh that went on and on, until Luke thought he might run mad with fury.

'Oh!' Leadingham could hardly speak for mirth. 'Oh! So it was like that, was it? It was *love*! You, Luke Lexton, of all people, to fall in love with a witch.' And then suddenly, as suddenly as he'd laughed, he was serious again. 'Your mother and father'd be turning in their graves, boy.'

'Shut up,' Luke snarled again. 'You know nothing – *nothing*.'

He thought of telling Leadingham – telling him where his precious witch-finding sight had come from. Telling him that his father had more than likely had it before him. Perhaps that was even what had led to his death.

But something stopped him.

He would not give John Leadingham another reason to kill him. If there was a way out of this it lay in reminding Leadingham of the cold truth of what he was doing: killing a man he'd known from a boy, the nephew of his friend.

'If you won't untie my hands,' he said, trying to keep his voice steady, 'at least take off my blindfold. Look me in the eye and tell me what you're going to do to me. You owe me that, John.'

There was a long silence, and for a moment Luke thought that John was going to ignore him, take refuge in that iron-clad silence he'd preserved throughout the night.

'All right.'

Luke felt John's rough, scarred fingers at the back of his

head, fiddling with the knot of the blindfold, and then the rag fell away and he was blinking in the light from the carriage lamps. John Leadingham's wrinkled face was leaning over him, grim and cold.

'As a Brother, I owe you nothing, Luke Lexton. For you gave the Brotherhood nothing. But as a man, you're right. I owe you something. So here it is: you are to die. Because of your own stupidity in trying to save a witch who was fallen beyond saving.'

And he looked to his right.

Luke's eyes followed his bright button-black eyes. And then he saw.

Rosa.

Trussed and tied like a prisoner, her arms bound to her sides, her eyes blindfolded, and her mouth gagged and stuffed with a rag.

And Luke realized suddenly what he'd failed to notice during all the long hours of captivity – the stink of the chemical stuff John brewed was not on his hands or his jacket, but coming from the corner of the carriage, where Rosa lay bound and unconscious, her head lolling back against the hard bench seat, her throat bare and naked to any knife.

'No!' He began to struggle like a wild thing, kicking out in the narrow space, hardly knowing what he was doing, not caring that the ropes bit into his skin, not caring as John Leadingham's hard hand came down over his mouth, stifling his agonized bellow. 'No! For God's sake, no! No!

Rosa! Oh Christ, Rose, wake up, wake up—'

'Somebody shut him up!' John Leadingham yelled in a hoarse, furious whisper. 'Or we'll have half the inn out here!'

'Rosa!' Luke flung himself towards her, the ropes ripping at his skin as he strained to get close enough to yank the gag from her mouth.

And then something huge and heavy cracked down on his skull, on the old half-healed wound where Sebastian had hit him so many weeks and months ago.

He looked up for one long moment in silent astonishment, the blood running hot and dark down his cheek, to his throat.

And then he slumped to the floor.

15

'We get rid of her.'

The voice was low and firm. Luke screwed his eyes tighter shut, seeing stars against the blackness of his closed lids.

'What – for good?'

'No, you fool. A damn sight more profitably than that.'

'But she's a witch – shouldn't we try her?'

'Damn it, man, who's master here? Look, a trial means delay. It means keeping 'em both locked up, and keeping her dosed, day and night, or she'll break out. We don't have the time for that, nor the money to spare for men to guard her. Whereas if it's just the lad, all we need is a good stout door and a skein of rope, and someone to come in once a day to feed him and empty the slops.'

Luke's head was spinning. He tried to lift his skull but it gave a great throb of pain that made him sick to his stomach, and he let it drop. The lad . . . the witch . . . he felt they must be talking about people that he knew – but he couldn't join the pieces together.

'So what will you do? With her?'

'Never you mind. But there's people been looking for her. People who'll pay good money.'

'And the lad?'

'He'll stand trial.' The voice was troubled. 'If he makes it.'

'*If* he makes it,' the other man said. 'You hit him a blinder, John. What it he don't make it?'

There was a long, long silence. Luke felt his head loll and roll on the hard boards. Then the first voice spoke again.

'If he don't make it, then maybe . . . well, maybe it's for the best.'

When he woke again, it was to the feel of hands beneath his armpits, dragging him, and the cold rush of air against his face. He opened his eyes to a world that spun, but even in his concussed state, he knew. He was in London. He could smell it in the air, taste it in the snow-filled fog. He was in Spitalfields – and William was somewhere near. He was home.

The knowledge was like a river running through him, with all the slow force of the Thames. He felt a momentary strength return to his limbs and he kicked out, making the wound on the back of his head scream with pain and the world around him shudder as it whirled.

'He's coming round,' he heard a voice cry out, and felt the hands beneath his armpits falter and then grip harder.

'Never you mind him!' the cry came back. 'He's weak as a cat. The girl's the one you gotta mind, she's the killer. Make sure that rag's bound in good and tight.'

'She's out like a light,' said another voice. 'Never fear.'

'Then come on, stop gassing like a pack of women and get them inside 'fore the peelers start asking questions.'

Luke had no strength to fight any more, and he let his head fall back and his eyes close. But he was not done yet. He was still captive. He was still condemned. But he was in London.

Rosa woke to darkness and a splitting headache. Her hands were bound behind her back and there was a rag in her mouth choking her, making it hard to breathe. As she pieced together where she was, she couldn't stop a kind of panic spreading through her, her heart beginning to race, the air dragging fast and painful through her nostrils.

Luke – where was Luke? Where was she? *Someone* had tracked them down. Not Sebastian, she was sure of it. That spell had *held*.

But who?

The answer came with the stench of the rag in her mouth, and she realized with a sinking heart. The Malleus. She and Luke had been so busy worrying about Sebastian they had almost forgotten there were other dangers out there, not all of them witches.

She lay in the darkness, trying to calm her thumping heart and summon a little magic to get the bindings off her.

Come on . . . come on, Rosa.

She couldn't say the words of the spell, not with the spit-covered gag in her mouth, but she thought them with every muscle and nerve and bone in her body. *Unwríð! Unwríð!*

But the ropes did not shift, and she could feel there was almost nothing there, only a thin thread of fuddled magic, poisoned and quelled by the stinking rag.

Try harder.

She wasn't even trying for the words of the spell now, just concentrating every fibre of her being on the gag. *Please . . . please . . . come on!*

She felt a great tide of frustration and fear rise up inside her, threatening to choke her, and she tried to force it back, but it tore out of her in a snorting, gasping sob that hurt her throat and eyes and nose.

Please let me go!

But there was no power there. Whatever was soaking that gag, it was the same dizzying, acrid stuff that had been in Luke's bottle, that had made her magic quail like a frightened animal. She thought of Alexis, lying in a pool of the poison, and the sob rose up again. Whatever he had done, he was her brother and she had left him there, perhaps to die. The sound that broke out of her was not a cry or a sob, but something more animal, a kind of

240

bellowing moan that echoed around the little room, taunting her in the darkness, filling her ears with the sound of her own dumb misery and despair.

Then through the thickness of the wall she heard a cry, muffled by the bricks. She held her breath, listening, trying to silence the thumping of her heart, and it came again. It sounded . . . it sounded like her name.

Was it real? Had she really heard it, or was it her mind playing tricks?

'Rosa!' This time it was a long, drawn-out cry, made faint by the distance, but she could not mistake the words. It sounded like a man.

Her heart was pounding as she began to inch her way painfully across the floor, the cold stone scraping her skin as she pushed herself along with her fingers and feet, until at last she was hard up against the wall where the sound had been coming from.

'Rosa!'

It was Luke! It really was Luke. She did not know whether to laugh with relief that he was alive, or cry with horror that he was in the same mess as her. But it was him – and so close she could hear his voice, and yet . . .

'Rosa?' he called again, more faintly, and there was a note of despair in his voice. 'Rosa, are you there? Answer me!'

But how could she? She couldn't speak. She could only . . .

She twisted round and banged the wall with her feet,

hard enough to send shock waves through her body to her pounding head, hard enough to make her joints ache in protest, desperately hoping the sound would be enough to travel through the bricks and carry to wherever he was.

'Rosa?' The sound came again, a shout this time, full of a kind of desperate hope. 'Rosa, is that you? Answer me!'

She banged again, willing him to understand.

'Oh God, the gag!' She heard his muffled groan of frustration, and then, 'Are you hurt? Bang once for no, twice for yes.'

She banged once and then listened with a thudding heart, begging him to hear the questions screaming in her skull. *Luke! Are you hurt? Where are we? Will they kill us? What's going to happen?*

'Thank God.' His voice filtered thinly through the walls. 'I'm all right too.' Her heart leapt with joy. 'I'm manacled, but I'm not gagged. They've chained me to something and the door's locked, but I can sit up. Listen, can you cast spells?'

The sob rose up again with fury at herself, frustration at her power for being so weak and pointless and easily cowed.

She banged once with her heels on the wall. One blow for no. The single thud echoed in the little room with a horrible finality.

There was a long, long silence.

Then at last Luke spoke. She could hear the despair in

his voice and the way he strove to hide it for her.

'Don't worry. It'll come back. It'll be all right. We'll be all right. We'll think of something.' Then his voice came again, quicker and fainter, not quite a whisper, but not the shout of before. 'They're coming back. I can hear feet. Don't bang until I call.'

And then nothing.

In a cell just up the corridor, Luke lay back, panting with the effort of shouting through the thick brick walls. He was pretty sure they must be in the cellar of a pub. Earlier, he'd heard barrels being rolled down a ramp not far away, thumping on to the hay-filled sack at the foot of the chute. Most likely it was the Cock Tavern. But the knowledge was of precious little use down here. The cellars were huge and rambling, and the Brothers would make sure that no one would hear their cries. But at least now he knew that Rosa was here – and alive.

He lay quiet, listening to the footsteps coming closer, and then a key grated into the door and he tried to sit up. His wrists were chained to the floor.

'Who's there?' he said, trying to keep the fear out of his voice.

'Shurrup,' growled a voice, and a man shuffled into the cellar, his face hidden by a black mask. Luke knew the boots though, and the bottoms of his trousers: Benjamin West. He could see his glasses glinting through the eyeholes of the hood.

'Ben,' he said hoarsely, 'Ben, don't do this. Think about what William—'

'I said, shurrup, traitor!' Ben shot back, but his voice trembled as he slammed down the plate of food and the tankard of water.

'Loosen my hands a bit, Ben, so's I can at least eat. *Please*, I—'

'I said *shut up!*' Ben bellowed, and he kicked Luke in the side, so that he gasped and fell silent, choking for breath.

Then he was gone, the door slamming behind him.

Luke lay crouched for a while, trying to get his breath back. He should try and eat something, he knew, though he didn't feel hungry.

His hands were manacled to a ring on the floor on a length of chain maybe six inches long. It passed through the ring, so that by crushing one hand against the ring he could reach six inches in either direction. Benjamin West had left the food maybe eight inches away.

Luke sighed. He pulled himself around, the rusty metal manacles biting into his skin, and by straining all his weight against the ring he could just reach the plate with his shoulder. He pushed against it with his upper arm, trying to get a purchase on the thin, slippery plate without spilling the contents, but it flipped and the bread fell to the damp, dusty floor. Luke gritted his teeth and shoved it again with his shoulder, dragging it across the flags. Slowly, slowly he edged it nearer until he had it within reach of the ring. He sat up, his muscles shaking with tiredness, and picked it up in his fingers. It was damp and covered in black dust from the floor, but it still made his mouth water. By crouching down and pulling the chain upwards as hard as he could, he could just get it to his lips. He chewed slowly, filled with thankfulness, feeling the energy slowly return to his limbs and the cold exhaustion ebb a little.

When the bread had gone he lay on his side and tried to find a comfortable place for his head on the stone floor. The back of his skull hurt like a bastard where he'd been hit and he could feel crusted blood on the back of his neck, but that might be the least of his worries soon. How would they do it? Quick and clean, or slow and drawn out? He remembered John Leadingham's abattoir, with the pink, naked pigs swinging from their hooks and the grating in the middle of the floor where the blood pooled and drained.

Once he'd imagined himself on the end of one of those hooks, his ribs split open and his blood dripping on to the concrete floor. But now – now as the bread sat heavy in his belly – now it was Rosa's naked, gutted body he saw swinging from the hook. He remembered the night he had spent in her arms, the feel of her long slim side beneath his hand, the soft rise and fall of her ribs, the hot smoothness of her skin, and the sound she had made as he touched it with his lips.

And he thought of her corpse swinging in that abattoir . . . and he was filled with a cold, dread-filled rage.

He pulled at the manacles with all his weight, the rusty metal biting into his skin, the blood running down his hands, making them slick and wet. But the chain did not snap and the manacles were too tight for him to force his hand through.

At last he gave a great cry, a shout of frustration that echoed through the vaults, and he let his head fall to the floor. There was nothing he could do.

It was dark, so Rosa could not tell whether it was morning or night, but she was sleeping the sleep of the dead when a man came through the door. He put his foot on her back, between her shoulder blades, and pressed her face into the stone. She heard a knife coming out of a sheath and her breath caught in her throat in a scream that died before it was born.

Then there was a snick. She felt hair fall to the ground either side of her face and the gag was off.

The man ran for the door and she rolled over, blinking and bewildered, and wondering what on earth was happening. Her mouth felt rancid and as dry as dust, and there was cut hair beneath her cheek, but then her face knocked against something that glinted in the scrap of lamplight beneath the doorway and slopped when she rocked it.

Water.

With her bound hands she could not lift the dish, so she crouched above it, sucking and lapping like a cat, and feeling the coolness drip down her throat. It tasted strange – metallic and bitter.

It was only when the stuff hit her stomach that she realized her mistake.

It was drugged. With something similar to the liquid in the bottle – maybe even the same stuff, diluted.

She knelt on the floor trying to master her thirst, but her head was already starting to reel and the dry ache in her throat was too much. She put her face to the dish and sucked and sucked until it was dry, knowing that she was sealing her fate but unable to stop herself. She felt the chemicals flooding her body, chasing out the magic from every cell.

'Luke!' she called thickly, too dazed to work out whether calling for him was a good idea or not. 'Luke!'

But there was no answer. If he could hear her, he wasn't giving anything away.

Her head spinning, she crawled across the floor to lie pressed against the stone wall where she'd heard Luke's voice, trying to keep herself awake, keep herself listening, as she slipped back into darkness.

Luke woke from a half-drowse to the sound of footsteps in the corridor outside. A candle flame showed thin and wavering through the crack beneath the door and he heard a voice.

'. . . today, probably.'

'I don't understand.' It was Ben West, his voice plaintive. 'She's condemned – why can't we try her alongside the boy? Why sell her on?'

'Never you mind.' Leadingham's voice, sharp and angry.

'And who'd pay a price like that anyway? It's madness!'

'I said,' Leadingham spoke low and full of menace, 'never. You. Mind. If you know what's good for you, West, you won't go blabbing about this, neither.'

'But—'

'I said, *shut it*. Or do you want to be in violation of your oaths, like our friend here?' And he hit Luke's cell door with something hard that chinked against the iron work.

West said nothing, but Luke could almost hear the uneasy reluctance in his footsteps as he walked away.

He heard the two men go up the corridor in the direction of Rosa's room and then the sound of their footsteps as they passed back up, towards the door to the street.

'No need to come back tonight, Ben,' said Leadingham's voice. 'I'll get Arthur to come with me this evening. I know you'll have yer work to do.'

'All right, John.' Benjamin West's voice, thin and unhappy. 'But listen, man, I still think—'

'And I still think,' Leadingham broke in, hard and suddenly very dangerous, 'if you keep asking questions you'll end up with a knife in your side. And mebbe it won't be one with a false blade, neither.'

There was silence from West, and then Luke heard their feet on the stairs and a big heavy door swing shut.

He waited a few moments to make sure they were out of earshot. Then he filled his lungs and yelled.

'Rosa! Rosa, can you hear me?' He stopped, listening to his own voice echoing up and around the narrow room. 'Rosa!' he yelled again, his head throbbing with the shout. 'Rosa, wake up, wake up!'

But there was no answer. Only a silence that struck a coldness into his gut.

She could not be gone. She could not have been sold already. He'd know – surely? He'd have felt it.

'Rosa!' he yelled.

'Rosa! Rose!' A hoarse shout filtered through into her dream, with a note of hopelessness in it, as if the caller had been trying for a very long time and was beginning to despair of an answer. 'Rosa . . . Oh God please, answer me . . .'

She surfaced from a horrible dream of clutching hands and arid deserts and croaked, 'Yes . . . yes, I'm here. They took the gag off. Is it safe to talk?'

'Rosa!' His voice was croaky with relief. 'Thank God! I've been calling for hours, on and off. Yes, they've gone out, but I don't know how much longer we've got before they come back. Listen, I heard 'em talking; they're going to sell you.'

'Sell me?' She tried to think straight, but her head was aching and swimming. 'What do you mean? To who?'

'I don't know. But they said today. We've got to get away. I've rubbed my wrists raw but I can't get out of these manacles. Is there anything you can do? Is your magic coming back?'

Desperation rose inside her, a kind of despair as the fragments of memory clicked into place.

'No . . .' she managed. 'Luke, they're drugging me.'

'In your food?'

'I've had no food. In my water. I tried not to drink it – but oh God, I'm so thirsty.'

She heard him swear, long and low.

'It's that stuff that John brews. I don't blame you for drinking – thirst can drive you half mad. But – oh Jesus, what are we going to do?'

She shut her eyes in the darkness, searching inside herself for a scrap of power to kindle into a spell. But she could feel only sick confusion; magic, but a muddled, twisted, directionless mass that she couldn't shape to her purpose or force to do anything.

Luke would die if they stayed here. Whatever, whoever, she was to be sold to, Luke's fate was clear. And he was mortal and defenceless, and in this nightmare in part because of her – because he had refused to keep his oath and kill her.

Very well then. If magic couldn't help her, she would have to find something else.

But how, with her hands bound behind her back? They were tightly fastened, no hope of wriggling her legs through the circle of her arms, even without her hampering skirts. And there was nothing in the little cell – nothing apart from the dish of poisoned water. It was not glass, but a kind of earthenware. But perhaps, if she were lucky . . .

She twisted around, feeling for it with her fingers behind her back. When her fingers met the lip of the plate she grasped it firmly, then picked it up and brought it smashing down on the concrete floor.

'Rosa, are you all right?' She heard Luke's shout filter through the damp cellar bricks.

'Yes,' she called back. 'It was nothing.'

No point in getting his hopes up. If there was a chance, it was slim.

There were two shards she thought might be usable. The rest had just crumbled to splinters and chips.

But two pieces . . . Behind her back she felt them with her thumb, rubbing the rough gritty edge. They were not sharp – but they were all she had.

She began to saw at the rope binding her wrists.

16

There had been silence from Rosa's cell for a long time. Luke was tempted to call out to her, but then he thought better of it. Perhaps she was sleeping off the effects of the drug. If so, he wouldn't wake her.

Once he'd thought he heard a muffled cry, of pain, or perhaps frustration. But when he lay, holding his breath to listen, there were only the faint muffled sounds of the street. He must have imagined it, or heard some noise from outside.

He was almost dozing when he heard a different sound: a key in the lock of the door at the top of the stairs. He was awake at once, his heart pounding, but he lay with his eyes squeezed shut, trying to give nothing away. If they thought he was asleep perhaps they might let slip something about their plans . . .

It was only one set of feet that he could hear coming

down the stone steps though. Heavy feet, for a heavy man. Not skinny, wiry John Leadingham. West then? But no – John had told him not to come.

Someone else. What was the name Leadingham had said? Arthur. Luke didn't know any Arthurs in the Brotherhood, but that didn't mean much. He didn't know all the Brothers.

The steps paused for a moment in front of Luke's door. A slight sound came from the latch, as though someone'd laid his hand on the handle outside and then thought better of it. The footsteps moved on down the corridor in the direction of wherever they were holding Rosa. He heard them get fainter, and then the rattle of keys, and the scrape of a lock.

But who was he? Why'd he come alone without John? What did he want with Rosa that he couldn't have a witness?

If you touch her . . . His fists inside the manacles clenched. *If you harm her* . . .

Then what? What could he do? If this unknown man assaulted Rosa, then he would lie there in the dark and listen to it, because there was nothing else he could do. Just as he'd lain and listened as his parents were slaughtered by Sebastian's father, the Black Witch.

Fear and fury rose up inside him, suffocating him.

And then he heard something. A crash, as if a door had been slammed shut violently, and a long drawn-out howl of agony.

Luke leapt to his feet, forgetting the manacles around his wrists, and screamed as the cuffs ripped into his bloodied skin, jerking him to the floor with a bone-crunching impact.

'Rosa!' he bellowed. 'Rosa! For Christ's sake, say something!'

The scream had died away and he lay there, trying to listen, but with his heart beating so loudly in his ears that he could hear nothing but its pounding and the roar and rush of his own blood.

If you've touched her, you bastard . . .

There were flurried footsteps in the corridor and he heard the scrape of keys in the lock and scrambled to his feet, in the crouched defensive position that was all the manacles would allow.

'Luke!'

For a minute he couldn't believe it. Rosa? She was standing in the doorway, lamplight streaming past her into the cell. Then she staggered into his room and fell to her knees beside him. There was something in her hands – something that chinked as she tried with shaking fingers to hold it out. Keys.

'Rosa.' He could only kneel there, gaping stupidly, trying not to sob with gratitude and disbelief. 'Rosa, what . . . ? How . . . ?'

She had no magic. He could see something there, but it was a black, poisoned mass of sickness.

There was blood on her dress and on her face.

'I sawed through my bindings.' She was sorting through the keys, looking for one to match the keyhole in the manacles, but her hands were trembling and she kept losing her place. 'I hid behind the door. When he came in, I slammed the door shut on him. On his face! Oh, Christ, Luke, his face! I didn't mean . . .'

She was crying, tears making pale runnels in the dirt and blood on her face.

'Well done,' Luke said. There was a fierce triumph starting to burn in his gut. 'I don't care if you slammed the door so hard you broke his bloody neck. He went into your cell alone for a reason – and not a good one.'

'But his face . . . Oh God, the blood!' Her fingers slipped on the key again and she wiped the tears from her cheeks. 'Damn these keys. I can't see what I'm doing.'

'Give them here.' Luke took them and found the right key. He held it out to Rosa and she put it into the lock with shaking hands.

'He was just an outwith, Luke – just a poor outwith. I think I killed him.'

Then the manacles clinked open and Luke staggered to his feet, feeling the magnificence of standing upright after the long hours chained to the floor. He pulled himself to his full height and stretched, the blood rushing into his weary muscles and his joints snapping and cracking.

He took the keys from Rosa's hand.

'Stay here – no, wait. Stay in the corridor. I'll go and check.'

'No!' she cried, but he was already gone. Not to reassure Rosa – though he didn't believe the man's injuries could be as bad as she feared – but to lock the man in the cell. If he did come round, they didn't want pursuers.

The man was lying on the floor. He was breathing, bloody foam bubbling down his face, and Rosa had smashed the door into his nose so that he'd have a crooked profile for the rest of his life. But he wasn't dead, not by a long chalk.

Luke pushed the man's prone form out of the way, so that he was lying on his back in the centre of the cellar. He shut and locked the door behind him – and then stopped.

Damn him.

The man deserved to die but – choking on his own blood . . . He wouldn't let a dog go that way.

He unlocked the door, his fingers nervous now, conscious of the time ticking away and John Leadingham's probably imminent arrival. Inside, he grabbed roughly at the man's left arm and shoulder and rolled him on to his side, with his own arm and one leg as a prop, the way he'd seen William do for drunks. The blood would drain out of his nose that way, not pool in his lungs. And if he vomited, he wouldn't choke on it.

Then, angry with his own soft-heartedness, he slammed the door, hard this time, and locked it, his hands shaking with haste.

Rosa was standing in the corridor where he'd left her, her hands by her side, her face white in the dim light. Her hair was in ragged streams around her shoulders.

'Is he dead?'

'No. He'll have a bloody sore nose for a few weeks, but he's not dead. Now, come on, let's get out of here.'

Hand in hand, they ran up the stairs. The door at the top was not locked and Luke could hear music coming from outside. He flung it open – and they staggered out into the parlour of the Cock Tavern.

For a moment everyone stopped. The pianist at the bar stopped banging out his Cockney crowd-pleasers. The lady hanging on his shoulder and warbling out the words stopped in the middle of a verse, her mouth hanging open.

And at the bar Phoebe Fairbrother stopped too, the glasses on the tray she held sliding to the floor one after another: crash, crash, crash.

'Luke?' she gasped. Luke winced, hearing the crashes, as loud as pistol shots in the silent bar. If they'd had any hope of slipping out quietly, that hope was gone now.

Then, behind his shoulder, he heard an echoing strangled gulp.

'*Luke!*'

He turned. It was Minna. Her face was white, her hands pressed to her mouth.

'Jesus wept, Luke!'

He didn't know what to say. He couldn't find the words.

Then she dropped her hands and he saw that her face was swollen, her legacy from Knyvet's match factory.

'Minna . . .' He put his hand out, towards her cheek, but she jerked back.

'Don't you touch me, Luke Lexton.'

'I wasn't going to.' He felt anger flare. 'Why d'you do it, Minna? Why d'you sell me out for two shillings?'

'I dunno what you're talking about,' she said nervously – but she did. He could see it in her eyes and the way she refused to meet his gaze, looking shiftily over his shoulder towards the lighted street.

'You want to know why Leadingham wanted that address?' he said brutally.

'Not really.'

She tried to push past him, but he grabbed her wrist, pulling her back.

'Because he reckons I betrayed him. And he's planning to kill me for it.'

'*Kill* you!' She gave a derisive laugh. 'Don't flatter yerself, Luke.'

'Look at me,' he snarled. 'Look at me, Minna. Do I look like a man who's been hit and starved and locked in a cellar in irons for three days? Because that's what he did.'

'Luke.' He felt Rosa's pull on his arm and heard her voice, low and urgent in his ear. 'We need to go. They could be back any moment.'

He clenched his fist, aching to throw a punch – not at Minna, she wasn't worth it. And he would not hit a woman, not even one who'd sold their long friendship up the river so brutally. But he was desperate to hit *something*.

258

He took a breath.

'All right.'

'Luke . . .' Minna put a hand on his arm and spoke, her voice low. 'I'm sorry. Look – I needed medicine, yeah? I can't get by no more without something to take the edge off. My jaw aches something cruel. I don't take much . . .'

'Laudanum,' he said flatly. She said nothing, but the fact that she didn't deny it told him all he needed to know. He could have wept. But really, what difference did it make? If she did have the phossy jaw, she'd likely die anyway. 'Minna, the kids—'

'Screw the kids,' she snarled. 'I never asked to be saddled with a pack of brats! I worked myself to the bone for them kids, Luke, and what do I get? "I'm hungry, Minna." "I want a dolly, Minna." "I peed my drawers, Minna."'

She imitated a child's whine with uncanny accuracy and Luke flinched.

'So what if I have a drink every now and again, and something to help me sleep? I don't get no help from nowhere else. Now, if you ain't gonna buy me a drink you can piss off with your sanctimonious talk, Luke Lexton. You always was a self-righteous shit.'

For a minute Luke drew a breath – and then he stopped himself. Rosa was right. They had to get out. Leadingham could be back any moment and, though Rosa was still and silent next to him, he could feel anxiety emanating from her like an electrical current. He turned to go.

'Go,' Minna shouted as he pulled open the pub door

259

with a hand that shook. 'Go on, piss off and take Lady Muck with you! Where was you when I needed you? Where was you when I was selling Bess's bones to the knackers? Playing kiss-me-hand to another man's fiancée, that's what. Bet she don't look so tasty now you've dragged her down into the gutter with you, eh!'

For a second he stopped, his hand on the door frame, his head bowed between his shoulders, trying to master his anger.

Then he felt Rosa's urgent pull on his sleeve and he followed her into the night.

Outside in the narrow alleyway down the side of the pub, Rosa pulled her shawl around her face. It was drizzling – a fine mist of rain that drifted in the night air, making blurry rainbow auras around the gas lamps. She tried to cast her mind back to the night they had left the Cock at dawn in the drifting snow, but she could not remember which way they had turned. Her head felt thick and stupid from the poisoned bottle.

'Luke, where now?'

He looked dazed and almost punch-drunk.

She tried to imagine standing in his shoes, seeing all his kindness turned to poison and thrown back at him. She wanted to put her arms around him and tell him that it was not his fault, that Minna had to fight her own demons, and Luke could not have fought them for her, even if he had been there to do it.

But now was not the time for this. Now was the time to run.

'*Luke*,' she said more urgently. 'Come on.'

He seemed to pull himself together and nodded.

'All right.' He took a deep, shuddering breath. 'We . . . we need to get out of Spitalfields. Fast. The markets are full of Brothers and it won't take them long to get word out. Let's go down to the Thames; maybe we can get aboard a barge or something.'

'So which way to the Thames?'

'That way.' Luke pointed up the alley and they began to walk towards the road.

They'd only gone a few yards when a carriage drew across the opening ahead of them. Rosa's first thought was that it was oddly grand for Spitalfields. It was high and polished, with a beautiful matched pair of horses and a liveried coachman on the high driver's seat.

Then it swung to a halt and she saw the side door. And the crest emblazoned on it. Sebastian's crest.

She heard Luke's strangled gasp and she knew that he'd seen it too.

For a minute she stood, frozen by the awful impossibility of it. *How?* Had he tracked them down?

Luke grabbed her arm and they turned as one to run down the alley in the opposite direction.

'Are you sure it's not a dead end?' Rosa gasped. The high brick walls seemed to disappear into drizzling darkness.

Luke shook his head and panted, 'No, keep going; leads

261

into Commercial Street.'

As they got closer, a long rectangle of gas-lit street emerged out of the gloom.

Knyvet's carriage door slammed shut and they quickened their pace.

Then a man turned into the alleyway.

Rosa carried on running, ready to barge past, but Luke stopped dead. She skidded to a halt.

'Luke!' she implored. 'What the hell are you doing? Come *on!*'

'Hello, Luke,' said the man at the far end of the alley. His voice was a pleasant croak. He began to walk up the narrow gap between the buildings, and Rosa could see that he was a small, wiry man with a muffler round his chin and a packet in his hand. 'Din't expect to see you here.'

Rosa ran back to Luke and grabbed his hand.

'Come *on!*'

Whoever this man was, he was just an outwith. Their chances with him had to be better than facing Sebastian.

'It's Leadingham,' Luke whispered dully. He didn't move. 'He's one of the Malleus. He knows.'

Rosa stopped. She looked down the alley at the man walking towards them. Then she looked back to the other end, where Sebastian's coach still stood beneath the gas lamp, the rain glittering on its polished sides.

'Is it possible Sebastian doesn't know we're here?' she asked desperately.

'Oh, he knows,' Leadingham said. He spoke in a

conversational tone, but the alley funnelled and shaped his voice, bringing it to them as clearly as if he spoke in their ear. 'Oh yes, he knows.'

'What?' Luke swung round, facing Leadingham. He put Rosa behind him, as if his body could protect her. She wanted to laugh at the futility of it. She wanted to kiss him for trying. 'How the hell d'you know Knyvet?'

'Leadingham and I came to a temporary arrangement some weeks ago.' A low drawl came from the other end of the passage and a familiar top-hatted figure stepped out at the end of the alley, silhouetted against the shifting lamplight. Rosa's fingers closed on the back of Luke's coat. That soft, rough voice, like velvet rubbed against the grain. Pictures rose in her head: Sebastian's fist against her face; his teeth grazing her lip; the sound of a whip against flesh and a puppy's screams.

Her head reeled and for a moment she thought she might pass out, but the sickness passed and she stood, panting with fear and anger, ready to fight.

'*What?*' Luke turned from Leadingham, to Sebastian, and then back again. Rain dripped from his hair and ran down the bridge of his nose. There was a kind of incredulous disbelief on his face, as if someone had just struck a huge blow at the foundation of everything he thought was true. 'Leadingham, tell me this isn't true?'

But Leadingham only shrugged.

'No.' Luke was shaking his head. 'No. How can you condemn me when you – you—'

'Don't start on that with me,' Leadingham sounded weary. 'I never betrayed my oaths, Luke. I did my best to protect my people and my patch, that's all. Sometimes that means compromises.'

'But – but . . .' Luke's hands were in his hair, tearing at his face as if he could pull out his eyes and not have to see or hear this any more. 'Why? *How?*'

He stopped, gasping, unable to find the words.

'We stumbled over each other looking for you,' Leadingham said dryly. 'And, well – I knew who he was, of course, but there was no sense in fighting a war on two fronts. We had a . . . discussion, let's call it, and agreed to drop arms against each other for the time being, concentrate on our joint aim. I've been able to do Knyvet the service of returning his fiancée. And him – well, let's just say he made it worth my while.'

'Very,' Knyvet said, and he smiled, a smile that thinned his lips to a bloodless white line.

'Sebastian . . .' Rosa's hand crept to her throat and then she dropped it. She would not show him her fear. She would not show him her revulsion.

If there was a way out of this, it did not lie in running.

She stepped away from Luke, up the alley, towards the top-hatted figure.

'Sebastian, let me go.'

He said nothing and she moved closer to him, her hand outstretched.

'You could have any wife you wanted. You could have

beauty, riches . . . anything. Find another wife. One who loves you for who you are.'

'One who loves me . . .' There was a silence and then he began to laugh, a long, rolling, bitter laugh. 'One who loves me for who I am. And what is that, Rosa darling? What am I? A madman?' He stepped into the light at the end of the alley and Rosa saw the thin white line that traced his cheek from lip to ear, where she had slashed him in the factory: a dueller's scar. 'A killer?' He came closer, his hand outstretched. 'You've made a monster of me, Rose.' He reached out and traced a finger down her skin from cheek to jaw, his fingers imitating the raindrops that caressed the line of her throat and soaked into her shawl. 'Your disloyalty, your perfidy, your *beauty*. You've turned me into this, Rosa. I burnt innocent men and women, children, because of you. I will have to live with my actions until I die. And so will you. A kind of justice, is it not?'

'No . . .' She was not sure if she was telling him, or begging him. 'Sebastian, no—'

'How dare you blame her.' Luke's voice behind her was hard and cold. '*You* owned that factory, *you* chose to lock us in and leave us to die. You did that – not her, *you*.'

Sebastian thrust out a gloved hand, palm first, and Luke slammed back and upwards into the wall of the alley, his feet dangling, his head smacking against the brick. He gasped and a thin line of fresh blood trickled from the wound on the back of his head, mingling with the rain that ran down his throat.

265

'Sebastian!' she gasped. Sebastian only smiled and closed his fingers into a fist. Luke's groan strangled and then died in his throat. There was silence in the alley now, so quiet she could hear the pub songs floating in the night air and the patter of the rain that dripped from the eaves and puddled on the floor.

'Sebastian!' she begged again. Luke's chest rose and fell, heaving for air. His eyes were screwed shut, as if he were fighting something . . . as if he were losing.

'Sebastian!' she screamed. 'Let go of him!'

'Come with me,' Sebastian said, low and soft, his voice caressing. 'Your life for his – wasn't that what it was always about?'

For a moment Rosa stood in the passage, looking from Sebastian's tall silhouette to Luke's agonized, crucified form, splayed unnaturally against the brickwork. Luke's face had darkened from red, to a kind of purple.

'Please . . . You're *killing* him.' She turned to Leadingham in despair. 'How can you stand by and watch this? Isn't it your mission, to protect your kind from ours? Do something!'

'Luke forfeited our protection.' Leadingham's voice was as implacable as his face, hard and cold. 'When he chose you over his Brothers, he forfeited any right to our blood spilt in his defence.'

She would have screamed if she thought it would do any good. She could have sobbed and pounded them with her fists. But she knew that none of this would move

266

either of the two men standing sentinel at each end of the narrow alley.

'Let him go.' She spoke to Sebastian, not Leadingham. 'Let him go, and I'll come with you.'

'Do you swear?'

'Yes.'

He released the spell and Luke fell to the wet ground, his head lolling painfully. Rosa ran to him, kneeling in the muck and silt of the alley by his side, but before she could do more than smooth his rain-drenched hair back from his forehead she heard Sebastian's voice, hard and sharp as a gunshot.

'Touch him again and he dies. Now, get back here.'

Slowly, she stood. But she had seen what she wanted to know – Luke was breathing. His colour was fading to normal. He was alive.

'Come here.'

She went, hating herself for her obedience, but knowing that fine gestures could achieve nothing now.

With an elaborate flourish, Sebastian held open the door of the carriage and bowed.

'Your carriage awaits, milady.'

Hating him, hating herself, Rosa put one foot on the step. Then she turned back, to Leadingham, still standing implacable at the far end of the alley, his arms crossed in the dim, shifting lamplight.

'If you kill him,' she spoke very low, but somehow she was sure her words would reach him, 'if you kill him, I *will* find you. No matter if it takes me a year, five years or twenty. You will never hear a door bang, but wonder if it's me, coming for you. You will never hear a creak in the night, or a branch tap on your window, without thinking of my promise. I *will* come for you. And you will suffer ten times whatever you inflict on him.'

'For Gawd's sake,' Leadingham's voice was full of a biting sarcasm, 'shut her up, Knyvet. If there's one thing I can't stand it's a crowing hen.'

Sebastian gave a short laugh, and Rosa let herself be pulled into the carriage, and Sebastian slammed the door closed.

The last thing she saw as the carriage pulled away was Luke's body, lying in the muddy, rain-soaked alley, and Leadingham standing over him, his arms folded, like his murderer.

Rosa stayed at the carriage window as long as possible, until the rain closed behind them. And as the coachman touched his whip to the horses and they picked up their pace along Brick Lane, she could think of only one thing: she had not told Luke that she loved him. And now perhaps he would never know.

17

It was growing light as the carriage swung into the drive at Southing and wound down between the frost-rimed trees to the great house. The rain had turned to snow on their journey down and the carriage wheels made a soft shirring on the freshly fallen flakes that lay undisturbed on the drive.

The horses were tired, their breath rising white in the cold dawn air, but at last they came round the last curve, into sight of Southing itself, still and silent in the white landscape. Last time Rosa had seen it, it was ablaze with light and life, the doors flung wide, footmen lining the drive in serried ranks to receive their visitors. Now the windows were dark and shuttered inside.

Sebastian helped her from the carriage and she walked, in a kind of waking dream, or perhaps a nightmare, across the soft carpet of snow and into that tall pillared porch where just a few weeks before Sebastian had given her a rose made of ice.

She remembered the entrance hall as it had been then, full of footmen and maidservants, the butler standing by, a fire roaring in the grate. It was silent now, the furniture shrouded in white dust sheets, the grate dark. Only a single oil lamp burnt, high in the rafters.

'Welcome home, my darling,' Sebastian said as the door closed behind them, and he kissed her left hand, dirty and bloodied as it was. His lips curved in a thin, wry smile. 'I suppose you thought you were very clever, chopping off your finger?'

'Not clever, no,' she whispered. 'Stupid, for not realizing the truth before.'

'Alexis found the ring, you know, when he came round after your trick with the bottle. I had it reset.'

'He's alive then?'

'Oh, yes.' A voice came from behind her. She turned, and there was Alexis, his hands in his pockets, standing in the doorway to the drawing room. His red hair was dishevelled and he was white and sweating. Rosa realized he was drunk, though the sun had barely come up. 'Were you worried?'

'Yes! Of course I was!'

'Touching solicitude, considering you left me for dead in a pool of – what *was* that stuff? It knocked out my magic for a good couple of weeks.'

Rosa shook her head.

'I don't know. I don't know what it was. Luke had it . . . Alexis, *please*.' She stepped close to him, lowering her voice, although there was no hope of Sebastian not overhearing. 'Please. Think of what you're doing. *Think* of what this will mean to me. Is it really worth selling your own sister for a post at the Ealdwitan? For God's sake . . .' Her voice was pleading, though she hated herself for it. 'Think – think of what Papa would say!'

'Him!' Alexis gave a laugh – not a pleasant one. 'This whole situation is dear, precious Papa's fault, if you must know.'

'What?'

'If he hadn't tied up half the estate in your marriage portion . . .'

'*What?*'

'You heard me.'

'B-but we're penniless. He died and left us penniless.'

'He left *us* penniless, yes,' Alexis said. 'He spent Mama's dowry, mortgaged the house, sold my future up the river. About the only thing he didn't touch was your damn marriage portion.'

'Is that what this is about?' she cried. 'Some trust? I'll sign it over! I'll *give* it to you, for God's sake, Alexis, please!'

'You can't,' Alexis said dismissively. 'Don't think we didn't look into that. Mama's had the best lawyers in the Ealdwitan looking at the terms of that trust. It's marriage or nothing.'

271

'How can that be?' Rosa said bewildered. 'What if I'd died a spinster?'

'Oh, it reverts to you on your thirtieth birthday if you're still unmarried. But unfortunately we can't keep afloat that long.'

'But – but if I marry, it becomes *mine*. How can that benefit you?'

'If you marry,' he spelt it out, 'it becomes your husband's.'

'And he has promised it to you.' Her heart was sinking. She felt like the bottom had fallen from her world. Not just advancement. Not even friendship. But *money*. That was all it came down to. Money Alexis felt should have been his. Money he could not touch, except by betraying his sister.

'I did not choose this,' she said, her voice very low. 'I didn't ask for this. You're punishing me for something I had no part in. How could Papa know, Alex? I'm sure he didn't mean . . . he never meant . . .'

'I really don't care what he meant or what he thought." Alexis looked at her and there was something close to disgust in his face, or perhaps it was hate. 'Father was a fool and a drunk who fell under a carriage when he was soused without a care for his wife and son. And if you'd ever acted like you gave a damn about me, all these years—'

'As if *I* gave a damn?' Rosa gasped. She looked at him standing there in his stained britches and waistcoat, his freckled face damp and waxen with drink, and she shook with anger. 'Alex, you had everything! You had Mama's love, you had all the money there was, you had clothes and education – there was *nothing* left for me, nothing! Why should I be sorry for you? You condemn Papa for a drunkard – well, look at yourself. Perhaps he tied up that money because he looked at you and refused to throw good money after bad.'

'He tied up that money,' Alexis snarled, his spittle striking her face as he enunciated the words so that she could not mistake a single syllable, 'because he didn't *love me*. Because all the affection he had was sucked out him by you, you little leech. And you expect me to feel sorry for you because of that? Well, damn you, Rosa. Damn you to hell. Do you think I enjoy crawling to Seb for what should be rightfully mine?'

He turned on his heel and began to walk away, leaving Rosa speechless, almost winded by his vitriol. How long had he and Mama known this, known that she was sitting on the last asset the estate possessed? Since Papa's death? Before, even?

'Oh, and by the way,' Alexis said carelessly as he caught the library door in his hand, 'you owe me a new horse. Bye, Seb.'

The door slammed and he was gone.

Rosa stared at Sebastian, who gave a shrug and then held out his arm.

'Shall we?'

'He's mad,' Rosa whispered. 'You're mad. Don't you care how people will see your actions? How can you go from

273

loving me, to trying to kill me, and now to this? To a forced marriage?'

Sebastian smiled.

'I have to *own*, Rosa. I have to control. My family have always been commanders of one kind and another: generals, judges, bishops, admirals, ministers of parliament – and yes, businessmen and factory owners too. We have fought and killed and subdued to our will – that is what it *means* to be a Knyvet, Rosa. It's what I was bred to, from my cradle. And when I saw you – in the drawing room at Osborne House, with your eyes so wild and afraid, and your spirit so unquenched, your fire undimmed by the London fog – there was something about you, Rosa. You were so impossibly different from all the women in India, starched and sweating and damp with their ardour and their greed. Beside them you were a little vixen. You were that little wild girl running in the woods at Matchenham, with her hair loose and her skirts ripped. And I knew I had to have you. There are many kinds of possession, Rose. Many ways to tame and silence and control. They are all facets of the same thing.'

He came very close and put his fingers on her neck, where the pulse beat hard and fast beneath her ear and the skin was thin. She felt his breath on her face and smelt the sourness of old cigar smoke, but that was not what made her shudder.

'Do you know what the French call the act of love?' His fingers against her throat were hard and cold. She shook her head, trying not to show her fear. He whispered the answer and she felt his breath, cool against her cheek. '*Le petit mort* – the little death.'

He would never let her go. It came to her as she stood, rigid with fear, her magic a small, cowed thing deep within. He *could* not let her go, for she would tell the truth about everything. In truth this marriage was a death; a living death. She thought of Sebastian's mother, a prisoner upstairs. Had this been her fate? Perhaps the madness had come later . . .

She swayed and almost fell, and Sebastian's arm went around her, carefully, solicitously.

'Darling, you are tired. Let me show you to your room.'

'My cell.'

But she followed him up the stairs, her feet shushing on the thick carpet as he turned down corridor after corridor, until they came to a thick baize door, soundproofed with padding. He unlocked it with a key.

'I thought you would like to get to know my mother. So I have put you in her wing. The rest of the house is shut up, in any case. She is asleep, I believe. But later I hope you will meet. This is your room.'

He opened a door to his right and Rosa looked at the tall windows with their iron bars, at the flowered yellow wallpaper, incongruously cheerful. At the bed. A double bed.

She walked to the window, her heart beating hard, and looked out over the parks and woodland. The bars were

275

laced with spells, she could feel the magic. Oh, just a night or two of rest and her power would be back!

She shut her eyes.

'Please, I'd like to rest,' she said, her voice sounding hard in her attempt not to give way to the churning fear inside. 'If you could leave now.'

'Of course, my darling. You're tired. All that travelling . . . Oh, just one more thing,' Sebastian said, almost carelessly, as he turned to go. 'Your wedding ring. As I said, I had it reset.'

He reached into his pocket and held up a necklace, a narrow band of filigree gold, shaped like a slender collar, with the ruby burning at its heart.

'*Fríes-þu!*' he snapped, and almost before Rosa had realized what was happening, she found herself rigid, her arms locked by her side, her feet fastened to the carpet as if made of stone.

Sebastian crossed the room behind her, his feet silent on the thick carpet, and she felt his shadow fall across her spine and his fingers, cold against the nape of her neck, as he tenderly fastened the collar around her throat.

There was a snap as the two halves clicked together and she felt the metal burn against the back of her neck, the catch fusing into one smooth unbroken line.

'You'll have a little more difficulty cutting off your head, I imagine,' he said, and there was a smile in his voice. Then he turned and left, locking the door behind him.

18

When Luke awoke it was dark, and for a panicked moment he thought they'd taken his eyes and he was blind, for he could make out nothing; eyes open or closed it was the same velvet blackness. He turned his head wildly from side to side, and at last he made out something – a glimmering line of light – a crack beneath a door. The sight anchored him, and he crawled across to it until the chain at his ankle pulled taut. He lay on the cold floor, looking longingly at the light.

There was a smell of blood in the air and he could feel something rough and yet soft beneath his fingers – particles of something that felt like sawdust.

With a sudden lurch to his gut, he knew where he had been taken. Not back to the cellars beneath the Cock. Not to a room beneath the house in Fournier Street where the Malleus had their headquarters. But to John Leadingham's abattoir. To the swinging pink carcasses, to the shining metal hooks, worn with use. To the drain in the floor and the pump that swilled the blood away.

So this was it. He had always known it would end here, somehow. The floor was cold beneath his cheek and he shut his eyes and thought of William, who would never know what happened to him; of Minna, whose last act had been to betray him; and of Rosa. Always Rosa.

So many choices, so many forks in the road, so many mistakes and betrayals and all leading to this small squalid death, with his parents unavenged, his life wasted, and his blood spilt into the Thames with the pigswill and the guts.

And Rosa in her living death, her living hell.

Was there a twist in the road that could have saved them both? Was there a choice he could have made, a road he could have taken that would have let them both live? But he could not think of one. Maybe if he'd gone after Sebastian in the burning factory . . . If he'd pursued his revenge instead of going back for Rosa . . . But he'd known, even then, that there *was* no choice. Even if Rosa had saved herself, he could not have lived knowing that he'd left her to burn to satisfy his own grudge.

The only thing he could have changed was Minna. If he'd not written to her, they might still be free. He might be sleeping now, in a room above a forge in Scotland, his head on Rosa's breast, her arms around him, her breath soft on his forehead.

What was it they said? No good deed goes unpunished?

He found he was smiling in the darkness, in spite of the tears that wet his cheeks. He deserved to die for the men and women he'd betrayed, for the names he'd written in that black book of death and – most of all – for what he'd tried to do to Rosa. But instead he would die because of his pity for Minna.

He wanted to laugh. But if he did, he might begin to sob – and never stop.

Rosa surfaced out of a raw, painful dream of Luke's arms and his lips and his skin against hers. She lay for a moment, gasping, her skin shivering with the memory of his touch.

With a sudden sharpness she remembered the first time he had taken her in his arms in the stables and she had run, hot with fear and full of shame at the gulf between them, the gulf of class and magic and money.

How absurd it all seemed now, like the scruples of another girl, in another time. Why had she cared? She had had so much – and all she had thought of was what might be taken away: her reputation, her virtue, her good name.

Now all that was gone – and she could not have cared less. And she would have traded it all again, a thousand times over, for one last chance to hold Luke, to tell him that she loved him.

All those hours they had spent together, all those nights in his arms and days on the road, and she had never said what was so painfully clear and urgent now.

'I love you.' She spoke the words aloud, not caring if

anyone heard, not caring what Sebastian thought. 'I love you. You will not die. I won't *let* you die.'

The words sounded painfully loud in the small room and suddenly she could not bear to lie still any longer. She got up, pushing the hair off her face and feeling the ruby necklace bite into her skin.

At the window she pulled back the heavy velvet drapes. It was evening. She had slept the whole day through and now the sun was setting across the Downs. She stood holding on to the metal bars, feeling their cold strength and the spells that ran through and through them.

'*Ábíeteaþ!*' she whispered, and then louder, '*Ábíeteaþ!*' But they did not break. They did not even shiver in their frames. Abandoning magic, she climbed on to the window seat and pulled at them with all her strength, bracing her feet against the wooden shutters and feeling the muscles in her arms and back strain and crack with the effort. She heard the threads of Mrs Cleave's borrowed dress snapping across her shoulders, and when she stopped and put her finger to the seam beneath her arm, there was a hole.

'Rosa?' There was a sound outside the door, a small voice, uncertain and full of doubt. 'Is that you? Are you awake?'

'Cassie?' She turned and jumped down from the window seat, her bare feet making a soft thud on the thick carpet. 'Cassie, is that you?'

The door handle turned and Cassie stepped into the room.

'Cassie!' Rosa hurried across to take her hands. Cassie's beautiful blue eyes were red, as if she had been weeping, and her lids were puffy. 'Are you all right?'

'Rosa!' Cassie's voice broke with a sob, but she smiled. 'It's absurd that *you* should ask me that! I am . . . I'm so . . . I can't tell you how sorry I am. I don't know what to do – Sebastian has threatened me with all sorts of awful revenges. He doesn't know I'm here but—'

'Oh, really?'

They both turned, Cassie's sightless eyes flickering towards the sound, Rosa's towards the shadow that darkened the doorway. It was Sebastian, shaking his head.

'Don't be a fool, Cassandra. And don't abuse the freedom I give you. What is given can be taken away.'

'How dare you call me a fool.'

Cassie looked very small, facing Sebastian. Rosa was reminded, painfully, that she was only a girl, not even fifteen years old. She was no match for Sebastian – physically, magically or legally. Sebastian smiled unpleasantly, but Cassie smiled back, and Rosa saw, suddenly, the strength that lay beneath Cassie's soft face. Cassie might be just a girl, but she was a Knyvet.

'I see more than you think,' she said, and there was something hard and taunting in her voice. 'Don't you want to know what I see?'

Sebastian gave a snort.

'Not particularly.'

He turned on his heel to go.

'I see you, brother dear. I see your corpse.'

Her voice was not loud, but the words fell clear and separate like stones into a well – and full of a heavy weight. In spite of herself, Rosa shuddered as the soft, childish voice uttered those cold words, like a promise.

'You've been prophesying doom since you could talk,' Sebastian said loftily, but he turned back, his hand on the door frame, and Rosa could see the vein that beat in his throat above the starched collar. 'Aren't you bored of it yet?'

'You can scoff,' Cassie said. 'In fact, I'm sure you will. If it's my curse to know the truth, it's your curse not to recognize it.'

'Death is the one prophesy you can make rather safely, don't you think?' Sebastian drawled, but he swung his watch chain with a savage, nervous energy. 'Since it comes to all of us in the end. Perhaps that's why you're so fond of trotting it out.'

'Let her go.'

'Why should I, since according to you, I can't change my destiny?'

'You can't. But you can change how you're remembered.'

'Good God,' Sebastian snapped. 'Please stop imagining that I *care*.'

There was a sudden spitting crackle in the air, magic against magic. Rosa felt it, as thick and heavy as the atmosphere before an electrical storm, with the same sense of menace. Cassie's face was flushed and her breath came quick, but Sebastian's pale countenance never changed, only the muscles of his jaw tensed for a moment and then released.

Cassie fell back, gasping, on to the window seat behind her, and Sebastian swung around with a laugh, kicking the door closed behind him. They heard his footsteps up the corridor and the dull thunk of the baize door slamming shut. Cassie sat hunched and white. Her hands were trembling and there was sweat on her forehead.

'Cassie, are you all right?' Rosa knelt at her feet, worried by the girl's white, pinched face. 'What happened?'

'Nothing,' Cassie gasped, but her voice was hoarse, as if she had screamed herself silent. She tried to smile. 'Nothing. I'm all right.'

'Was it true what you said?' Rosa's heart was beating fast and shallow. 'About Sebastian. About – about his death?'

'It was true.' Cassie's small face was very pale, and there was an unhappy line between her brows. 'I've been dreaming about it.'

'Wh-when does it . . . happen?'

'I don't know. But it can't be long. He's a young man in my dreams. I see the house in flames – and Sebastian too.'

'And . . .' *And me?* she wanted to ask. Did she live, or did she die alongside Sebastian? But somehow she could not bring herself to utter the words.

'Don't.' Cassie laid her small, fine-boned hand on Rosa's strong, burnt one. 'I know what you're thinking. Don't ask me. It's better not to know too much.'

'Cassie, *help* me,' Rosa begged. 'Please. I know Sebastian is your brother, but he will kill me – you know that, don't you? Please, help me get this collar off. Help me get away – I can take you with me, if that's what you're worried about. But I must get away – Luke will die if I don't.'

'I can't.' There were tears in Cassie's bright-blue eyes, and she shook her head, her white-gold plait snaking across her shoulders as she did. 'I would if I could, but I can't. Please believe me. My magic doesn't lie that way – I'm not like you and Sebastian, I can't cast spells or do anything useful. I can only see – inside people's heads, into their future. My power is knowledge – that's all. You saw me before – I'm no match for Sebastian. I never have been.'

'Then your mother,' Rosa said desperately. 'She would help me, wouldn't she?'

'I . . .' Cassie took a breath. Her hand tightened on Rosa's and then she let go and stood restlessly, pushing past into the centre of the room. 'I don't know, Rosa. I truly don't.'

'But she helped me before – she healed me, didn't she? Surely – if she knew the truth—'

'I don't know,' Cassie repeated unhappily. 'It's hard to explain. Perhaps . . . perhaps you should meet her.'

'Perhaps I should.' Rosa stood too. She smoothed down her threadbare skirt, feeling the thin limp cotton beneath her palm, and the stains: crusted mud, mildew streaks from the cellar floor, the spattered slush of the alley. She knew the dress must smell, too: the stink of wear and sweat

284

and fear. There were dresses in the wardrobe; silk and satin, lawn and muslin. But she wanted to face Sebastian's mother like this, with the evidence of her son's crimes before her eyes.

'I'm ready,' she said. Cassie took a deep breath.

'Very well.'

Luke lay in the darkness with his eyes closed, counting the bells that tolled out the hours from the church on the far side of the Thames. He had no idea if it was morning or evening, but he'd heard it toll six times soon after he woke first, and now as it began to ring again he counted out the strokes.

One . . . two . . . three . . . four . . . five . . . six . . .

He had been here twelve hours, with no candle, no water, no food. Was this the plan then? No execution. No trial. Just a slow painful death by thirst and his corpse slipped into the water as the tide was on the turn.

Rosa . . . Her name was like a thirst on his tongue. He let his dry, cracked lips shape the words in the darkness, the whisper hoarse and sibilant in the locked dark room.

'*Rose . . .*'

The door was locked, but Cassie put a hand above the door frame, feeling for something, and drew down a key and fitted it into the lock.

'Mama,' she said as she turned the key, knocking with her free hand. 'Mama – may I come in?'

There was no answer and Cassie sighed.

'Mama, I'm bringing someone to see you. It is Sebastian's . . .' She stopped, biting her lip and then finished. 'It is Rosa. Sebastian's fiancée.'

The door opened.

Inside it was darkness and for a moment Rosa quailed at the thought of going in there, into the stuffy blackness, where that wild, black-haired witch was waiting.

'*Coward*,' she whispered in her head, but the word reminded her of Luke, and it gave her courage. Luke was no coward, whatever he thought. Perhaps neither was she.

Nevertheless she wished that she could cast a witchlight as she stepped over the threshold and into the velvet black interior.

It was not quite dark, she realized as her eyes adjusted to the dimness. There was a fire in the grate and, as her eyes became accustomed to the dark, she could see a shape crouched over it – a woman, squatting on her heels with long black hair dripping between her knees. Her face was a pale skull in the flickering light, the eyes nothing but dark holes.

'Mama . . .' Cassie said. She shut the door and locked it behind them. 'Mama, this is Rosa.'

'Rosa . . .' The woman's voice was hoarse and cracked. Her eyes glittered as she looked steadily at Rosa. 'I remember you.'

'You saved my life,' Rosa whispered.

'I saved you for the cage,' the woman said. She rose and

walked across the hearthrug to where Rosa stood, trying not to show her fear. She reached out, her arm white as bone, and touched the ruby at Rosa's throat. 'He is bleeding you. And you are letting him.'

Rosa swallowed, her throat dry and hoarse. 'Ma'am, you helped me once before – won't you help me again?'

'Help you?' Her eyes flickered up to Rosa and there was a crafty look in them. 'Why should I help you?'

'Because we are both caged. Because I want to get free . . . There's a man –' she spoke fast, before she could regret what she was about to say, '– a man that I love. He is the one I want to spend my life with – not Sebastian.'

'Help you?' The woman began to laugh, a hoarse cackle. 'Help you cuckold my son? Help you disgrace my name?'

'*Your* name?'

'Why not? I am a Knyvet, after all.'

'But . . .' Rosa put her hands to her face. The woman turned away, indifferently, and Rosa sank on to the ottoman at the foot of the bed, watching her.

Suddenly, to Rosa's horror, she put her hand towards the fire and picked up a red-hot coal in her fingers. She turned back and flicked it towards the bed. Rosa gave a gasp and jumped up to stamp on it, before she realized her feet were bare. She looked around for a book, a rug, anything, but by the time she turned back the coal had burnt out, leaving a dark weal on the floorboard.

Rosa let her breath out in a ragged trembling rush. And as she sank back on to the ottoman she noticed something,

something she had not noticed before in the darkness. The boards and the rugs in the room were pitted and spattered with black welts, the twins of the one left just now by the burning coal. The painted skirting boards were disfigured by little smoky smuts, patches where the paint had bubbled as a coal burnt out against the wood. Even the curtains had patches and holes where the flame had caught at their foot and been beaten out in time.

The woman crouched at the hearth watching, her eyes glittering, and she smiled, so that Rosa saw her bared teeth beneath her thin, bloodless lips. The resemblance to Sebastian was suddenly marked – and terrifying.

'Get out,' the woman snapped, and Rosa saw that her fingers were spitting sparks, that there was smoke coming from beneath her nails. When she opened her mouth to speak, there was smoke on her breath. 'Get out.'

'Come, Rosa,' Cassie whispered. 'There is no dealing with her when she's like this. We will come back another day. Next week perhaps.'

Another day! Next week! Rosa's heart filled with despair. In another day, another week, Luke might be dead – and she might be married to Sebastian, or dead herself.

'Please!' she begged the woman, pulling her arm out of Cassie's tugging fingers. 'Ma'am, I beg you. I know he's your son, but can you countenance this? A woman married against her will to a husband she does not want?'

'Get out!' the woman screamed, and the room began to fill with smoke.

'Rosa, we should go,' Cassie said. Her voice was shaking. She opened the door and pushed Rosa into the corridor, coughing against the smoke. Then she slammed the door shut and locked it from the outside.

For a moment Rosa could not speak, she was too horrified by what they had seen.

'I'm sorry,' Cassie said. She opened the door to Rosa's room and pushed her gently inside. 'I didn't think . . .'

'What – what's wrong with her?' Rosa sank on to the bed. Was this her future if she stayed here?

'They say . . . they say she is mad.' Cassie's voice was a whisper. 'But I think it is something more than that. Something else. Her magic is black and uncontrollable. It's a kind of curse, I think. She wasn't always like this – she was very beautiful when she was young. But she did something unforgivable, I'm not sure what. It was before I was born. My father locked her up here and he tried to contain her magic.'

She stood and walked carefully to the dressing table, then felt her way delicately to a miniature that was hanging between the two windows, taking it gently from its hook.

'I am told that this is a portrait of her when she was twenty-one.' She held it out to Rosa, and Rosa looked down at the portrait in its gilded frame. It showed a woman – astonishingly beautiful – her ebony hair piled high on her head. She was dressed in walking clothes and there was a little white-haired boy on her lap – Sebastian perhaps?

Her face was a china oval, her eyes large and lustrous,

but she was not smiling, and there was something hard about her face, something that reminded Rosa of Sebastian. It was not a pretty face – it was too uncompromising for that. Her lips were set firmly, and the artist had caught the light that burnt in her eyes, as if there was a flame inside, waiting to consume her from within.

No, it was not a pretty face. But it was a remarkable face; the face of someone who would burn bright and fierce.

There was something in her hand, something that caught the light and threw it back at the artist, and Rosa held the portrait closer, trying to see what it was.

'What is it she's holding?' she asked Cassie, and then blushed, realizing what she'd said. 'I'm sorry – I forgot you can't . . . It doesn't matter – it looks like a cane, but it's familiar somehow. That's why I wondered.'

'There's no need to be sorry,' Cassie said lightly. 'I know the cane you mean. It is familiar because it is the same as the one Sebastian has now. With the head of a silver snake eating its own tail. I used to play with Mama's when I was a child – I loved to run my fingers over the snake, feeling it twist and turn.'

'But . . .' Rosa stopped. She was trying to remember where she'd heard that phrase: the snake eating its own tail. She remembered Sebastian saying, *'It was my father's . . . I would not lose it for the world.'* But someone else had described a cane so similar . . . someone who could not have seen it. An ebony cane with a head of silver in the

290

shape of a twisted ouroboros . . .

Luke.

It was like a cold touch down her spine.

She remembered his voice in the forest night as they lay huddled in each other's arms. She remembered him describing the witch who had come to his parents' house in the depths of the night and killed them both, so that the blood ran down the walls while he huddled beneath the settle and saw only the snake's-head cane rolling towards him.

It did not make sense. Nothing made sense.

'But – but Sebastian said . . .' She swallowed, her throat too dry to speak, and then tried again. 'Sebastian said the cane was his father's.'

'I said the same *as* his cane,' Cassie corrected. 'Not the same cane. They were a pair – her wedding gift to him. Sebastian has my father's cane now. My mother's – I suppose it is still in her room.'

The blood beat in Rosa's ears. *She did a terrible thing . . . It was before I was born . . .*

'Rosa?' She heard Cassie's voice as if from very far away. 'Rosa, are you quite well? You sound—'

She managed to shake her head, feeling the exhaustion run through her muscles like water.

'I'm very tired. I need to rest – to think . . .'

Luke.

19

'*Luke!*' The voice was a hiss, like the sound of a snake spitting, and for a moment Luke thought he had imagined it, that it was all part of his dream: the twisting, silver snake, poised to strike, Rosa with her hands outstretched and the snake wrapped around her throat, hissing, hissing...

'*Luke!*' It came again, a sibilant whisper in the dark. He scrambled to his feet, looking wildly about. The crack of light was gone from beneath the door and he had no way of knowing where he was in the darkness. He put a hand in front of his face and felt nothing.

'Luke! Are you in there?' The sound was slight, but in the silence it bounced off the bare walls, filling his cell with its whispers.

'Yes!' he called, his voice shaking. 'Who are you?'

'It's me, lad.' A different voice: deeper, louder, less afraid. One that made his heart leap into his throat and his pulse quicken. One that made him want to fling himself against the door.

'Uncle?' he called back. He could tell where the voices were coming from now. William's deep, sure voice was easier to place than the first echoing whisper, and he felt his way across the dark space to the direction of the sound. The brick walls were cold and damp to his touch, until he came to a metal door. 'William!' He wasn't sure whether to sob or laugh. 'What are you doing here?'

'We've come to get you out.' There was a grim purpose to his voice. 'Stand back.'

Luke heard a scraping from the outside, as if something were being forced into the crack of the door. Then there was a crunching screech, metal on metal, and he heard William's desperate groan as he heaved with all his strength.

'Shove the blocks in, there's a good lass.'

A good lass? Luke's heart leapt. It couldn't be . . . Rosa?

There was a thud as wooden blocks were forced into a narrow gap and then another shrieking crunch as William put his crowbar to the gap once more. Then with a suddenness that made him almost jump out of his skin, the thick metal hinges gave with a shrieking bang and the door crashed backwards on to the concrete floor.

Outside, in the dim light of a single lantern, William and Minna stood, both of them grinning from ear to ear.

Minna. Luke's crushing disappointment was swiftly followed by shame, that he could feel so, when he should have been thanking her with all his heart for freeing him.

'Minna. Uncle.' He staggered forward on shaky legs and fell into his uncle's strong arms, feeling the tears come hot to the back of his eyes as he leant on his uncle's hard shoulder and felt his hand clap him firm on the back, holding him as if he'd never let go.

'My God, thank you – you don't know . . .' His voice cracked and he couldn't carry on.

But William was shaking his head, his face grim.

'I can imagine, lad. But come on. We've got to get out of here before Leadingham comes back.'

'He's in league with Knyvet,' Luke gasped as William shouldered the crowbar and pulled his muffler over his face. He flung another one to Luke. 'All this time.'

'Minna told me.' William nodded at Minna, standing in the corner of the abattoir. She tossed her head.

'Don't I get a kiss for being yer knight in shining armour?'

'Thank you.' He moved across to where she was standing, but he didn't kiss her. Instead he put his arms around her, feeling the sharp edges of her limbs, her cheekbone hard against his chest. 'I'm sorry, Minna. In the Cock, I didn't mean—'

'Yes, you did. And I deserved it. But c'mon. We ain't got time to stand here gabbing.'

She grabbed his hand, her fingers thin and wiry in his, and pulled him towards the door where William was standing.

'Come on,' William said. He turned towards the door to the street, his hand outstretched for the latch.

Then everything happened very quickly.

As he put his hand out there was a sudden rush, the door flung open and a man came barrelling in.

He had a club of wood in both hands, held high above his head, and before William could do so much as cry out, he brought it crashing down.

William fell to the floor with a thump and blood began to pool around him.

Luke froze in horror. He wanted with all his heart to run to William and gather him up. But the man stood over his prone body, the club in his hand. He was wearing a hood and muffler, but Luke knew who it was before he looked up, pulling away his scarf.

'Hello, Luke.'

It was Leadingham.

'You bastard,' he managed, though his voice was choked and raw with fear for William. 'What did he ever do to you? It was me you wanted. Not him.'

'He got in the way,' Leadingham said flatly. 'There's no more morality to it than what happens to a man who steps out in front of a galloping horse. Don't look at me like that, lad. If you do something stupid, you may get it in the neck. That's all there is to it.'

'I'm not your lad.' Luke's voice shook with rage. He looked to where the butcher's knives stood against the wall, great heavy things in wooden slots in the butcher's block.

'Give up,' Leadingham said flatly. 'Give yourself up and

I'll get a doctor here; maybe it's not too late.'

For a minute Luke wavered. He was within reaching distance of the knives. But was it worth it – to carry on fighting and bleeding and hurting, and to risk William's life? It was true after all; he had betrayed his oath. He had betrayed the Brothers. He'd known the price he would pay before he did it, so why was he trying to wriggle out of paying it now?

'Come on, lad . . .' Leadingham said warningly. 'Your uncle's bleeding to death while you tap yer foot. You ain't got long to think about this.'

Luke put his hands to his head. He just needed a minute to *think*. But all the time, William was lying on the cold stone floor, the blood black and glinting around his head.

'Luke!' Leadingham snapped. 'Come on, lad, this is your last chance. I'm running outta patience. If you want your uncle to live . . . I'll throw in the girl's safe passage too, for good measure, so make up your mind before I run out of goodwill. Five. Four—'

'Oh, shurrup,' Minna growled from behind Luke. 'Luke, don't listen to 'im. He knows full well we ain't never getting out of here. He can't afford for us to blab what we seen.'

'Shut up, you little bitch!' Leadingham snarled, but it was too late. Luke saw that what Minna had said was true. It was not just William's life ticking away. Either he fought, or they *all* died.

He took a step towards the butcher's block and grabbed a knife.

Leadingham's wrinkled brown face split into a great, wolfish grin, and Luke saw that he was in some perverse way *pleased*, that he had known it would end like this, that for all his protests he had *wanted* Luke to fight, to die like a man.

'So that's how it is then, is it?' He let his club drop to the floor and pulled a knife from a sheath at his belt. It was a long wicked thing, sharpened to a stabbing point. Luke looked down at his own knife, grabbed at random from the block. It was a skinning knife, long and curved, sharpened along the blade for slicing, not stabbing. But it had a point, albeit a blunt one, and it would slice a tendon, or an artery, or cut a throat as well as any.

Leadingham crouched with his blade held out in front of him, and Luke was reminded of that night, months before, when Leadingham had taught him how to wield a knife.

Pulmonary artery, kidney, Achilles . . . Stick 'em as hard and fast as you can, and get out.

The words rang in Luke's head as he circled cautiously in the lamplight, watching their shadows dance against the wall, watching John Leadingham's little grinning face opposite him, his eyes glittering like polished stones in the candlelight.

He felt the knife slip in his sweating hand and the exhaustion in his shaking muscles. His heart beat fast and shakily, and he knew he didn't have much strength left. If he didn't bring this to a close quickly he would stand no chance at all.

He lunged, striking for Leadingham's knife arm, but the little man jerked his arm up, parrying the blow with his forearm before the blade could make contact, and then twisting in so that his own knife sliced along Luke's wrist and up his arm, through the material of his greatcoat.

Luke twisted himself away and staggered back, clutching with his free hand for the place Leadingham had hit. For a minute he felt nothing at all. And then the spreading warmth of blood blossomed sticky beneath his palm and he heard the first *splat* as a fat drop fell on the floor.

They carried on circling, the blood dripping steadily from Luke's arm. He tried to keep his knife hand up, to try to stem the flow, and to keep the blood from running over his hand and making it slip on the hilt of the knife. There was nothing he could do about his sweating palms, but it would be fatal to add blood to the mix.

'Give it up, lad,' Leadingham said, and his voice was that hoarse, friendly rasp that Luke had known since his childhood. It was a voice that had croaked out songs and nursery rhymes, had joked and praised and taught. It was hard to remember that this circling figure was trying to kill him, and not just teasing him in play as they'd done so often. Could he really do it? Could he kill Leadingham, a man who'd dandled him on his knee and slipped him pear drops before bed?

A man who's trying to kill you.

298

Out of the corner of his eye he saw Minna pressed against the wall, her eyes fierce with hate, and it came to him that it should have been her, here, wielding the knife. She would've killed, stuck it home with a good will. She was more of a fighter, more of a man than he'd ever be.

Leadingham struck, taking advantage of his distraction. The knife flashed before Luke's face, going for his throat, and he was grappling for Leadingham's arm, trying to turn the blade away.

There was a long, long eternity as they both struggled, with no sound but their gasping breaths and the splat of Luke's blood on the floor, and then Luke's foot slipped in a splash of his own blood and his feet went out from under him.

He fell, taking Leadingham with him, his knife clutched to his breast. His head cracked on to concrete, sending a blaze of pain roaring through him, and then they were rolling in the blood and sawdust, locked in each other's arms, too close to stab. Luke was imprisoned in Leadingham's grip, and somewhere in between their two chests was his knife, but where?

There was a clatter as something fell to the floor; he could not see if it was his knife or Leadingham's, but there was something hard against his pelvis, something that felt like a hilt, digging into his gut, wedged between them.

He strained one hand down between their tight-locked bodies, trying to reach it, and then there was a sudden searing pain in his cheek and he pulled back, roaring with

299

fury, to see Leadingham laughing at him with bloodstained teeth.

'You bit me, you bloody animal!' Luke shouted, and Leadingham laughed again, Luke's blood running down his chin.

'All's fair in love and war, lad! There ain't no Queensberry Rules here!'

Through the hot, red haze of pain and rage, his hand closed on the knife. Leadingham pulled back to go for a punch and Luke brought it up, hot and slippery in his grip, and suddenly the point was at Leadingham's throat.

Leadingham went very still. He was on top of Luke, but his right arm was trapped beneath Luke's spine, and his own knife was far away across the floor.

'Go on then, lad,' he whispered. 'What are you going to do?'

'I'll kill you!' Luke panted. There was blood in on his face and in his eyes. He felt the tearing of his own heart and breath, and the force of Leadingham's life pounding through the body pressed against his own. 'I'll kill you, you bastard!'

'Go on then!' Leadingham snarled. 'Do it, lad! Don't just lie there prating at me. *Do it!*'

Luke clenched his fingers on the knife.

Do it. *Do it.*

Leadingham's face above his, his eyes bright with life and the thrill of the fight.

His heart pounding next to Luke's.

The heat of his breath on Luke's face. His voice in his ear.

'*Do it!*'

The point of Luke's knife was against Leadingham's throat – and he could not do it. He could not drive it home.

He shut his eyes. He gritted his teeth . . .

And then suddenly there was a deafening crack and Leadingham's body jerked down on top of his, driving all the breath out of him.

Luke opened his eyes wide, panicking.

Leadingham lay on top of him, heavy and limp. The tip of Luke's knife had gone clean through his throat.

Above them both stood Minna, a club in her hand, and her face was white as bleached bone.

'I done it, Luke,' she whispered. 'Gawd help me, I done it.'

She let the club fall from her hand with a crash, and fell to her knees in the blood and the muck.

'I killed him.'

20

Luke pushed with all his strength and the heavy, limp body of Leadingham rolled off him and fell to the concrete floor with a thud. He struggled to sit up, but as he did so he felt a sharp stabbing pain in his upper chest, and when he looked down he was covered in blood. His own, or Leadingham's?

At first he wasn't sure, but when he pulled open his shirt, he could see no breaks in his own skin, just a huge spreading bruise across the right side of his chest, below his shoulder. He put his hand to his ribs; something creaked ominously and it hurt to breathe.

For a minute he could not work out what had happened. Had Leadingham hit him? But when? Then he realized – the knife that he'd held in his right hand must have been driven back against his own body by Leadingham's weight. The hilt had smacked into his chest with all the force of

Minna's blow, driving the blade through Leadingham's throat and breaking his own ribs.

He drew an experimental breath. It hurt. But not so much that he couldn't stand.

He dragged himself to his feet and staggered past John's sprawled body, past Minna slumped white-faced and frozen where she had let the club fall, to where William lay on his side in a pool of thickening blood.

'William!' he croaked, falling to his knees at his side. 'Uncle!'

'Luke . . .' It was a whisper, the smallest, softest whisper, so different from William's deep, booming voice that it brought a sob to Luke's throat, but his uncle was alive – and that was all that mattered.

'Uncle! Oh, thank God, thank God . . .' The words tumbled out and he was crying, the tears falling hot on William's shoulder and arm, but he did not care. He bent and kissed his uncle's stubble-rough cheek, feeling William's breath come faint against his own blood splashed face.

'You'll be all right, you understand?' He blinked furiously against the blurring tears. 'I'll get a doctor. Minna will stay with you, won't you, Minna? Won't you!' he shouted, when she did not respond, and she jumped, and stumbled across the floor to kneel beside them.

'A'course. I'm sorry Luke, I can't . . . I didn't . . . Oh God, I killed him. I killed a man.'

'Listen, stay with William while I go for a doctor.' He

tried to stand, his rib creaking painfully, but he felt something pluck at his hand as he did, and he looked down to see William shaking his head, the smallest movement, but just visible in the gloom.

'No . . .' It was a croaking whisper, barely audible. 'Don't go.'

'I must.' It broke Luke's heart to try to pull his fingers from his uncle's grip, but he had to, he had to try to get help. But William only closed his eyes, and held fast.

'I'm dying, Luke . . .' His breath wheezed, painful and shallow. 'You don't . . . don't recover . . . wound like this. Stay wi' me.'

'No!' It broke out of him like a shout, a cry of sheer agony in the echoing warehouse. For a minute all he could think of was Rosa and Sebastian's mother, and he longed to have even an ounce of her power to bring someone back from a mortal injury. Surely, *surely* if William could hold on for just a few hours longer . . . 'William, no! For Christ's sake, please. Please, you can't do this . . .' There were tears in his eyes, running down his face, mixing with the blood and sweat. 'Please don't leave me, William.'

But William said nothing. He only lay, his hand in Luke's, his eyes closed, and there was an expression of peace on his face that Luke could hardly bear, for he knew that it meant that his uncle had given up, that he was no longer fighting, that his struggle was done.

'No!' he sobbed. 'God damn you, no! No!'

William's chest rose and fell, rose and fell.

'Let me go, Uncle,' he pleaded. 'Let me go for the doctor. Please, I'm begging you. Don't give up.'

But William lay in peaceful silence. Only the sound of his slow, shallow breaths, and his fingers clenched on Luke's, showed he was still alive.

'Let me go,' Luke begged again, but he did not move. He knew he would not move, could not leave his uncle like this, not without his blessing, and William would not give it now, that much was plain. He was almost beyond speech.

His blood was pooling warm and wet beneath his body, and his face had grown very white – even his lips were white. His hand in Luke's was cold – soft and malleable as clay.

'Good . . . lad . . .' His lips tried to form more words, but no sound came out, just the clicking of his tongue, as it tried to make the words.

'No!' Luke sobbed. 'No!'

There was nothing he could do but watch in the silence and the darkness as William's life slipped from his body and his fingers grew cold and limp in Luke's. The only sound was Luke and Minna's sobs, and the almost imperceptible flutter of William's breath, growing fainter and fainter . . . and then at last there was just Luke and Minna, and William was gone, his unblinking eyes fixed on some point beyond them both.

Luke wanted to bellow and scream and rage, but he did

not. He knelt in his uncle's blood, on the abattoir floor, and his tears mingled with his uncle's spent life on the concrete slab. He knelt there while Minna's harsh sobs grew quiet and the only sound was of blood running into the central drain where it would flow into the sewers and at last into the great, dirty life-force of the Thames and away.

'Luke,' Minna croaked at last. 'Luke. What we gonna do?'

Luke looked up. The blood and tears had dried on his face leaving their stiff, salty tracks, he could feel it as he passed his hand across his skin, and he felt too the pull of the wound on his arm, where Leadingham had slashed at him, and the scrape and grate of the broken ribs.

'You need to get out of here,' he said hoarsely. 'Don't tell anyone what you did – understood? If people knew—'

'I don't want to stand trial for murder. But we can't just leave 'em – what're people gonna think?'

'They'll think they had a fight,' Luke said. He got to his feet, his ribs screaming in protest, and looked down at the two bodies on the floor. 'And in a way it's true. Maybe it's best we leave it at that.'

His heart was near breaking at the idea of leaving William lying in his own blood on the floor of the abattoir. Who would take care of him, wash his body, keep the vigil while he waited for burial? William had no one but him. But he couldn't stay.

'Listen, Minna.' He took her hands. 'There's something I've got to do. And I don't know if I'm coming back.'

'What d'you mean?' Her small, pale face was a mix of fear and outrage. 'You ain't gonna go after her, are you? Me and William, we didn't save you from the frying pan for you to throw yourself into the fire!'

'I've got to do it.' He felt tears prick again at the back of his lids, though he should have cried himself dry. 'I can't leave her. It's because of me she's here, they came for *me*, not her. If she hadn't come after me, looking for me, they'd never have caught her.

'What are you sayin' then?'

'I'm going after her. And I want you to go back to the forge and then tomorrow I want you to report William missing to the coppers.'

'Why?'

'So his body gets found. I don't want him to rot here or get given to the bodysnatchers for an unclaimed corpse. I want you to say that he'd had an argument with Leadingham, make up something – about me, if you like. And that he and Leadingham had agreed to have it out here, tonight. Then if –' he swallowed, his throat working painfully against the tightness, '– if I don't come back, will you see to it that he's buried, decent?'

'How? I ain't got no money!'

'There's money at the forge. In a strongbox under William's bed. It should cover the funeral and leave a bit besides. You can stay at the forge until I come back, you and the kids.'

'And if . . . if you don't come back?'

'Then the forge is yours. Find a man to work it. Charge him rent and use the money for yourself and the kids.'

'What if they kick me out? Yer uncle's mates? I've got no papers to show I've a right to be there.'

Luke bit his lip. They were wasting time arguing, when he should be trying to track down Rosa. But she was right.

He looked around the abattoir, searching for a piece of paper, anything, and his eye fell on a small desk in the corner by the door, scattered with receipts and orders. There was an accounts ledger open on the desk, and a spattered ink well. He strode across to it, ripped out a page, and began to write hastily.

He shoved the page at Minna, and she read haltingly.

'I do solmen . . . solemnly declare that I, Luke Lexton, give Minna Sykes permission to live at the Old Forge, Farrer's Lane, Spitalfields until such time as I return from my travels. Sig . . . signed Luke Nathaniel Lexton. I never knew yer middle name was Nathaniel!'

'Well, it is,' Luke said shortly. 'Now, I've got to go, Minna. Will you do it?'

He didn't trust her. He knew that it lay on a knife's edge as to whether she would take the money in the strongbox and blow it on opium, forgetting William's funeral, forgetting the kids in the workhouse, forgetting everything, until someone swindled the forge away from her and she died in the gutter.

But she looked up at him, nodding seriously, and he

308

wanted desperately to believe that this would be the making of her, the chance she needed. That she would get the kids back from the workhouse orphanage and make a go of it.

'I'll do it, Luke.' Her eyes were wide and limpid. 'You can trust me.'

He shut his eyes, praying to all the saints and gods and forefathers he had betrayed that she would keep her word.

Then he opened them and let his breath out.

'Thank you.' He kissed her forehead, the curls damp and cold beneath his lips. 'Goodbye, Minna.'

'I'm not sayin' goodbye, Luke, because it ain't goodbye. You got that?'

'Goodbye,' he said again. Then he tightened his muffler around his throat and walked out into the cold, frosted night.

In her room, Rosa paced backwards and forwards. There was a tray of supper on the floor, but the food was uneaten. Outside, night had fallen, but she had no means of lighting a candle and so she paced in the gathering darkness, as the snow fell.

Luke. Sebastian. The Black Witch.

Their names beat inside her head, making her dizzy.

Had Luke known about the cane, about Sebastian's link to his parents? Was this what he had meant that night above the forge, in each other's arms?

I gave up everything for you, his voice whispered in

her head, and she remembered again his face in the candlelight and the feel of his touch in the darkness. She remembered the ridges of the brand beneath her lips as she kissed his back and his shoulders, and the weight of his body on hers. *The Malleus, William, revenge for my parents – I gave it all up.*

He had seen Sebastian carrying the cane, he must have. And instead of pursuing the truth, he had chosen her. He had given everything up, just as she had for him. The past, the present, the unwritten future.

And now he was lying in some godforsaken cell in the Malleus's stronghold, awaiting his death, and there was nothing she could do.

She pulled again at the necklace round her neck, feeling it pinch against her windpipe and her breath grow short as she tugged at the constricting metal, and she remembered Sebastian's drawling: *You'll have a little more difficulty in cutting off your head, I imagine.*

The ring had been his grandmother's, he said. Was this, then, the secret of his family's power? Had they been bleeding their womenfolk all these years, taking their magic for their own through the power of this stone?

'You will not have mine . . .' she snarled, the words shockingly loud in the silence of the room. She did not know if Sebastian was listening, but as she pulled again she felt the necklace tighten around her throat, making her breath strangle and her vision break into stars, and then loosen, like a teasing threat leaving her gasping and furious.

310

'Damn you!' she screamed, her voice hoarse with fury. 'I would rather die, do you understand that? I will not be your wife! I will never be your wife!'

She picked up a chair and flung it at the tall, barred window with the glimmering snow beyond, but it only bounced harmlessly off the glass and fell to the thick, muffling carpet, and she felt as if the whole house were laughing at her, conspiring against her, suffocating her with its luxury and its taunting extravagance.

She could not escape. But she could find out the truth, at least. Luke had given up that chance, for her, and now they were both condemned. Luke would die at the hands of the Malleus, she had no doubt of that, and she would die before she married Sebastian – she had no illusions that the choice would come to that.

But before she died, she could at least do this. She could find out for Luke the truth of his parents' death, why they'd had to die, and at whose hand. Even if she could never tell him what she found, that one last thing, she could do for him.

But she could not do it without her magic.

Luke hitched a lift across London on the back of passing hansom cabs, holding on perilously above the rushing road until the cab turned off the route he wanted, or until the cabbie noticed the extra weight and chased him off with a curse and a crack of his whip. Then on to the next one, until that one too saw something amiss or a passing mate tipped the driver off. He earned himself a bleeding cheekbone from a cabbie who moved quicker than he did, and his rib was roaring with pain by the time he got to Knightsbridge, but at last he limped into Osborne Crescent just as the moon was rising high over Hyde Park, hoping to God that Becky was still awake, hoping to God that the new stable-hand wasn't.

He picked the lock on the mews gate easily enough and eased himself through the narrow gap into the cobbled yard, trying to walk softly in the shadows and not rouse the horses.

He had only the faintest recollection of which window was Becky's. He knew that Mr James slept to the front of the house, and the two maids at the back, and he thought the left-hand dormer was Ellen's, but he couldn't be sure. At last, realizing that he wasn't going to get any nearer deciding by dithering, he took a handful of pebbles and flung them up at the right-hand window.

They hit the glass and rattled back down, terrifyingly loud, and Luke waited, his heart in his mouth, but neither Becky nor anyone else came to the window. He tried again with a single stone in an effort to make less noise, the action giving his rib an agonizing twinge. But to his horror there was a dull crack and the pane split clear across.

There was a deathly silence. And then he heard the rattle of curtain rings and saw someone in a white nightgown and mob cap pulling up the sash.

'What in gawd's name . . . ?'

Becky. He felt almost weak with relief.

'Becky!' he shouted up in a hoarse whisper, and she looked down, blinking with astonishment in the moonlight.

'Who the hell . . . ?'

'It's me, Luke! Luke . . . ' He remembered just in time to give the false name he had used while he lived in Rosa's house. 'Luke Welling.'

'Luke!' Becky pulled a shawl around her shoulders, shivering in the night air, but she leant out of the window, smiling down at him. 'What are you doing back here? We heard as you'd gone back home, sick!'

'I did. I was. But R— Miss Rosa, do you know where she is?'

'She's missing, ain't you heard? Run off, or maybe kidnapped, some says. No one knows where.'

Did her family know she'd been found? Clearly the servants had not been told – and he could hardly go and quiz Rosa's mother. Would Sebastian have taken her to his house in London or his place in the country? Instinct told him the country, but it would be a long journey if he was wrong.

'Mr Alexis then, is he here?'

'He's gone down to Mr Knyvet's place in Sussex. You know, the gentleman Miss Rosa was to have married? He's been a marvel, I must say. Wouldn't hear of calling off the engagement, though there's not many would have stood by their fiancée like that, even if it weren't her fault. But no, he's made sure it's hushed up, told everyone she's gone to the country for her health, though he could've married a hundred other girls in the meantime, with his looks and money. But he'll have no other girl but her. It must be true love for him.'

She sighed romantically and Luke curled his fingers into a fist. But she had told him what he needed to know. If Alexis was down in Sussex, ten to one Knyvet and Rosa were there too. He only prayed he was not too late.

'I'm sorry to have disturbed you,' he whispered up to Becky. 'I'll go now, you be getting back to bed – you'll catch your death, and I don't want to get you into trouble. I'm sorry about the window. Tell 'em a bird flew into it, cracked the pane.'

'All right.' She looked down at him, twisting a lock of her hair round her finger. 'You always was a funny one, Luke Welling. Listen, now you're better, you ever come up west?'

He drew a breath, not wanting to lie, but desperate to keep her sweet and get her back to bed, happy and unsuspicious.

'Sometimes,' he lied. He tried to force a smile, though his face felt stiff as a mask and his rib was crying out with pain. 'Maybe. Why, is there a reason for me to come?'

'Could be.' She smiled down at him, her fingers twining and releasing, twining and releasing. 'Maybe a girl could be persuaded out for a cuppa, or a glass of ale, if a young man was to come calling.'

'I'll remember,' he said. 'I remember your afternoon off

is Wednesday, in't it? If I'm up this way on a Wednesday evening, I'll call for you, I promise.'

He could make that promise safely, he thought, with a pain in his chest that was not just from his rib. It was not likely he would ever see London again, let alone come up west on a Wednesday night.

'Good night, Luke Welling.' She smiled down at him, and then pulled down the sash and let the curtain swing back. He stood for a moment, waiting to be sure that she'd gone back to bed. Then he turned, but not back to the gate. Instead he went across to the stable.

There were new horses inside: a beautiful Arab in Brimstone's stall and a slender thoroughbred grey in Cherry's, shining in the moonlight like a ghost. But it was neither of these that he went for. It was Castor, the big bay gelding who had the stamina of the ox and a heart even bigger than his body. Castor gave a soft whickering neigh as he saw Luke and pushed his head eagerly over the stall door, shoving his whiskery nose into Luke's palm and butting him with his head.

A lump rose in his throat. Castor, who'd carried him so faithfully, through so much.

'I'm sorry, boy,' he whispered. 'I've got no sugar, but will you come? One last ride, eh?'

The horse threw up his head, for all the world as if he were nodding, and Luke slipped the bridle over his head and led him quietly from the stable, the saddle slung over his arm.

Outside in the lane, he saddled him up, and then he took one last look at the darkened house, pulled himself up into the saddle with a scream of protest from his injured rib. Then they were away, riding swift through the moonlit shadows and the cold, shifting fog.

21

'Yes, miss?'

The maid outside the bedroom door looked frightened, her face white and pale in the darkness. Rosa wondered what she'd seen in her time at Southing, what horrors the locked wing held.

'Would you light a candle for me?' she asked. 'I have no magic to strike a flame. And would you –' She swallowed, feeling the collar tight against her throat. 'Would you tell Mr Knyvet that I have thought long and hard, and would like to see him.'

Her pulse beat in her throat, against the collar's constriction. She could be wrong, horribly, fatally wrong. She had so little to go on, after all. And if she *was* wrong . . .

The candles flared up as the maid lit them, casting a golden, shivering light across the room. Rosa shut her eyes, the flames still burning against her closed lids.

317

If she was wrong, the fight would be lost a little earlier than she thought – that was all. It wouldn't change anything, not really.

She heard the spit of kindling in the grate and the roar of the draught as the fire began to draw.

'Will that be all, miss?'

'No.' She opened her eyes as the girl stood, brushing down her apron. 'Could you – could you bring me something to drink?'

'Of course, miss,' the girl whispered. 'Tea, miss?'

'No.' Rosa bit her lip, thinking of Alexis. Was he still here? Or had he gone back to London? 'No, brandy. Please.'

The girl curtsied and scurried away. When she was gone Rosa turned to the wardrobe in the corner, the wardrobe full of the dresses Sebastian had given her, the dresses she had scorned and refused to wear.

She took one of them down, a long slim dress the colour of old ivory in the light from the fire and the candles. It was hard dressing without a maid to help her, harder still with her clumsy, injured finger, but she was just putting her hair up in the mirror when a knock came again at the door. She drove the last pin into the heavy coil and turned to face the door.

'Come in.' The catch in her voice was slight and she clenched her fists, feeling the strangeness of the missing finger, a gap where something should have been. She would have whispered a spell to give herself courage – but she had no magic. She heard the words in her head, nonetheless, and perhaps it was her imagination, or perhaps just the comfort of a familiar mantra, but in the moment before the door swung open she thought she felt it: a prickle of bravery like a cool breeze across her skin.

It was Sebastian. He had a decanter in one hand and two brandy glasses in the other. He was dressed in faultless evening clothes, white tie and tails, and his white-gold hair gleamed like burnished silver in the candlelight, though a lock had come loose across his forehead. He bowed.

'You asked for me, my darling?'

'Yes.' She swallowed and forced her fingers to relax out of the fists she had made. Now was not the time to fight. 'I did.'

'You look . . .' There was something hungry in his blue eyes, a starved yearning so strong that even the candle flames seemed to quell and gutter as he crossed the threshold into the room. She would have taken a step back, but the dressing table was at her spine, and she could only stand straighter as he came towards her. 'You look . . . beautiful. Quite extraordinarily beautiful.'

His thin lips curved in that rare, true smile – not the mocking twist or the wolfish grin she had come to know, but the smile of the boy she had known as a child, and for a moment a look of pain crossed his face. She was not sure if it was the scar where she had cut him, or just her own apparition in the candlelight that caused it.

'Thank you.' She stood for a moment, feeling his eyes on

319

her naked throat and bare shoulders. Then she turned away, moving to the ottoman at the foot of the bed. 'Won't you sit?' He had already been drinking, she could see that in the too-careful way he set the decanter and the glasses on the table. He was not drunk, not yet, but she recognized from Alexis all too well that deliberately stilted movement, trying to hide the slurring of alcohol.

Sebastian waited for her to sit and then sat himself, in the armchair to the right of the fire.

'The maid said that you wished to speak to me.'

'I did. I do.' She swallowed again. 'Might I – might I have a drink?'

He nodded and poured her out a snifterful, and then one for himself.

'I want to make a toast.' Her face felt stiff as a mask. But when she raised the round, golden globe of brandy, her hand did not shake. 'To . . . to us.'

'To us?' He leant forwards, his eyes aflame with the candles and the fire and something inside, something that burnt and consumed him from within. 'Then you mean . . . ?'

'I will marry you.' She put the glass to her lips and watched as he drained his own and then put it down on the table between them. She set her full one next to his and he reached for her hands.

'Rosa, darling . . .'

She tried not to shudder at his touch even as she pulled away to pick up his empty glass.

'Won't you pour me another glass?' she asked. Sebastian gave a short laugh and let go of her fingers to refill the snifter.

'I didn't think . . .' He topped up the other glass and picked it up. 'You seemed so very . . .'

He stopped. She had rarely seen him at a loss and now he looked much younger than the man who had bargained with Leadingham in the alley, dragged her back to London, imprisoned her in this room.

'I love you, Rosa.' He leant forward and touched his hand to her face, cupping her cheek. 'I know you may find that hard to believe, but I do. I have never wanted anyone the way I want you.'

You want me because you cannot have me, you who have never been denied anything . . .

'And now you are mine,' he said, his voice soft and rough and full of a contained passion.

'We are not married yet,' she said with a shaking laugh, and she put the brandy to her lips and took a rash gulp, watching through the curved glass as he too raised his glass and drained it, wiping his lips with a laugh. He refilled without her suggesting it and threw it back again, and when he tipped his head back she saw the muscles of his throat move and flex as he swallowed.

So vulnerable . . .

He set his glass down on the table next to hers, with a clumsiness that made the glasses chink against each other, and she refilled before he could tell her not to.

'What made you change your mind?' he asked. She closed her eyes. *Mama. Alexis. Luke. Luke. Always Luke.* But she knew it would be fatal to speak his name.

'I don't know,' she said. 'Perhaps . . . perhaps the realization that I have no choice.'

'Ah, darling Rosa, don't be bitter.' He looked at her in the firelight, the flames softening the planes of his face from marble back to flesh. She sipped at her glass, staring into the flames, not looking at him, and he sighed and leant back in the armchair, warming the brandy with his palm. 'Did I ever tell you about my lark?'

'No.'

'I bought it from a bird-catcher when I was a boy, one of those men who walk about the country lane with their hats filled with wild singing birds, and it lived in a cage in my room and sang so beautifully your heart would break to hear it. Cassandra always nagged at me to free it, but I loved it too much. But finally we were going to India and I thought: why not? I can't take it with me, after all.'

'And did you? Free it, I mean?'

'Yes, I opened the cage door and it flew out of the sash window into the sunshine, singing with all its heart. But the next day I found it lying on the cobblestones of the stableyard, its innards spilt on to the ground, with the stable cat prowling around, defending its kill. My lark had grown soft in captivity, and trusting. When it had to fend for itself, it could not. I should have killed it in its cage, spared it those last moments of horror and pain.'

'But in exchange it had a moment's freedom.' She thought of the lark, its moment come at last, bursting from the bedroom window into the summer sunshine, spiralling to the blue sky. 'It had a moment's unparalleled joy.'

'Much good it did it, when the cat was pawing its entrails. No –' he took a gulp of brandy, '– I learnt my lesson that day. Some creatures are not meant to fly free. They are too beautiful, too fragile. Love can take many forms, Rosa. Sometimes that form is a locked door.'

I was raised in a cage, Rosa thought. *A cage of privilege and magic. And Luke opened the door.*

He had not just opened the door. He had smashed it with a hammer. He had tried to kill her – and it would always be between them: the shivering mirage of the death she could have had.

But he had saved her life too. He had given her freedom. He had kissed her, and loved her, and given up everything for her sake, and he would never be done repenting the mistakes he had made.

She thought of his gentleness and strength, of the hardness of his muscles and the softness of his skin. She thought of his body against hers in the warm bed of the forge at Langholm, and of his gasping cry in the silence of the night.

She knew she must hold on to that: that brief moment of unparalleled joy.

'I have one condition,' she said to Sebastian, watching his face carefully.

'What?' There was the smallest, slightest slur in his voice, and looking closer she saw that he was drunk now, really drunk. The brandy was whispering through his veins, turning his muscles to water and dulling his reflexes.

'Take off the collar.'

'No.' He shook his head. 'I'm sorry, Rosa. I can't.'

'I'm yours.' She forced herself to put out a hand, caress his cheek. 'What difference can it make now?'

'The day you swear to love, honour and obey me in front of a priest, that is the day I will take off the collar. Not before.'

Damn him. She shut her eyes, clenching her fists. She forced herself a smile.

'Then let us drink to that day.' She stood and held up her brandy glass. Sebastian looked up at her, his hair falling over his brow.

'Are you trying to get me drunk?'

'I've matched you drink for drink,' she lied. 'Are you saying a girl like me can drink you under the table? Come.' She would not drink to obedience, never to that. And there was little enough honour in what she was about to do. Instead she raised her glass. 'To love!'

He gave a laugh at that, short and bitter, and then heaved himself to his feet.

'Very well. To love!' He threw back the brandy, the whole brimming glassful. He must have had near enough half the decanter, she judged, watching him as he tried to set his glass back on the table, missed the edge, and then tried again, brushing her arm as he did.

And Rosa flinched.

She stilled, hoping Sebastian was too drunk to notice her reaction, but he did, and he laughed as he straightened.

'Kiss me,' he said.

She felt as if she were turned to stone. He stepped closer, put his hand to her face, his eyes cold and blue as moonlit snow.

'Kiss me,' he repeated, and though his voice was smooth, there was something beneath the surface that sounded to Rosa almost like a snarl.

His grip on her jaw grew tight, his fingers squeezing the flesh against her bone.

Rosa shut her eyes. She made herself small and still. *Luke*, she thought, remembering the softness of his lips, the arch of his throat in the candlelight. *Luke*.

Then she felt Sebastian's lips on hers, and he was not Luke, he never would be. His mouth was cold and hard, and she felt his teeth as he forced her lips apart.

'No,' she managed, the words muffled and twisted by his kiss. She put her arms up to his chest, feeling the hardness of bone and muscle beneath the pleated dress shirt as she pushed him away. '*No!* I'm sorry, I can't, I can't do this!'

Sebastian staggered back and grabbed at the fireguard to save himself from falling. For a moment he said nothing, he only stood, panting. Then he put out his tongue to lick a fleck of saliva from his lips and began to laugh wildly, holding himself up against the mantelpiece, his head flung back.

Rosa put her hands to the collar, feeling the metal ripple and flex beneath her fingers as it tried to tighten.

Please God, let me have guessed right. If it's Sebastian who controls this thing, Sebastian who takes my magic . . .

He was drunk, stumbling drunk. He could not control himself, let alone his magic. She dug her fingers beneath the necklace, into the soft flesh of her throat, feeling it tightening against her grip, and she pulled with all her strength and power.

'Stop that!' His voice was slurred, and he came stumbling across the carpet towards her, his eyes wild and pale with rage, his fingers outstretched. She could not take her hands from the collar, or risk suffocating, but she kicked out, kicking him hard in the stomach so that he staggered backwards into the coffee table, their brandy glasses skittering and smashing beneath their feet.

The collar was tight as a rope around her neck, only her frantic, scrabbling fingers buying her enough space to breathe. As Sebastian struggled to disentangle himself from the shards of wood and broken glass she pulled again.

A spell! I need a spell! She racked her brains, trying to think of something to break the hold, but nothing came into her head but nursery charms – for witchlight, luck, courage – the small folk-magics she had whispered before her magic had even come in. Nothing that could help her now.

Let go of me! she screamed inside her head, her throat too tight to form the words.

Her breath tore in her throat and the pressure on her windpipe was making her gag, but as she flung back her head, trying desperately to drag in a little air, she felt the metal slip beneath her fingers. For a minute she thought that it was her own grip giving way, and she sobbed out a despairing cry, but then she realized she could breathe, that she had dragged in enough oxygen to make that gasping, hacking noise. The collar was loosening.

'Bitch!' Sebastian growled. He was crawling towards her, the smashed glasses cutting his hands so that he left a trail of bloody handprints on the silk rug. Then he was at her feet, dragging himself upright using her skirts, even while she kicked out against him. He was past spells too – too drunk to speak, almost. She only felt his black rage boiling around her, smothering her in its grip, a blind directionless hate that wanted to crush and to kill, to smash her across the room and to grind her to the floor, all at the same time.

It seemed like an eternity that they struggled, but at last he was upright, at her throat, pulling at her hands, pulling them away from the collar, trying to wrest her fingers away from the metal. Rosa clung on, fighting against Sebastian's desperate strength.

'Let me go,' she managed, her voice a raven's croak.

'Never!' he screamed, his face so close to hers that she could feel the flecks of spit in his roar. And then his weight toppled her and they fell to the floor together. Sebastian landed on top and Rosa could not get upright, not without putting a hand to the floor, and she could not afford to let go of the necklace. Her hold was the only thing saving her from suffocation. Sebastian crouched over her, one knee braced against her ribs, pulling with all his strength at her grip on the collar.

And then it snapped.

Rosa felt it go, the jagged edge scoring the back of her neck as Sebastian staggered backwards, sprawling over the foot of the bed with the broken collar in two halves in his hands. He looked down at the broken pieces of metal and then up at her, his eyes full of a stupefied disbelief. And then, as Rosa raised her hand, feeling her magic flood through her like wine in her blood, something else came into his expression: fear.

'Rosa . . .' He tried to scramble to his feet, but he tripped, too drunk to steady himself. 'Rose – my darling—'

'Don't call me that,' she snarled.

'*Ábréoðe!*' he roared, and she felt his magic buffet her, but she flung the spell away before she had even time to think about.

'*Ádræfe!*' she shouted back, and he flew across the floor to slam against the wall between the two windows. There was a cracking thud as his head met the plaster, and a Ming vase on the dressing table rocked gently, but did not fall.

Rosa crouched, waiting for him to rise again. But he only lay, slumped against the skirting board, blood running from a cut on his temple. Was he alive?

'God forgive me,' she whispered, horrified by what she had done. But she knew in her heart that if the time came she would do it again. She had been fighting for her magic, for her life.

She felt the magic flowing through her bones and muscles. She closed her eyes and let it run to her fingertips, filling her with a wild, formless joy.

The necklace lay on the floor, its two halves winking in the candlelight. Rosa picked it up, weighing them in her hands, and then she rolled Sebastian on to his side, so that his hands were behind him. She picked up the collar and wrapped the broken halves around his crossed wrists, pushing them together with her mind and magic. The gold shivered beneath her finger, shrinking away from her touch as it melded into one so that he was bound, his hands clasped behind his back. She wasn't fool enough to think it would hold him for long – Sebastian knew the secrets of the jewel and she did not. But perhaps it would slow him for long enough to let her accomplish what she wanted to do.

She looked at herself in the mirror. There was a smear of blood on her cheekbone – hers or Sebastian's, she could not tell. But when she wiped it away, the girl that looked back at her from the glass might have been dressed for a ball or a dinner. Her throat was bare – no locket, no collar

– and the ivory lace dress fell in folds and ruches to the ground. She pinned her hair again, where a lock had come loose in her struggle.

Then she took a breath and turned to open the door.

Luke held on to Castor's mane with numb fingers. It was snowing, the flakes driving into his face as they galloped through the night, and he had no gloves. His rib screamed with the pain of the long ride through the darkness, but he did not dare stop.

Behind him lay the Malleus, who might even now be sending Brothers out to find out why Leadingham had not returned. When they found Luke's cell empty, they would start the pursuit. Whether they found him depended on one thing: if Leadingham had told anyone about Sebastian. If anyone knew that Leadingham had traded Rosa for a sack of cash and the promise of cooperation, they would know where to find him.

He could only hope that Leadingham had kept his treachery silent, but he would not know for sure until he heard hoof-beats on the road behind and felt a knife in his back.

Castor was tiring, he could feel it in the horse's lolloping gait and the way he had begun to stumble in the snow. Clouds of white came from his flared nostrils and his flanks were hot and wet with sweat beneath Luke's legs. But he could not allow the horse to rest.

'Come on, boy,' Luke whispered, his teeth gritted against

the pain of his rib. 'Come on. Black Bess carried Dick Turpin from York to London in a single night, I'm not asking the half of that. Fifty miles – that's all I ask. You can give me that.'

And then? But he couldn't think about what lay at the end of his journey – the high walls of Southing, the wreathing web of spells. Rosa. He would think of Rosa – and he would pray that she was still alive.

The room was in almost complete darkness as Rosa stepped inside, but there was a fire in the grate and as her eyes adjusted she could see a woman lying on her side on the burn-spotted hearthrug, staring into the flames. She said nothing as Rosa entered, closing the door behind her with a quiet click. Only the fire flared up, the logs spitting and crackling, fed by the woman's magic.

'Mrs Knyvet? Are you awake, ma'am? It's me, Rosa.' Rosa spoke very quietly into the deep, rich darkness. The woman said nothing, she just sighed, and the flames in the grate gusted up and settled back. 'Do you remember? I came earlier. I am the girl . . .' She stopped. The girl Sebastian wanted to marry. The girl who kissed him. The girl who took his ring and slashed his face, and would not give in.

The woman didn't answer. Rosa walked into the darkness, feeling for a chair beside the hearth.

'I saw your picture. It was you, wasn't it? You were the one with the snake's-head cane. You murdered a couple, one night in Spitalfields, long ago. Do you remember?' She shivered, in spite of the heat from the fire. She could feel it flaring in the grate, flickering with the woman's uncertainty and suspicion.

'What do you want?' the woman said, and her voice was bitter. 'Why do you come, raking up the past?'

'Why? Why *them*? Just a poor man and his wife, and his child who hid under the settle. You dropped your cane, he remembered it.' *He dreamt of it, every night, for fifteen years . . .*

'I don't remember,' the woman said sullenly. She did not look at Rosa, she only stared into the fire. 'Rich or poor, they all bleed red.'

Rosa shuddered.

'Lexton,' she managed, trying to push away the images that were crowding her head: a sobbing woman, a man bleeding his guts out on to the floor, a child beneath the settle, closing his eyes as the blood pooled on the flags . . . 'Lexton, their name was. Don't you remember?'

The woman said nothing at all. At last Rosa shook her head and got to her feet. She had tried, for Luke's sake she had tried, but she was not going to get an answer from this shell of a woman. And Sebastian might wake any moment and find her gone. She would be better off making her escape, trying to make her way back to London and free Luke from his prison cell. If he was still alive.

The thought almost made her choke, and for a moment she stood holding on to the door frame, steadying herself.

But before she could leave and close the door behind her, the witch-woman raised her head from the hearthrug. Her eyes glittered in the firelight.

'I wore black kid gloves,' she said, her voice hoarse and yet strangely excited, as if even now the memories thrilled, fifteen-years dimmed though they were. 'To hide the blood.'

'Why?' Rosa said, almost in spite of herself. She felt like stopping her ears and slamming the door and trying to expunge the memories of the dark firelit cave from her mind for ever. Part of her felt a desperate pity for the ruined creature crouched in front of the fire, and part of her could barely master her disgust for what she had done, and the still-vivid excitement of those memories. 'Why them?'

'They were enemies,' the woman said. She picked up a coal from the fire and poured it from hand to hand, the flames spitting as she did. There was a smell of burning flesh, and Rosa gagged and put a hand to her mouth. 'I did it for my husband, for my son. Outwith! He was no outwith. I could see in his eyes as he walked around the factory, asking his impertinent questions. He knew.'

Rosa's blood seemed to freeze.

'What did you say?'

'He knew,' she repeated sullenly. 'Knyvet laughed, said he was a poor fool of an outwith, and to let him write his stupid article; we would sue the publication and they would lose every penny. But he was no outwith. I don't know what he was – he was no witch either. But whatever he was, he *knew*. He could see the spells, the bindings – I

333

saw it in the way that he looked at the machines, at *me*.'

He knew. The words pounded in Rosa's head. He knew. As Luke had known.

'He was going to expose the conditions at the match factory,' Rosa whispered, 'wasn't he? And so you killed him.'

'No one is allowed to stand against us.' The woman flicked the coal at Rosa's feet, so that she had to jump back or risk being burnt. Then she picked up another, clenching it in her fist. When she breathed, smoke came from her lips. Rosa remembered Cassie's panic and she took another step back, into the corridor. She knew she had to slam the door, but she could not. She could not bring herself to do it, to trap the woman back into her dark prison cell, as she herself had been trapped just hours before.

'Mrs Knyvet, please, be calm,' she begged.

The woman looked up at her and there were flames in her eyes, flames as bright as gold that seemed to glow in the darkness.

'Calm?' the woman said. She laughed, a terrible sound that made Rosa think of someone screaming in pain.

And then she threw back her head and roared.

A wall of flame came blasting from her lips. Rosa smelt the stench of scorching wood, of burning skin and hair. She heard a scream – her own? And she flung every particle of magic that she possessed into a huge shield, trying to keep the flames inside the room, away from the corridor, away from her own skin.

Dimly, through the crackle of burning wood and the blaze of fire and smoke, she could see Sebastian's mother standing in the centre of the flames, and hear the scream of her laugh.

Oh God, what have I done! she thought.

She picked up her skirts and ran.

22

The snow was driving hard in Luke's face as he came over the top of the Downs and began the slippy, perilous descent to Southing village. He was exhausted and so was Castor. Neither of them would have lasted another five miles, but he did not need to travel five miles. The fingerpost said *Southing – 1¼ miles*.

Please, he found himself thinking, in time with Castor's plodding hooves. *Please. Please. Please.*

Please let him get there. Please let this night be over and the pain in his ribs cease. And above all – please let Rosa be alive. For all Sebastian's talk of marriage, Luke couldn't shake the suspicion that what he had in mind was a colder bed and a grave cloth instead of a bridal gown. He had tried to burn Rosa in the factory in Brick Lane. He wanted her, yes. But he could not afford for her ever to leave Southing. And there was only one sure way to accomplish that. If he married Rosa, it would not be for long.

Please . . . Oh, Rosa, wait for me. Stay alive . . .

And then, coming down the Beacon, he felt it, like a punch to the chest, a burning smack that made him catch at Castor's reins and sent the horse stumbling in the slushing snow. He caught himself and pulled Castor up, his heart beating fast and hard as they stood looking into the swirling snow.

There was nothing there, nothing but the darkness shadowed by the moon and the close-clustered trees that lined the road. But there was no mistaking what he had felt; a huge buffeting surge of magic, from somewhere close. And not just any magic – Rosa's. It burnt in his chest, like a brand in his flesh, and he knew that she was very near and that she was fighting for her life. But she was alive. And more than that – she had her magic back.

'Come on, boy!' He put his heels to Castor's side, kicking the poor, tired horse into a trot. 'Come on, we're nearly there. *Come on.*'

Wait for me, he thought grimly. *Hang on, Rosa. I'm coming.*

'Cassie!' Rosa screamed. She pounded against the green baize door, feeling the spells bend and groan beneath the onslaught, but not break. 'Cassie! The house is burning! Unlock the door! Get the servants out!'

Could Cassie hear her? She remembered the huge thickness of the door, its muffling spells. She felt a sob rise in her throat and then fought it down. *Cassie!* she screamed inside her head. But the only voice she heard was the one she longed to hear, but knew could not be real. Luke's.

Hang on, Rosa. I'm coming.

If only it were true. But he was in a cell in London. And unless she got out of here, he would rot there for ever.

There was a crash, breaking glass, and the reflection of flames flickered against the corridor wallpaper as the fire blazed higher, fanned by the fresh air.

She clenched her fists.

She *must* get out.

If only I had the Grimoire, she thought despairingly, and then she shook her head angrily. No. She didn't need the Grimoire any more than she needed the locket she had sold to Phoebe. Papa's love for her, her memories of him, none of that was in the locket, just like her childhood happiness was not in the bricks and stones of Matchenham. They were inside her. In the same deep well where her magic lay. Yes, she had thought of Papa as she traced the locket's curlicues with her fingertips, but it was not the source of her memories. It was just a prop, a crutch.

She remembered Mama's words to her when she was a little girl: *If you want something badly enough, if you will give enough of yourself, it will come.*

She ran back into the bedroom, past Sebastian, stirring

on the hearthrug, to feel in the pocket of her old, stained dress, where a scrap of paper lay. 'Charles Darwin, crossed with a potato,' Alexis had said, but to Rosa it would always be Papa, with his soft dark beard and his soft, dark eyes.

She touched her lips to the paper and held it in her hand for a long moment, and then she ran out into the corridor, to stand in front of the massive, spell-locked door.

'Ætýne,' she whispered, and then louder. '*Ætýne!*'

She clenched her fist around the scrap of paper, feeling it grow wet with her sweat. *I want this. I want to get out. I want to save Luke, and Cassie, and my own life.*

'*Ætýne!*'

She felt the flames at her back. They were creeping along the skirting board of the hallway now, licking at the floorboards.

She opened her hand and she flung the paper at the flames.

I will give you anything. Anything.

'*Ætýne!*' she screamed, her voice swallowed in the roar of the flames coming from Sebastian's mother's room.

And the door sprang open.

The house was quite dark, but the front door gave beneath Luke's stiff fingers and he stumbled into the vaulted, shadowy hallway.

It was dark, but not silent. He stood for a moment panting, expecting to hear running footsteps, servants. But nothing. Only the faint sound of pattering snow against the panes. And from above, something far more worrying. The sound of . . . could it be . . . flames?

The air smelt of smoke.

'Rosa!' he called, his voice shockingly loud in the echoing hall. The sound bounced back at him from the high stone ceiling: *sa! sa! sa!* 'Rosa!' he shouted again.

And then – from somewhere high above, he heard an answering shout.

'Luke?'

And then there she was – running along the upper landing and down, down, down the stairs, like a ghost in pale lace that fluttered in the smoky darkness. There were smuts on her face and her hair had come out of its pins and streamed out like flames in the darkness. Her magic blazed – so bright he would almost have shielded his eyes, except that he could not look away from her face.

'Rosa . . .' His voice was a croak, his throat suddenly tight with wanting and a desperate, painful relief.

'Luke! Is it really you? How? *How?*'

She came running into his arms, half laughing, half sobbing, and then her lips were on his, and her hands were at his face, kissing and then pulling back to look again, her fingers digging into his shoulders so hard it was almost painful, as if she couldn't believe he were really here, really in her arms.

He kissed her back, her lips, her throat, her temples,

everywhere his lips could reach, trying to ignore the roaring pain in his ribs. But he couldn't suppress a gasp when she flung her arms around him in a fierce embrace.

For a second the pain was so fierce he could hardly speak, and he knew from the way she fell back, her face white and horrified, that it must have shown in his face.

'S'all right,' he managed, putting a hand to where his rib clicked and ground. 'I'm . . . s'just a rib. Don't – don't crush it. I'm all right.'

'Let me heal you!' She put out a hand, but he shied away.

'Not now.' His breath was still coming quick with the aftermath of the pain. 'When we're away.'

'Away?'

'I've got Castor outside.'

'But – but, Luke, I *can't.*'

'What?'

'Cassie. She's upstairs. The house is burning.'

So it was true. He looked upwards.

'I must go and find her. I must!'

'She's a witch,' he said, and his voice sounded brutal in his own ears, but it was the truth, wasn't it? 'She can save her own skin.'

'She's *blind*, Luke!'

'So? She's still got magic.'

'The fire, it's my fault! You don't understand – I went to see Sebastian's mother – I left her room unlocked. It's her – she's burning the house and if Cassie dies, it's all my fault. I *have* to get her out. And the maids – we must warn them!'

He clenched his teeth, feeling the tiredness in his muscles and the scream of his rib. He'd come *so* far . . .

He thought of William, lying on the floor of the abattoir. He thought of all he had lost. He could *taste* the freshness of the air outside, the sweetness of Rosa in the saddle next to him. He thought of them riding into the night, in the silence, together. It was like a mirage, just beyond his fingertips.

'I'm going back,' Rosa said. Her face was streaked with smuts and she looked as white as a ghost in the moonlight that filtered through the unshuttered windows, but her expression was resolute. 'You stay here, outside with Castor. Wait for me.'

'No.'

'But you're hurt—'

'No,' he said again, his teeth gritted against the pain. 'No. I've lost you too many times. Not again. We go together.'

She hesitated . . . and then nodded and stretched out her hand. He took it in the darkness, and together they ran up the thick-carpeted stairs, towards the sound of the fire. At the landing they met a housemaid coming the other way in her nightgown and shawl, her face pale and frightened.

Rosa grabbed her arm as they passed.

'Are there others – other maids? Where's Miss Cassandra?'

'Let me go!' the maid cried. She tried to tug her arm free, her magic crackling, thin and pale with fear.

'What about the others?' Rosa hung on like grim death.

'Cook's gone down to the village with the head footman. I'm the only one here. Let me go!' She pulled her arm free and ran down the rest of the stairs.

'Miss Cassandra?' Rosa cried after her, but she was gone, out into the snow.

'Cassie!' Rosa shouted again. She had no idea where Cassie's bedroom was, and it felt as if they'd been wandering the corridors of Southing for hours, past rooms with furniture shrouded like ghosts against the dust, and whole wings closed off for the winter.

'Cassie!' She shut her eyes, throwing out her magic into the darkness, but all she could see were the silent, empty rooms, dark grates, stripped beds.

'Maybe she's gone,' Luke said, and she could hear the hope in his voice. 'Maybe she smelt the smoke and got out. We should look outside, check we're not hunting for a bird that's flown the coop.'

Rosa wanted to believe him, but she couldn't. It didn't seem in Cassie's character to flee the house when her mother and brother were still inside.

'No,' she said stubbornly. 'She wouldn't have gone without checking on her mother. She must be asleep, or not have heard the fire.'

But the noise of the flames was now so loud that was

beginning to seem implausible too. Rosa shouted again and, when they stopped to listen for an answering cry from Cassie, they could hear the roar and crackle coming from the other wing and see the flames reflecting back from the snow-covered lawn.

Still, Luke went to the window, peering out into the falling snow. He stood with his hands either side of the frame, his shape silhouetted against the dim glow of the snow, and she took a breath. There was no time for this now – they should be going after Cassie, or getting out, saving their skins. But it might be now – or never.

'Luke, I found out something. About – about your parents.'

He turned back. She wished she could see his eyes, but they were shadowed.

'They died—' Rosa said, then she choked. She forced herself on. 'They died because your father was a good man. He – he was a . . .' She stopped, searching for the word. What *was* Luke? Not a witch finder, with its cruel associations of burning and hanging and breaking, not any more. But something more – a man who could perceive magic, and resist a spell. 'He could *see*, Luke, just like you. And was trying to expose the practices at the factory. He was a journalist – isn't that right? And he went to the match factory and threatened them, threatened to write an article. And so . . .' She stopped. She could not say the words, the horror that Luke had lived with and grown up with all these years. He had lived with that

344

memory all his life, and she could not even say it.

'So he killed them?' Luke's face was very white. 'Sebastian's father killed 'em – my father for what he planned and my mother because she knew? Is that right?'

'Not Sebastian's father.' She swallowed. 'His mother.'

'His *mother*? A woman? But – but . . .'

He stopped, his face quite blank and white as he stared at something in the middle distance, and Rosa knew that he was reliving it again, seeing the scene in his mind's eye. Hearing the crack of bone and the splat of blood on the floor. Seeing the black glove and the rolling cane . . . and realizing that it could be true – that he had never seen the witch's face. That it *could* have been a woman all along.

'I never saw his face,' he whispered. His face was a frozen mask, as white as the snow that was blowing against the windowpane. 'I never saw his face, that's what I told 'em. But it was a lie – I never saw *her* face.'

'Luke—'

'Where is she?' he interrupted.

'What?'

'Where is she? Sebastian's mother?'

'Luke, no, you don't understand. She's burning the house. If you go after her—'

'*Which way?*' he roared, but she stood her ground, her breath coming fast and panicked, trying to work out what to say, how to persuade him of the stupidity of what he wanted to do. For a long moment they stood at loggerheads, like two bulls facing each other down. *I have magic*, she thought, a fleeting, unworthy realization. *And he does not. I could compel him.*

But even as the thought flickered through her mind, he took a deep shuddering breath and took her hand in his, the injured hand. As he held it in both his hands, her heart missed a painful beat.

'I turned back,' he said very quietly. 'In the factory. I turned back for you. I gave up my chance at revenge for *you*. I came back here, for *you*, and you wouldn't come away with me. You went back for Cassie. You did what you had to do, even though you knew it was dangerous, maybe even might cost you your life to try to find her. And I didn't try to stop you. Please.' His hands around hers were warm, and he shut his eyes, his expression wringing her heart. 'Don't try to stop me, Rose.'

She said nothing. The roar of the fire was in her ears, louder and closer now.

'Which way?'

'Back the way we came,' she said at last. The words stuck in her craw, and she had to force them out. She wanted so badly to find Cassie and get *out*. The thought of Luke plunging into that inferno – to what? To his death? To pursue some long-dead vengeance? To put hate above love, as the Malleus did? 'Past the green baize door at the end of that long corridor. But, Luke—'

But he had already turned, striding back along the corridor they had already taken, back to the stairwell and the passage that led to the green baize door.

For a minute she stood, watching his back disappear into the wreathing smoke, and she thought of turning and leaving, finding Cassie, letting him pursue his obsession to the death. It was his choice, after all.

But as his shape retreated into shadow and her heart seemed to pull from her very body, trying to follow, she realized she could not.

'Luke, wait!' She began to run, feeling the heat on her face and the smell of smoke grow stronger as she followed him. 'Wait!'

Luke was almost at the green baize door before he heard the footsteps behind him and, above the roar of the fire, a voice calling desperately.

'Wait!'

He turned – and his heart leapt and clenched with joy and fear at the same time. Rosa.

'What are you doing here?' he called, coughing against the smoke. 'Go back!'

'No.' She ran up next to him. Her face was flushed and her eyes were red and watering. 'No, I will not.'

For a minute Luke wavered, and then a crash of a falling beam decided him. They could not stand here arguing; every moment that they did the danger grew.

'Come on then.' He put his hand towards the door, but even before he touched it he could feel the heat coming off it, and as he looked properly he saw it was smouldering, the baize blackening and smoking before their eyes, far too hot to touch.

'Don't be a fool,' Rosa said shortly. She shut her eyes and whispered the words of a spell under her breath. Luke saw her magic shimmer and flare and it seemed to wrap around them both, with a sensation like a cool breeze in his face. Suddenly the heat of the fire was less, and then she bent her head and he saw the struggle in her face, her lips moving in a silent exhortation.

'What are you doing?' he whispered, but he did not expect her to answer. Her lips kept moving in that silent prayer, those strange foreign words, like a half-remembered tongue, whispering in her magic.

And then the door sprang open.

The wall of flame beyond was like hell. The blaze curled up the walls, arching overhead like a cathedral of fire, blazing into glory as the air from the open door fed the inferno.

'Where can they be?' he shouted over the roar of the fire. 'No one could survive in that!'

Rosa made no answer – she just pointed down the corridor of flames to where a door stood open at the end. For a moment Luke couldn't understand – they were on the second floor. The door could not lead anywhere but to open air. Then he remembered: a fire escape ran along the two end walls of Southing, a metal zigzagging ladder that scaled the east and west end, leading down from the servants' rooms in the attics to the grounds below.

'They must have gone that way!' Rosa shouted. 'Come on!'

She took his hand and he felt her magic gather and build, wreathing him in its cool embrace.

'We must run!' she cried above the roar of the flames. 'I can't hold this for long, the fire is too strong for me to protect us for more than a few moments. Are you ready?'

He nodded.

And then they ran.

Luke felt the burning floorboards shift and crackle beneath his feet, and the flames fanned by their passage leaping and licking after them, snatching at their clothes and hair with greedy fingers and tongues. There was a roar in his ears like a waterfall, and despite Rosa's magic the heat was so great that he screwed up his eyes as they ran, trying to keep them from scorching in his skull.

And then Rosa was gasping beside him and the coolness in his face was real. There was snow speckling his scalded cheeks, hissing as it blew through the open door into the burning corridor that was now behind him.

'You're incredible,' he croaked above the crackling roar. '*How?*' He looked back at the burning inferno, unable to believe that it was Rosa who had brought them safely through that hell.

'You walked through fire for me once,' she said, her voice hoarse.

Luke touched her cheek, his heart so full he could not speak. Then he turned away to wipe the snow from his eyes, coughing roughly to clear his throat.

'The ladder beneath,' he managed, pointing at the fire escape. 'It's still pulled up.'

'In which case . . .' Rosa looked up, at the ladder stretching up above their heads, to the servants' wing and beyond. 'They must have gone up.'

23

The ladder rungs were slippery and icy with snow, and when Luke reached the edge of the roof he stopped and flexed his fingers, trying to get the feeling back into them before he hauled himself over the parapet and on to the slates, keeping his body low and inconspicuous.

For a minute he lay panting, waiting for the grinding pain in his rib to subside. Then as his eyes got used to the swirling snow he looked around, his heart thumping, half with the pain and half with fear. Were they there? Was Sebastian hiding around the corner of a gable, waiting to strike?

Suddenly, out of the dimness, he saw a figure crouched further along the roof with its back to the parapet. Sebastian? But as Luke peered closer he realized it was too small, with pale hair straggling across its shoulders.

Cassie.

He was about to call out to her when he saw another shape on her other side. Knyvet.

Luke crouched back into the shadows of the gable, but there was no danger of Knyvet seeing him. Sebastian's attention was fixed on something – or someone – far up on the topmost ridge. A woman, with wild black hair streaming out in the wind-blown snow, her face turned to the scudding clouds and the stars.

'Mama!' Cassie's voice was thin and snatched by the wind, but Luke could hear the sob in it. 'Mama, *please*. Please come down, it's not safe.'

'Safe!' It was a wild, eldritch scream, blown on the night air. 'Safe? For ten years I've been caged to keep me safe. I am done with safety, do you hear me? Come!' She spread out her arms, her face turned exultantly to the sky. 'Come, Asag! Come, Shedu! Come, Išum and Belial and Lilu and Pazuzu! Take me, possess me! Let me ride you to the land beyond!'

Her magic was a huge billowing cloud of ink spreading across the sky, like a polluting oil slick shadowing the moonlit clouds. Luke had never seen so vast and terrible a power – the wild black power he had seen that day in the drawing room, when she had revived Rosa, was nothing to this enormous spreading blackness. It was as if some dam had broken and all the power pent up in the years of miserable captivity had flooded out.

'Mama!' Cassie sobbed. 'Please!' She turned to Knyvet, who was crouched by her side. His hands seemed to be bound in front of him with something that gleamed in the dim light. 'Sebastian, say something, *do* something!'

'Do?' There was a snarl in his voice and Luke could smell the brandy coming off him, even at this distance. 'What can I do? That little bitch has chained me like a dog. I can't cast a damn witchlight. Get these things off me and then I'll *do* whatever you want.'

But he stood and shouted.

'Mama! Get down off that roof. D'you want to kill yourself?'

'Kill myself?' She laughed delightedly and began to walk the ridgepole, her scorched gown trailing out behind her like a macabre wedding train. 'Why not? I have little left to fear, now your father is gone.' A huge buffet of wind suddenly caught her and she staggered, but did not fall. She had something in her hand that she was using to balance herself. His heart caught in his mouth as he realized what it was – the snake's-head cane, clutched between her hands like a tightrope walker.

'The house is burning, Mama!' Cassie cried. 'Please, we must get down. *Please!*'

Behind him, Luke heard Rosa's feet on the ladder and he turned, putting his finger to his lips as she clambered over, her skirts dragging in the slush-filled gutter. They crouched, side by side, watching the figure on the roof.

'I am free,' she called, her voice floating on the night wind, swirling with the snowflakes. Below they could hear

353

the crackle and roar of the fire as it raged higher. 'Free at last!'

Luke felt for Rosa's fingers and squeezed them tight. Then he stood up.

He said nothing, but he didn't need to. First Sebastian's and then his mother's gaze turned to him. Sebastian swore and began to stumble along the edge of the roof towards Luke, but behind him Rosa stood, her hand outstretched.

'Stay where you are!' she shouted, her magic blazing out across the tiles, and Sebastian seemed to freeze, statue-like, balanced at the edge of the slates.

'Who is this?' his mother called, her voice ripped and torn by the wind. 'Who are you, outwith? What are you doing here?' She took a step forward along the roof. 'Don't you know, I eat young men like you?' She raised her hands to the sky and great bolts of lightning shot from her finger tips, arcing into the heavens where they crashed and rumbled and lit up the snowy landscape.

'NO!' Rosa screamed. She scrambled across the tiles to stand in front of Luke, her arms outstretched. 'If you touch him, I will – I will die first!'

The woman on the roof gave a long, low cackling laugh and then she opened her mouth and roared. A wall of flame shot out across the frozen slates and Rosa ducked, grabbing Luke in her arms as she did, her magic flooding out to encompass them both. Luke heard the crackle of the flame as it passed over, and smelt singeing hair and clothes, but they were both unharmed, though Rosa was panting and her face was white, the freckles standing out like breadcrumbs on snow.

'Luke, we should not have come!' she whispered desperately. 'She is far, far stronger than me. I can't hold her off – that was just play-acting on her part. If she attacks us in earnest, we're both dead.'

'Mama,' Cassie called from far along the roof. 'Mama, come down. Don't do this – you know what will happen if you kill another outwith. The Ealdwitan will *have* to act. Without Father to protect you—'

'Protect me! Cage me, you mean,' the woman snarled. She paced back along the ridge, away from where they were standing, and Sebastian's voice hissed above the wind.

'Rosa. *Rosa!*'

'Shut *up!*' Rosa snapped. 'If you open your mouth I'll—'

'Listen to me!' he spat back furiously. 'You can't hold her – you said so yourself. Take off this spell, take off the cuffs. I'm the only person here with a chance of getting her down. I give you my word, I *won't* harm you, or your outwith.'

Luke saw Rosa's indecision in her face. She looked up at him, her eyes wide and dark, and full of questions and fear. He bit his lip.

'I don't know,' he whispered. 'Can you trust him?'

'No,' she whispered back, despair in her voice. Then she turned to Sebastian. 'Do you swear. Do you *swear* on – on your honour?'

'I'll swear on my honour, your honour, my dead father's

honour – anything you damn well choose, just get me free before we all die! If my mother lets loose we are *all* dead, not just your outwith.'

'Very well.' Rosa seemed suddenly to make up her mind. She edged along the roof to where Sebastian stood and put her hands to the golden necklace wrapped around his wrists. There was a moment's struggle, and then Luke heard the snap of breaking metal and the necklace was in two halves in Rosa's hands.

Sebastian stood for a moment, massaging his wrists. Then he looked up and smiled, his thin, curving, mocking smile.

'Oh, my darling. My beautiful, foolish, incurably optimistic darling. Don't you know yet, I have no honour?'

Rosa's face went pale.

But then Sebastian turned and began to climb towards the roof.

Like a cat, he climbed using his fingers and toes, and his magic billowed and shimmered in the snowy wind.

At the apex of the roof, his mother stood, her hair streaming, laughing into the night.

'Mama!' Sebastian called as he climbed, shouting against the howling gusts. 'Mama, stay there, don't move.'

At last he was at the top.

Very slowly, he got to his feet and then stood, swaying on the ridge. Luke held his breath. It was impossibly dangerous – even for a sober man, and Sebastian was not sober. And then he started to edge along the tiled precipice, his hand held out.

'Sebastian!' His mother began to laugh and sob, all in the same word. 'Sebastian, my darling, you have come to dance!'

'Yes, Mama.' He held out his arms. 'I've come to dance.'

She put her hand on his shoulder and round his waist, and for a moment they stood, tottering, in a macabre, precarious mime of a waltz.

'Da da, da da, da da, da daaah,' she sang in a trembling voice, snatched by the winds, and Luke shuddered.

'Come down now, Mama,' Sebastian said, and there was a smile on his lips, though Luke could hear the strain in his voice. 'You've had your dance. It is time to go home.'

'One waltz!' she laughed. 'One dance does not make a ball. I was always the belle of the ball, you know, my darling. All the men danced with me. Dance with me, outwith!' she called down to Luke. 'Dance with me and then we will go home!'

'No!' Rosa's fingers closed on Luke's sleeve. 'Don't!'

He shook his head.

'Take Cassie down.'

'No! What are you going to do?'

'Dance with her, if that's what it takes to get her down.'

'Luke, are you mad? She killed your parents! Will you let her kill you too?'

'If she stays up there throwing thunderbolts, we'll all die.'

'Dance with me!' the witch screamed.

357

'I'm going to get her down. Get Cassie away.'

'No!' Rosa cried, but Luke pulled his arm gently out of her fingers and kissed her cheek.

'One dance, Rosa. That's all.'

And then he began to climb.

Rosa watched as he climbed in Sebastian's footsteps, fitting his fingers into the cracks in the slate, holding on to the ornamental curlicues of lead that decorated the ridges and turrets of the roof. Her heart beat in her throat like a trapped thing and she felt sick. Luke was sober, and he climbed more surely and carefully than Sebastian. But he was tired and injured. She could see the pain in his face as he climbed. And he had no magic to shield him if he fell.

Well, she would have to be his shield.

She drew a breath, readying herself.

When Luke reached the top he straightened, just as Sebastian had done, and then began to edge along the ridge to where their little group was standing.

Rosa was holding her breath, her fingers clenched.

Be safe, she begged Luke in her head. *Come back to me.*

Up on the ridge, Sebastian's mother turned her beautiful ravaged face to Luke and she smiled.

'I know you.'

'Yes.' She heard Luke's voice, tugged and frayed by the gusts. 'Yes, we met once before. In the drawing room, here. You saved Rosa's life. And I've come to say thank you – and ask you to come down. Won't you come with me now?'

'No . . .' the woman said. She put her fingers to his cheek, staring deep into his eyes, her wind-whipped hair flapping against his face. 'No, I *know* you. From before that. From Spitalfields. I – I *killed* you. How did you come back?'

Up on the ridge Luke froze, and then he seemed to find his voice.

'You – you remember?'

'Yes, I remember. I killed you – and your wife. Oh! She had the sweetest blood . . .'

Rosa put her hand over her mouth to stifle the cry that almost broke free. The woman was standing on the ridge, her hand on Luke's cheek. All it would take would be one push from Luke, one push – and could she blame him, really?

'And now you have come back for me.' Her thin, white face broke into a smile, as sweet as a young girl's. 'Have you come to take me away?'

'Yes,' Luke said. His voice was a croak, and Rosa wondered if he was fighting off tears. 'Yes, I've come to take you home. Come down with me. Please.'

'I knew death would come for me one day,' she whispered, her huge dark eyes fixed on Luke's face. 'But I did not think he would be so young and lovely. I will come with you, gladly. Come, let us go together. Sebastian, my darling, take my hand. It is time. It is time.'

She reached for Sebastian's hand and Luke's, and for a moment Rosa was flooded with thankfulness and relief that the horror was over.

And then as the witch turned to face the void, Rosa realized the meaning of her words.

'No!' she screamed. 'Luke, no!'

And in the same instant, the woman jumped.

Sebastian cried out, a brief, wordless shout of fear.

Rosa's own despairing '*No!*' echoed around the rooftop as she threw all her magic after them, every particle of it in a formless blazing rush.

And Luke – Luke made no sound at all.

They were gone.

24

Rosa ran to the edge of the roof, staring out into the swirling white.

There were three dark shapes far below, crumpled black masses against the snow.

A scream rose up in her throat, but she pushed it back and began to stumble back through the slush-filled gutters to the fire escape, when she caught sight of Cassie, huddled against the edge of the roof, her face white and filled with horror, her blind eyes staring blankly into the night.

'Cassie!' Her voice was rough with unshed sobs and she grabbed the girl's wrist. 'Cassie, did you see? Did you see what happened? Are they alive?'

'I tried to tell him!' Cassie's voice was an agonized whisper. 'I tried to tell Sebastian what I saw – his death in the flames . . . Oh, Rosa!' And she began to cry, the tears welling from her beautiful blue eyes.

'Luke?' Rosa managed. She knew she was being cruel, but at that moment she could not find it in herself to care about anything else. 'Is Luke alive?'

But Cassie could not speak, the sobs were choking her, and at last Rosa grabbed her arm and half led, half pulled her to the fire escape, dragging her down the slippery snow-covered rungs with a mixture of brute force and magic.

'Come on!' she begged as they stumbled past the open door that led to the prison wing, burning entirely out of control now. She had to shield them both from the flames roaring out of the open doorway. It would not be long before the whole wing collapsed – and with it the fire escape. If the structure fell she might be able to save herself, but not Cassie too. Not in this state of exhausted fear. And in the meantime Luke might be bleeding to death in the snow. 'Come *on*.'

She wrestled with the drawn-up ladder, and then it clanged down, and she was dragging and propelling Cassie down the next flight, and the next. They fell, more than climbed, the last few yards, landing in a heap of snow by the scullery door, and Rosa left Cassie sobbing by the foot of the ladder and stumbled round to the front of the house.

They were there; she could see them, lying like jacks flung down by a petulant child at the foot of the steps that led up to the great pillared entrance.

Sebastian had been thrown against the balustrade and

362

he lay with his head flung back and his neck at a strange unnatural angle.

His mother was crumpled in a heap against the bottom step. Her skull must have hit something on the way down for it had been caved in like a smashed egg.

And last of all, further out in the snow that lay thick across the driveway: Luke.

Luke: face down in the snow, spreading scarlet with his blood.

She was almost afraid to touch him, terrified that he was alive but beyond healing, that she might cause him pain if she tried to move him. But she *had* to try.

'Luke – oh, Luke! Please, please . . .' She fell to her knees in the snow and put her hand to his shoulder, turning him on to his back as gently as she could.

'Luke?' she whispered.

He lay, his eyes closed, his face pale as death and covered with blood. And then he coughed.

'Help,' he managed. Blood came bubbling out of his nostrils. 'Help me sit up . . . choking . . . nose . . .'

Almost crying, she helped him sit and lean forwards, so that the blood poured out of his nose on to the snow instead of running back down his throat. He coughed and spat, and coughed again, and then pinched the bridge of his nose, trying to stem the flow.

'Is it broken?' Rosa asked through her sobs.

'Maybe.' He touched it gingerly and then shook his head, drops of blood spattering his shirt. 'Maybe not. My rib is. Ahhhh . . . ' He pressed his hand against the side where it hurt, his eyes screwed shut with the pain.

'When you fell . . .' She held on to him, her fingers gripping through his coat as if she would never let him go again. 'When you fell . . .'

But she could not finish. She only knelt opposite him in the snow, tears streaming down her face.

And then she kissed him, through the blood and the tears and the melting snow. She felt his mouth, hot against hers, and she tasted blood and Luke, and she found she was shaking.

'I love you,' she said, her words blurred by their kiss and her tears, but she knew he would understand. 'I love you, Luke, so much.'

'I love you too.'

He wrapped his arms around her carefully, pulling her into his uninjured side, and she felt his strength like a rock, his warmth encompassing her as her magic flooded out to him.

'I'm sorry,' she managed. She spoke into his chest. 'I let you down. I tried – I tried to stop you fall—'

'I'm alive,' he said. He pulled back, looking into her face, his rough hands stroking her hair. 'I'm alive because of you.' He looked over at Sebastian and his mother, sprawled in the snow, and his face was pale. 'Can you do anything for 'em?'

'No,' Rosa shook her head. 'No, they're gone, beyond saving.'

They were still looking at each other, shivering in each other's arms, when there was the sound of bells from far away. Luke struggled to his feet, peering into the darkness, his hand shading against the moon and the swirling snow.

'What is it?' Rosa stood too, stiffly, brushing the melting snow from her skirts.

'Fire engine, I think. That maid must have raised the alarm.'

Sure enough, in a few moments they heard the sound of galloping hooves and a fire cart rounded the corner, the bell ringing like bedlam, two shire horses between the traces and a farm boy seated aloft, whipping the horses for dear life. The men were not like the uniformed firemen Rosa had seen in London – they were just villagers: farm hands and servants, she guessed from their clothes. But they leapt down and began shouting orders.

'Where's the fire?' one of them called to Luke. 'Round the back?'

'Yes, round to the right.' He pointed, and the farm boy seated on the back of one of the shire horses gave it a whack with the whip and began to steer the apparatus round the corner.

'All hands to the pump!' one of the men shouted. 'Jim, you go for the doctor, for them two out the front.' And then, 'Who's that girl? Get her out the way!'

'Cassie!' Rosa gasped. She had completely forgotten. She ran after the fire cart and there was Cassie, still huddled at the foot of the fire escape.

'Stop!' Rosa shouted to the men, already training their hoses at the burning building. 'Wait!'

She crouched beside Cassie, trying to pull her to her feet.

'Cassie darling, come with me. There's nothing you can do here. Come away – we'll get you to the village.'

'They're dead, aren't they?' Cassie raised her thin, white face to Rosa's. 'Both of them. They're both dead.'

'Cassie – I . . .' She didn't know what to say. She thought of when they had come to tell her about Papa; she could remember almost nothing, just the look on her mother's face and her voice saying, *My dear, I have some dreadful news* . . .

'I have no one,' Cassie said. Her voice was strange and wondering, almost calm. 'I have no one.'

'You have me,' Rosa said. She put her arm through Cassie's. 'Come, you are cold and they need to set their hoses to the buildings. We can't stay here. We must go to the village, someone will take us in. And then . . .'

And then? And then what?

But she could not think of that now, she could not think of the future. Just of tonight, and tomorrow, and the day after that. Time enough for the rest in the morning.

25

'Fire at the manor!' the small boy shouted. 'Fire at the manor! Two dead! Master and mistress dashed their brains out on the drive! Fire at the manor!'

'Hush, for God's sake!' Rosa stuck her head out of the window at the inn, beside herself with fury. Cassie had not slept all night and now she was finally collapsed into unconsciousness. The last thing she needed was to be woken by this horrible, bloodthirsty urchin. 'Take yourself somewhere else, for pity!'

'Hush yerself!' he retorted. 'I've got papers to sell, ain't I? How'm I supposed to shift 'em if I can't cry me wares?'

'Oh, go away!' Rosa hissed. 'I'll buy a stupid paper, if that's what it'll take. Just go away!'

'Six,' he said firmly. 'Six papers. That's what I'd've sold on this corner, I reckon. So you should compensate me for me loss.'

'Very well then, six!' she snarled. 'Just go away!'

'That'll be a shillin'.'

Her fingers shaking, Rosa scrabbled on the dressing table for a coin and flung it down. In return the boy bound up six copies with string and launched them through the open window. They thumped on the rug. Rosa slammed the window shut and looked over at Cassie, still slumbering in the bed.

She would have to get rid of the copies before Cassie woke. The easiest way would be the fire. She snipped the string, and began to separate the pages for burning. One, two, three fed into the fire, but by the time she got to the fourth it was burning too fiercely and the grate was too full of ashes.

She stood, smoothing her skirts, and walked up the corridor to the room where Luke was staying.

Luke was sitting in the window seat, a book in his hands, but he had not turned a page for a long while. Instead he was staring unseeingly out into the street, thinking.

At last he turned with a sigh back to the book, but when he bent his head to read, the stiff collar dug into his neck. Not so much mutton dressed as lamb, as a pig in a bonnet, he thought, pulling at it. And a too-small bonnet at that. The collar, along with the rest of his outfit, belonged to the innkeeper's own son, away at university. Luke had tried to protest, to say that he would rather have a spare shirt from their groom, but the innkeeper had refused. Nothing was too good for Miss Cassie, and by extension for Rosa and Luke. The innkeeper's son was tall, as tall as Luke, thankfully. But he'd not spent his life beating hot metal, and the collar, as well as the fabric over Luke's right shoulder, was uncomfortably tight, so tight that he feared he might split the jacket when he breathed.

But that was not what had been distracting him from his book this last half-hour. That had been something else.

He knew he should be thankful, most of all for the fact that they were free, free of the Brothers, free of the Greenwoods, free from Sebastian's pursuit. John Leadingham was dead. The witch hunt was over.

Except it was not over. Somewhere, Rosa's name was still written in the Book of Witches – and Cassie's too, for all he knew. He should have burnt that book when he had the chance, flung it into the fire in front of all the Brothers to undo the harm he'd done. It was not just Rosa: there were other lives forfeit because of him, because of his sight. He remembered walking the streets of London as a child, John Leadingham's hand at his back. 'Him,' he would point and John would nod at a Brother and set him off to trail the witch to his destination. 'Her. And that girl with her too.'

How proud he'd been of his gift. And how wretched the memory made him now.

He thought of his father, who had taken that same gift and made something noble out of it: who had protected the powerless without resorting to hate. Rosa's words rang in his head: *You were a child – you didn't know any better!*

No. He'd not known any better. He had grown up with ignorance and fear and hatred, drunk it down with his bedtime milk, chewed on it with his morning bread, learnt it alongside his ABC and the Lord's Prayer.

But he knew now what he'd done, what it felt like to lie in chains, awaiting your death. He knew the stink of the bottle and the feel of a knife against skin. He knew what it was like to wish a girl's death – and how impossible it was ever to atone for that sin.

'Luke?'

His head jerked up.

Rosa stood in the doorway, her magic a ripple of flame against the wood panelling. She was dressed and her hair swept up in a silver comb. For the first time in many weeks she looked completely and utterly what she was: a lady, through and through, and the knowledge made his heart thump with a painful missed beat, and his breath catch in his throat just for a moment.

He was almost afraid to touch her, but she walked into his arms and put her hand against his cheek, meeting his eyes with a look so hungry his heart twisted in his chest.

'Rose,' he whispered, and then her lips were on his, soft and warm and open, and his senses slipped from him. She was light in his arms, but strong and tough as wire. 'My God, I love you,' he said, his words smothered against her skin, but she heard, and her fingers tightened on the

370

muscles of his arms, her nails digging through his shirt sleeves until he groaned against her throat.

Then something slipped from her hand and landed with a thump against the floor, and they both laughed, a shaky trembling laugh, and pulled apart.

'What's that you've got there?' Luke asked.

Rosa picked it up and put it on the windowsill beside him.

'Some horrible child was shouting the headlines in the street, so I bought a bundle to shut him up. I didn't want him to wake Cassie, least of all with grisly details about her family's death. I burnt half in my grate but it couldn't take the rest. Can I use yours?'

'Of course. What does it say though? The article about the fire?'

'I don't know. Why?'

'Does it mention us?'

Rosa's eyes widened and she unrolled the top copy. The first page was advertisements, but the second was an account of the fire. Rosa scanned it, Luke reading over her shoulder, his hair falling in his eyes.

TERROR AT SOUTHING

RESIDENTS of the small hamlet of Southing in Sussex were woken in the night by news that Southing House, the family seat of the Knyvets, great landowners in these parts, was burning to the ground. Villagers and firemen

*rushed to the scene and battled the inferno with great
determination and at risk to their own lives, but all
efforts to quench the blaze proved unsuccessful, and
your correspondent is led to believe that this great
manor, once described as 'the jewel of the Downs', is
no more.*

*The owner of Southing, Mr Sebastian Knyvet, showed
enormous courage and fortitude in his attempts to
rescue his invalid mother from the rooftop, whence she
had fled in terror from the inferno below. His
determination and filial loyalty showed no bounds, even
to the extent that he ventured up on to the slates where
Mrs Knyvet had taken refuge, at great risk to his own
life. Alas, the inclement conditions, combined with his
mother's fragile state of mind, led to a double tragedy
and both mother and son fell, and were dashed on to the
driveway beneath, where they died instantly. Miss
Cassandra Knyvet, who is only fourteen years of age, is
the sole surviving member of the family.*

*The late Mr Aloysius Knyvet, who served for a time as
Governor of Bengal, under the then Viceroy of India,
Lord Lytton, died last month after a short illness.*

'How dare they!' Rosa's cheeks flushed as she looked up at
him. 'Sebastian showed enormous courage and fortitude?
What about you? Risking your life for—'

372

'He did show great courage. And I'm bloody thankful they didn't put my name in the paper. As far as the Brothers are concerned, I died somewhere at John's hands. And as far as your family are concerned, you were in that house when it burnt to the ground. D'you realize what this means?'

'It means . . .' She stared at him, her gold-brown eyes wide and dark, dilating to black. 'It means we are free.'

The words were still ringing in her head as she made her way back up the corridor to the room she was sharing with Cassie. It had been hard to leave Luke, the warmth of his fire, and the comfort of his company, but she did not want Cassie to wake and find herself alone.

Free. Free to do – what?

She opened the door to the room, quietly, trying not to wake the sleeper inside, but as her eyes adjusted to the dim light she heard a rustle, and saw Cassie struggling up against the pillow, her hair in tangled rats' tails.

'Oh, you're awake!' Rosa exclaimed stupidly. 'I'm sorry – did I disturb you?'

'No, no, I was waking anyway.' Cassie rubbed at her eyes. 'I had been lying there, trying to understand, to believe . . . For a moment I thought it was all a dream – and then I remembered . . .'

'Cassie, I am so very sorry . . .' Rosa trailed off, twisting her fingers. But Cassie was shaking her head.

'No. I am done crying. Mama – Mama leapt. She leapt

into the void. She chose death over that miserable existence. And she took Sebastian with her. I cannot help but think . . .'

'What?' Rosa went to the bedside to take Cassie's hand in hers. 'What, Cassie?'

'I can't help thinking that she did not want him to live. That she knew she had that one chance to end it all and to take the darkness with her. They say suicide is a mortal sin, don't they? But perhaps – perhaps it was a noble thing that she did. In a way.'

'Perhaps it was,' Rosa whispered. She felt her eyes well with tears and for a minute she blinked, trying to clear her vision. Then she coughed and turned away to the fireside.

'What will you do, Cassie? You can't stay here for long – do you have family? Will you go to London?'

'Southing is entailed, I've been told,' Cassie said wearily. 'Along with the London house. I don't know who they will go to – some distant cousin, I believe. But I dare say the factories are mine, if I wanted them.'

'Do you?'

'No. They would not let me manage them, a blind girl not of age – and I am done with money bled from the veins of the poor. No, I will sell them – or try to. And then I would like to go far away, so I never have to smell the smoke of Southing again. I have a cousin in America, near Boston. Distant relatives of ours and of the Mr Rokewood that you met at our ball. They are a kind family and would take me in, I'm sure. They offered to have me stay once before, but I did not want to leave –' her voice faltered, '– to leave Mama.'

'America!' Rosa was taken aback. 'But, Cassie, how – how would you get there?'

'There are steamships. Ocean-going liners. The crossing takes only a week or two.'

'But – but the icebergs! And, Cassie, you are—'

She stopped. She could not bring herself to say it. But you are *blind*. How can you travel halfway across the world, alone?

But Cassie nodded, catching Rosa's thoughts in that uncanny way she had.

'I know. But I was hoping . . . Rosa, would you come with me?'

'*What?*'

'Just for the journey, although of course if you wanted to stay with me in America, I would love that too. I will understand if you don't want to, but Luke could come too. It would be a new start for all of us.'

Rosa said nothing. Pictures swirled in her head: Mama, Alexis, Clemency, Belle . . . the tall white house in Osborne Crescent, Papa's narrow grey gravestone in the country churchyard near Matchenham . . . To leave all that – to leave the weight of expectation and duty behind, step out of the corpse of her old identity, to start anew . . .

'I only thought,' Cassie said, 'perhaps . . . it might be

easier. For you and Luke, I mean. To start afresh in another place. They see matters differently, I think, over there. A lady and a blacksmith – perhaps it would not be so impossible? And –' her voice wavered, but she went on, bravely, '– I must confess it would be good to think I had a friend in America. Perhaps even two.'

'It – it's a wonderful idea,' Rosa managed. 'I must talk to Luke though. I cannot decide for him. If he comes, it must be his own free will.'

'Yes,' Cassie said quietly. She swung her legs over the side of the bed, and walked carefully across the hearth, to where Rosa stood, feeling for her hand. 'But you, Rosa? Will you come? No – forgive me, I should not ask. You will want to wait, speak to Luke before you decide.'

Rosa took a breath.

'No,' she said. And then, as she saw Cassie's smile falter, she took Cassie's hand in hers, her words coming fast. 'No, whatever Luke decides, I will come with you.' *I owe you that much,* she thought. *Your mother, your brother, your home: they are gone, because of me. I cannot give them back, but I can give you this friendship, though God knows it's not much.*

'Really?' Cassie's face lit up, her cornflower-blue eyes like a summer sky. 'You will come?'

'Yes,' Rosa said. She gripped Cassie's hand in hers. 'Yes, I will come.'

The knock at the door broke into the silence after her words, making them both jump, and it was Cassie who spoke first.

'Come in.' She dragged a wrapper from the bed around herself and turned to face the door. 'The door is not locked.'

It was Luke. He came into the room a little awkwardly, pulling at his collar as if it chafed him.

'You're awake, Miss Knyvet.'

'Yes, but please, call me Cassie.'

Luke winced and shook his head.

'I'm sorry,' he said. 'I can't. It – it wouldn't feel right. They've dressed me up like a shop-window dummy, but I'm still a blacksmith underneath.'

'You tried to save my mother's life,' Cassie said softly. But Luke shook his head again.

'I'll call you Miss Cassie, if it makes you feel better. But don't make me uncomfortable, miss. I'd sooner go to dinner in my drawers.'

Cassie laughed at that.

'Miss Cassie then, and can I call you Luke, or must it be Mr Welling?'

'Mr Lexton,' he corrected uncomfortably, and Rosa knew he was remembering the circumstances of their last meeting.

'Mr Lexton then.'

'No – no, I didn't mean that. I meant – call me Luke. Please.'

He was red and flushed, and Rosa realized afresh how impossible this would be in England. Even without the

Malleus and her family to keep them apart, all of society would conspire to separate them.

'Luke,' she said impulsively. 'Cassie has had an idea. She asks . . .' She stumbled. It had seemed so clear on Cassie's lips, so logical. Now as she tried to think of a way to phrase it to Luke, to invite him but not compel, she faltered.

'I asked if Rosa and you would come with me to America.' Cassie crossed the carpet to take Luke's hand in hers. 'I would count it a great favour, Luke. I have money and means, but I cannot travel alone. I have a cousin in American, a Genevieve Rokewood. She is married to an American, a young, up-and-coming politician called Franklin Entwhistle. He is a supporter of the Vice President, a Mr Thomas Jefferson. Have you heard of him?'

Luke shook his head.

'Franklin is a great proponent of his. He says he is sure that Mr Jefferson will rise to great heights. I asked Rosa if you would both come with me because I think –' she paused, and Rosa could see she was trying to think how to phrase it delicately, '– I think, perhaps in America . . .'

Luke met Rosa's eyes and Rosa bit her lip.

'Perhaps this is a subject to be discussed over luncheon,' Cassie said at last. She let Luke's hand drop. 'I should dress.'

'That's what I came to say,' Luke said, as if remembering for the first time the reason he had come. 'The landlady sent up to ask if we were eating here or not. I'll tell her yes, shall I?'

'Yes, ask her to send something up to our parlour. Thank you, Luke. I see you, you know,' she said as he turned to go, and he turned back, looking at her deep-blue sightless eyes. She smiled, feeling his gaze upon her in that strange, uncanny way she had. 'I see you and Rosa in America. I see happiness for you. I see a future.'

For a moment Luke stood, looking at her. And then he rounded on his heel and left.

Luke's heart was beating hard and fast in his chest, his eyes staring unseeingly, as he strode down the long corridor towards the stairs. He was no fool. He knew what Cassie had meant. America was the great classless society, where self-made men lived in great houses alongside old money and dukes' daughters rubbed shoulders with the sons of Irish peasants.

But he could not see himself pulling his fortunes from the mud, raising a railroad company, drilling for oil. He did not want to be a self-made millionaire. He wanted to be a blacksmith, and to have pride in that. Even in America, he doubted that a blacksmith could marry a lady. A man had to put down his tools, to enter the drawing rooms of the rich. That didn't change just because you'd crossed an ocean.

And yet . . . and yet he also wanted Rosa. For her, he could change, put down his tools, forget his past. Couldn't he?

He stopped at the top of the stairs, his hand on the newel post, and his rib gave a stab, as if it was his heart, not his rib that was broken.

How . . .

'Luke!'

He looked up. It was Rosa, running down the corridor, her slippered feet light on the polished boards, her magic glowing around her. 'Luke, wait!'

'Rosa.'

She came level with him and put her hand on his arm as she looked into his face. She saw pain there, but didn't understand it, or not completely.

'Luke, what is it?'

'My rib,' he said stiffly. She put her hand on the place where it hurt beneath his jacket, gently tracing the swelling there, and he felt the soft warmth of her palm through the thin shirt material and closed his eyes, shutting back the tears that pricked at the back of his lids.

Rosa.

'Can I?' she asked. He nodded, and then felt her magic flood through him, a warm wave breaking over his head, mending, making right and new.

He took a breath, and in the old, unfathomable miracle that he would never grow used to, never take for granted, he felt it: his rib was healed. But the pain was not gone.

They were so close, he could feel her breath on his cheek, the heat of her skin . . .

'Luke, come with me . . .' Her arm stole around his neck and he felt her lips against his throat, his jaw, each touch soft and warm as light. 'Come with me.'

'Yes,' he found himself saying, as her mouth found his. For how could he let her go? This light, flame-filled girl he loved more than life. 'Yes, I'll come . . .'

26

The RMS *Albion* stood at the dock at Portsmouth, dwarfing all the other ships in the harbour. Rosa had never imagined anything so huge – like a travelling, floating hotel. She had read aloud to Cassie the brochure that had accompanied their tickets, describing with astonishment the restaurants, billiard rooms, covered walkways, quoits deck, library – every kind of amusement and pastime man could devise, crammed into seven decks.

Now they had been shown to their cabins – she and Cassie sharing a two-room suite, Luke in a single first-class berth on the opposite side of the ship. Rosa was on the manifest as Rose Farrier, a joke that had made her and Luke smile when they came up with it. Luke had just shrugged when Cassie asked what name to put down.

'Put me down as Luke Lexton. If they find I'm gone, so much the better.' But Rosa knew the real reason, or thought she did. His surname was all Luke had to remember William by. He would take the risk rather than lose that last link.

Below they heard the roar of the engines as the great ship began to build up steam, and she opened the window in their cabin and leant out, looking towards London, thinking of Mama and Alexis. She knew she should miss them; she knew she should feel sad at the thought of them mourning her death, burying an empty coffin with just a handful of the Southing ashes instead of a corpse. But she could not. She felt – not empty. Not even numb, for what she felt was not *nothing*, it was – indifference? Perhaps there was no word for this feeling, a kind of benign detachment. They would have their legacy now. And she would be free; poor but free.

I am no one, she thought. *I am nothing. I have nothing.*

But it was not true. She was Rose Farrier. She had her freedom. And she had Luke. Suddenly she wanted him, wanted to feel his skin beneath her hands, to believe that this was real, at last, that they could be together in safety.

She found him in his cabin, watching out of the window as she had been, but he was not sitting by the porthole, he was standing, gripping the wooden surround so tight his fingers were white and the muscles in his back were tense as iron.

'Luke?'

He had not heard her come in over the thrum of the

383

engines, and he turned, startled.

'Rosa!' Beneath the surprise, his face was troubled, and she felt something uneasy stir in the pit of her stomach.

'Wh-what's the matter?'

He swallowed and turned away to the window, but it was when he turned back to her, tears in his eyes and said, 'Come here, love,' that she felt a sudden coldness.

'You've never called me that before,' she said as she came across the little room. He sat, drawing her on to his knee and folded his arms around her.

'I should have,' he said, and his voice cracked. 'I should have told you I loved you every day since we met, because it was true, even when I didn't know it myself.'

He put his face on her shoulder and she felt his breath shudder as he tried to pull himself together.

'Luke, what is it?' She took his chin and pulled his face to look at her. 'You're scaring me. What's the matter?'

He took a long breath, as if he were readying himself for a fight, or a dive into nothing.

And then he spoke.

'I – I can't come. To America.'

She did not speak, but whatever showed in her face made him tighten his grip round her and his words came rushing out like tears.

'I wish I could . . . My God, Rose, you don't know how much I . . . but I can't. *I* wrote that book. I condemned those men and women and children. And I can't leave that, I can't leave it undone. Leadingham is dead, but the book is still there, and while it is, I can't run away.'

'Luke . . .' she whispered, but the words wouldn't come.

'I could spend a lifetime trying to atone for what I did to you, but as long as your name is in that book, along with all the others, I'll never manage. If we're ever to be happy . . .'

He choked again and then scrubbed furiously at his eyes. His voice was cracked with tears.

'I'd lay down my tools for you, Rose. I would become something else. I'd make any sacrifice for you, and gladly. D'you understand? But this – this I can't lay down. It's not *me* I'm sacrificing. It'd be them, *you*. I must go back. I *must* destroy it. And then I can rest.'

She felt his arms around her, feeling her heart swell and crack with love for him, and she did not cry. She could not cry. She only listened to the thrum of the ship and thought of the peaceful life an ocean away that they could have had. But she knew that he was right – that there would be no peace for him, no future for either of them, while that book seeped its black poison into London's streets, and men, women and children that he had identified were condemned to death on his word.

'Do you understand?' he said again, and his voice broke. 'Say something, Rose, please.'

She nodded. She had to force the words out, and when they came they were a whisper, but she made them come.

'Yes. Yes, I understand.' She swallowed and spoke more strongly. 'But I cannot leave Cassie. Not now, not when I've promised her to come.'

'I know.' His voice was hoarse with tears. 'I'm not asking you to stay. I don't *want* you to stay. I want you to go – be happy – make a new life.'

They sat for a long time, wrapped in each other's arms, remembering the days and nights they had held each other and thinking of the emptiness to come.

'You look different,' Luke said softly. 'Your magic. It's different. Did something change, in the fire?'

'Perhaps –' her throat was tight and sore, and she swallowed against the pain, '– perhaps it's because I'm not afraid any more.'

The thrum of the engine increased to a whine and she forced herself to stand, pulling herself away from his clutching arms.

'I love you,' he said hopelessly. The tears ran down his cheeks.

'I love you too. Now, go, before the ship leaves.'

'I'll come and find you, I promise.' He kissed her, his tears on her lips, his arms so tight around her that it ached, but she did not care. She wanted to remember this always, to feel his bones imprinted on hers. 'This Entwhistle – he's a big man, by the sound of it. He won't be hard to find. However long it takes, I *will* come. Will you wait?'

'No, I won't wait,' she said, and she put his hand to his face, trying to smile at the sudden hurt she saw in his eyes. 'For if you don't come to me, I will find you. We *will* be together, Luke. Remember what Cassie said?'

'She saw us,' he managed. 'Both of us. Happy.'

She nodded again.

The ship had begun to shudder and a bell was ringing up and down the corridor. 'Shore visitors and workmen off the ship!' someone was calling. 'Ten minutes to embarkation! Visitors to shore!'

'Go!' she said, and her voice was fierce, almost angry.

'I love you.' He kissed her again, and again, on her face and her lips and her eyes and her throat, until she began to sob.

'Go! Luke, please, p-please just go.'

He nodded, grabbed his bag and turned.

'I love you!' she cried after him, unable to bear it if that was the last he heard from her.

'I love you too, Rose!' he called back. 'We'll find each other, I swear it. I love you!'

And then his voice was drowned in the ringing of the embarkation bell.

Standing on the desk, Rosa watched as the great boat slid smoothly away from the bustling port. Somewhere in that throng of people was Luke, but from this great height she could not pick him out of the mill of caps and greatcoats.

Luke, she thought, sending her longing out, across the widening gulf of sea, not a spell, but just a heart's cry of love. *Be safe. Come back to me.*

And somewhere out there, although she could not see him, she knew he was there. She felt it inside her, like a warmth that burnt against the chill breeze, picking up as they headed out of the port.

She looked away from the quay and turned into the wind, feeling its cold exhilaration on her face. And the boat turned to face America and the future.

Have you read the Winter Trilogy?

Read on for an extract from Book 1:

A WITCH *in* WINTER

The first thing that hit me was the smell – damp and bitter. It was the smell of a place long shut up, of mice, bird-droppings, and rot.

'Welcome to Wicker House,' Dad said, and flicked a switch. Nothing happened, and he groaned.

'Probably been disconnected. I'll go and investigate. Here, have this.' He pushed the torch at me. 'I'll get another one from the car.'

I wrapped my arms around myself, shivering as I swung the torch's thin beam around the shadowy, cobwebbed rafters. The air in the house was even colder than the night outside.

'Go on,' Dad called from the car. 'Don't wait for me; go and explore. Why don't you check out your bedroom – I thought you'd like the one at the top of the stairs. It's got a lovely view.'

I didn't want to explore. I wanted to go home – except where was home? Not London. Not any more.

Dust motes swirled, silver in the torchlight, as I pushed open a door to my right and peered into the darkness beyond. The narrow circle of the torch's beam glittered back at me from a broken window, then traced slowly across the damp-splotched plaster. I guessed this had once been a living room, though it seemed strange to use the word 'living' about a place so dead and unloved.

Something moved in the dark hole of the fireplace. Images of mice, rats, huge spiders ran through my head – but when I got up the courage to shine the torch I saw only a rustle of ashes as whatever it was fled into the shadows. I thought of my best friend, Lauren, who went bleach-pale at even the idea of a mouse. She'd have been standing on a chair by now, probably screaming. The idea of Lauren's reaction to this place made me feel better, and I reached into my pocket for my phone and started a text.

Hi Lauren, we've arrived in Winter. The welcome party consists of half a dozen rats and—

I broke off. There was no signal. Well, I'd known this place would be isolated, Dad had called that 'part of its charm'. But even so . . . Maybe I could get a signal upstairs.

The stairs creaked and protested every step, until I reached a landing, with a corridor stretching into darkness, lined with doors. The closest was ajar – and I put my hand on it and pushed.

For a minute I was dazzled by the moonlight flooding in. Then, as my eyes adjusted, I took in the high, vaulted ceiling, the stone window seat, and smelled the faint scent of the sea drifting through the open window.

Through the casement I could see the forest stretching out, mile after mile, and beyond a thumbnail moon cast a wavering silver path across the night-black sea. It was heart-breakingly lovely and, in that fleeting instant, I caught a glimmer of what had brought Dad to this place.

I stood, completely still, listening to the far off sound of the waves. Then a harsh, inhuman cry ripped through the room, and a dark shape detached from the shadows. I ducked, a flurry of black wings beat the air above my head, and I caught a glimpse of an obsidian beak and a cold, black eye as the creature hunched for a second on the sill. Then it spread its wings and was gone, into the night.

My heart was thudding ridiculously, and suddenly I didn't want to be exploring this house alone in the dark. I wanted Dad, and warmth, and light. Almost as if on cue, there was a popping sound, a blinding flash, and the light-bulb in the corridor blazed. I screwed up my eyes, dazzled by the harsh brightness after straining into the darkness.

'Hey-hey!' Dad's shout echoed up the stairs. 'Turns out the leccy wasn't off – it was just a fuse. Come on down and I'll give you the grand tour.'

He was waiting in the hall, his face shining with excitement. I tried to rearrange my expression into something approximating his, but it clearly didn't work, because he put an arm around me.

'Sorry it's a bit of a nightmare, sweetie. The place hasn't been occupied for years and I should have realized they'd have turned everything off. Not the best homecoming, I must admit.'

Homecoming. The word had a horribly hollow sound. Yup, this place was home now. I'd better get used to it.

'Come on.' Dad gave me a squeeze. 'Let me show you around.'

As Dad took me round, I tried to find positive things to say. It was pretty hard. Everything was falling apart – even the plugs and light switches were all ancient Bakelite and looked like they'd explode if you touched them.

'Just look at those beams,' he exclaimed in the living room. 'Knocks our old Georgian house into a cocked hat, eh? See those marks?' He pointed above our heads to scratches cut deeply into the corded black wood. They looked like slashes: deep, almost savage cuts that formed a series of Vs and Ws. 'Witch marks, according to my book. Set there to protect the house from evil spirits and stuff.' But I didn't have time to look properly at the scarred wood, because Dad was hurrying me on to his next exhibit.

'And how's that for a fireplace? You could roast an ox in there! That's an old bread oven, I think.' He tapped a little wooden door in the inglenook beside the fire, blackened and warped with heat. 'I'll have to see about getting it open one of these days. But anyway, enough of me rattling on. What do you think? Isn't it great?'

When I didn't respond he put his hand on my shoulder and turned me to look at him, begging me with his eyes to like it, be happy, share his enthusiasm.

'I like all the fireplaces,' I said evasively.

'Well you'll like them even more when winter comes, unless I can get the central heating in pretty pronto. But is that all you've got to say?'

'It's a lot of work, Dad. How are we going to afford it?' Even as I said it, I suddenly realized that I'd never really said those words before. I'd never had to. We hadn't been rich, but Dad had always earned enough for what we needed.

Dad shrugged. 'We got the place pretty cheap, considering. And I'll do most of the work myself, which'll cut down costs.'

'Oh God!' I said involuntarily in a horrified voice. Then I caught Dad's eye and began to laugh. Dad can barely change a light-bulb, let alone conduct major house renovations. He looked offended for a minute but then began to laugh too.

'I'll get someone in to do the gas and electrics, at least, I promise you that.' He put his arm around me. 'I have a really good feeling about this place, Anna. I know it's been a jolt for you, I do, but I honestly think we can make something of our lives here. I can do a bit of writing, grow veg – maybe I could even do B&B if money gets tight. This place just needs a little TLC to make it fantastic.'

A *little* TLC? I thought about the filth and the rats,

and all the work we were going to have to do to make this place even liveable, let alone nice. And then I looked at Dad, and I thought of him back in London, sitting up night after night, his face grey with worry as he tried to make the sums add up, tried to find a way out for both of us.

'I think,' I said. Then I stopped.

'Yes?'

'I think . . . if anyone can do it, you can, Dad.' I put my torch down on the mantelpiece and hugged him fiercely. Then I noticed something . . .